THE PREPPER

PART TWO: KINGS

BY
KARL A.D. BROWN

Chapter One

"How prone all human institutions have been to decay; how subject the best-formed and most wisely organized governments have been to lose their check and totally dissolve; how difficult it has been for mankind, in all ages and countries, to preserve their dearest rights and best privileges, impelled as it were by an irresistible fate of despotism." James Monroe

Alfred Aimes, called Alfie by his friends, sat in his cabin in the woods watching his son sleep. It had been two months since Robert had been shot while the family was trying to get to their bug out location. The young man had mended slowly and was just getting most of his mobility back. Alfred knew that his son had worked hard to pull his weight around the *Rabbit Hole*. There were no slackers around their hideaway. Their lives could not accommodate that anymore. There was always a lot to do, but Alfred could tell that his family was beginning to actually thrive. It was good to be self-sufficient. There was a sense of pride around the homestead.

It was early morning and Alfred was going hunting. He was hoping to get one more deer to round out their food supply's fresh meat. Candice, his daughter, was up and ready to go. His wife, Samantha, was going to reorder their main pantry. With hindsight comes wisdom and they realized that they had not arranged their provisions as well as they should have when they had rushed to stock up on supplies. There were certain things they used every day versus stuff that they only rarely used. He didn't know how long he and his daughter would be gone, but he was sure he would find his wife still at it when he came home.

Candice had gotten up early and had eaten and made a cup of tea. She was ready to go. Her scoped Ruger Hawkeye was slung over her shoulder, and she was dressed in a white and brown camo outfit that would help her to blend into her surroundings. She was looking forward to this hunt. It was always a treat to go out with Dad. It was an interesting time for the children. They were part of a generation who had grown up glued to their cellphones and iPads, and now they were essentially living in a nineteenth century world.

It meant a less sedentary lifestyle. Life took on an immediacy that they had never really experienced before, and the Aimeses realized that they were actually relishing it. The family had grown closer than they had ever been before. That new closeness came partly down to more direct communication. They actually talked now instead of texting, and they shared important chores like hunting for meat.

Alfred went into the small room in the back of the cabin to check in on his still sleeping wife and left the little log cabin with Candice in tow. He was a man of medium height. He was now one hundred sixty pounds and solidly built. When everything had gone bad he was twenty pounds heavier. Living like a pioneer made him shed the excess pounds and had turned disused muscles hard and toned. He, too, was dressed in camo like his daughter. He also carried a scoped Hawkeye over his shoulder. Father and daughter trudged off into the woods in the wee hours of the morning, and they were happy.

Alfred had made a few tree stands at strategic points on their land. This time he decided to try the one that was just inside the tree line that opened on to a small meadow at the north eastern end of the property. It had snowed pretty well the day before, and they walked through six inches of new powder. He had seen a lot of deer tracks down by the meadow the past week. Alfred couldn't help wondering about what he would have been doing on a Saturday in the old world before the Collapse. Probably dropping the kids off at their friends and then a trip to the supermarket, he thought. No matter how hard he tried not to think of his old life he just could not help it. There was just no way to turn off forty-five years.

They reached the stand and Candice went up first. She dropped a rope down and he sent up their rifles. He then went up himself. It was a great tree stand. He figured it was the best one he had built. It was just big enough for two and the tree was kind enough to have two sturdy branches that allowed him to hammer in a floor so they could sit. There was enough room for them to kneel and shoot if they wanted to. He secured them in and they sat down to wait. Candice hadn't gotten a deer yet and she was full of hope. There was no awkwardness between them. It was actually comforting to sit with each other in total silence listening to the song of the woods around them.

He marveled at the peacefulness of the world. This is what modern man had been missing, he thought. We were so caught up in being busy, we forgot about what really mattered. He sighed, and as he listened to the leaves of the trees rustle, he could hear the tinkle of the stream that flowed through their land and smell the air that was crisp and sweet. For a while father and daughter were at peace in a very serious time. That's what

3

nature could give, the gift of a moment's rest from the horrors of the world.

There was movement and Alfred watched in fascination as his daughter shifted quickly and silently into a shooter's crouch. She rested the barrel of the rifle on one of the security beams he had installed. He saw her smile as she watched the small herd of deer walk gingerly into the meadow. He also went into his crouch. He would give her the first shot and if she missed he would take his. He heard his daughter breathe out and knew she was picking her target with the scope. Then there was a single sharp crack. The herd turned and bolted, but one deer fell after two strides.

There was a feeling of surging pride in Alfred's heart. It was a joy any hunter would know. That feeling of excitement when their child joins the ranks of the hunters that had bagged their own meat. He understood the age-old sense of accomplishment, one that parents had felt since humans became hunters. They waited in the tree stand another twenty minutes to see if her shot had attracted any attention. Normally they would have gone to the carcass immediately, but these were dangerous times. They quickly and quietly descended and went over to their kill. It was time to field dress the deer.

Alfred and Candice slipped on gloves and got to work, father instructing child in the proper way to clean the animal, a skill that was dying out before the Collapse. He remembered how disconnected people were from their food, and this included his own family as well. Everything they ate would have been bought at the store. Alfred had never really paid any attention to where his food came from, how it was grown, and what was in it. He regretted that sorely now. He and Samantha were planning on planting a small garden to grow fresh vegetables in the spring, and they were seriously worried about how to go about it since they had only a limited supply of heirloom seeds.

He showed his daughter how to roll the animal on its back, then he started at the tail and cut up the body to the chin. He was careful not to knick the organs. He wished he had a small axe and a hammer to break the chest, but would make do. He removed heart, lungs, and windpipe. He then cut around the anus and pushed it into the body gently before pulling the intestines and the colon out. After he removed all the organs, he skinned it and wrapped it up in the tarp to pull it back to the homestead.

Candice was excited. She couldn't wait to tell Robert about getting her deer. She knew that because Robert could walk properly again he would be going out hunting, but she had one upped him on this one and she was proud of herself. 'I field dressed a deer for heaven's sake.' The two of them lugged the load back to the cabin. As they were going by a small storage shack Alfred had made, he asked her to stop and get the butchering knives and meet him by the house.

Alfred's head was down as he dragged the tarp to the cabin. He didn't see the signs until it was too late. He noticed that there were a lot of boot tracks leading up to the lodge. His heart knocked against his ribs, and he suddenly felt cold all over. He dropped the tarp and was about to reach for his .45 when a sneering voice cut through the cold winter air. "I wouldn't if I were you. Jessie and Birdman, show this idiot what we got so he won't make any stupid mistakes."

A huge monster of a man dragged Samantha out of the cabin by her hair. Alfred gasped. He could see that she was badly beaten. The man threw her on the ground and placed a foot on her back. "Sam!" Alfred rasped.

"Yeah, we also got your boy in the back. Now you drop that weapon nice and slow now."

Alfred's world spun out from under him for a second. He could have kicked himself for being so careless. There were two guns pointed at him, and he knew that he didn't have a choice. They had the edge. He slowly drew the weapon out of his holster and placed it on the ground. The two men laughed and the tall man who had been standing on his porch came down and picked up the gun, tucking it in his waist. Without any other warning he swung his shotgun around and hit Alfred across the face. The pain was blinding and he fell to his knees. The man then began kicking him mercilessly. Before he blacked out Alfred could hear Sam screaming his name.

Candice was happy. She had spent the morning with her father and the hunt had gone well. She was getting the plastic container that held the butcher knives when she heard her mother scream. A chill went through her, and she dropped the container and snatched her rifle from beside the shack's door. Before she could run up to the house everything Dad had taught her snapped into play. They had run countless drills on what if someone or people surprised them in the cabin. Her father was a very careful planner; he had made countless contingency plans for such a scenario. The first thing she had to do was to establish that there was a threat. She circled around the house in an arc, sticking to the dense tree line. Eventually she saw the tracks and stopped. She could see the front of the cabin now and she saw the man drag her father's inert body into the house. She saw the other man slap her mother, banging her head into the wall of the small front deck. He then shoved her inside and closed the door.

This was very bad. Suddenly despite the cold she felt a bit hot in her camo. Biting her lip she understood that this scenario was one they had talked about, but never thought they would have to deal with. It was hard to find the cabin, and they had been careful but obviously not careful enough. She then made a couple of circles around the house in wider arcs and eventually found a small fire and a crude canvas tent. The men must have come in during the snow last night and camped there. The Aimeses were all inside during the worst of it, and their visitors had gone undetected. All the men had to do was to walk four hundred yards to the left straight ahead and there was the cabin. She figured that they had not seen them leave but probably stumbled on it after she had left with her dad. They probably waited and surprised Mom when she came out to do the early chores.

It was fortunate that she was not with her father at the time. She also knew that her family would not tell the truth about who was outside the home. That was also in the plan. She picked a spot far back from the house and hunkered down to watch. Eventually they would all have to use the outhouse. After a few hours she ascertained that there were three men and that they appeared heavily armed. The *Rabbit Hole* was a thing that they would kill for, she had no doubts about that. Around noon she saw her mother open the curtains in the front and she knew that the one in the back would also be open as well.

This was something they would never do normally; she knew that her mother wanted there to be an unobscured view into the home. She had seen enough.

The next phase of the plan had to go into place. She pointed her rifle in the air and fired a single shot. She then melted into the trees. Her dad had dug a few spider holes around the house's perimeter. In them he had stashed food, water, blankets, and a few boxes of extra ammunition. The wind began to pick up again and the snow started coming down in blinding sheets. She crawled into the spider hole. If they were good enough to track her in the storm she could see them coming, and she knew how to use her firearm very well.

When it was dark enough she checked her rifle and went out into the snowstorm. Even in the blizzard she knew unerringly where to go. Her father had made her count the amount of steps to the first container a thousand times. She squatted in the snow and used the scope as a monocular. The front window was lit by a soft glow, and she could see a man sitting at a table.

She went around to the back of the house where there was another door and a window that showed the inside of her parents' master bedroom. What she saw through the monocular appalled her. Her mother had been tied to the bed, face-down, and one of the men was on top of her. Candice turned her face away, and a rage white hot and pure coursed through her. She knew she was going to kill the men in the house. She could not see her father or her brother, and she prayed they were okay.

There were three bullets in the rifle. She knew who her first target was going to be. Steeling herself she leaned the rifle on the low branch of a tree and waited for the shot. The man got up and stretched, scratching himself. The rifle popped, the window smashed, and the bullet took his left eye and his life. Candice then ran around to the front of the house. She could no longer see the man who had been by the table in the front room. Very carefully she edged back to the side of the house by the outhouse. There her father had stashed a stack of wood under a tarp to keep it dry, and he had said, *"If we ever got separated and if someone has some of us inside the house, light this stack of wood if you can. In the night, no one will know who is out there. For all they know it will be marauders or cannibals trying to break in or burn them out. Hell, burn the goddamn outhouse down if you need a distraction, do what you have to do, to kill the people who are in the house."*

Candice, in her rage, took this advice from her father very literally. She went into the shed she had left that morning and took a small gas can. She poured some of its contents onto the wood pile under the tarp and lit the match. It didn't take long for the wind to whip the flames up despite the snow, and in just a matter of a few minutes she had a bright blazing fire roaring and sizzling. It cast an eerie glare around the cabin and she knew that the men in the cabin must have been going out of their minds trying to figure out what was going on outside. Then she did something utterly insane. Grabbing one of the burning logs by its safe end she threw it through the front window. The response from one of the home invaders inside was immediate, and when he popped up to toss it back through the window a .300 Win Mag bullet ended his life.

Then Candice saw something through her scope that made her catch her breath. She saw through the window that two men were struggling. She couldn't quite understand at first what she was witnessing, but it became clearer as she tweaked her scope. Her dad was using the rope they had tied his hands with like a garrote. He had the rope around the man's neck, and he was twisting his hands together to tighten the rope, cutting off the man's air supply. The man had his shotgun in his hands and he tried using it to swat at his assailant. Candice saw her dad take a few good whacks to the head, but he was not going to let go. Then the two men fell to the floor, and after what seemed an interminable wait there were two loud bangs from the 12 gauge that the man had. She still could not see anything and her heart was in her throat as she waited to see who would stand up. A figure came into view and he waved his hands. Candice gasped in relief, "Ohh, Dad," and then she began to cry.

William Diefenbacher, known as Splinter to his acquaintances, was a smalltime hood before the Collapse. After the economy tanked and the world descended into chaos, his fortune rose as others went up in flames. Splinter was a small, wiry man, pale with limp brown hair and flat blue eyes that left no doubt that he was crazy. The small, round wire-rimmed glasses he wore did not mask the wild intensity in his eyes. He had made his living making and distributing methamphetamines, and he had been in the process of carving out a name for himself when things went south.

Always being a paranoid fellow he had almost instinctively done what other more prudent folks had done; he had stocked his New York City apartment with food, guns, and lots of ammunition. Luck comes into play in that he never got caught. He was ruthless in the way he conducted business, and one man's life meant no more to him than a cockroach. When things crashed he reached out to a few of the street gangs that he had done business with and, after killing their leaders, he assumed control. In two months he had three hundred well-armed foot soldiers working for him.

Now while the other gangs were still thinking about territory and drugs, Splinter read the tea leaves and understood that the world as we all knew it was over. There was no coming back from this one. It was going to be a new canvas, and he intended to paint it in his image. So in the first few days when other more well established gangs were still fighting over the products they pushed and the territory they controlled, Splinter had set his people to stockpiling food and as much guns and ammunition as they could. He then waited.

When New York began to burn, and the traditional gangs and crime families fought each other, he carefully went about drilling his people into well-organized teams. If anyone was thought to have divulged the group's secrets they were immediately liquidated upon his orders. No one in his original group had any family or connections; he chose them carefully that way. He intended to survive because he was really excited by the opportunities the new world could give a person like him. His group was armed, fed, and well-trained. Soon he began to target the other gangs. His vision of assuming complete control of New York City demanded that he act systematically and brutally.

His small army, because that was what it was, began to wage open and organized warfare with the other gangs throughout the city. Borough by borough, they assumed control. Splinter understood the situation better than his peers. He understood that the lack of food, water, and resources would cripple the opposition. He understood that while the National Guard maintained its ring of steel around the city no one could get in or out easily, and that worked to his advantage. He had the guns and he had the ammunition, and that was all that mattered. He took from the gangs and the people of the city, and he stockpiled more food and guns.

Four months after the Collapse, because of how quickly and decisively he had moved, he was the undisputed crime lord of New York City. The next phase of his plan came into place, and he ruthlessly made the survivors understand that the world had changed. The USA was no more, and he was the man in charge. He offered to take any man or woman who would fight in his army as long as they were single and childless. Later on he would take in people with children but he made it clear that if the children became a liability to the militia or its objectives they would be sacrificed. Now he was looking beyond New York City and he wanted as much as he could take. His army's ranks swelled to over two hundred thousand.

When the blockade by the National Guard known as the Ring of Steel around New York City finally crumbled, his soldiers went out to plunder and to make New York their own. They had a charismatic and shrewd leader, and they followed him willingly because they knew he was special. He was a prince. Splinter and his captains, in a campaign reminiscent of medieval times, went about the systematic conquering of New York. They had pretty much rolled over every small town they had encountered as Splinter's territory extended further into the heart of Central New York. He made sure that the locals of the conquered towns understood in no uncertain terms who their lord was and who was in charge.

He understood that if he was going to realize his dream he would have to make sure that his territory was peaceful, organized, and productive. He also understood a basic fact—he had to keep his people in serfdom. That meant there was no hurry to bring back modern technology and conveniences. The only technology he was interested in was the technology that kept him in power. He restarted gun and bullet manufacturing. Metal and the refining of oil was a top priority. His army needed to keep on the move. The way he had it figured, it was imperative to get his soldiers through the winter as best he could, then push on when the warmer weather broke. He needed a buffer between himself and the rest of Central New York. So he expended a lot of resources in a gamble of taking enough strategically valuable land close to his powerbase of Middletown, NY.

It was amazing to see the toll the Collapse had taken on the population. In the months following the disaster, a good portion of the people had died of starvation. But that was not the only killer. Diseases whipped through the villages and towns caused by bad sanitation practices. And then there was the influenza outbreak that was still taking lives. In a world where the manufacturing of drugs and the wholesale destruction of the medical profession had taken place, people died of simple ailments that normally they would have survived. There was no way to know what strain of the influenza virus was moving through the population, ensnaring its unsuspecting victims in its deadly caresses. There was also yet unconfirmed reports of a subtle campaign of biological warfare being razed upon the unsuspecting survivors.

It wasn't just the United States that had suffered this mortal blow. Canada was also in flames. Central and South America had become a dark zone; there was no real news coming out of their sovereign countries. Europe had been poleaxed. The English had abandoned their Prime Minister and reinstated the royal family. The average man in the street could not understand, even now, how it had all gone so bad so fast. The

English needed someone to rally behind as they sank into their medieval existence and so the King was back in charge.

The English and Canadian preppers had done all they could to protect their loved ones and prepare for the bad times, but the odds were against even this intrepid lot. The survivors who had made it through the horrible first five months were now facing one of the worst winters on record with dwindling supplies and rampaging plagues.

No country in the world escaped. When no one can trade for goods and when money has no value in a world that had become very dependent on its technology, the pyramid scheme humanity had been playing with the gods of fate came crashing down. In five months the world lost half of its population. In five months the brain drain that resulted ensured that all humanity was firmly back to a nineteenth century existence. It would take generations to regain all the knowledge that had been lost, and the world had changed fundamentally and forever.

Splinter had always felt that he was special. He had always watched those documentaries on Hitler and Stalin and felt that he had the stuff. As a boy he would play in his parent's backyard with his toy soldiers, moving his armies about. His father had been cruel and he became cruel himself. His mother had spent most of her time living in abject fear of her husband; she was cowed and he was beaten. By the time he was fifteen he was a thin terror whose classmates were relieved when he dropped out of school. It wasn't because he was stupid. On the contrary Splinter read every day and everything he could get his hands on, especially history. He came to think that the only people who truly mattered were the people who made their fortunes themselves. It didn't matter how the wealth was made. Only a fool did not take a chance for self-liberation.

He saw nothing wrong in making money illegally, and he had tried many different ways until he settled on making meth. Anyone who saw him would have thought that he partook of the stuff himself, but that was not the case. He was careful and he was prudent. There was another interesting anomaly about the man, and it was that he really had no interest in sex. He really didn't care one way or the other about it. So there was no one he cared about and no emotional ties to distract him from his singular purpose, and for him that was part of being truly liberated.

Today, on what had turned out to be an extremely cold day, he was a bit hot under the collar. There was something in the way the objective was achieved that left him disturbingly dissatisfied. He had taken to wearing a white suit with gold epaulettes and black military style boots. On the right side of the jacket the insignia of his army was sewn. It was a golden dove. No one called him Splinter anymore. All his soldiers referred to him as Commander. The people he governed called him the Dove. Buckled around his waist was a sword in a black sheath. His headquarters was the large waiting room in the City's municipal building.

When his army had rolled into Middletown they had met very little resistance. His scouts had told him that much. He knew before they got into the small city that most of the residents were dead or had left when the flu began picking off the survivors. The ones that had stayed behind had slowly banded together and had managed to stay alive by hunting or cannibalism. His men were bringing in two of their leaders to see him now. He sat behind the huge and heavy dark red cherry desk, adjusting his sword and trying to calm himself.

Four of his men dressed in brown army fatigues came into the hall. They flanked the two stinking unwashed men in the middle. Both men were so dirty that it was really hard to tell them apart. Their beards and hair had grown long, tangled and caked with dirt, and they had carved tattoos into their foreheads and cheeks. Splinter quickly took in the two men with a glance and he realized that there was no fear in them. They were not armed, but they carried themselves with an air of boldness. When his army had gotten into the city, they were not attacked. The people had known that they were coming and had kept out of sight. There was no way to fight the well-organized men with all their weapons. As far as Splinter was concerned these two men were here to hear his orders and accept his rule.

One man stepped forward and said, "My name's Jerry and his is James. We don't run things in this city, but we speak for the man who does."

"What's this man's name?"

"We are not here to answer questions. We are here to give you a message. You are to pack up and get your men out of here. This is our town, and you and your kind are not welcome." The one named James, a bigger, smellier, and uglier version of the other said, "Our boss said that you are all welcome to stay if you let us have all your food and give us a few of your men, so that we can have us a—"

In a flash Splinter was out from behind the table, and in a move that surprised even his own men he drew his sword and James' head went flying from his shoulders. "Crucify him." He pointed to Jerry who was looking at James' corpse, a look of genuine shocked surprise on his face. The big man turned and slammed a fist into one of the guards, then pulled a knife from somewhere he had cleverly concealed and stabbed another in the throat. A guard smashed the butt of his gun into the man's temple and he crumpled senseless beside his headless friend.

Later on that night the man's shrill screams of agony could be heard echoing all around the city square. He had been mounted on a tree in the city park. On express orders he was tied upright onto the tree, and ten inch spikes were driven through his arms above his head on both sides of the tree. The same thing was done to his feet. The order coming from the Dove was that he was to be kept alive and alert for as long as possible, and they did just that for two days. When the man died, the Dove gave orders to send out squads of ten heavily armed men or more, and any local they caught they were to nail to the other trees around the square. In five days there were ten people, howling and screaming for mercy. On each of the trees large signs were hung asking the leader of the Middletown survivors to come in and kneel, and so spare the rest of his people. After ten days and twenty more crucifixions, a man finally came in to see Splinter. He wore dirty jeans and a heavy black coat. He fell on his knees but did not beg.

"My name is Gregory. I am the one they call leader. Why have you put those people on the trees?"

His question rankled Splinter. He was supposed to be begging. It was not enough for Splinter that he was here; he needed him broken. So he had the man bound to a table and a hot poker was brought along with some hot coals in a brazier.

He started with the man's toes. With extreme care he touched each one with the red poker, and he could hear the skin sizzle. The man began screaming after he started on the bottom of the soles. Splinter didn't quite care; now he was just enjoying himself. The man began to babble and his breath started to hitch in his throat. Splinter then got an idea that gave him goose pimples. He touched the tip of the poker to the man's eye, and as his eyeball began to sizzle, the man began crying out for mercy. He had really begun warming to the task when his chief intelligence officer, Cole, came in. He had an important message.

"There is a man outside, Commander, who said that he needs to talk to you. He says that he is from Albany."

"Can it wait? I am kind of in the middle of something right now," he said as he raised the poker. He was about to take the other eye out and the man was straining and gasping, trying in vain to move his face away from the glowing instrument of torture.

"He looks kind of important. Says his name is Lambert. I swear, Commander, you need to see this guy. He looks like he is still working for the Feds. Black suit, tie and all. He says he is here to offer you a pretty good deal." This got Splinter's attention and he dropped the poker back into the brazier.

"Cut him loose." Two of his personal body guards cut the ropes binding the man to the table. They then stepped in front of their leader to protect him from the man possibly attacking him. But they didn't need to. The man prostrated himself on the ground and said, "Thank you for my life, we will do as you wish."

"You and your people are now under the control of the New York City Militia. We will spend the winter here in this town, which is now my town. Then in the spring we will march north and we will bring the rest of the state under my command. Because of your stupidity I will not help your people through the winter. You will do what you need to do to survive. If you harm any of my men I will hunt you all down, and there are a lot of trees between here and Binghamton for more crucifixions. I will also burn this city to the ground. Do you understand?"

"Yes, sir, I do."

"You will not call me sir. I am your lord and master. You will call me My Lord. Yes, yes, I like the sound of that. My Lord."

"Yes, My Lord."

"Good, now get out of here. If you or your people give me cause to doubt your felicity, you will regret the day you were born." Two guards escorted the weak, trembling man from the small room. Splinter then went to look at himself in the mirror in the bathroom. He looked a mess. His hair was matted to his forehead and his uniform looked grubby. He decided he would change before seeing this Lambert from Albany. It was good that he had broken the people in this settlement. The survivors of the winter would be fresh troops in the spring. He guessed that they would be very grateful to the man who would give them fresh clothes and real food. They would find a place in his army and they would be willing to fight for him. Yes, he nodded to himself in the mirror, things were beginning to come together.

Chapter Two

"Love seeketh not itself to please, nor for itself hath any care, but for another gives ease, and builds a Heaven in Hell's despair."
William Blake

Alfred was worried for his wife. Samantha was usually the one who brought hope to the family unit. She was always able to see the glass as half full, not half empty. This was a vital gift to their small prepper unit, and now it was absent. Ever since they had overcome the attack on their lives, she had been silent and despondent. He had known what had happened to her but had no idea how to talk to her about it. He also blamed himself for allowing it to happen. He had gotten careless. The first month after they had gotten to the *Rabbit Hole*, he had been almost paranoid about their camp security. He had run drill after drill on what to do if they were attacked. He was even planning to build an escape tunnel from the cabin to the tree line in the summer. He was glad that he had run the drills, because it had allowed Candice to make the right decisions and escape the home invasion with their lives. The next time they might not be that lucky. It was incredible what a traumatic experience could do to one's mindset. Alfred couldn't help but think that they were all living on borrowed time.

He remembered the despair he felt when that animal had tied him up and when they took his wife to the back room. There was nothing more humiliating and crushing to a man than knowing that his wife, lover, or child was being raped. He remembered how he had felt—it was as if the bottom had fallen out of the world. He had fallen head first into a yawning chasm of despair. He was so happy knowing that Candice was not in harm's way. Their plan had worked brilliantly. When they had heard Candice's gunshot, they knew she was okay and was going to hide. They also knew that she would be back, looking for any opportunity to kill the intruders in the house.

Robert and Samantha had told their captors that a hermit lived somewhere on the state land that was on the borders of their property. They also told the men that they sometimes traded with him, and they all just tolerated each other, but he was very adverse to others and wouldn't like strangers hanging around. They also told them that he always shot his gun into the air as a signal that he had something to trade, and they usually replied with a single gunshot when they wanted to meet. The men had bought the story. They had no intention of meeting their friend, at least not yet. They had allowed Sam to cook for them and they had the two males tied up and secured in the front room near the stove. Alfred had intuited that the men would be planning to shoot them in the morning. He was hoping that Candice would give them something to think about before they could get around to that. Meanwhile he had been working on getting his hands loose.

The men had looked through the cabinets, which were stocked well with food. More food than they had seen in three months. This was another trick the Aimeses used to at least possibly delay the discovery of their major food storage location. They really didn't care so much for the food that was in the cabinets.

Their root cellar was where the majority of their food was kept. It had been a big project Alfred had worked on with Samantha during the summer before the Collapse, when they had first set up the hideout.

He had rented a backhoe and had found a nice spot close to the cabin in the trees, one that was located on a small north facing knoll. He picked that location because everything he had read had said a north facing hill will keep the cellar cooler in the summer. He had carefully excavated a hole twenty by twenty and seven feet deep. He had poured cement for the floor, laid down some wooden planks over it, then installed his uprights at the recommended four feet apart to support the weight of the roof. The two sheets of plywood did it for the roof, covered with a thick sheet of plastic and dirt. He installed his shelves three inches from his walls, and to provide their cellar with a means to vent warm air, he cut a small hole into the side, inserting a small PVC pipe and covering both ends with wire mesh so that small animals could not get in. When he and Samantha were done they had a place to store perishable food, secure and camouflaged.

The men who had attacked them knew nothing of this major source of food. But they had seen enough of the Aimes's set up to know that they had inadvertently stumbled across a gift that they would kill to keep. It was not the first time the Aimeses had to fight to hold on to the *Rabbit Hole*. He remembered how Samantha and Candice had to fight and kill the Pywoskis. Janice and Peter had been close family friends. They had sold them the land on which the hideout was located. When things went south, the Pywoskis remembered that the Aimeses had bought the land and checked it out, discovering the hideout and its supplies. Samantha had to shoot them when they had attacked her and Candice during the night.

It really amazed Alfred that more people had not done anything to prepare for the possibility of a crisis. Most people had watched as the world fragmented before their eyes and had done nothing. The majority had been completely reliant on the country's infrastructure for food and the other necessities of life, and when that was no longer available it had all unraveled pretty fast. Alfred was scared for his family and not only for his wife, although she was his most pressing worry at the moment. Robert, his son, had been injured while the family was trying to escape from a Government roadblock. Candice had to leave behind a safe secure world for one where violence was the order of the day. Alfred groaned. His daughter had just killed two men. He had been watching her closely but she didn't seemed too bothered by it, and that in itself bothered him. His wife was just assaulted by three men. Samantha was a tough lady, but he knew that he was going to have to be there emotionally for his wife.

Alfred knew that he had changed over the last five months. He had always been an easygoing man with a ready smile. Now he had killed men, and seen things that tested his sanity, and chased him into his dreams. He knew that if it wasn't for his family he would have probably thrown in the towel a long time ago. He needed the people in this cabin and they needed him now more than ever. Samantha was busy stoking the fire, her back to him, and Robert was drinking some tea at the table. Candice was inside the backroom taping some plywood she had cut over one of the windows she had shot out as a temporary fix, until he could devise a better way to repair them. The three bodies were outside on a tarp sled he had made. He was about

23

to drag them over to the abandoned farm that boarded the southern edge of their land. They had used this farm to dispose of bodies before, and going back to it always gave Alfred a feeling of disquiet. It was easy to drag the bodies by himself over the ankle deep snow, but Robert had volunteered to go with him.

He knew that his son was trying to get himself back into shape. It was now a little more than two months after Robert had been shot. At first it had been touch and go, but the boy had pulled through. Then came the issue of how much damage the bullet had done to his spine. A week after his injury, he could finally move his toes and this was a cause for celebration in the cabin. Then slowly as he recovered he could get up and begin to move around the small house. Eventually, he went for little walks outside. His injury would sometimes hurt, but slowly he could now move and stretch. This jaunt over to the farm would be the longest walk he would have been on since the injury.

"Sam, we are about to go. We've got to get those bodies over to the farm. Will you be okay?" Samantha turned and looked at her husband, and there was a flatness to her eyes that Alfred didn't like one bit.

"Yes, I have a lot to do around here. Just keep a close eye on Rob. I know he thinks he has recovered but he may be overestimating himself. You be careful and hurry back." She reached out and hugged him close, then she went back to her work.

"Back soon, Candice."

"See yah, Dad."

"Okay, Rob, let's get this done."

He felt a moment of panic seize him. He did not like leaving the cabin. He did not want to leave his wife and daughter alone. He almost found a reason to stay, but Robert called to him and he went outside. He grabbed the two pieces of the rope that had been tied to both ends of the tarp and began to pull. He was only armed with the .45. Robert carried the one of the Mini 14s they owned. He picked the easiest and most direct route to the farm and trudged ahead of his son, anxious to get the work done.

Samantha felt a twinge of panic when Alfred left the camp. She held it in and instead made herself some tea. She looked at the cup in her hands and thought ruefully that they had been drinking a lot of the brew lately. She thought often about why her friend Janice Pywoski and her husband had tried to murder her that first night in the cabin. She had always tried to understand but she hadn't really known why until now. She had initially hated the Pywoskis, but now she truly grieved for her friends.

She imagined what it must have been like for the Pywoskis losing their home to the gangs and looters and finally living in fear on the streets and in the woods. How long had they gone without food until they had found the cabin? How much physical violence did they have to survive before they found what they must have thought was a small miracle, only for it to be snatched away again when the owners showed up.

Since the Collapse, Samantha had never felt so shockingly vulnerable and desolate as she did yesterday morning and last night. That horrible man had surprised her in the yard, knocked her down then beaten her until she cried out and begged him to stop. She had watched them kick in the door and saw the fight that had gone on in the house with her son. Not knowing if Robert was still alive was horrible. When the one called Don dragged her into the house she had seen Robert and he had been a bloody mess. They had surprised him completely and he was tied hand and foot, with a shotgun pointed at his face. Watching them beat her husband had also been soul sucking. The only ray of hope had been that Candice had gotten away. Her heart had lurched in her chest when she heard that solitary gunshot during the afternoon and she hoped that the men would not go to investigate. So she had volunteered to make them something to eat. It was after their bellies were full that they had tied her to the bed and assaulted her. It had been horrible and she remembered her ordeal with a clarity she knew she would take to her grave.

She felt not only anger but shame. She was ashamed that her husband had known what had happened to her. She couldn't explain it but she did. She felt humiliation knowing that her daughter had seen what the men had done to her, and knowing that when the men had been making their bawdy jokes about her private parts, Robert must have heard. After the fight, instead of feeling exhilaration that they had somehow beaten the odds, she felt a wrenching despair she could not understand. She tried hiding it as best as she could but she knew that Alfred wasn't fooled. He knew her too well. She could tell that he was worried. It was all over his face before he had left.

Candice had now finished up the window patch and had come to take a seat at the table. Samantha decided to carry on with the chores that she had intended to do the day before. The container closest to the cabin on the right side was what they considered their main storage unit, because that's where they stored most of the things they found themselves using most of the time. On one side of the container there was dehydrated foods and on the other side tools for planting and doing chores around the house. When Samantha popped the lock, the day was bone chilling cold. She also noticed that the sky had begun to darken. There was a lot of stuff in the back of the container that needed to be inventoried. It was now mid-January and she was already thinking about doing some serious farming around the cabin. She figured that she could produce enough fresh food to keep her family healthy for an entire year. A lot of the equipment she would need was at the back of the container.

She and Alfred had talked about this very thing ad nauseam when they were setting up the *Rabbit Hole*. He wanted to use the space to store only canned and dehydrated food. She also wanted to store her seeds in the root cellar. This was a big problem that Samantha, in all the study she had done online *when there was an internet,* could not find a comfortable solution for. She found out that there were two types of seeds, desiccation-tolerant and desiccation-intolerant. The tolerant could be stored much easier for a long period of time while the intolerant could not. There was also the temperature issues with some saying you should store seeds between 33-40 degrees Fahrenheit. Because of where their root cellar had been built and how deep it was, she decided to store them there. She had found a number of companies that had sold non-GMO, heirloom seeds. She had bought a lot from Pleasant Hill Grain, Annie's Heirloom Seeds, Eden Brothers, and Survival Seed Vault.

She was really now beginning to understand the task ahead of producing fresh vegetables and food. She hoped that her gamble of storing the seeds in the root cellar would pay off. They had no means of providing constant refrigeration. The solar system Alfred had rigged up was good to recharge tools and provide light indoors, but they were not very comfortable with the system. Now that she thought about it, it would have been great if they had bought a Sunrnr solar system for the cabin as well. But they had not thought that it would have gotten as bad as it did as quickly as it did. She shrugged as she moved heavy bags and tools around; the idea of always preparing for the worst-case scenario and to be completely self-sufficient, she realized, was the prepper's creed.

As Samantha and her daughter built up a sweat on the cold bleak day, she found that she could still think about the future, even after her horrible experience. She was just worried that maybe that future was a dark and hellish one that her family would not survive.

Father and son both looked like they had been in a prize fight. Alfred had lost a tooth in the final fight with the one called Birdman. He had managed during the confusion in the cabin to get behind the man and throw the length of rope that had bound his hands around the man's neck. It had not been easy to kill him and Alfred realized one thing, if the Birdman had been in tip top shape and not suffering from the flu as he had been, he most likely would have lost his life last night. He had wrapped both ends of the rope around his hands and brutally garroted the man.

To kill a man that way was a horribly protracted act. The rope which is twisted around the victim's neck constricts and cuts off the flow of air to the brain. Most times, as in the case of the Birdman, the rope would cut into the neck causing even more pain and trauma. The victim, in pain and fully aware that someone is trying to kill him, thrashes around trying to shake the attacker from his back. The Birdman had smashed Alfred in the face with the butt of his shotgun more than once. The third and last time the gun's stock had smashed into Alfred's mouth and cracked a tooth. The pain that bloomed inside his mouth was jagged and horrible but he knew that if he let go the man would turn the shotgun on him, so he held on. The Birdman had wheezed and stumbled around the small room slamming into the hot stove and burning himself. Then he tripped over the rug and fell face down on the ground. His fingers had been trying to get between the rope and his neck, but to no avail. Alfred had planted both knees in his back and twisted that rope for all he was worth.

Then suddenly the man had stiffened like a board then went limp. Alfred had run over, got the shot gun and shot him twice. Ignoring his son, who was gagged and begging to be freed, he ran into the small back room he shared with his wife. He saw her tied to the bed and saw the corpse of Jessie on the ground with his pants still down around his ankles. He untied his wife and held her in his arms. He was crying; she was not. She had held onto him, and there was a look of stunned desperateness in her face. He got tense when he heard a noise in the front room, but he realized that it was Candice coming in. He could hear her and Robert talking in high shrill tones. He had led his wife into the larger front room and sat her down next to the stove, and he and the children had dragged the bodies out of the house. They spent the next three hours cleaning up the mess. Then they nailed heavy blankets over the smashed windows to keep out the cold. In the morning he would very quickly cut some plywood, and he would at first tape it over the holes to keep out the cold. He wanted to see if there was a better solution before he nailed them in.

He had fixed Samantha a cup of tea and still she didn't cry or say much. Alfred had known his wife had experienced a significant trauma. That was where his mind was when they came to the boundary between the farm and his family's land. He wanted to do this quickly and get back to his wife. He and Robert lifted the tarp with the bodies over the hip high barbed wire fence. They then took them across the overgrown field, up the walkway. He had intended on dumping them in the large barn that had been burned when the farm had been attacked. They dragged the tarp up the driveway. He came up short; near the farmhouse there was a pickup truck. In the back there was a boy about Robert's age. He had a gun in his lap.

Before Alfred and Robert could just ditch the bodies and run, the boy began screaming for help. A man and a woman came out of the house. Both were armed and they pointed their rifles at the man and the boy who had been dragging three bodies on a tarp up the driveway.

Chapter Three

"To live is to suffer, to survive is to find some meaning in the suffering." Friedrich Nietzsche

The Bunker-England

Being a prepper was just not an American thing. People all over the world had felt that something bad was coming and had prepared for it. Joseph Lafferty was a thirty-six-year-old IT guy who had worked for HSBC in London. He knew something was wrong when he saw the top brass of the bank pulling their money out of the stock market and transferring it to secret offshore locations. Some liquidated their huge portfolios and bought huge amounts of gold or other precious metals. When the bankers started dying mysteriously in droves that did it for him. Over a period of five years, top bankers all around the world began dying in really suspicious circumstances. Most of these men and women were healthy and in the prime of their lives.

He had money socked away and he and his wife decided to leave the crowed city for the remoteness of Cornwall. They bought a small farm and began to learn how to live in a self-sustaining way. He also looked around for a company that could build him an underground bunker; the only one he found was Blueprint Carpentry and Safe Rooms. He told them exactly what

31

he wanted and, after a year, they finally delivered and buried the underground shelter on his small farm.

When things had gone badly and roving bands of marauders had begun moving across the country, Joe, an avid Tottenham Hotspurs fan moved his family into the bunker and closed the door on the world. He and his wife, Trisha, who was two years younger, and daughters Cathy, fourteen, and Bea who was the youngest at ten years old, had enough food for two years. The bunker was made to sustain life indefinitely. They had fresh water from a well and a sewer system. This was a different approach to the bug out location idea that the Aimeses had gone with. Preppers had made many creative arrangements to keep themselves safe and hidden during the bad times. Others had formed groups in which they had invested a lot of time and money to ensure that when the shit hit the fan, they had somewhere to go and a group that could protect them. All of these approaches met with varying degrees of success. As many would find out, survival was not only how many guns you had, or even how many people or smarts. A lot of what made people survive was mental. Having the correct psychological mix in the group was essential. People resorted to many tricks to keep their sanity. One was the diary, and that's what Joseph Lafferty started when he left the world behind. The place he writes is a small desk at the back of the bunker. He writes when everyone is asleep for the night. He has a small light that runs on a battery that is charged by the solar unit that runs his bunker.

Journal Entry 75

January 23rd. We have been underground now for more than two months. The children have had their good days and bad days—see entry from yesterday.

Cathy had a meltdown. Her iPod stopped working. I don't know the reason why this occurred. It had been fine all week. We had recharged it and then the damn thing just went dead. She lost it, saying that she didn't know what she was going to do now. All today she was in a mean, mopey mood. I finally had to put my foot down and tell her to clean the bathroom and floor of the bunker with soap and water. I put her to work. Trisha didn't agree with my methods, but the work tired her out and at the end of her chores, she was too exhausted to cause much of a fuss. I can understand what she is going through. It has been hard hiding out down here. When they dug the well for the bunker, I had them sink another deep shaft. I have set up a natural geothermal earthtubing air circulation system. I can use a small fan if I want to pull the warmer air from four large pipes in the shaft into the bunker. I have found that it does it passively and I've never had to use the fan. The cooler air vents naturally through a small camouflaged pipe on the surface. This winter the air temp in the bunker has hovered around 58 degrees. On the really cold days we lit candles and it sometimes got up to 66 degrees. I am glad we spent the extra cash to do this, because this winter was one of the worst I have seen.

Not being able to see the sun has been hard. We miss all our family and friends. We all wonder what has happened to them. Are they still alive? We have been lucky. I used to be able to get some news on the regular radio but now all the stations are dead, and the only thing that works is the ham. The last I heard the King was going to take control. I guess in times like these the country needs one person to make the decisions instead of some committee that can never agree. We are luckier than the Yanks and the Canadians in that we already had the monarchy in place. I always knew something bad was going to go down but I never thought it would have gotten as bad as it has here. English men and women killing each other over a crust of bread, bloody intolerable.

I do know a few English and Canadian Preppers. We had chatted online before the big crash. They all had interesting theories about the best way to survive a total societal collapse. I think looking at it now all scenarios are difficult. None guarantees success. At most, some will just keep you and your family alive for a short time until hopefully the danger has passed.

In this bunker we have had to deal with the toilet backing up, and the well not giving water for a few days—that was a real concern. We had a family of mice that had somehow gotten in with the food. I had to kill them, pop the hatch, and quickly dispose of the bodies. If we were starving that would have been protein. Trisha and I had had a row about opening the hatch. She wanted me to just chop them up as fine as could be and then flush them down the toilet. I could not take a chance on the toilet backing up again, so I took the risk and went above. It's amazing how frightened I was unlocking the door for the first time since we came down. I must have had a panic attack and almost passed out. Were a couple stupid rats worth my family's safety? I almost decided to just throw them on a skillet and eat the damn things myself, but I just could not bring myself to do it. So eventually I turned the lock and looked directly at the sky for the first time in five months. The air was the sweetest I ever smelled. It was all I could do to stop myself from running into the field, and rolling in the weeds. I walked the twenty feet through the trees, looked down the hill and saw that our house had been burned. That sobered me up quickly, and I went straight back down the ladder and bolted the door.

It's tough living in a bunker sealed off from the world. I told Trisha and the kids about our house and now I think it was probably a mistake. I should have kept it to myself. The kids started crying and Trisha, who had always been optimistic about us coming through this, has become moody and snappy. Yesterday when Cathy began to go on about the iPod, she just ripped into her. Then she began to cry. She has not eaten anything since yesterday. I can tell that she is depressed. I miss the days when I could have a proper pint before a Spurs game. I miss being able to go for a walk with my children in the park. I used to hate when Trisha would always suggest we go for a walk as a family. I would rather have been home resting on the couch or taking a trip to White Hart Lane. What I would do to be able to go for walk now. My God, my kingdom for a walk in the park.

Splinter had changed his clothes and was now sitting behind his desk as the man who called himself Agent Lambert walked into his office. The man was very cool and self-possessed; he was dressed in a dark blue suit. His calmness was the exact counterpoint to Splinter's edginess. He smiled at Splinter and extended his hand which Splinter took. The handshake was firm and cool just like the man himself. There were a lot of important things on Splinter's mind, so he wanted this meeting to be over as soon as possible.

"So, Agent, what can I do for you."

"Ahh, Mr. Diefenbacher. We have a lot of interesting things to discuss. I think we will be of enormous help to each other."

Splinter felt his breath catch in his throat. No one alive, at least that he could remember, knew his real name. Some people might still remember him as Splinter, but they would never dare call him that to his face anymore. Everyone now called him Commander, and he had ambitions that went well beyond that. He looked at the man who sat in front of him with mounting interest.

"No one has called me that in years. Now what is your business?"

"I find myself in a very unique position, Mr. Diefenbacher. When I went to work for the Department of Homeland Security a few years ago, I was made the Chief of Operations for the Southern Tier Homeland Security Division. My job was to investigate any situation or person who might be a threat to the country. We at the NSA collected data on everyone and from every available source. Those boys in Silicon Valley, and through the research and development departments of Google and Microsoft, provided us with programs that collected and stored every bit of information on every American citizen. Soon the programs became very interactive. We were able to sometimes predict and stop threats before they occurred. Then came the Collapse. We all had known that it was always a possibility, but as far as the program went it was at best a very remote reality. Most of our efforts went into preparing for an actual EMP attack which the program highlighted as the most likely threat. That's why we reopened and moved a lot of equipment underground, especially to the Cheyenne Mountain bunker."

"But it happened. Your program was wrong."

"Yes, it was, and we could not understand it. The lone wolf nuclear attacks which caused so much confusion were also not high on the probability list. It was a one-two sucker punch. The attacks completely helped to destabilize the wobbly economy, and our Ponzi scheme came crashing down. Of course it wasn't only us but all the major economies around the world that toppled like a domino chain. When the chaos began we had plans in place. We knew that there might be a chance of a major social emergency; the program had given that as a probability. We had gone ahead and bought and armed as many government agencies and police departments as possible. The alternative websites were not wrong when they began to report that we had bought up billions of rounds of ammo and that we had given police agencies a lot of tactical gear. Some of our drills leaked out; one of the most famous, Jade Helm, caused certain people to get a bit nervous, but it was necessary."

"Yes, I remember reading about that. You guys also wanted to give guns to the TSA agents and the Postal Workers."

"Yes, we wanted to create a large paramilitary force that could be called upon in a time of crisis to help maintain order. Americans didn't know they were already living in a police state. I could listen in on anyone pretty much anytime I wanted. I could monitor anyone's home knowing exactly what was going on inside without having to switch on a camera. We could track anyone, anytime using their cell phones or their cars. We were watching. I was Big Brother.

"We did have a lot of contingency plans in place for a major civil event, and when it occurred we were able to get the camps going, and mobilize the government militia so to speak. We managed to keep order until it became too unsustainable. When we could not keep control anymore, things devolved into total anarchy. I saw the tea leaves and recruited a small group of agents and soldiers. Then one day a man walked into my camp in Albany. He had this computer which I will now show to you."

He placed his briefcase on the table and when he opened it, Splinter reached under his arm and drew his Glock. He pointed it at Lambert, who smiled ruefully. "That won't be necessary, Mr. Diefenbacher. You will want to chat with the man who will be calling in the next two minutes."

Lambert booted up the computer, opened up the web cam program and punched in a code. A small square screen popped up within the screen and after a few seconds of white snow a man's face came into view. Lambert looked at Splinter and saw that his mouth had been open in astonishment. The same thing had occurred when he spoke with the man for the first time himself. What Splinter was witnessing was a miracle. Electricity all over the country was out. There was no way a signal like this was supposed to be possible. Well, unless you had your own working satellite and your own power source. Yes, it was still possible but the fact that someone was able to communicate this way made Splinter re-holster the pistol and cross his arms over his chest. Obviously the man on the screen was someone important, and suddenly all the other 'important business' which he had planned over the next few hours did not seem so pressing after all.

The man on the screen was elegantly dressed. He was older and had a grin that was infectious. Splinter found himself responding to the man's smile with one of his own.

"Hi, Herr Diefenbacher. Do you prefer that appellation or do you prefer Splinter? I know you go by either."

"You can call me Commander, that's what everyone calls me now."

"Ahh, yes, you have been doing very well in making order out of the chaos. We have been watching you very closely, Commander. We are very impressed."

Splinter could see a bit behind the man, and he seemed to be in a lab of some kind.

"Have you ever heard of Plum Island, Commander?"

Splinter frowned, his mind snatched at a memory but could not fully grasp it, and he shook his head in the negative.

"Plum Island and many important installations around the world are now under the full control of the Bilderberg Group. Herr Lambert will give you all the details. What I will tell you is that in four months we will begin stage three in forging the New World Order. Mankind had been on a path to wrack and ruin. We have taken steps to reset the clock on our species and on the planet. We will need men like you, Commander, who will be able to take what's left of humanity and lead it into the future. If you agree to work with us, we will help you fulfill your ambitions of becoming a powerful, respected ruler who will be remembered throughout the ages. I will let you have words with Herr Lambert. He will contact me with your answer. It was really nice chatting with you, Commander. I sincerely hope we will meet in person someday soon."

He saw the man move toward the screen and then it went blank. He settled back into the large leather chair and watched as Lambert closed the computer and slip it back into his attaché case. Splinter's face was positively lit up. His mind was churning. He knew with the instinctiveness of despots that here was a deal he could not refuse. That man whom he had just spoken to was powerful, or had powerful connections. His ambition burned raw within his breast. It was all he could do not to leap out of his seat and shake Lambert like a rag doll, to make him tell him about this man and what plans this Bilderberg Group had. The other crucifixions he had planned for the evening could wait. He suddenly caught wind of a bigger game in play, and he intended to be in on it.

"Okay, Agent Lambert, let's have that chat."

Samantha noticed that she was feeling a bit hot and winded. She wondered if her ordeal over the last twenty-four hours had anything to do with it. Suddenly, as she was lifting a thirty pound bag of rice she felt the world swim out from under her. When she came to, Candice was kneeling over her. Candice's face had that pinched look she got when she was alarmed. "What happened?" She realized that she was laying on her side beside the very sack of rice she had been trying to shift.

"You just fainted. Mom, you're shivering."

Samantha realized that she was trembling. Her mind flashed back to the men who had invaded the cabin. The one who had called himself the "Birdman" had been sick. He had been coughing, trembling, and had a runny nose.

She got up slowly and when she finally got to her feet she understood, like it or not, her work was done for the day. Her body was dealing with something. In her pre-collapse life Samantha had been a nurse, and when they had stocked up on medical supplies at the *Rabbit Hole* she had stocked an abundance of natural immune boosting medicines. Since she was already sick she decided that it was too late for Sambucol, a natural immune boosting anti-viral medicine made from black elderberry. She decided that she would try Super ViraGon and if that didn't seem to be working, she would try Lomatium Dissectum. ViraGon is a potent combination of garlic, olive leaf extract, onion, ginger, zinc, and other nutrients. She would take the largest dose possible.

Candice helped her back to the cabin and went to fetch the medicines from the root cellar. She went into the back bedroom and laid on the bed. Just as she was getting under the sheets, a wave of nausea hit her and she rolled herself to the edge of the bed, just in time to vomit her last meal on the floor. The room spun a little and she suddenly began to cry. That's how Candice found her when she got to the room. The sight of her strong mother sweating, trembling, and crying made her insides turn to water. The smell of her mother's vomit made her want to gag.

"Look at the directions and give me the largest dose recommended," Samantha said. She was hoping that it would go down and stay down. Her daughter used the dropper and measured out the largest recommended dose in a cup of water and Samantha drank it down. She then sat up with her back to the wall, waiting for her stomach to settle. "Listen, if I become delirious or really sick, so much so that I cannot tell you what to do, keep giving me the medicine every three hours. If I am still sick after a day and it seems like I am having trouble breathing, switch to the Lomatium, the largest recommended dose. Keep me hydrated, and if my temperature gets above 103 degrees you may have to use some cold water to help my body bring it down.

"Now I want you to take a shot of Sambucol, and when your dad and brother get back they should immediately take a shot as well. You guys should take some every four hours until I come through. Get your father and brother to help you to wash the house down as best as you can. Bleach and water should do the trick. Get every surface we or *they* may have touched. Tell your dad to make sure you all wash your clothes…" She seemed to be searching for something else to say when she groaned and sank down into the blanket. Her head ached and her jaws clenched as the trembling increased. Candice looked at her mother slipping out of consciousness and realized that there wasn't anything else she could do except follow her directions. She wished Dad was here but until he and Robert returned it was up to her to hold the fort.

She made her mom as comfortable as she could and went into the front room. She took some of the Sambucol as her mother had suggested and then she went immediately to work. Running to the well she got the largest pot she could find and placed the water she had drawn on the stove to boil. There was going to be a lot of work to do.

The man and the woman who came out of the farmhouse looked normal. Their clothes were clean and both were clear-eyed. Alfred had dropped the ropes he was using to pull the tarps. Robert had his rifle pointed at the couple on the small stoop.

"You okay out here, Philip?"

"Yeah, they came up the driveway." The boy pointed with his rifle as he spoke. "There are bodies on that tarp, Dad."

"I can see that. Who are you mister?"

"My name's Alfred, and this is my boy Robert. We had us a spot of trouble last night and decided to take these dead fellows and leave them here."

"That so, huh?" He looked at Alfred long and hard, then remarked, "You don't look like the ones that eat the dead or the living."

"You don't appear to me to do that yourself. Did this farm belong to you or your family?"

"No, we are just passing through. Heading up to the big Free America camp up there in Marathon. My name is Jim Meehan we were hunkered down in Orange County, but things were just getting too dangerous. We quit our camp when we lost our little girl. The place was crawling with cannibals and that slimeball's, the Dove's, soldiers. You're not with his outfit are you?" Alfred saw the woman whom he assumed to be the man's wife raise her rifle at the question.

"No. We are not with his outfit. We had heard a bit about this fellow. Some sort of militia leader, is he?" Alfred had caught Donald Rovey's early ham radio broadcasts and he remembered hearing about a militia outfit out of New York City, but Rovey had not mentioned it for a long time and the Aimeses had bigger fish to fry.

The woman moved forward and spoke up. "When all this started we were members of the Orange County Christian Preppers. It seemed a natural thing for us. As Christians we are always prepping anyway. We were never into any of the extreme stuff. Just putting aside a little extra in case we had to help the community or ourselves. Then when the terrorists nuked Syracuse our pastor decided to form a more formal group. There were originally twenty of us. Our church ran a summer camp in the mountains, and kids would come from all over to stay or just visit. It became our bug out place. When things got really bad and the looting and rioting began in earnest, all the families who had contributed to the cause were let in. I can't tell you how many people we had to turn away or had to fight off. The bad thing was that we were too well known. A lot of people knew where we were located and word got around. They have food and they have medicine. We always managed to survive. Our pastor saw it all as a test, I think. But one day this huge group broke through the fences during the early morning. Before we knew it we were overrun.

"They were not really interested in gasoline, or to grab things they could trade. All they wanted was the food, and they killed to get it. They were like wild animals. There was no real organization to the attack either, but they still caught us out and it was by sheer numbers that they overwhelmed us. The camp had an indoor pool and that's where we ran and locked ourselves in the tiny adjacent basement room. Jim here poured bottles of chlorine down the hall leading to the room where we hid. We thought if the fumes didn't get us then maybe the good Lord had something else planned for us. It worked, we heard footsteps and voices now and again, but no one came downstairs to check out the little room where we hid.

"We must have stayed there for two days before Jim opened the door and we realized that they were gone. We got out and after we knew that we were alone we began picking up the pieces. Jim decided to move the bodies to the outside of the fence that surrounded the camp. Then we got really creative. We made signs that we hung from their necks saying, '**Killed Carriers of Plague and Sickness.**' I think it must have worked too, because we remained in the camp for the next two months until we lost our little Diane." The woman lowered her weapon and she began to cry.

"Of all the strange things to happen, she drowned in the pool." Jim said. "We just couldn't stay there anymore so we decided to take our chances and try to make it to Marathon. The people that run the camp we knew them through the American Preppers Network website that we used to blog on all the time. I think Jasper Filitree is in charge up there. They are inviting everyone as long as you contribute to the community."

"Jasper, I'll be damned. I used to go hunting with him a lifetime ago."

Suddenly Alfred began to feel self-conscious, and he could see that that the Meehans were too. It was weird but Alfred realized that these were the first people they had spoken with in over a month. He didn't count the ordeal he had with the men that had tried taking over the cabin. They were trying to kill him and his family; the Meehans were not. Humans are really a social animal, he reflected. "Listen I know how it must have looked. Me and Robert here dragging these bodies, but we just didn't want them on our land attracting attention. Hell of a first impression. If you will allow us we will just drag them into the barn there and we will be on our way." Jim shook his head as he held his wife's hand. Such were the times that despite the friendly exchange of words, the Meehans had not lowered their weapons and Robert still had his Mini 14 trained on them. Alfred reached down and grabbed both ropes and pulled his load into the barn. After he rolled the bodies onto the floor, he rolled up the tarpaulin and joined Robert. It was time to go. "I wish you and your family luck," he said to Jim, and he felt himself smile. "Hope you make it all the way there." He turned on his heels and walked down the driveway. He could hear Robert coming along with him. It had been hard turning his back to people who had weapons trained on him. But he needed to get home, and he had sensed that they were not a threat to him.

When they jumped the fence and were back on their land, Robert said, "They seem like nice people, don't they, Dad?"

"Yes, in another life I think I would have liked to have known them. They seem like good folks." An air of solemnity settled between father and son. They walked through the woods in silence. They could hear the harsh cries of blue jays, and as they got closer to their cabin it began to snow lightly. When they came into the small clearing around their home they could see that Candice was cleaning like a woman possessed. Alfred looked around and he could feel that tightening in the chest that he knew meant something was off. They went inside the house and saw Candice using a cloth and wiping down the walls.

"Oh, Dad." She dropped the cloth and ran to him. "Mom's sick."

Chapter Four

"Power acquired by violence is only a usurpation and lasts only as long as the force of him who commands prevails over that of those who obey." Denis Diderot

Splinter was intrigued with Lambert and all the possibilities he brought with him. He could not believe his good fortune. He sent for tea and cakes for him and his guest. Lambert was amused and pleased that the introduction had gone as smooth as it did. When Splinter's cook brought in the refreshments, both men partook with gusto. Lambert sat looking at Splinter, his gray eyes taking in the man coolly.

"Okay, Lambert of Albany. Explain it all, I want to know."

"The man you spoke to on the computer is Count Gustave. When everything went to hell, the people he works for bided their time and began to put their plans into place. They helped to facilitate the inability of the world leaders to act at key moments to avert or minimize the disaster. Most people do not know that a month into the Collapse our President and half his cabinet were assassinated. That was true of all the heads of state of all the major world powers as well. In key cities a variety of infectious diseases were let loose on the inhabitants. This created and set in motion other destabilizing effects, most importantly thinning the population.

"These men in the Bilderberg Group are extremely powerful. They have spent a lot of time and resources making this happen. Now they are about to enter a crucial stage in creating their empire. They need to assess the will of the people to accept a more central-ized government. That's where you and I come in. As leaders in the state they want us to get all the front runners to a meeting. They want us to take the lead in getting New York State under control and pacified. We need to invite the delegations of all the surviving militias in the state to a roundtable and see who wants to reestablish the old Constitution and who wants to go a different route.

"Let me be clear the people I work for do not want the old system back. They will protect their allies and kill their enemies. We need a certain number of people on each continent to properly restart an orderly sustain-able world. At the beginning of the crisis there were around seven billion people. That number is now around four billion. It is our intention to get that number down even further to just under two billion." Lambert looked at his host's stunned expression and appreciated what he saw there. Splinter was beginning to understand that these people in the Bilderberg Group were even more ruthless than he was. He was very small potatoes compared to the men who had gone about and orchestrated the deaths of at least two billion people and were hoping to kill that much again soon.

"What's your role in all of this?"

"Well when all this broke, as I said earlier, I was an NSA Agent. Working for the Department of Homeland Security, my job was to monitor suspicious activity and investigate it to assess if there was a threat to national security. I learned a lot in the NSA. We tapped everyone's phones and computers. We realized just how twisted and crooked the government was. I was under no illusions about the state the world was in. We had been teetering on our first global war in seventy-two years. Our resources were beginning to run out, life on the planet was becoming unsustainable, and if the Collapse had not occurred we would have been fighting a bad nuclear war with our enemies.

"I helped to coordinate the security of the FEMA camps and Rings of Steel around all the large cities in New York State. I also read the writing on the wall and began to make arrangements for the future. A lot of the men who worked for me became part of my private army. Just like you, we understood that in order for us to survive, the territory around us must be pacified, so we began to take control of strategic areas and military bases in the state.

"You control lower New York. I control the areas around Albany and parts of Central New York. There is a large militia group based in Marathon, New York, that hasn't really gone out into the surrounding areas yet. As far as we know there are others further upstate, in Buffalo and Watertown. What we will do is send out an invitation to these groups to see if they will attend a discussion. We will invite them to send a delegation for a two-day meeting to feel out their intentions. The groups that are interested in getting rid of the Constitution and setting up their own territories are our friends; the ones that want to reestablish the union are our enemies. When we know who is on our side, we will know which groups to target and destroy."

Splinter was nodding his head in silent agreement. He felt honored that these men had taken him in. This was a big bold adventurous move. The world was not made for men who wanted to be led around like sheep.

It was made for the ones who wanted to lead, who had vision and nerve. In this new world he would be a prince, a king, not some taxpaying subservient nobody. "I'm in," he said, and then he settled in as Lambert outlined the plan for world domination.

Alfred held his head in his hands. The pain in his mouth throbbed mercilessly. The children were in the outer room, and he was in the backroom that he shared with Samantha. She was sweating and shivering in the blankets. He had never seen her so sick. He didn't know what it was that she was suffering from because the symptoms were all over the map. He and Robert had followed Candice's recommendations. They had taken a natural antiviral medicine and helped with the decontamination of the house. He had also thrown the tent and stuff used by their attackers on a huge bonfire and burned the lot. He disinfected the two shotguns the men had used to terrorize them.

Candice came in again and gently lifted her mother's head from the wet pillow and spooned more of the medicine into her throat. "Mom's pretty tough. She'll pull through, Dad." She put her hand on her father's shoulder before she left the room. Robert was outside in the kitchen watching the snow fall. They had reinstituted the watch system, and he had the first shift. Soon he would go and melt into the tree line around the house. It was now an unshakable rule that the watch should be maintained at all times. If there was a snowstorm, then the sentry was required to make one circuit an hour as well as maintain a watch from the windows of the house. Alfred had begun to think that if he had the time and the equipment he would cut out a section of the roof and make a small glass box that they could use to watch all sides of the home from the inside. He already had it planned in his head. He would make a simple rope seat with a piece of wood that could be stored out of the way and pulled down when needed. It would be a neat project. He would also dig an escape tunnel from the house into the tree line.

Robert was glad that he could begin helping out. He had seen his sister do more than her share of the work, and he was glad to be back pulling his weight. There was still considerable tightness where the gunshot wound had healed, and he knew that it would still be a week or two before he could up his physical fitness regimen. Now he was just worried about Mom. His dad had hardly left her side since they had been back. He had been monitoring her temperature and trying to keep her as comfortable as best as he could.

Robert was in awe of his parents, something he would never let on. In a time when a lot more people considered being married an antiquated custom, he saw firsthand the value of the family unit and the benefits when two people worked together for the same goal. He also realized that his parents were really a team. No one was subservient to the other; there was just this iron-clad respect that they had for each other. There were things that Dad was good at as well as Mom. In some things one would be better than the other, and that was also part of the strength they shared. Robert could not even begin to contemplate life without either of his parents, and he hoped and prayed that his mother would pull through.

Prayer was something the Aimeses had slowly discovered, and it helped them through their darkest times. They were not Bible-thumping Christians, but they had found their way back to some semblance of a religious life. The Bible was one of the books that was constantly read in the cabin. Alfred urged all things in moderation. He would say, "God will help you in your worst time but it is up to you to make your own miracle." Robert would run his dad's words through his head from time to time, and that particular bit of wisdom made him smile.

It would be three days before Samantha's fever finally broke for good and the shivering stopped. She was so weak she could not sit up by herself. Alfred had made a strong broth using some of the fresh venison he and Candice had harvested, as well as the newest vegetable preserves he could find. She slowly made her recovery back to health. It was another eight days before she could say that she was over the illness. It had struck Alfred as a strange case of the flu. There was something troubling about the way she had become ill that bothered him. No one else had gotten sick, and both she and Alfred had been thankful for that. Alfred also thought that perhaps taking the antiviral medicines when they did also helped.

Samantha was still not quite her old self. Alfred could tell. There was a listlessness about the way she moved and spoke that was never there before. He knew that she was still very unhappy. There was Samantha before the home invasion and then Samantha after it. He also knew that it was just not because she was getting over a major illness either. He knew what the animals had done to her, and he knew that they had not just violated her body; they had violated something in her soul as well. He knew that his wife now had a massive spiritual battle to fight. He would try to help as much as he could, and he suspected that it would not be easy.

It was now late January, six months after the Collapse. The family had survived a number of attempts on their lives. Although they were introspective people they were not completely aware just how much they had changed. There were the Aimeses before the shit hit the fan, and the Aimeses after. Before the Collapse Alfred had been a Quality Manager at a yogurt factory in Binghamton, New York. His wife had worked as a nurse at Binghamton General Hospital. Their two children attended the local schools. Robert was fifteen, soon to be sixteen now, and Candice had been thirteen. Alfred constantly grieved for his family. With the collapse of society, an entrenched way of life and expectations had died. Now after the Collapse, he thought of his family as the pioneer Aimeses, who lived like the men and women of the nineteenth century. With the evaporation of the safety net of modern life, Alfred realized that they now had so much to learn and wished he had not been so lax in studying more about how people had got things done in the past. There was so much information that was now lost, he believed. He thought about his young daughter and he grieved for the life that had been taken from her and how she would now have to live.

Candice had killed people. He had taught his daughter well in that respect. It was a heavy weight that he had to teach his children to kill other human beings. She should have been going to high school this year. He thought about all the things she would miss, and he wondered how much time he had given her. The average lifespan at the turn of the twentieth century was forty-five years for a man and fifty years for a woman. The world was, for the most part, back to that stage at the moment. He heard his daughter going about her chores in the outer room and he grieved. He wondered if she was troubled about the lives she had took. He deliberated if he should talk about it with her. He was amazed at how quickly the young adapted. For Alfred, one of the things that concerned him was the effect the Collapse had on the children. He shuddered to think how many had died, and how many would be forced into militias as soldiers, to kill other children and people. Could he kill a child that was going to kill him or his family? He remembered reading that soldiers in World War II faced the same conundrum when Hitler sent old men and boys to defend Germany.

Was he entirely innocent in all this himself? He had drafted his daughter and son into his own little army and had rationalized it as a 'necessary evil.' Robert was doing his rounds now. Under his arm he was carrying a Mini 14. He knew that his son would not hesitate to defend the people in this cabin. Robert was fifteen years old, a boy now forced to be a man. A boy who would probably have to shoot and kill other boys and girls to protect himself and his loved ones. He understood that a lot of people had romanticized what the end of the world would be like if it actually happened, and the reality was far worse than anything the books could conjure. The thought that made him quake and still gave him nightmares was when he saw a man being killed, then cooked and eaten by cannibals. He still had nightmares about that experience and sometimes he could not bear the smell, or sight, of cooking meat.

He realized that he had to get his wife back fully into the family. He had to be there for her one hundred percent. The family would need her strength and wisdom. He recognized that one overlooked component in his prepping had been hope. How do you keep hope, a valuable block in the foundation of survival, alive and well? There has to be something beyond just surviving for the moment or for the short term. People needed a long term goal or plan. Something they could shoot for that was bigger than them, an idea that was still achievable. He understood that they had to start with small achievable goals then layer it with other more far reaching, but loftier goals. He decided to think about it some more, and when he was done he would run it all by Samantha.

Samantha was still weak, but she was grateful that she had pulled through. She had never remembered getting a bout of the flu that had been so horrible. She was still anxious about her family's well-being and had continued with the anti-viral boosters and the manic house cleaning. It was in some way cathartic, too. She could never undo in any way what those men had done to her. But she could heal her soul. She knew that her family was there for her, especially Alfred. She knew she could talk to him when she was ready. She just wasn't yet.

Her harrowing ordeal made her now more connected to the post-collapse world than any of her family. It was as if she was in a long dark tunnel and she could not see the light at the end. Alfred had been correct in his assumption that she was now depressed and feeling utterly hopeless. She wondered what would become of her or her family. How long could they go on like this? What was the point? She was back in the container, finishing up the chores that had remained undone since she'd fainted and gotten ill. As she moved around in the small space, the revolver in her waist holster knocked against one of the makeshift shelves they had rigged up. She stood up and leaned against it. Her thoughts went to the gun at her waist. It would be an easy thing to say that she was going for a walk, pick a peaceful spot, put the gun to her temple and pull the trigger. It would be quick and painless. It would be rest. Her hand went to the butt of the gun and rested on the cool stock. She took it out and looked at the ugly weapon. She could and would never understand what some people saw in those killing devices that they could call beauty. There was a direct transfer of her emotional feelings about her life and circumstance towards the weapon. It was ugly when it transferred power to the unworthy and it was beautiful when it gave power to the weak to defend themselves. She did hate the fact that she now had to carry one everywhere she went. As with everyone at the *Rabbit Hole* a firearm was never out of arm's reach. It could be comforting, knowing that release was just a bullet away. She sighed and shook her head. It was crazy to have such thoughts, and she imagined Alfred bumbling around with the kids and she could not suppress a weak chuckle. Alfred didn't bumble, if anything he tended to be a bit neurotic. The Collapse had really brought all of his natural talents and instincts to the fore. She began to reflect on the man she married and there was a fierce mixture of love and sympathy. Despite everything, she realized that she was lucky. Her marriage had lasted longer than most, and she realized, standing in the container with a .38 in her hand, that her children and spouse were the most important things to her. She slipped the firearm back into the holster and sat on a bag of rock salt. She was happy that she had a moment alone because there were some heavy emotional issues she had to deal with. She hated that at one moment she would be feeling okay and the next she felt like she wanted to crawl off somewhere and die. She shook her head, trying to understand how she could have even thought about killing herself when her family needed her the most. She then realized that it was the trauma of surviving from day to day in a constant state of fear in a world where the old rules and expectations didn't apply anymore.

She thought about her children and the world they would now inherit, and it broke her heart. She wondered if her children thought about any of this or were they just moving through their days, living in the moment. She hoped that they would never come to such a low point as she had recently. She held her head in her hands and a low groan escaped her. She would have to help them, Alfred, Robert, and Candice through their dark days, when they came. She was living through her own hell at the moment and although she felt alone, a small part of her understood that she wasn't. What those men did to her she could not erase, but her family needed her and they were proof that there was still goodness in the world.

The Bunker-England

Journal Entry 87

The regular radio has started to broadcast again. This time it was some guy named Archibald. He is calling himself king now. He said yesterday that King Peter's army had been annihilated at Falkirk. Then there was a bunch of white noise and another guy came on saying that his name was Malone and that Peter's army was still intact. He said that they had made a strategic retreat, and that most of the army was unharmed. He said the people of Britannia should not give up hope.

It must be utter chaos up there. I can't even imagine what it must be like when those armies fight each other. I try to picture it in my mind. Do they shoot at each other, or do they go at each other with swords and axes like in the olden days? It's tough living down here, but it must be hell living out there. All those people having to choose up sides, and although I don't really care for the royal family, at least we know who they are, but these other people, these rebels pushing for a New World Order, I don't really trust them. Are they any better than what we already have? Hell, now it's either you are a Rebel or a Royalist. I don't trust the Rebels. They seem like a bunch of opportunists. I don't want to spend the night writing about politics.

Today everyone was in a bad mood. If I had known how bad it was going to get I would have brought down some more books and rigged up our computer so it could play a movie once in a while. I think we are all suffering from really bad cabin fever. Trisha was in a really foul mood, a real funk. She started screaming this morning that her hair stank. Now she has not had the opportunity to care for her hair, and I know that she said that she had run out of the stuff she uses to condition and wash it. She has really nice long brown hair but now it's all tangled, and she is miserable. She also went after the kids this morning, saying that it was time they learned to wash their own clothes. She really did throw a blinder. The kids had dropped their dirties on the floor near the hamper in the bathroom. She went in, got upset about her hair, and started yelling at everybody about washing their clothes. She started screaming that she was tired of it, she was tired of the kids, and she was tired of me and tired of the goddamn bunker. She started throwing stuff around in the bathroom.

I felt bad for her and for the kids. Me, she can curse at if it makes her feel better, but the truth is if it wasn't for the bunker we probably would be dead by now. I always thought I was so clever but now I don't know. I should have thought about making the bunker more sustainable. I was hoping that I would have enough supplies to outlast the bad times and we could just wait out Armageddon, so to speak, but that's not the way it is shaking out. The bunker should have been bigger. We should have made at least another space that is away from the main cylinder. It would have been better if it had been built in an L shape rather than this single cigar tunnel we live in. The curtains we have for privacy just aren't enough. It's tough as hell having to listen to everyone and knowing that they are listening to everything I am doing. It so tough because we cannot see anything except the trees around the bunker with the periscope. Nothing but tall weeds, trees, and a whole lot of nothing. We can't even see the sky through the damn thing. It would have been nice to be able to see the sky or look down into a valley, just something different once in a while.

I had been so caught up in "just surviving" that I had not properly considered the mental challenges we would have to face. It's tough sharing every waking moment with four other people, even if it's my family. We will just have to find a way to deal with this without losing our minds. It was just that when we were 'top-side,' that's what we have started to call outside now, we had other things going on. We were in different places most of the day, doing different things, and there was a lot of distraction. Here there is none of that opportunity for diversion. We have a whole lot more time available to watch and over-analyze every little thing that is said and done. Little things take on big meanings, things we would have let go topside have now become glaring and annoying. I keep asking myself again and again was this the best choice for this family? Should I have invested in an above ground hideaway or thrown our lot in with a group of like-minded people? I think I was wrong in that I tried fitting a square peg into a round hole. I should have really studied my family closer to see if this was a good fit for us. I realize now, but it's too late, that based on our psychological makeups this was not the best choice. But we are here and the world has gone insane topside, and we have to get through it. May God help us.

Lambert watched as his well-trained men carried out the mission they were assigned. The Nine Mile nuclear station had been manned by a small company of men who took their job very seriously. The assets Lambert had used to get his small army to the nuclear plant had been provided by the Bilderberg Group. Two CH-47 Chinook helicopters had been sent to airlift his men to within a mile of the plant. Their objective was to take control of the facility. His mission was in tandem with other Bilderberg strike forces who were attacking and securing the other nuclear plants in the state.

There were certain things that had remained strangely intact, and one of those things was the protection of the nation's nuclear assets. There were soldiers that had stuck to their missions when the world fragmented. These were troops that were specifically trained and hand-picked. Troops whose loyalty was without doubt. They were flown in and all their supplies had been airdropped. The nuclear plant was effectively shut down and the troops were there to guard it until told otherwise by the government. It was a dangerous and uneasy job they were assigned, because apart from guarding it they had to make sure that the plant didn't go into meltdown.

This had already happened in other parts of the world where such contingency plans were not really adhered to. Nuclear plants in Pakistan, India, Russia, and China had gone into meltdown. Canada and the United Kingdom were not immune. There were two meltdowns at the Point Lepreau plant in New Brunswick and the Sizewell B plant in Suffolk. The area for miles around those plants was now effectively uninhabitable and many would die from the exposure.

The guards at Nine Mile lived and worked, knowing full well that they watched a sleeping dragon. It was the Bilderbergs' plan to take control of all the viable power plants in New York State. This was also Lambert's chance to show the Board that he was a valuable asset in the field. There were thirty men guarding the base, and they had .50 caliber machine guns mounted at certain locations around the plant's perimeter. The guards were heavily armed and well trained. He had thought about a night attack, but he understood that would make it harder for them to get real time intel from the drone that would be airborne to monitor the attack. They brought up the heavy armored vehicle. The plan was to crash it through the fence surrounding the plant, and the men would then lob grenades, taking out the two .50 caliber machine guns. They would open up with a blistering barrage of their own .50 caliber machine guns. Then his soldiers would go in through the fence, taking out the enemy until they were all dead and the plant was in their hands.

Lambert gave the order to go and the plan was put into action. The M1117 Armored Security Vehicle barreled its way up the road, and as soon as it was within two hundred yards of the fence a .50 caliber machine gun opened up. Lambert knew that .50 caliber machine guns were devastating and he got a clear reminder just how deadly they were. The bullets tore into the ASV, chewing up the metal, and it shuddered and began to burn under the well-directed barrage. He figured to the men inside the vehicle it must have sounded like hell on earth. He felt a momentary shiver of doubt as he watched the vehicle almost stall. It sounded like someone was cutting it apart with a saw. He saw the ricocheting bullets blow through some of the soldiers who were hiding in the bushes, ending their lives with meaty thumps that tore out vital organs, tissues, and bones. There is the particular sound a bullet makes when it hits a human body that anyone hearing it will never forget. Lambert and his men had been under fire before, but it was always up against undisciplined troops nothing like this.

The M1117 did its job and it revved and smashed through the fence, bringing down a great portion of the barrier. It got some of the wire fencing snagged in the right wheel well and it was dragged forward as the vehicle rolled before coming to a stop. Its wheels were shredded. The crew inside opened up with their own Browning .50 caliber machine gun, sweeping the area at the front of the main building that was stacked with sandbags. Its launcher sent a couple of 40 mm grenades over the sandbags, effectively taking out the threat. That was the signal to get his men moving. With the M1117 providing cover his men rushed through the opening in the fence. Some took cover behind the vehicle.

Everything he had thought about this mission was proving to be true. It was going to be a tough nut to crack. The men guarding the facility knew the complex inside and out. They were well trained and no doubt would fight to the last man. He realized that their initial advantage had been lost as the other .50 caliber machine gun opened up, pinning them in their position. That was when he gave the orders for the gas to be used. His men donned their gas masks and two men with modified bazookas inched forward and fired. The shells arched over the guard emplacements and exploded. A thick gray cloud soon enveloped the front of the complex.

Lambert looked at the men and nodded again. They sent another round of the gas into the sandbags, and what happened next was grim and surreal. Men whose lungs felt like fire had been poured into them got up and ran about screaming. Lambert's men picked them off very methodically. He didn't wait for the gas to clear. He had to keep the momentum going. He led his men through the initial defenses until he came to the door that led down into the plant itself. Two men taped explosives to it and blew it inwards, killing a man who was on the other side.

Then it became a running battle as the defenders fell back to specific areas and held their ground. It dawned on Lambert that they were firing live rounds and using grenades inside a nuclear facility. The sheer insanity of what they were doing made his stomach go cold. His men broke through one hotly contested barrier and a deadly gun battle ensued. He found himself in front of his men, chasing four defenders down a long metal gangway. The men turned and fired, and there was a hot burning feeling as a bullet grazed his neck. He returned fire, hitting one man square in the back and another in the head. The dead men's comrades gained the corner, and temporary safety, to return fire. The man next to Lambert went down and without really thinking, he unhooked one of the grenades from his belt and lobbed it around the corner. There was a hollow metallic boom and the men around the corner began screaming. He edged gingerly around and into the passageway. One man was not moving. The other was trying to raise his pistol to shoot. Lambert shot him first.

All around, above and below him on different levels of the plant, there were the sounds of a viciously contested battle being fought. Lambert himself helped to clear the last of the defenders from the reactor room. When the battle was over, he and his men moved the corpses out of the facility. The body count was forty-four defenders to fifty-eight of Lambert's men. He set up camp on the outside of the facility. He did not want to be inside the skin of the plant; there was just something about it that gave him the willies. He got his boss on a satphone and relayed the news.

"The Nine Mile nuclear plant is now secure, Count Gustave."

"Excellent, Herr Lambert, you have done a fantastic job. We will send in a relief team and engineers to relieve your men in forty-eight hours. Just to let you know the other teams have also been successful. All of New York's nuclear facilities are now safely under the control of the Bilderberg Group."

"I am glad to hear that."

"Everything is falling into place. We've had some hiccups here and there, but we are doing something unprecedented in the history of mankind. We are reengineering humanity. We are putting in place a plan that will benefit the planet for thousands of years." The man on the phone paused to catch his breath, then continued, "We will go ahead with the New York Plan as discussed. We will not act until May. We will let things settle for a while. I don't want anyone to acquire any more territory for now. There will be time enough for that later. In the spring we will meet with the large survivor groups that have established their own settlements, and we will chat with them to see who will join our cause and who will be against us. Exciting times, Herr Lambert. Oh, yes, the Board has decided that we will resort to the old ways of addressing ourselves. I have been instructed to confer upon you officially the title, Lambert of Albany, congratulations."

"Thank you, sir."

The Count broke the connection. Lambert knew what that meant. When the relief party got here they would have a new uniform for him. It would be black pants, a gray shirt, and a black armband with a red C imprinted on it. He would also be given a purple cape, a sign of royalty, and a Luger. He sat down on the hard steel chair looking across the complex. His eyes came to rest on the churning water of Lake Ontario. The Count was right, it was exciting times. Never in his wildest dreams did he ever think that he was going to be a king. That was exactly what was happening. These men who had brought about the destruction of the old world were now busy building a new one. One that required men of great resourcefulness and courage. He had been in a unique position when the Collapse occurred, and when the chance had presented itself, he had grasped it with both hands. When the world was divided up, he intended to have a piece for himself.

Chapter Five

"To live without Hope is to Cease to live." Fyodor Dostoevsky

The remainder of that first winter after the Collapse came on like a ferocious beast. The temperature nose-dived to twenty below zero for days on end. To Alfred it seemed like God himself wanted to wipe out the rest of humanity. Life was a very fragile thing at the *Rabbit Hole*, and it took every member of the family working fanatically to survive. There was just so much to be done. During a particularly bad stretch it snowed for seven days, dropping about six inches every day. The snow was packed solidly around the log house. Alfred and Samantha took turns going up unto the roof to shovel the heavy ice and snow off. They had to dig a path to the remains of the outhouse. There was no way to do a roving watch in weather that bad, but one person did keep a check on the perimeter at all times. The Aimeses were determined not to be surprised again.

They did begin to get cabin fever and after a while they began to get on each other's nerves. It got so bad that at one point there was a stony silence in the cabin, and they wouldn't even look at one another. Alfred understood that they had to get a grip on the situation before it got completely out of hand. One evening after they had a meal he leaned back in one of the small chairs at the dinner table, looked at his family, and said,

"I know this has been hard on everyone. How can we lose everything and still keep our souls, our basic sense of selves? We have all changed. These few months have altered who we are." As he looked at his children his mouth formed a sad grin, and he sighed. Samantha was looking at him, her eyes burning hot as tears began to form. She watched her husband struggle for words and reached out for his hand. Candice, who was doing the watch, looked away from the window. For a fleeting second she felt like the kid she was a year ago—the one who would have ran over to her parents and thrown her arms around them.

The cabin was small. Dad could talk as she did her job, and she could hear as she moved about the house, her feet and body on autopilot. Robert was by the small woodstove, carefully laying a log on the fire. He had become an expert at keeping the fire going. He looked up at both his parents as his dad continued.

"We have to find a way to keep our spirits up. Our sanity depends on it. We should find one thing we can do to entertain the family and schedule it into our day."

Alfred paused and as he was about to speak Samantha piped up. "I could prepare something really yummy every other day. Small so it's not overwhelming but sweet, a treat." She smiled.

"Yeah that would be great, Mom. You know I think I could find my iPod; it's around somewhere. I had a secret project going. A few months before it all crashed and we had to come here, I had downloaded music from the different decades. I figured I'd have something for everyone. I could plug into the ham aux plug and we could have a few minutes of music a day." Robert looked at his parents shyly.

"I could be in charge of game night." Candice's voice drifted into the front room from the back. She was looking out the window examining the darkening tree line. "We have all those board games that we never play—Monopoly, chess, backgammon, and Scrabble. We could get us a tournament going."

"Sounds good." Alfie was once again amazed at how everyone decided to chip in. "I'll be in charge of reading a story every night. We have a few novels that we had stashed in one of the containers." Alfred looked around and was surprised to see Robert and Samantha smiling. They were actually looking forward to playing their part in lifting the oppressive gloom around the camp—no, he would stop calling it that. It was their homestead.

The next day Samantha got some peanut butter, honey, vanilla extract, cinnamon, and hazel nuts from the pantry. She poured the honey into a saucepan and got it to the hard-crack stage. Then she stirred in the peanut butter, vanilla, and the hazel nuts. She placed the saucepan outside to cool in the snow. After an hour she took the pan in, and using a mallet, she broke up the sweet mixture into a sort of brittle and placed it on the table under a cloth. After dinner, everyone was treated to a sweet dessert. She could not believe just how well her treat was received. It actually made them giddy, and Alfred and the children giggled and joked about the most mundane things. There was banter in the cabin that reminded Samantha of the old days before the darkness. For a fleeting moment she went back in time to when they would sit around their home in Binghamton. It had been filled with laughter and hope. She looked at them now, her husband on the floor sucking the brittle carefully, trying not to aggravate his broken tooth, his eyes closed, laughing at something Candice had said about having to take a crap in a burnt down outhouse. Robert, who had the watch, was cracking up in the next room. Candice was laughing so hard there were tears coming down her face. For a moment in the cabin the harsh world receded, and the Aimeses found comfort in each other.

Spurred on by his mother's success with her pastry dessert, the next day Robert found a small box under his parent's bed where they had kept the technological relics of their past lives. There were two laptops in the box, filled with pictures and clips of happier times. Robert wondered if anyone would ever get the nerve to look at the clips and photos ever again. He went by other things until he found what he was looking for—his iPod. He turned it on and to his delight it still worked, but he could see that the battery was low. He plugged it into their small Allpowers 16W solar charger and within a few minutes the power bar on the iPod indicated that it was fully charged. That night he plugged it into the aux function of their ham radio so they could listen to the music from the speakers. Samantha had the watch and she was in the next room gazing out the window. The snow was coming down in an almost impenetrable white mass. True to his word, Robert had downloaded music from a variety of different decades, and he arranged the twenty minute playlist randomly so that when the music began it filled the cabin with a nostalgic remembrance of the last sixty years. There was *Sing, Sing, Sing* from Benny Goodman that had them tapping to the sound of the big bands, and on through the decades the music wove its spell. From *Born in the USA*, to Jim Brown's *Living in America*, the hypnotic music soon had them all wrapped up in memories of happier times. In the small front room close to the fire, they clapped and sung along to *Bad to the Bone*. When Jim Reeves strong voice came through crooning *He'll Have to Go* they all looked at Robert like he had been dropped from another planet. He smiled and said, "Just couldn't help it."

Alfred smiled and looked at Samantha. "Can I have this dance?"

"I have the watch."

"I know, but I want to dance with my wife."

Samantha found her face heating up as she shyly fidgeted in place. The kids were looking at them, and it made her nervous and self-conscious. Alfred took the rifle from her hand and handed it to Candice, pulling his wife close. As she hugged him and swayed to the music she realized just how much she loved this man. She sagged against him as all the strain she had been carrying alone for the past couple of weeks left her body. She sighed and hugged him close, burying her face into his chest. She could feel the heat of him and smell his particular scent. Alfred could see that his wife was letting something go. He could feel it in her body, and when he looked into her eyes he saw deep into her soul. He saw the glimmer of the person he had married, and he knew that his wife was finding her way back to the family. He felt a wave of gratitude to his son. He was the one who had collected the music and had made this possible. The couple danced in the lamp light and their children watched and smiled.

And so it went for the Aimeses. The next day Candice ran game night. They played Chutes and Ladders. They settled on a routine, and every other day each member would provide the entertainment. Alfred read *David Copperfield*. It was amazing how quickly they were transported back in time in their minds and soon everyone around the camp was talking about David's tribulations and couldn't wait to hear more of the story. These activities gave them a way to contribute and have some mental downtime. It kept them sane while the winter roared on angrily. They also made plans for the spring. Alfred understood now that for them to survive, they would need a lot more reference material than what they had brought with them initially, and one of the things they planned on doing was an excursion to the library in Whitney Point. They also had plans to get a garden going for fresh fruit. They now fully understood that they had to begin thinking of the homestead as their permanent home and as such they had to plan to survive here long term.

Alfred also understood that they would have to spend some time practicing hand to hand combat. It was time to break out Sam Franco's and Tim Lakin's old manuals. It was with great reluctance that he understood that there was necessity in teaching his family to defend themselves not only with firearms, but also with knives and their bodies. He spoke with Samantha about this and there was no arguing about it. She understood that these were dangerous times and to survive they had to be more prepared and trained than their enemies. It was now three months since they left their home; it had taken them that long to arrive fully at the survivor mentality. They were a family but they were also a small military unit. Alfred and Samantha had a lot of plans and as soon as the winter began to give ground to spring and the thaw set in, they began to put those plans into place.

Samantha drew up a roster and every other day a member of the family was scheduled to practice hand-to-hand combat and self-defense for an hour. Alfred and Robert had made a small enclosure at the back of the cabin. They hung a heavy homemade punching bag from a tree and made a couple of man-sized crosses from heavy planks wrapped with cloth and burlap, at strategic places like the head, arms, chest, stomach groin, and shins. They practiced attacking an opponent's weak areas with their fists and feet.

Alfred showed them how to wrap their knuckles and shins with cloth to protect their bones. They practiced throwing punches with the heavy punching bag and delivering devastating attacks on the man crosses. The two elder Aimeses were of one accord on this, and there was no letup in the schedule. Soon each member of the family could go through the moves and respond to any hypothetical threat instinctively.

On one of his foraging trips Alfred brought back some rubber that he had scavenged from the farm, and a piece of cherry wood. He charged up his tools and got to work. When he was done he had carved out four Y shaped frames and made four sling shots. He figured that if they got good at using the slings they could save on bullets. And they were quiet and easier to carry than bows. This along with the hand-to-hand training meant that the Aimeses were very busy. They had survived the initial Collapse and now were adapting to their new world.

Robert got stronger and regained full fitness. He cut his hair shorter, and while he had been a bit on the chubby side four months ago, he was now well muscled and stronger. It wasn't just the boy who had been transformed physically. The entire Aimes clan were toned and strong. A combination of all the grueling physical work on the homestead and the physical training they did made them fitter and stronger. Samantha also realized that they were actually eating a lot better now, too. While they still ate some processed rehydrated food from time to time, their meals now consisted of a lot of fresh venison and natural starches and vegetables. Gone were pizza and fast food meals they had indulged in frequently pre-Collapse. Alfred was happy that after a few weeks they all got pretty good with the slings. He understood that when they were hunting big game they would have to do it with rifles or bows, but the slings could take down smaller game such as squirrels and woodchucks. It was in this way that the family recovered from the initial trauma of the horrific months following the disintegration of the social infrastructure.

They had gotten a few things right, and it made a big difference in their lives. Alfred and Samantha realized that they had to think of themselves like the pioneers of old, living on a hostile frontier. There were enemies all around and there was no law, or institutions to protect them. For the moment they were on their own. Alfred would always wonder just how many of the people he knew and were acquainted with in his past life were still alive. Such thoughts would always lead him down a dark and fearful road and he learned to turn his mind away from such things. In a few days he and Robert were going to go on a very dangerous walk into the town of Whitney Point.

It was a risk, but it was one that after a family discussion they decided must happen. It was an interesting thing, the family discussion. It used to be that Alfred and Samantha were the ones who decided all things and the children were passive participants but something new had evolved in the cabin. Somewhere along the way the children became active contributors. They gave their opinions and voiced their concerns. The awed parents realized that their children, although young in years, had become responsible and serious individuals.

Samantha and Alfred had understood that although they had a brought a lot of how-to manuals with them, they were still lacking a lot of practical homesteading information. The internet was dead, so the only place where they could acquire the information they needed was from books, and the only place they could think of getting the manuals was the library. So Alfred decided to make a little excursion. It would be a six-hour walk from their cabin into the town, a very dangerous trip, but they weighed up the pros and cons and decided that it would be worth it. Tomorrow Alfred and Robert would set out at first light.

The Bunker-England

Journal Entry 130

Things have gone from bad to worse. Trisha almost strangled Bea. I have been trying to play the peacemaker. I seem to be handling this a lot better than Trisha. I have been trying to do a bit more, in that I tell Trisha to have a lie down, and I'll handle the children for a while. I can see my wife going, and I don't know what to do about it. It's hard to see the one you love breaking down. I am trying to make it easier for her, but nothing seems to work. I listen to the radio now with the headphones because all she says is that it is all over. There is just so much bad news lately that I can see how easy it is to lose heart. This morning she didn't get up until it was almost 10 a.m., and I really think she only got out of bed so that she could use the bathroom. She went by me while I had the headphones on; the kids were trying to wash their underthings. I had assigned them some chores to take some of the pressure off us and especially Trisha. I thought for sure she would have been feeling good knowing that the kids were taking care of some of their own personal responsibilities. But Bea had spilled some water on the floor, and when Trisha stepped in it, soaking her socks, she lost it. She kicked Bea's basin, sending soap water flying, then she started slapping Cathy, really beating on her. Bea started to cry and that's when she turned on her. I am at a loss trying to explain all this, Jesus Christ, my wife tried to kill our daughter. There is no doubt in my mind that's what occurred.

She shoved her to the ground and started choking her. Bea is small, and we have all lost a lot of weight in the bunker. We just don't eat as much anymore. Anyway, she shoved Bea up against the wall and started to strangle her. I got up then and tried to get her off, but she is strong. I couldn't get her hands from around Bea's neck. That's when I hit her. I body-checked her and her head slammed into the wall. Blimey! I thought that I had killed her because when her head hit the wall it was loud, and she basically just collapsed. Bea wasn't moving and Trisha had just fallen on top of her. Cathy started to scream; she thought they were both dead. I pulled Trisha off Bea. Bea started to choke and cry and I knew then she was alright but Trisha wasn't moving at all. It's an amazing thing, panic and guilt. I knew that I had hurt my wife. It was the most horrible thing in the world. It was terrible seeing her inert body. I pulled her toward the kitchen area, got some water in a towel and gently wiped her face. She opened her eyes. It is true when they say that the eyes are the windows to the soul. Trisha has these really clear blue eyes and when she looked at me I could see the hopelessness and misery in them. She moaned and rubbed her head. She looked up at me as I held her head in my lap. "What's the use?" she said. "The world is gone. It's all over. There is nothing out there except a bunch of savages killing each other. We should all just go out and let them kill us." She turned and looked at the kids, who were crying. "What kind of world is it going to be for them? What kind of future will they have? I'll tell you. They have no future. The world isn't going to go back to what it was. It's over all over. My babies, my poor babies. We can't stay in this tomb forever, at some point we have to leave it. Then what? We get murdered; my sweet girls are raped and killed. Let's just end it, Joseph. Let's be brave and end it. I bet a lot of people have opted out of all this misery. We can and we should." She looked at me and I couldn't help but cry.

We were a family once, a real family with hopes and aspirations. I had a good job, Trisha too. Even when we left London and came here to the farm we were happy. We were blessed with two beautiful daughters, and then the world imploded. I don't know what to do. I don't know what to say to my wife. The news that I had been hearing through those infernal headphones was not good. It's hard to believe that my people, the English, with our proud history and herit-age, a beacon of civilization, is now gone. The hope that people would come together in humanity's darkest days has proven to be a pipedream.

So I looked at my wife and I wanted to comfort her. I wanted to comfort the child she hurt and almost killed, and I could do neither. For the thousandth time I think about the way I prepared and I am coming more and more to the conclusion that I didn't prepare enough. Maybe I should have gotten together with other like-minded people and gone over the possibili-ties; maybe with that help I would have been able to make better plans. Maybe I would have gone with an above ground bug out location rather than the bunker we are presently in. I think that I got so caught up in the just getting out of the harm's way part of the experience, I failed to understand that surviving wasn't just about living through the initial danger, it was also about how to get by in the long-term afterward.

If I had been thinking about the days after, in a hard no nonsense way, it would have gone something like this: There most likely won't be any social order, not for a long time, years maybe, so what would that mean to my family and me? Well there would be no law, except if you lived with a community of like-minded survivors. The strong would rule over the weak because civilization is the great equalizer. I would have to be mentally ready to kill anyone who threatened my family or our possessions. Running and hiding as we have done would not be enough. I really didn't talk with my family enough before all this went down. I thought I did, but I didn't. I viewed the bunker and prepping as more of a contingency plan rather than a lifestyle. Meaning that we should have run drills and chatted more about potential scenarios than we did. If we had done that, then I think we would have had the survivor mentality hardwired in and things would have gone a bit easier. True survivors outlast the initial danger and the troubles that follow after. We survived the danger, but it doesn't seem like we will survive the troubles.

I held her head in my hands for a while, then she got up as calm as you please and went to lie down in her bunk. She just trudged and slipped quietly into her bed. She turned her face to the bulkhead and just laid there staring at the wall. I got Bea and tucked her into bed as well. Her throat had ugly black and blue bruises. Eventually she cried herself to sleep. Cathy did a halfhearted job of cleaning up the mess. Then she too went back into her bunk and turned facing the wall. If I had known how serious it was all going to be, I would have done my research and preparations more carefully. We are all still here, but I can't say for how long and that uncertainty is very frightening. It would help to have us all pulling in the same direction; it would help enormously for Trisha to be with me on this, but I am afraid that she has given up. She has lost all hope and I don't know what to do about that. God help us.

Chapter Six

"Courage consists not in blindly overlooking danger, but seeing it, and conquering it." Jean Paul

Splinter sat in his office reviewing a stack of reports he had received from his intelligence department. The department was run by a man named Cole. His intelligence officer's small but vital unit was responsible for investigating any serious internal crimes, as well as gathering intelligence on threats to the militia's plans. The fifteen page typed report that was on his desk was about the large Marathon Militia group that controlled Cortland and Cayuga counties. They also controlled most of Upper Broome County as well.

Splinter looked at the county map of New York that was tacked to the wall opposite his desk. His territory stretched from the tip of Long Island all the way up into Delaware County. Lambert controlled most of the counties north of Albany. There were three other big militia groups of note that had controlled and brought order to the areas around their bases, the St. Lawrence and Genesee Militias. It rankled Splinter that these groups were so presumptuous to take the names of the counties they were based in. It irritated him that he now realized through his intelligence network that these groups were not going to be easy targets. He had steamrolled over most of the opposition, taking few, if any, casualties. It was not going to be so easy to bring the rest of New York under control. He couldn't help mulling over the fact that even with all the gun control measures that had been thrown at the Upstaters, as they liked to call themselves, they still were well armed and prepared. He understood the subtle cultural dynamic between the people who had lived in downstate New York versus most of the folks who lived upstate.

This Marathon group was a big problem. He had sent spies disguised as regular people looking to join the community. Two had come back, and the third no one knew what happened to her. He then hit upon a rather brilliant idea. He had sent a group of spies. Their cover was that of a family unit, and they had started to send him regular reports. The two returning agents had reported that the group was well armed and well trained. They had fortified the town and the surrounding area, creating a five mile buffer zone between the town and the camp limits. They had gone out and systematically pacified the surrounding counties, clearing out most of the renegade and canni gangs that had terrified the area. Their grip over the two counties was not one of iron, but it was strong and they were slowly bringing a sense of order back to their territory.

The report said that they did everything by vote. They were old Democratic Republicans holding on to a failed bygone democratic system that they hoped one day to restore. Their hope of reestablishing the Republic was contrary to Splinter's view of the world. As far as he was concerned the old way was dead. It was now his time. He saw himself as a visionary who would carve himself a kingdom from the ruins of a past defunct world. So these preppers were an obstacle that had to be removed.

According to his spies, the Marathon Militia was led by one Jasper Filitree. He had been the one who had organized the group and when they set up shop in Marathon they elected him leader by vote. They had a small council of seven and five people representatives. Splinter shook his head and a cry of exasperation escaped him. He could not believe what he was reading. They had gone about the business of setting up a leadership team on the model of the past US government. As he read, he shook his head in bewilderment at the sheer stupidity and naivety of the Marathon group. They flew the stars and stripes in the middle of town and at the point of entry into the camp's perimeter on Interstate 181 South and North, which they controlled. They began each meeting reading one article of the Bill of Rights and a prayer to God.

Splinter got up from his desk and paced his office. He did that a lot now as he made his plans. The conquest of New York was now entering a definitive and more precarious stage. From here on out he understood that he would be fighting not disorganized shell-shocked gangs, but tough well-armed survivors. These were people who had survived the hellish five months of terror after the Collapse. They had not turned on one another but helped each other. They had not looted others or become marauders; they had prepared and had survived. They were diverse in background and culture but still loved the idea of the USA, and hoped one day to see it restored. It reminded him of ancient Rome when the Republic collapsed. There were people then, romantic dreamers who had hoped to restore the Republic. It never happened. These so called preppers were likewise delusional. He knew that in a time of crises a strong central leadership would trump a bunch of talkers in a town hall, any day of the week. He would wait until early May before sending out his ghost squads. These would be small groups of six to seven soldiers, highly trained in the arts of guerilla warfare. They would harass the enemy and weaken them, and then when the time was right he would move in for the kill.

He walked out of his office, down the hall to a locked door. There was a solitary guard sitting beside the door. When the guard saw him approach he got to his feet and stood stiffly at attention. He turned the key in the lock and peeked in. On a small cot bundled in a blanket was a small biracial girl with curly black hair. She was eight years old. She was snoring, and she seemed to be talking in her sleep. He closed the door and locked it. It's amazing what some parents will do for their children and what some won't, he thought grimly. That child was a way to control the father who loved her, and he was a very important part of Splinter's plans. He took off his glasses and began cleaning them with a handkerchief.

"Make sure she's comfortable and that she has everything she needs."

The guard nodded as he walked away. He went back to his dimly lit office and sat facing a large map of New York. Binghamton would be his next target. Once he got control of the city he would be able to have a very fortified base close to his enemies. Then he could go about crushing Jasper Filitree's dreamers.

It felt good to Robert to go on this mission with his dad. His recovery had been a slow but gradual one. There were many times in the days just after he had been shot when he had run a fever and taken a turn seemingly for the worse, just to pull through. Five days after the incident, when he had tried to move and found that his legs could not, he had cried hysterically.

The fear he had felt then of not being able to walk dwarfed the fear of dying.

Lying and recovering from his injuries made him undergo a mental transformation. As he watched his family take care of him and things around the hideout, he understood that the world had changed. The way they had to live at the *Rabbit Hole* was far simpler than the way they had lived at their home in Binghamton. He realized that his generation's job was to rebuild a better world than what his parents had lived in. He also gathered that he knew nothing about his country. He had learned a few things in the Social Studies classes he had taken over the years but he understood that he was lacking the knowledge of what had made the United States the beacon of light it once was. He was determined to find out. He knew that his father was going to the library to find books on homesteading and farming skills. He was going to find a few on the US Constitution and US history. There was a burning urge to put things back to right. He was responsible for the world the surviving generations would inherit.

As they walked along under the trees making for the edge of their property and the beginning of state land that angled downward toward State Route 206, which would take them into the town, Robert became switched on. Father and son moved quietly, both had Ruger Mini 14 tactical rifles slung across their bodies, and they were wearing green and brown camo to blend into the landscape. They were traveling light—extra ammo, and three dense high-energy meals to eat on the go. They both had backpacks. Alfred carried the small tarp they would use to pass the night, and Robert carried both sleeping bags in his pack. Otherwise their bags were empty. That space would be filled on the return trip with the books they were hoping to salvage from the library.

They trudged along, the father medium height with the weather beaten face under a camo hat and the son, a slimmer and younger version of the elder, dressed in similar attire. Watching them walk one could not imagine that they did not have any military training. The watchfulness and the careful, light, almost soundless movements came from their new lifestyle of tracking game and avoiding other people. They followed the road using the woods as cover as far as they could before it thinned out to the point where it became meaningless. They jumped the barbed wire fence and got onto the road proper. They had another ten miles to hike. They moved cautiously along the road. Alfred ran the necessity of this mission through his head again and again. It was risky but it would be worth it if they got the books and made it back home safely.

"Smoke," Robert said softly. "Smoke up ahead."

Alfred got that queasy tense feeling in his stomach when there was trouble. He had had to kill people to protect himself and his family, but for him it never got easier. For him there was never any glory or thrill in having to take another human being's life. It was always a nasty dirty business. His tooth was throbbing from where the home invading bastard had knocked it out during their struggle in the house. The fire was coming from just behind a small bend in the road. Father and son separated. One sticking to the curb, the other going into the grass on the other shoulder.

"Okay, we go in quick, assess, and if we need to pull back we run for that ditch there where we can find cover."

Robert nodded, his face calm. He watched his father get into a crouch and jog forward. He did the same on the other side. As he came around the bend he saw that the smoke was from a small campfire, and despite himself and all his training he pulled up short when he saw who the camper was. His father did the same, but Alfred's gun was aimed at the man's head, and he scanned the area around the man to make sure that he was alone.

The strange little man dressed in an archbishop's robe, complete with cap and staff, had his back to them, and he swiveled around on his bum when he heard them coming. He had something roasting over the fire. It looked like a squirrel. He took them in with an intense bemused look and then reached toward the fire and turned the roasting animal around on the stick. A small chuckle escaped him. "Oh, how nice it is to have company! The Lord provides, oh the Lord provides!"

Alfred stood about twenty feet from the man looking at him intently.

"Oh, come, if we were going to kill each other we would have already gotten about the business of doing it," the priest said with a smile on his face. "Come sit awhile." The man's laugh was infectious, and Robert couldn't help smiling. He began to relax but he could see that his father was still on alert. Alfred's finger was on the trigger of the Mini 14 as he tried to make sense of what he was seeing. This was just too strange, too bizarre.

The man looked at them and sighed, "Father and son. I can tell from where I sit. Father and son, a sight for sore eyes. Not many families are still together. Come sit for a while." Alfred finally began to relax. He lowered the gun and the priest clapped and rubbed his hands together in glee. "Come sit." Alfred walked over to the priest and stood back as the man began picking bits of cooked meat off the roasted animal. He didn't offer them any. Alfred figured that it was a test. If they were starving they would take his food, a simple test of friend or foe. So far he knew that the priest would most likely not see them as a threat.

"My name is Archbishop O'Riley," he said with a chuckle between bites. For a second Alfred had a bout of déjà vu he remembered seeing O'Riley's picture in the now defunct *The New York Daily News*. He looked hard at the man and realized that this was indeed the priest.

"How did you make it all the way here from New York City?" Robert asked as he sat down beside the holy man. He was fascinated by the cheery, gaudily clad man who was dressed in the pontifical vestments of his order, down to the pastoral staff and the stiff hat.

The priest nibbled at the sweet meat of the squirrel, and his eyes took on a faraway look as he said, "Before the terrible Collapse, I was a very busy man. Always on call taking care of all the people who depended on me and the church. When the troubles found us I did all I could to take care of my flock. I saw young strong men and women die off as the people turned on each other. I am proud of my brothers; they did all they could to help the people of the city and the surrounding areas. But when all the food ran out, all the hope and kindness went with it. New York City burned, and my priests and flock got murdered. We became targets. They all thought we would have either food or money. I lived on the streets passing myself off as a bum, chasing rats for a meal. I was scared. I had lost my way and my faith. I thought that everything of value was taken from me. Then one day I saw a man run into a burning building trying to save a woman. When he pulled her out, I asked him if she was his wife. He said no, she was just a human being. He stayed with her. She was too badly burned to live. I sat there with her and when she was about to die she looked at me and said, "Father, give me the last rites so I may go to heaven."

"I looked at her dumbfounded, I couldn't believe that she would have recognized me. Or that she still had faith even after everything she had been through. My hair and clothes were dirty and grimy, I was dressed in jeans and a dirty jacket, my face was covered with a beard, and she still knew me. I looked at her and I saw hope in her eyes, and I gave her the last rites before she died. I think I went a little mad after that. I wandered around the city for days, and most of the time I wasn't even looking for food. Something was at war within me. I looked all around at the crumbling burning husk of a city that man had built and then destroyed, and I remembered all those stories of old in the Bible. All those stories of cities that had met their ends because they were wicked and had affronted God. It took a long time for me to face myself, to face my world.

"My world was now one of lawlessness, despair, and pestilence. That man had pulled that woman out of the fire, a woman he didn't know, and it was time I pulled as many souls from the fire as I could before my time comes to an end. So I went down to the banks of the Hudson and baptized myself again. I went back to my ransacked and destroyed apartments and found that no one had taken my holy garments. They were still where I had left them a lifetime ago. I shaved, and put on my clothes, and went out into the desolation that is the world. I walked out of New York City about two months ago. I have taken shelter on the cold nights in abandoned homes. I have acquired things that are necessary as God saw fit. Like today I was hungry so I picked up that rock over there and this squirrel happened by, and now here he is. I was lacking for company and you appeared." The priest chuckled and his eyes crinkled up as he crunched on the bones of the animal.

Alfred and his son were completely taken with the man who just oozed otherworldliness. There was something about the archbishop that made him seem more than a man to Alfred. He resisted the urge to reach and touch him just to see if he was real. It seemed incredible that the man could have walked all this way from New York City in his gaudy clothes and with no apparent weapon other than his staff. Alfred shook his head at the sheer audacity of it, at the sheer wonder of it, and smiled.

"So where are you two gentlemen headed?"

"Oh, just into town."

"I'll tag along. I'll be pushing on though. I would like to check out that group up here in Marathon, see what they are about." He got himself to his feet. After throwing dirt on the fire, and slinging his rather large messenger bag across his shoulders, he followed the Aimeses down the road. "I've seen a lot in my travels. I've been through towns that are just ashes, burnt to the ground. I've seen places where the inhabitants would just as much kill you and see you as a good meal. But there are not that many of us left."

"What do you mean?" Alfred asked.

"Well the one thing that we have not really come to grips with yet is just how many people have died. It's almost like the survivors are in some kind of self-hypnotic psychosis. New York City was very empty of people and rats when I left it. On my way here, I met people from time to time but not that many. Some I had to avoid, and some I met with, they were normal like you. Bodies are everywhere, on the streets, in the houses, in cars. A lot of people died in the initial violence, but a lot more died in the winter, and of starvation. There have also been these diseases that have been going around that killed a whole lot more. It was if the universe got tired of man and decided to cull the herd."

Alfred couldn't help but wonder at what the priest said. He was always a practical man. The past six months had been spent surviving everything the elements and enemies could throw at him and his family. His mode for the last six months had been 'there's a problem, figure out the solution.' The country had fragmented because of economic mismanagement and terrorist attacks. He realized just how different he and the priest's quests were. His mission, as long as there was breath in his body, was to make sure his family was safe. The priest, on the other hand, was on a spiritual journey and as far as Alfred could see one quest was to save a family and the other was to save souls.

"You know my name, but I am at a disadvantage," the priest said.

"My name is Alfred, and this is my son Robert. How did you hear about the Marathon group?"

"I've met people on the road. I've heard good things about that group. Run by a man named Jasper Filitree. I heard that he got his little settlement organized and they are trying to make a go of it. I think I would like to see that." The archbishop smiled and Alfred remembered the family he had met by the farm about a month ago. He wondered if they had made it. They got into the outskirts of the town and they went on full alert. Alfred realized that the priest was right about one thing—if there was any one left in Whitney Point there was no sign of them. There were bones and bodies everywhere. "There may not be any evidence of people but I'm sure we are being watched," Alfred said.

"Yes, I am sure we are," the priest agreed.

They came to the center of the town and began making a beeline for the library. This, and going back through the town, as far as Alfred and Robert were concerned, was the most dangerous part of the mission. They got to the library without incident. The front door was smashed open and when the men went inside, Alfred had a lot of doubts as to what he would discover. They checked each floor carefully to make sure that the building was clean. Then they set to work. The archbishop volunteered to guard the door.

Alfred and Robert went through the self-help section of the library with a fine tooth comb. Alfred picked some books off the shelf, old but longstanding classics of becoming self-reliant, *Four-Season Harvest: Organic Vegetables from Your Home Garden All Year Long*, *Root Cellaring*, and *The Encyclopedia of Country Living*, and more on homesteading and fixing machinery. Robert found two books on US history that he threw into his pack as well. Alfred came across a copy of the Bible, and on their way out of the building he handed it to the priest who smiled sadly and placed it in the messenger bag across his shoulder.

The man stretched and said "We are being watched, you know. I don't know how many but we will have to separate since you are going back in the opposite direction. I will be going on to Marathon."

Alfred knew that it would have made sense for the three of them to stick together, but the archbishop was still a virtual stranger to them, and there was no way he was going to reveal the homestead to anyone. He shook his head and before they left, the archbishop asked if they would like to say a prayer. Alfred felt something powerful and undeniable about the request. They all took a knee and bowed their heads.

The priest said *The Lord's Prayer*. He ended the session saying the following words, "Find it in your heart, oh Lord, to help these fine people. May I find that there are a lot more like them. Help us remake and heal the world. Let us be our brother's keeper, let us trust in your justice, punish the sinners and reward the righteous. Help us all to find our way into your holy grace. Protect and bless the Aimeses, amen." He smiled and gathered his robes about him and said, "God bless" as he moved off down the highway.

Alfred and Robert adjusted their now heavy backpacks and began the trek home. The archbishop's warning that they were now being watched stayed with them as they made their way forward warily. They had just made it to the outskirts of the town when it seemed all hell broke loose. There was gunfire coming from the direction the archbishop had gone. Alfred ground his teeth together as they listened to the sounds of the fight. It was obvious what had happened. He and Robert carried their rifles openly. They wore camo so whoever had been watching them must have decided that the archbishop was a much easier target, seemingly defenseless, and they had gone after him instead. The gun fire petered out and Alfred and Robert walked forward quickly, adrenaline pumping in their veins. They made one mile then another, and then they got to the cover of the trees again. Alfred decided to stop to grab a drink of water from his canteen; they were both breathing hard. As they drank and caught their breath, Robert had a look of puzzlement on his face. "Dad, how is it he knew that our last name was Aimes? We never told him, right? Not that I can remember anyway."

Alfred looked at his son and processed the interaction with the archbishop in his head as he capped his canteen. "No, you never said anything and I never told him what our last names were either. Funny thing, isn't it. Hope he managed to get away. Damn it, he may have been a bit crazy but he was a good man."

Archbishop O'Riley had walked away from the father and son, going in the opposite direction. He had a lot of miles to cover over the next few hours. Marathon was about nine or ten miles away as the crow flies, and he was hoping he could get there in a day. He walked with purpose, carrying his staff. It had been a strange day weather-wise. Late April, most of the snow had melted, and the air had that heavy wetness typical of spring. The archbishop was feeling good, his belly was full, and he had met some good people. He was beginning to lose his sense of wonder at that as he was coming to the conclusion that people were just varying degrees of good or bad. Some people had more good in them than bad and vice versa. Despite mulling over the goodness of people, he was on high alert. He knew that he was being stalked. The people doing it were beginning to get a bit sloppy, and he figured they were beginning to become overconfident since they believed that it would not be much of a challenge to attack the old dude in the robes. There was a gas station up ahead. It had a large open square. It was here he was trying to lure them. He wanted to get them all into the open, and then he could deal with them. He got there and kneeled as in prayer. He had a regular black priest's outfit in his messenger bag, but he found that his gaudy archbishop robes caused a lot of distraction and gave him an edge.

Five people stepped out of hiding and came into the square. Three were men, and they were armed with various weapons. "Drop the bag and take off all your clothes and maybe you will live." A tall, thin sick-looking man with bad teeth said as he came forward. He had a small pistol that looked like a .22 in his right hand. The other two men had bolt action rifles. The two women had machetes. They were all dirty, smelly, and had that insane look in their eyes that the priest recognized as the canni, or cannibal, look. These were the eaters of the dead. They walked differently, smelled differently, looked differently and they had all seemed to have lost the ability to socialize with anyone except their own kind.

"Tell me, you have small weapons, why hunt people? You could go into the woods and get a deer or small game. Why hunt people?"

The tall thin canni shuddered visibly as though he was suffering from the shakes. "We lost everything, everything! There is no hope left, this is Hell, and we are in Hell! This is our punishment, we must help God fulfill the plan! We are doing what He wants!"

"No, you are not doing what He wants. He wants you to be kind and compassionate. He wants you to be your brother's keeper. This is not Hell. Hell comes after, after you pass from this time of troubles. What you do now determines that, and there is no sin so great that He cannot forgive. But you have to ask for that forgiveness. Why don't you ask for that forgiveness here, now? Save yourselves from the true Hell. Pray with me, let's save your souls."

"I think you have to save yourself priest. You will be meeting your God soon. I will put you over the pit and see if you think the same when you are roasting alive."

The archbishop sighed. "Well, go with God, brothers and sisters, may he have mercy on your souls." His left hand materialized from out of the folds of his robe. A Glock .45 popped, and a large red hole blossomed in the thin man's face. Before the body could fall the priest had dropped his staff, and when he reached into his robe another Glock.45 materialized in his other hand and another of his attackers fell dead, shot in the chest.

One of the women ran at him, her machete upraised, and he just barely got out of the way as he twisted his body. He shot her in the side and she tipped over as if she was pushed, crumpling to the ground like a broken doll. The two men with rifles aimed and fired. The priest anticipated their actions and was already on the ground as the men hurried to chamber another round. The .45s cracked twice and they fell, one with a hole in the chest and the other in the head. The woman he had shot was still moving and groaning. He walked over to her, and after a well-placed shot, she stopped moving permanently. He took the weapons off their bodies and carried them to the bridge and dumped them into the river. For the priest there was no thrill in killing or surviving. For him there was the incontrovertible truth that there was a spiritual tussle for the world going on, and he hoped the good people would win.

He said a prayer over the bodies, topped off his clips, and re-holstered the pistols in the double holster under his robe. For him the Collapse and subsequent fall of the country represented a spiritual reality made real and tangible. He saw his role now as a priest in the purest sense. A servant of the church who passed on the word of God and defended that word. He walked out of the town toward Marathon not knowing exactly what he would find there, but he hoped that it was something he could fight for.

With the men gone, Samantha and Candice got to work cleaning out the cabin. It was a nice day for it and since they were both working, they both were armed with .38s in their waist holsters. After the incident with the home invaders, they always went about armed now, something that Samantha hated but understood as a necessity. It was after midday when they got done with cleaning the cabin.

She then decided to collect what would be the last of the maple sap from the buckets she had rigged. Alfred had discovered a large stand of sugar maple trees and she had been determined to have some maple syrup. She had gotten bit by the idea and there had been a book in their valuable collection on how to harvest the sap from the tree. She took eight quart cans and homemade spiles to tap the trees. They harvested the sap every other day. Today she and Candice went for a jaunt to the maple grove which was located on the westernmost part of their land. It took them just under half an hour to reach the trees. The thought of making maple syrup made her mouth water. It was a treat item and could also be used to barter if they ever needed to trade.

They checked the trees and poured the sap they found into two plastic quart buckets. Samantha realized that this was most likely the last time she would be checking the trees; the days and nights were now above freezing as spring was taking hold. On their next trip here she would take all the equipment back to the cabin, clean it, and put it away for next season. A good portion of the homestead ran along parallel to the road.

Both women had Hawkeye rifles slung across their backs, and in their hands they carried the buckets of sap by the thin aluminum handles. They moved carefully through the dense woods, unerringly steering for home as they treaded silently, senses on alert. When they were out like this they seldom spoke to each other because they knew that voices carried and would give them away if there were other people about.

Candice was a bit ahead and Samantha saw her daughter stop and go tense. She felt the familiar sensation of coldness spreading through her body. She automatically held her breath as she watched her daughter. Candice quietly placed her bucket on the ground and unslung the rifle from her shoulder. She very carefully pushed and closed the bolt quietly, dropped into a crouch and moved forward. Samantha did the same thing. They moved quietly toward the road and the voices they heard.

It must be said that the women could have moved away from the issue at hand. They could have made a beeline away from the edge of the property toward the relative safety of the cabin that was located on this part of their land, but the sounds of distress and violence drew them towards the scene. Four men wearing brown camo surrounded a woman and a young girl. The men were heavily armed, carrying what looked like M16's and side arms. The woman hugged the child close to her body as the men touched her face and hair.

It was obvious what they were going to do. The men were intent on sexually assaulting the woman and the child. The woman began to cry. She was wearing a pair of dirty jeans and her thin black coat was open. Samantha wondered where they had come from and how they had gotten this far without being killed. One of the men pulled the child away from the woman and she screamed, uttering a heartbreaking groan. She offered herself in place of the child.

"Let her go and I will do whatever you want. Please, she is just a child."

Samantha was now on her stomach watching the tragic scene. A jolt of anger hot and murderous filled her. She knew she was going to kill the men who were victimizing the woman. She ground her teeth as she remembered her own helplessness. She quietly signaled to her daughter and they sighted in the men in their scopes. One man grabbed the woman's hair and he began dragging her towards the side of the road. His head filled Samantha's scope and she squeezed the trigger of her M77 Hawkeye. The man dropped like a stone as a baseball sized part of his cranium blew out. Candice fired almost simultaneously, taking out the man holding the child, and was loading another bullet as her mother shot another of the men in the chest. The last soldier brought his M16 up and the gun began chattering, spraying the area of woods where the women were hiding. Samantha held her nerve and breathed out slowly. Her Hawkeye cracked. The man rocked back sharply on his feet but didn't go down, and Samantha had just enough time for it to register that he was wearing a vest under his shirt. He aimed the rifle in her direction, and the M16 came alive again. She heard the bullets buzzing by and was forced to hug the earth close, the top of her head began to burn, and she knew that she had come very close to being killed. Then something extraordinary happened. The woman in the coat rushed at the soldier, ploughing into him.

The man who was hit in the back stumbled forward, his finger still squeezing the trigger as bullets ripped into the asphalt. A blade appeared in the woman's hand and as he turned to fire at her she stepped in and stabbed him just above the groin. He let out an anguished scream. The rifle fell out of his hands and he grasped the knife's handle that was sticking out of him. He screamed again. It was a pitiful, nerve jarring and pig-like sound. It was the cry of a human being who knew that he was dying, and the horror and hopelessness that came with being dragged into oblivion. The man fell on his side and, after a few short hitching grunts, expired.

Samantha stood up slowly, she didn't want to black out. Candice ran to her and put her arm around her. "Mom, you are hurt." She felt the world wobble a bit but she fought off the dizziness and a bout of nausea. "Get on your knees, Mom, let me look at your head." Samantha took a breath and went down to one knee as her daughter moved the bloody hair out of the way and examined the wound. "It's not too bad. It took a good chunk of flesh though. Geez Mom, that was close." Candice felt a chill; she had almost lost her mother. She tied a bandana around her mother's head. It would have to do until they were back at the *Rabbit Hole*.

The woman they had rescued was on her knees herself, hugging the child; they were both crying. She was soothing the girl's hair. She let go of the girl, stood up, and a sad smile crinkled her lips. "Thank you. They were going to kill my niece and me for sure. Oh, my God." She walked over to her rescuers and extended a hand. Samantha got to her feet and took it. Both women shook strong and firm.

"Mind if I ask what happened?" Samantha said. She would have understood if the woman refused to volunteer anything about herself.

"My name is Julie Matson. I was lucky. My husband, Adam, had stocked the basement of our house. We lived in Tannersville. We managed to hide out for a long time. One day my husband went out to forage, and he never came back. I figured that he met something that he could not walk away from. We stayed until all the supplies ran out. My husband had a ham radio and we used it to listen to that guy, Donald Rovey. He would talk about the group up there in Marathon. That's where we are going. We managed to stay off the radar, breaking into houses to escape the worst of the cold and scavenging for food. There were days we went hungry but things always came through. We were hiding in the woods at the side of the road over there when these guys came by. One of them decided to go for a pee and my darling Nancy here made a noise. She was hiding and some insect crawled into her coat and bit her. At first I think they were going to let us go, but they decided to have themselves a little fun. If you hadn't come by they would have killed us for sure." Julie shivered and hugged herself. The girl came over and clung to her side, eyeing the two women shyly. There was a wild hunted look in her eyes that broke Samantha's heart. Julie went over to the man she had stabbed and pulled her knife out of his corpse. She wiped the blade on the man's pants and slid it into a sheath under her coat.

Samantha went over to get a closer look at the bodies. The men had been well fed and armed, and they all had a white dove patch sewn on the right sleeve of their fatigues. Samantha glanced at Julie as she pointed to the insignia. "I've heard about these Dove people. I heard that they force you to fight for them or starve. Their so-called leader says he is a man of peace that he only wants to put America back together again. But everything he does seems to go against all that. I've heard horror stories about what he and his army are doing, and I don't want any part of it. If these people up there at Marathon are decent enough, then we'll see if we can join with them."

Samantha shook her head in the affirmative. She had been listening to Rovey on the ham too, and knew of the reports about this militia leader they called the Dove. The men she had helped kill seemed to confirm the truth of Rovey's reports. She quickly searched them, all her instincts now telling her to get off the road and to disappear back into the trees. Her search yielded 4 M16s, 1,200 rounds of spare ammunition, two Glock 23's, a 9mm Beretta, and a Ruger LCR .38 Special. They quickly searched the men's packs for anything they could use. They gave the Ruger to Julie who also took as much of the MRE's from the soldiers' backpacks as she could carry. They then moved the bodies off the road and deep into the woods where they would not be discovered.

The entire incident and cleanup of the scene had taken two hours, and it was time for them to go their separate ways. Samantha and Candice watched as Julie and her niece trudged away, now sporting a new backpack, food, and supplies that should last them the two days it would take to get to Marathon. They were decent people and it made Samantha sad to see them go. It was the first time she had spoken to another woman in months. She wished her well and hoped that she would make it. It was a dangerous twenty-five miles to Marathon.

She and Candice slowly trudged through the woods to the cabin. They had placed the guns and ammunition in the sacks they had used to take the supplies to the maple trees. The rifles were heavy, but they were determined to take them home. The M16's would be a massive addition to their armaments. Candice had discovered that they were fully automatic weapons. Samantha was feeling a lot better. She knew that she had come very close to dying, but as she trudged home she felt something inside her soul working its way lose. Ever since the incident at the cabin she had been feeling a bit powerless and hunted. Helping Julie and her niece had done something to her psychologically. She had stopped another woman from being assaulted. She had saved two lives today and it brought back the belief that she could affect the world in a positive way. These were dark and terrifying times, yes, but good people could make a difference. As they came upon the cabin she found herself hoping and believing that she could once again help her children find a way into a better world, though the men she had just killed also served to remind her that it would be a way paved in blood and sacrifice.

The next morning when the men came home, they swapped stories and Alfred kissed the bandage on the side of Samantha's head, insisting that she stay off her feet for the next couple of days. Despite Alfred's misgivings she managed a few hours before she was back at her chores. She smiled mischievously at him and he knew that his wife was finally back. He knew something had happened during the encounter that had turned her fully around. He said a silent prayer that night, thanking God for sparing his wife and giving her back to him, and he wept.

Chapter Seven

"For rarely are sons similar to their fathers: most are worse, and a few are better than their fathers." Homer

The days were now beginning to get warmer. It was mid-spring and life around the *Rabbit Hole* was one of constant planning and work. There were several big items on the agenda. The first was to get a small vegetable garden going, and the second was to check out the prepper colony at Marathon. After the family had reunited and swapped stories it was decided that checking out the colony would be a very important thing to do. If they could trade a few things, get some news, and take care of Alfred's broken tooth that had begun to get worse, then the trip would be worth the risk.

During the struggle with the house intruder, Alfred had taken the butt of a shotgun in his mouth. It had knocked out a tooth but not cleanly, and the cracked tooth had begun to become a problem. He had ignored it for a few months, thinking that it would eventually heal, but his jaw had begun to swell and the family decided that he would have to get it taken care of. Alfred himself had thought about getting knocked out and having Samantha remove what was left of the tooth, but Sam had said that would be the worst case scenario. Most likely a group as organized as the one in Marathon would have someone who could remove it.

Today, having drank some white willow bark tea to ease the pain, he was out using a pick axe to help prepare a small section of land near the creek that they could use as a garden. They all took a turn using the pick axe and the hoe to till the earth. It was some of the hardest work Alfie had done; the small 10x15 feet plot had to be completely weeded and the earth turned over and leveled, then they marked off where they would plant certain seeds. The garden would present a big challenge from getting the plot ready, planting the seeds at the correct time, and the big one—pest control. It was a bit metaphorical but Alfred saw the challenges of the post-collapse world represented in the garden he and his family were trying to cultivate. It was going to be hard work laying the foundation of a new world. A new world faced many enemies and challenges. The futures of the garden and the new world were both uncertain. To create a garden that would yield nourishing food took them a few days, but they eventually planted the seeds. For the new world, the seeds of freedom would also have to be sown.

They decided to go to Marathon in a few days. They would go as a family and see what this prepper settlement was like. They had heard Donald Rovey on the ham radio inviting people to come in and trade or become part of the settlement. They trusted Rovey. He was the voice of the post-collapse world. Rovey had been one of the few radio personalities that had stayed on air and given updates, news, and warnings to his listeners after the world went to hell. Alfred's need of a dentist and the opportunity to trade for a few things was enough of an incentive to go and see the situation for themselves.

They prepared for the two day walk and discussed any scenarios they might encounter along the way.

Alfred and Samantha studied the map and decided to stay in the deep woods as long as they could. Because of the gunfire Alfred and Robert had heard leaving Whitney Point, they wanted to avoid the town altogether. They would only get on the road when it was absolutely necessary. When the day of the trip came, a feeling of panic almost overcame them. Despite all the things they had had to deal with at the *Rabbit* Hole, it was now their home. They had killed and suffered greatly to protect their homestead. Leaving it was hard. They had planned on staying one night at Marathon, then hiking back. They would be gone five days. Samantha looked one last time at the garden they had just planted, and once again she replayed the discussion of the necessity of the trip. They had to go; Alfred could hardly eat anything now, they had to fix his teeth, and if the people at Marathon were allies then that was good to confirm. They were all in green camo and heavily armed as they walked away from the hideout towards the unknown.

Lambert sat at a large aluminum table staring at a map of New York. It was a very complex thing to gain control of an entire state. Everywhere he looked at the map he saw problems. Splinter controlled lower New York, and he most of the upper northeast. His army had helped the Bilderbergs to gain control of all of New York's nuclear facilities. That was a vital key for the stability of the state. His and Splinter's men had reestablished a loose kind of order in the area that they controlled. That was all good. They had not stamped out all the gangs and canni clans, but that would come soon. The bigger problems were these survivalist groups that controlled key parts of the state. He and

Splinter had sent out invitations for the settlements to send a delegation to a meeting in Albany to hear about the Bilderberg Group, and to join them in the task of securing the Northeastern sector of the country. He would have to figure out a way to convince the delegations that although the Bilderberg's vision was much different from that of the democratic and free America they wanted, it was the correct one for the country and the world. He would have to convince these people that in a time of grave social upheaval as they faced now, the best option was a more centrally localized government led by one or just a few individuals, in other words a king or kings. Well, it was worth trying. If he could get them to join the cause willingly it would be a big win. He had dispatched messengers to the encampments; he knew he would be hearing from them in a few days.

The men who had engineered the collapse had really underestimated the stubbornness of most humans to accept authority. Bringing about a cohesive social order was a tough and ruthless business. It was a soul-crushing enterprise. He wasn't asking people to join and accept him as their leader because of a shared ideology and equal status. He was the leader by sheer brute force. It was a quicker way of gaining power. While some people had indeed capitulated, most were indignant and had to be brought to heel by brute force. That's what his compatriot Splinter was doing rather well. As far as Lambert was concerned though, Splinter was a threat that eventually would have to be dealt with. The man was too unstable. Lambert would let it go for now. He knew that Splinter was going to take action in the central part of the state. He would let the man deal with it in his own way while he quietly carried out his plans.

There was also an interesting development that his superiors had informed him about. They would be sending cylindrical tanks to him and Splinter with a very special biological payload. If he couldn't get the better of the resistance groups—that's what they were calling the survival groups privately now—then he and Splinter would be authorized to use the weapons. Lambert leaned back in his seat, placed his feet up on the desk and gazed out the window. There were people in the Bilderberg Group who still thought that the population needed to be culled even further. In their social engineering plans they figured that smaller, more centralized inhabited zones were the way to go. The numbers they were playing around with were no more than two million per continent. There was still a lot of killing left to do. The goal was to empty the land, reorganize the survivors, and create a new better society that would last a thousand years. It would usher in a golden era of peace and prosperity around the world. It was a bold plan, a daring one that would save humanity from itself.

This was a deadly game of power with all the major players jockeying for their place at the table and history. He intended to be at the table. He was going to be a survivor. He was good at that. He had always beaten the odds. Harry Lambert survived a stormy childhood with a drugged out mother and an alcoholic dad. When he was ten, his father, driving drunk, drove his car into a family of four, killing them and himself. His mother spent most of her time strung out on the couch in the living room, and did not have the ability to raise Harry and his brother, Michael, who was three years younger.

When Harry was twelve his brother swallowed one of his mom's feel good rocks. The child collapsed and died, twitching and frothing at the mouth. Harry had found him. He had gone out to play some basketball with some friends and when he came back in, he found his brother's body in a pool of his own saliva and blood. His mother was passed out on the couch. The police came and took the body away. They arrested his mom and placed him in a foster home. For six years Harry moved from home to home, until he graduated high school and joined the army. After basic he was sent to Afghanistan where he served two tours. Harry Lambert proved himself cool and tough under fire. His men respected him. He earned himself the Silver Star when he and his men became trapped in a small village and he held out against the insurgents, despite being outgunned and outnumbered. During the night Sergeant Lambert led a group of his men to outflank the enemy, and using a .50 caliber machine gun that they had acquired by killing the three men manning it, they went from building to building, clearing out the enemy until there were no hostiles left.

He had seen a lot of good men die during his many deployments. He was a good citizen. He had found something he could believe in. When he left the army he joined the Department of Homeland Security and his initial views were crushed as he saw how the men in power manipulated everything. He became disillusioned and cynical. He now believed that everything was really about power and the ability to control others to keep that power. He understood the basic selfishness and corruptibility of people, and he began to believe in the NSA's mission of surveillance control. He had deeply believed that the world was spinning out of order and that the only way to keep control was to search and look into the hearts of his fellow citizens. As far as he was concerned, Americans had given up their rights to privacy by manipulating the Constitution, and because the technology of the times made privacy almost impossible. It amused Lambert that Americans were shocked when they realized that Big Brother was listening in on every phone call and storing every internet page they visited. He had gone about his job of identifying and arresting potential threats efficiently and ruthlessly. He had also attracted the attention of the Bilderberg scouts, who eventually very carefully vetted and brought him into the organization.

They shared their vision of the New World Order with him, and he found that he was completely on board. He had seen the underbelly of war. He had seen a country he had once believed in without its makeup, and up close it was ugly, corrupt and dying. He became a loyal and ready soldier for the Bilderbergs. Their plan for rebuilding the world was a multigenerational plot, and finally the time was here. They had waited patiently, and when the world's economic infrastructure collapsed they seized their chance. Lambert still had shivers when he saw just how connected and powerful the group had been.

It had shocked him when they eliminated the President. During the early days of the Collapse, when things were still very retrievable, the President had been working hard to restore some kind of order. At a high level meeting at the bunker at Greenbrier, Virginia, a squad of fifty specially trained soldiers attacked and killed not only the President but also the Speaker of the House and the vice president. All major government officials were ruthlessly hunted down and eliminated. The country descended even further into chaos.

They were still in stage two of the plan. They were concentrating on getting the world's population down to one billion and creating centers of power on all the major continents. It had amazed Lambert how all the mighty world powers had folded like a deck of cards.

Not a single country had survived unscathed. He knew that biological weapons had been used to thin the world's population. The Ebola virus had been mutated and weaponized in the labs of the Bilderbergs. It had been unleashed into the populations in Asia, Africa, and Europe. Wave after wave of diseases were decimating the population of major cities and towns. There was no way for the survivors to protect themselves. All the countries that thought themselves insulated from the rest of world soon found that viruses knew no borders.

Lambert and his army had gotten over half a dozen vaccinations. All across America armies loyal to the group were now getting ready to close the circle of death. At strategic points all around the US men were releasing, or getting ready to release, biological weapons to further decimate the North American population. The population goal in the US was five million survivors. Two such weapons were now being delivered to Splinter's group. They were going to be deployed as soon as the survivalist groups declared themselves. If they were friends they would be spared, and if they were enemies they would be destroyed and used as carriers of the disease.

There was no pity in Lambert's heart at the thought of his fellow countrymen being murdered and used to spread the deadly infection. In his imagination he saw the future world. One of order and sustainability. One where man would not be allowed to abuse and poison the planet. The populations would be stable and completely able to enjoy an abundance of resources. All individuals would work toward the advancement of the human race. All the vices of the past would be stamped out and there would be peace. Humanity would finally be able to reach its full potential. He shifted in his seat. There was still so much to do.

The Aimes family had an uneventful two days on the road. They had avoided as many towns as they could and stuck for the most part to the cover of the heavily wooded countryside. This was what ate up the time. It wasn't a direct march to Marathon. They moved as a unit, each person knowing precisely what to do. Finally they got to the first checkpoint of the Marathon settlement. For one sane second Alfred was tempted to leave his family in the woods and go down by himself. The last few months had made him squirrel-ly but he had listened to Donald Rovey's description of the group and decided to trust the old Ham. They slung their rifles over their shoulders and crossed out of the dense thicket onto the blacktop of I-81 South. The first check point didn't look like much, just three men sitting in a crude shack on the shoulder of the highway. They made their way over to the men and Alfred saw that they were being watched intently.

As planned, he let Samantha take the lead as the men came out of the shack. They all had rifles and wore camo, but a short thickset man came forward to meet them and he had a Glock G22 aimed at them. Alfred felt his heart rate shoot up, the pain in his jaw seemed to pulse and throb with his heartbeat.

"Are you guys with the Marathon Militia?" Samantha asked. She had a thin, grim smile and her thumbs were hooked in her backpack straps.

"Yes, ma'am, we are." The man looked at her hard, then his eyes glided by to take in the other three individuals. The man stood a little way off from the woman and the younger people all stood loose limbed. He noticed that they did not crowd each other. They all stood in a way that would make each member free to respond if there was a threat. The man realized that the members of this group were seasoned fighters. If they had wanted to cause trouble, most likely they would have done it from the cover of the trees. He relaxed and slid his pistol back into his holster.

"We have heard a lot about the Marathon Free Zone and we've come a long way to check it out and maybe trade for a few items."

"Where are you folks from?"

"Just outside of Binghamton."

"Well it's always nice meeting regular folks. Listen, keep to the blacktop. You'll hit another checkpoint beyond the exit 9 ramp. Good luck to you."

"Thanks," Samantha said and they walked away from the guard shack. They could hear the men talking in low whispers and Samantha heard what sounded like the squelching of a radio. No doubt they were radioing ahead to let the others know that they were coming. Samantha began warming to the idea of being with people who didn't want to hurt her family. It would be nice to hear human voices again, to see and watch other people go about their business. It would be good to feel normal again even if it was for a little while.

The Bunker-England

Entry 136

My wife killed herself last night. I am in hell. All of this must be hell. I will say that I am not surprised that she did it. I remember a conversation we had long ago when I had just started getting the bunker built. We were having dinner and somehow the conversation drifted to how things would be if the world somehow ended as we knew it. I remember saying that 'we', meaning 'us', the family, could ride out the first few bad months in the bunker. At least we might have a chance surviving the catastrophe. Trisha shook her head over her plate. She said, "I don't know, Joe. I mean if things got really bad, so bad that people are killing each other over food or if we couldn't go outside because the air was toxic, would it be worth surviving after all? I mean, what would be the point?"

She looked around our dining room at our house and said, "Everything I love is right here inside this house. I love the people and I love our lives; I love our things and all the things we do. If I couldn't go online or watch a movie I wanted to, or go to our favorite coffee shop, I don't know if I would like to live in such a world. For me it's about the quality of life, not just about being alive. If the children can't have a normal life, go to school, experience the rites of passage and get jobs, have a future of their own, then what good would it be living in a bunker? All you would be doing is just eating and breathing, waiting for the end."

I can't believe that I can remember that little conversation from two years ago, but I do. I can understand why she would do it. What I can't understand is why she would leave us, her family, behind. How could she be so selfish? How could she be so weak? How could she not want to help me protect our family? Now I am alone with the children. It's all on me. I love Trisha. I love her. She was my partner. Now I have this hole in my life. I have this hole I can never fill. How do you replace a loved one? You just can't.

In all the scenarios I ran through my head, losing Trisha this way was not one of them. People think about these potential scenarios all the time. I did. That's why we moved from the city. I figured that one day maybe one of us would have to make the ultimate sacrifice for the family. Or maybe one of us could have gotten sick and died, but for Trisha to take her own life, that wasn't in the script. Jesus, I wrapped the lower half of her body in plastic sheeting and I had to go topside to bury her. It was one of the scariest things I ever had to do. I told Cathy and Bea that I would have to go up and put their mother in the ground. They went nuts. They hugged and kissed their mum. They didn't want me to go out of the bunker. They were scared.

Hell I was scared. I wasn't strong enough to carry her up and out of the bunker, so I had to tie a rope under her shoulders and drag her up after I was topside. I was at the top of the ladder, and I froze just as I was about to open the door. I think I must have had a panic attack. The kids were also going nuts telling me not to open the door. We've been locked up and been scared so long that the thought of going outside terrifies us. My hands were sweating as I opened the hatch. When I climbed out, I almost fainted. All the snow of winter was gone and weeds had grown up around the entrance, which was good because it made it harder for anyone to notice.

I crouched down and got my breath back, then I listened and looked around carefully. I walked the few feet to the edge of the tree line and looked down the hill. I could see our house from where I was. It was a burnt out husk, and the roof had fallen in. There was garbage strewn around the yard. Even from where I stood I could tell that a lot of people over time had used the yard as a campsite. It's a miracle that we hadn't been discovered. I came back to the bunker, and after sucking in a deep breath and knowing that I had to work quickly, I pulled my Trisha's body up. She was heavy, and I think in the process I must have hurt my back.

I got her out of the bunker and then I took the plastic sheeting and quickly wrapped her upper body up in it. I dragged her about fifty feet from the shelter and began to dig. I dug a hole, one that I thought would be large enough for the body and placed her in it. I sat at the edge and cried. This was the last time I would see my wife. I think I must have spaced out a little because I never saw the man who had come up behind me. "Is that a relative?" he asked.

I turned, and standing there was this man. He was skinny and wearing dirty jeans and an old black coat. In his hand I saw a bat with long nails driven through it. Time sped up—there was no time to debate or think. What he said next sent me over the edge. "Is that your bunker?" He pointed with the bat to the opened hatch, and there was another young person standing by it. I think the way I came at him completely surprised him. I swung the shovel in my hand. The bloke was shocked. I can't even remember how I got up from the side of Trisha's grave so quickly. The edge of the shovel caught him square in the face with a loud clang. He tried to swing at me with his club. I knocked it aside and swung again with the shovel. It caught him on the side of the head, just above his ear. It caught in a downward angle and took off a good chunk of skin and his ear. I could hear the other person screaming. She ran over to us and she tried to attack me. She, too, had a bat, and she did clip me on my left arm. I lashed out at her, and it was a lucky stroke that caught her in the neck. The edge of the shovel almost took her head off. I remember her squeal, sharp and surprised, and then she fell in a heap, bleeding out. The man was trying to stay on his feet. I hit him square in the head again. This time I could feel his skull breaking under the battering of the shovel. I hit him again and again until he stopped moving. I then went over to the girl and hit her a few more times in the head as well.

When I came back to myself, I couldn't believe it. I still can't believe this and my hands are still shaking as I write this entry. I am a murderer now. I killed two innocent people. I replay it over and over in my head. Him coming up on me from behind, asking about Trisha and the bunker, the other one by the hatch's entrance. I just reacted. I reacted violently and I think I killed an innocent man and his daughter. I had beaten them both pretty badly. There was all this blood everywhere. The man must have been in his mid-thirties and the girl was in her late teens. I realized then that there was no way I could dig more graves to bury them in. I didn't have the energy. I felt so tired, so worn out. I wanted to sit down on the mound of dirt by Trisha's grave and rest, but I couldn't. I couldn't leave the bodies where they were, they would attract attention. So I went quickly back down into the hatch, got some more plastic sheeting and rolled up the other bodies in it. Then I shoved them into the grave I had dug for my wife. I piled my victims on top of the woman I loved, the mother of my children, and covered them with dirt. I hope the hole was deep enough. I would hate for any wild animals to dig them up.

Hell, when I came back inside the kids took one look at me and ran into the back of the bunker. I smelled rank, and I was covered in blood. When I looked at myself in the mirror over the bathroom sink, my eyes were wild, my hair was oily looking and matted down on my head. I had this weird grimace on my face. I was also grinding my teeth. I looked insane. I had to take off all my clothes. There was a lot of blood on my shirt and pants, so I had to change. I filled the face basin with water and took the closest thing I could to a shower. I washed the blood off, but I think that the smell is still on me. No amount of soap can get that off. The smell of killing, the smell of murder.

I think I have to stop here for now. I have to have a talk with the children. I have to let them know that I buried their mother. I'll lie and say that I prayed over her grave and gave her a last kiss. I'll say that I killed people who were trying to attack us in the bunker. I'll tell the children that it will be all right. That we will get out of this somehow, and one day we will be able to leave the bunker and get our lives back, and they can remember their mother who was brave and good, and who loved them and their dad.

Splinter had a new residence and a new base. His army had taken Binghamton without much of a fight. He had immediately set about pacifying the groups living in and around the newly conquered city.

Everything was in place now. The Bilderberg Group had come through with all their promises so far. A chopper with a squad of twelve men wearing black camo and black berets landed in the town's square. The leader of the group ran up to him and gave a sharp salute that Splinter felt he had to return. The man, a hard eyed rugged sort, said, "The devices need to be unloaded carefully."

Splinter nodded and motioned for his men to help the team with their precious and deadly cargo. His orders were to see if he could gain control of the Marathon group, by force if necessary. They had sent a delegation to the Albany sit down to hear what the Bilderbergs had to offer. If they rejected the chance of joining the Royalists then the two biological cylinders were to be deployed. The message would be clear to everyone and it was; come over to our side willingly or die a horrible, slow and painful death. There are no other options. A thrill went through him as he saw his men help unload the two huge crates containing the devices. In his mind he had the mental timetable of New York being under his and Lambert's control in the next four months. Splinter was okay with sharing the territories with Lambert at least for now. It was all about grabbing as much land as possible and then consolidating power. Last night he had seen the reports of the deployment of the weaponized, genetically mutated Ebola virus along the East coast of the country. The way the Bilderbergs went about their business of mass extermination of the surviving populace was admirable. The more he thought about the Bilderberg inner circle of power, called the Board, the more he admired them. These were true blue men of vision. They had waited and watched and when the governments of the world allowed their countries to slip into the economic disaster and wars that destabilized their governments, they acted decisively and ruthlessly.

Splinter now understood that destroying a well-established country was contingent upon a lot of things happening at once. The economic collapse and the terrorist attacks were enough to drive America to its knees; it was a huge blow but not enough to kill it. Sooner or later enough survivors would have banded together along with what was left of the government, and the military to turn things around. The Bilderbergs' Board anticipated that and blocked any attempts at social recovery all over the world. They did this by targeting all the leaders of the most powerful nations. Killing them or ruthlessly hunting them, forcing them into hiding. They then deployed deadly biological weapons killing billions on every continent in every city on the planet. The cures for the diseases they unleashed were not available to their victims. Only the vaccinated and the immune survived. With a relatively small force they were able to carry out their world restructuring plans. It showed the power of biological weapons.

The domino effect was much more successful than anyone could have anticipated. With the countries' infrastructures destroyed, there was no way for the people to deal with the death and sickness the attacks caused. People died in their camps and homes. Those who had survived by living off the grid in some remote location became infected when they came in contact with carriers; when they went into the towns or when those carriers found their way to them. Because of the lack of a communications network, survivors usually didn't know of the threat until it was too late. Life meant either being naturally immune or immunized. The deadly viruses were spreading exponentially across the globe.

All over the world the dead piled up. The cocktail of viruses released didn't care about religion or political affiliation; they killed indiscriminately. For those who had survived the economic collapse of their countries, most died in the biological warfare perpetrated on humanity by the Bilderbergs. Humanity had gone insane and it seemed it was trying to eradicate itself. Splinter was just doing his part, and he was seizing his chance. He had accepted an offer that would make him a king in his own right when the full plan was completed.

There was an old salt warehouse in the city that had been prepared. The soldiers would move the canisters there until it was time to deploy them. An older soldier, a man who must have been in his late sixties wearing a dove uniform, went on one knee and said, "We will make sure the weapons are stored securely, Commander. I will supervise it myself and organize the security detail."

"Good man, Aimes. Make sure that no one except us know what is inside those crates, and shoot any unauthorized personnel who shows up for any reason. Is that clear?"

"Yes, Commander."

"You may go."

The older man got to his feet and motioned to a group of eight men who were waiting for his orders. They drove two forklifts over to the chopper and loaded and secured the heavy boxes onto a waiting truck. They would then drive the deadly cargo to its place of storage.

Splinter watched as the truck pulled way with the gray-haired man driving. Five months ago he had met that old man. He had come into the City Hall when Splinter was still wintering in Middletown and volunteered his services. He had had his men interrogate him. He had convinced them that he had come from Utica, NY. They had radioed the town and had the records checked. They found that a man named Tobias Aimes had owned a house there. The man had also served in the Gulf War. Tobias had said that he and a group of close friends had banded together and had made it through the months after the Collapse, but he decided to leave to join a larger group. He said it was his last hurrah, a final chance to do something meaningful with his life. He said that he was good with mechanical things and that he was also a pretty good shot. All these things were put to the test as he helped to fix a few of the jeeps that had broken down. He might not be able to run around like the younger soldiers, but the man was still robust and very strong. He was also ruthless.

Splinter had seen the man nonchalantly shoot trouble-makers. There was also that time when he had worked with a special team to ferret out Marathon spies. They had tracked a transceiver signal to its source in the area around Middletown. The people in the house swore even under torture that they did not know anything about the device. Aimes had not only handled the interrogation, but he took care of the executions himself. There were a lot of hard men in Splinter's army. Aimes took his place among them quickly, and Splinter found that he could trust him. The man was loyal. He thought it had something to do with his age and generation. Splinter found that people of Aimes' age were loyal and stuck by their beliefs and their employers.

He had put him in charge of The Hammer Project. That's what they were calling it. If he couldn't break the Marathon group then he was ready to deploy one of those canisters over the troublesome town. Then they would wait and watch as the virus did its work, and hopefully they would also infect the surrounding survivalist settlements as well. The sooner they had New York pacified, the better. Then he and Lambert would push northeast and southeast until they came to the limits of their pre-assigned territory. He saw in his mind's eye the map sent by the Bilderberg Group. He saw the green sector he and Lambert were assigned to pacify and control. They had divided the USA into three sections, western, middle, and eastern represented by three columns dividing the country into three equal parts. Then those columns were further divided into three equal parts: southern, central, and northern. Lambert and Splinter's area of control was the north central area known as the green sector. This section was planned to comprise the states of Pennsylvania, New

York, and Vermont—large territory that would be split between the two of them. The surrounding states were going to be depopulated. The plan was already being initiated quite successfully. The virus had been deployed in every big city and large town on the east coast that was not part of the New North American Precinct vision.

It had decimated the survivors. It was all going according to plan. The two armies trying to consolidate New York would also then turn their attentions to Pennsylvania and Vermont. The scope of it boggled the mind, and sent shivers down Splinter's back. He was helping to tear down a civilization and building something new in its place. This force would be the main part of their army that would enforce the laws and organize the survivors of the pandemic into a new work force that would be the foundation of the New World Order. It would then be about building up their manpower, training and resettling the green sector to make it productive again.

Splinter couldn't help thinking about what that accomplishment would mean to him. He would have his own territory to rule as he wished; his word would be law. He would be a king, not the supreme king, but a king nonetheless. Generations would then grow up learning about the brave men and women who took the world from the brink of terrible destruction and annihilation and made it a safer, fairer, more productive place for all humanity. His name would be said in reverence until the end of time.

He remembered his father, a hard hateful man. He remembered one day when he got home from school and his mother was in the kitchen, making sure that dinner was ready to go. God forbid that she didn't have it done when Father got home. He went to his room to get his homework done and read until he was called to the table. He never spent anytime outside his room. He was afraid of his father. He never watched television or hung out on the porch. His dad had worked as a welder at the local metal works. He was taller than Splinter but just as thin. He had a perpetual scowl and long stringy brown hair. His dad was always simmering. He never remembered seeing the man smile. He knew that his father hated his mother and hated him. His dad had told him once that his mother had tricked him into being a father.

"She was just this girl I'd met in a bar," he'd said, his eyes scrunched up and his fists at his sides. He looked like a dangerous snake ready to strike. "She was just supposed to be a good time gal. You know what I mean boy. Your mother was just supposed to be a good time girl. A couple of times in the sack, then hit the road. I came from a good family. I went to college. I was supposed to make something of myself. Then one day she comes over to my mother's house and she says she is pregnant. She said she was going to keep it. Keep you, boy, Goddamn, my life went down the toilet that day, I tell you what. I begged her to get an abortion, but she refused. Said she didn't believe in it. She said she didn't believe in taking the life of the unborn. I thought a lot about just punching her in the stomach then. Just beat the hell out of her and that would probably solve all my problems. But instead she told my mother and my family found out.

"I married her then. I married her because it was the thing to do. I married that stupid woman because my family said it was the right thing to do. They said that it was right. I argued, boy. I argued and told them that no one got married now because of babies. I asked why I had to get involved if I never wanted a kid in the first place. It's not like we were in love. I never wanted to be a family. I never wanted to be your dad.

"So we got married and for a while I thought maybe, maybe I could learn to love you and your mother. But that never happened. I realized that I was right and that I had made a horrible mistake." Then his dad went back to his beer.

Splinter remembered that conversation because it became the central force that would shape his life. He remembered how he hated his father after that, and how he hated his mother, too. So that one evening when he was sitting in his room hunched over his homework, his stomach in knots waiting for the sound of the front door opening, he was under no illusions how his dad felt about him.

The inevitable happened and he could hear the sounds of his dad's arrival. The heavy shuffling. He could hear the man peeing, even with both the bathroom door and his door closed. He sighed and went out, expecting the usual daily dinner abuse. He went and sat at the table, and sure enough his dad was ready to go. He was a man of strict routines; get home, pee, eat dinner while belittling wife and stupid son, grab a couple of beers from the fridge, go out to the porch to drink and belch until 10 p.m., then news and bed. That was the routine. When Splinter was younger he was terrified of having dinner. He would get bad stomach cramps and heartburn as he ate at the table.

This particular day he sat down as usual in the chair in the middle, and his parents sat at both ends of the small metal table. His dad dished out some potatoes and passed the bowl to him. It was hot and Splinter let the bowl slip out of his hands. It clanged on the table. When it did, he saw his mother jump out of the corner of his eye. His father only glared at him and shook his head with his usual 'the boy is a complete fool' scowl on his face. He then began tucking into his stewed chicken with gusto. He didn't wait for his wife to serve herself before he began to eat.

"Stupid suits are cutting staff, starting next month. Just hoping to God they leave my department alone." He looked around the table. "I can't imagine what you all would do if I lost my job. If you lost your rides on the gravy train." He shook his head again and shoved more food into his mouth, and after a few more bites he said, "I noticed that the garbage wasn't taken out. We have all that crap stinking up the garage. They make their run tomorrow and it needs to be out at the curb before we go to bed tonight." He looked directly at his wife when he was saying this. She kept eating her meal, her eyes down on the table. "I don't want the boy to do it. I want you to do it. You hear me." His wife nodded and kept chewing slowly.

He took another bite, his teeth crunching the vegetables and meat loudly. "You, boy, Max Newman, that other good for nothing, said he saw you on Birch Street with some other lowlifes yesterday afternoon."

"Wasn't me, Dad."

"Well it sure as hell better not be, that was what I was thinking. You should be in school, not hanging about with the druggies and the goddamn lowlifes. I think you are lying boy. I think that it was you he saw. He described you even down to that god-awful bag you carry. Now think again, boy, think real hard. Was it you? Now it wouldn't surprise me if it was you. You have always been a disappointment. You have always been a thorn in my side. I wouldn't be surprised if it was you he saw hanging out with the druggies and the crackheads. Your type of people I would think. Losers, just a bunch of losers who won't amount to anything.

You won't amount to anything. You are just like your godawful shitty mother over there. You won't even be a shit stain on the world boy." He suddenly let out a croaking sound.

Richard Diefenbacher grabbed hold of the cheap vinyl tablecloth as he tried to eject the food that was blocking his windpipe. He retched and fell sideways off his chair onto the floor. Flopping around like a fish out of water, he rolled over onto his back, the worst thing he could have done. His mother had gone over to the choking man. She started crying and calling his name. Splinter thought then of the Heimlich. In his mind's eye he could see himself lifting his dad into a standing position, then getting his arms around and under the ribcage and pulling inward, allowing the choking man to eject the blockage.

He got up and moved over to his father on the floor, and watched as the man began to turn blue, his hands around his neck as though he was trying to strangle himself. His mother began to cry, her hands reaching, trying to give comfort uselessly. Splinter reached down and got his mother gently to her feet. "Let him go, Mom. It's time to just let him go." The man turned his head at that and looked hard at his son. A harsh choking sound issued from his straining throat as his eyes bulged. His face looked like all the blood vessels under the skin were going to explode. His hands left his throat and they clawed at the hardwood floor, leaving deep scratch marks; his nails broke and left bloody jagged streaks. His feet began drumming in a cadence of death. He went stiff as a board, mouth opened in a scream that would never come, and then he slowly went limp.

Mother and son stood over the body for about another minute before Splinter picked up the phone and dialed 911. By the time the ambulance crew arrived, it was too late. They pronounced him dead at the scene. As Splinter watched the crew take his father's body away, he felt a wave of relief. His second true life began after that moment. Half a year later he dropped out of school and pretty much became a drug dealer. He made enough money to pay the bills. His mother, he found out, was just as terrified of him as she was of his father. As soon as he was eighteen, he decided not to burden her anymore with his presence and he moved out.

His mother had found a job and a new independence as soon as the last Diefenbacher man left her life for good. She even went back to her old name of Bruster. Splinter never went back, and he became so engrossed in his own life that he wrote her off. When the Collapse occurred, he never checked in on her to make sure she was okay. Now eight months in he just figured that she was dead, and that worked out very well for him. He moved on with his life.

He went back to his office and looked once again at the map of New York, and the one of the Green Zone that was next to it and smiled. *"You won't amount to anything. You are just like your god-awful shitty mother over there. You won't even be a shit stain on the world boy."* His father's last words were burned away in his memory. "Well, Dad, you are worm's meat and I am about to become a king and a great man. I am about to fulfill my destiny."

Chapter Eight

"The true character of liberty is independence, maintained by force. Voltaire

Alfred and his family walked through the Marathon settlement and were amazed. From the minute they crossed the final checkpoint into the town they were awestruck. It was amazing just how organized and planned everything was. The settlement itself was well protected. Samantha wondered where they got all the heavy artillery and mounted machine guns. There was an obviously well-trained security force that could be seen manning the guns and making their rounds around the town. They were well armed with M16s and AR15s. You could tell the security detail apart because they wore black arm bands on the right arm, with the American flag patch sown on.

There were a lot of people in the town. Along the banks of the river that bordered the settlement, the brush was cleared and tents were set up. It seemed like every building in the town was taken and their rooms were either used for business or living accommodations. The population had exploded, going from around nineteen hundred souls to almost fifty thousand people who now lived and camped around the area. They walked along Main Street and turned onto Peck Street. They were heading to Lovell Field, where venders had set up booths to trade and offer services.

They checked out the people that passed them, going to and fro about their own business. Almost everyone was dressed in camo. There were some people in jeans and rugged shirts. Everyone they had passed so far seemed to be armed. If they did not carry a gun openly they had swords, bows, or machetes. All the women that they could see wore shirts and pants; there were no dresses or skirts. They passed people of every color, but what made Alfred pause and smile was the sight of a few children. Never far from their parents, these children, survivors of one of the most catastrophic events in the history of humankind, could be seen laughing and playing in the streets and yards of some of the homes.

The town leaders had some iron clad rules that had to be followed or else one could be expelled from the settlement. Robert had the book of rules in his hand. It was handed to them at the last check point into the town. They were planning on spending the night and then leaving the next morning, so they were told that they could go to tent city number two called Camper's Lot on the far side of the town towards Cortland. There they could find a spot to make camp for the night. It turned out that if they were planning on staying more than a night, they would have had to check in with the settlement admin office.

They turned into Lovell Field and the sight they saw was amazing. It was like a state fair. Huge tents were laid out side to side to use every inch of space. Under the tents, trade and the offering of specialized services was conducted. There was a section for mechanical repair and metalwork that seemed to be doing very brisk business. Before the family sought out the specific things they needed, they asked and got directions to the medic tent.

When they got to the only tent made from white canvas with a red cross on the outside, they were dismayed by the line of people waiting to be seen. Then they realized that the line for the dentist wasn't that long, and Alfred saw that there were only four people ahead of him. He and Samantha had a chat and they decided that he should wait there while the rest of the family went and checked out the rest of the vendors.

He hugged and kissed Samantha and decided on a meeting point. After an hour they would walk back to the tools stall. If no one showed they would meet back at the medic tent. He could tell that everyone was a little uncomfortable with the idea of splitting up. He, too, had a bout of anxiety but he looked at his wife and said, "We'll be okay. Go find the things we need and I'll meet you at the tools stall. Hopefully one of these guys can take care of this." He pointed to his tooth and smiled. Samantha kissed him and turned. The children followed her out of the tent. He then settled in to wait his turn in line.

The large tent had two entrances. At the end where Alfred waited was a small section for people requiring dental help. There were two dentists taking patients. One was an old man, and the other was a younger man in his mid-thirties. Alfred hoped that he would get the older fellow. If he was going to be in pain, he would rather have the older doctor taking care of him. It seemed that luck wasn't on his side, and when he was finally called, it was the younger dentist he would see. He shagged down his gear beside the chair and sat down. The dentist adjusted the battery charged lamps so he could get a good look at his patient's mouth. He inspected Alfie's teeth and stopped when he saw the damaged tooth and jaw.

"Damn, this is pretty bad. It's not only the broken tooth here, but the one beside it has been chipped pretty badly as well. All the nerves are exposed. This is going to take some time. I'm going to have to remove the fragments of the broken tooth and drain the abscess, then cap the chip on the other. It's going to cost you."

"What are your rates?"

"Two ounces gold, three ounces silver, or anything of corresponding value. Greenbacks are no good anymore."

"I've got some gold. My wife also has some spare maple syrup."

"Goddammit, did you say maple syrup?" The man's eyes lit up like candles. He leaned over and looked intently at Alfred like he just told him the secrets of the universe. "My Chrissy would love some maple syrup on her pancakes in the morning. Hell, I would love some real maple syrup in the mornings. I tell you what, I'll charge you an ounce of gold and a mason jar of maple syrup and you'll have yourself a deal." They shook on it, and after hearing the other patient screaming in the other chair, Alfred figured maybe he got lucky.

The dentist used a huge needle to numb the area, then he deftly extracted what was left of the tooth from Alfred's jaw. He tilted Alfred's head over the portable sink and drained the abscess. It was amazing to Alfred that he could feel the pressure leaving his lower jaw. The man then quickly capped the other chipped tooth. He rinsed again and realized that the other dentist was still working on the poor sap in the other chair.

The dentist had a pair of pincers and was pulling another brown rotted tooth from the man's mouth. The tooth left the man's jaw with a grinding crunch and the dentist dropped it onto a silver tray that had four other teeth he had pulled. Both patient and doctor were sweating. The dentist sprayed some water into the man's mouth then he said. "Just two more to go, Bob. I told you to come in ages ago, and now we've got all this to deal with." He grabbed hold of another tooth and began to pull as his patient gasped and his hands banged against the chair's armrests.

"That's what happens when you sleep with a dentist's wife. Haw, haw, haw!" Alfred's dentist slapped his legs and laughed. The man then gave Alfred four pills. "These are antibiotics. Take one a day. Pills are like gold now. I wouldn't feel right just sending you away. Just soft food until it heals. If you've got any Listerine or alcohol, mix half with water and rinse. If not, just some salt and water. Take good care of your teeth, man. In these times bad dental hygiene can kill you." Alfred paid the man and promised to come back with the maple syrup.

He then went looking for his wife and children. Making his way through the crowed tent bazaar, he figured that this was what an ancient market place must have looked like. Colorful crowded tent cities where people bartered for goods. There was the powerful smell of food everywhere that made his mouth water. He knew that the food tents would be seeing good business. There was even a place on the outskirts of the park where they had livestock for sale. He couldn't believe that there were any domesticated animals left. It seemed like towns like this one, that had banded together and fortified themselves against marauders and the cannibals and gangs, had managed to hold on to some of their livestock. People had trapped or bred rabbits, squirrels, woodchucks, and chickens. How they managed to hold on to their cows and goats he could not even begin to guess. People also hunted deer and wild hogs and sold the meat. He was going toward the prearranged meeting spot when someone familiar caught his attention. It was Jim Meehan, the man who he had met the day he and Robert dragged the bodies of the home invaders over to the farm. He paused to think, then the name came to him and he stepped toward the man to make his greeting.

"Jim, I see you made it."

The man turned and a big smile lit up his face. "Alfred, right? Alfred, well I'll be." They shook hands like old friends. "Yeah, we made it. We ran our truck all the way here. Call it dumb luck or stupidity. After we left the farm we drove like a bat out of hell all the way here. They couldn't believe that we had made it that far in a truck at the first check point. I found out that from time to time, marauders or canni gangs block the roads and try to ambush people or vehicles. But they must have had an off day, and here we are." The two men took to each other and a budding friendship developed. "So what brings you to Marathon?"

"We decided that we needed to come and check this place out, see what was available to trade."

"How long are you staying?"

"Well we'll be here for the night. We plan on going back tomorrow."

"Why don't you come and crash with us? We got ourselves a nice big tent over there at Camper's Lot. Ellie would like some company. We can catch up."

"Okay, sounds good. I'll talk with Samantha, and we'll drop by. What time would be good?"

"Oh, how about five? We can meet, have a meal, and you guys can crash on our floor instead of setting up somewhere. We are row four, tent eight."

"Alright, let me find my family and I'll let Samantha know. See you tonight."

The men parted ways. It felt so good to chat with someone in such a normal way. Alfred felt a hitch in his chest. It had been so long since he'd had a regular conversation with another human being. "Hell, we got invited to dinner, for Christ sake." He smiled as he went in search of his wife. The meeting spot was up ahead. He made three more steps before there was a series of loud bangs, then a big concussive explosion sent him flying.

Samantha walked through the stalls with the kids trailing behind her. The noise, people, and smells were staggering. She looked back at the children and saw that they, too, were overwhelmed by it all. She couldn't help musing that before the Collapse this would have been normal. After eight months of hiding from the world and fighting off attackers, they had become accustomed to the quiet and solitude of the *Rabbit Hole*. All this close human interaction and noise was a bit distressing.

She remembered all those documentaries and books she had read about people who had lived alone and off the grid for a long time, and how they always seemed to find coming back into civilization unsettling. It was amazing how quickly she had gotten used to hearing just the voices of her children and husband. Now I am the woods person, and these are the townies. She noticed how they all carried weapons, but they had a relaxed air about them that she could never really share. She noticed, too, how different her children were from the other young people they had seen in the town. Her fourteen-year-old daughter was a copy of her. Fatigues, hair up in a bun under her cap. Small pack with a tarp, sleeping bag and food. Her rifle, one of the recovered M16s, slung across her shoulder. She was small and athletic, and carried herself with a withdrawn wariness that broke Samantha's heart. Her son was very much the same, a younger version of Alfred. He had taken to getting himself in shape and there was an air of tough maturity about him now—too young to be so serious about the world.

She felt the familiar sadness press down on her like a blanket. Their world and future had been taken away from them. Samantha could not see the world of her children's adulthood if they survived. What would it look like? Would America get it together and pick up the shambles of the country and put it back together again, a little older and wiser this time? Was the old world of the early twenty-first century gone for good? If the USA was shattered beyond repair what would take its place? Would it be freedom or slavery? She could not tell, but she hoped that if things became so different and the union did break apart and form something new, that it would be a good place for people to live in peace and prosperity.

It was in this sad frame of mind that she entered one of the clothing tents. She was looking for yarn to knit. She had also learned to spin a long time ago in her former life, but she never really got good at it. She was more comfortable knitting and she figured that she could knit her family a few warm hats and gloves for the coming winter. She was also hoping to find a few more socks and underwear for the family. The thought of it caused her to sigh. When she and her husband were frantically getting their bug out location ready they had thought about a lot of things, but one of the things they had missed was extra socks and underwear. When they had fled their home in Binghamton, they had packed like they were leaving on an extended vacation and that they would soon be back. Samantha had six pieces of underwear, and they had begun to shred and unravel. Hand washing and daily constant wear had almost reduced them to ragged tatters; it was downright embarrassing. The underwear were made for attractiveness not for strength or extended wear. So she was here to get her family some strong-lasting small clothes that could be hand washed and beaten on a washing board for a while.

They located a vendor selling her sought-after merchandise. The woman and man who owned the stall had exactly what she had been looking for. She bought basic cotton small clothes for herself, children, and husband.

"If it gets bad enough and you can't get more new underwear, just run a string through the top and tie 'em. The first thing to go is the elastic." The woman said. "Push comes to shove there's nothing wrong with women wearing boxers."

Sam smiled and nodded. She had been thinking the same thing. She found a woman selling yarn three stalls down, and she carefully selected what she needed. She paid in gold. She also wanted to get some colloidal silver. She had heard about its antiseptic and anti-viral properties. She asked the woman who had sold her the yarn, and she said that there was a medicine tent about three rows over where she could get medicine for any kind of illness. She made a deal with the kids that after they checked for the antiseptic they would meet Dad and then go into the food tent to see if they could have a treat. She had asked them if there was anything they wanted. They both shook their heads. This was also a big difference. One that reinforced how things had changed. Before the Collapse, if she had taken the kids to the mall or a fair, they would have been buying or asking for stuff they thought they needed. Now, here they were among people for the first time since things went south and they didn't ask for anything for themselves. Everything she had bought was something that they sorely needed or was needed to make something in the future. She felt tears stinging her eyes. She would have to find something special for them when they went into the food tent.

As they shuffled out of the dry goods tent and made their way over to the medicine pavilion, there was a collective gasp as two concussive blasts went off nearby. Samantha didn't think, she hit the deck. Looking to her left she saw that the kids had instinctively followed her lead. Most people were still standing about. She could tell they were shocked and confused. There was the smell of smoke in the air, and after an initial stunned pause, she heard the panicked screams of people. Then there was another blast. It was obviously larger than the others. She turned around and noticed that the smoke seemed to be coming from the area of the medical tent. That's where she had left Alfred earlier.

Something twisted in her gut. People were running to and fro now with a lot more purpose. She just wanted to get to her husband. She got to her feet and was about to go looking for him when two men and a woman wearing the green camo and the black arm band of the settlement security force ran up and pointed their rifles at them. "Get back down on the ground now!" one of them shouted. Samantha felt her insides turn to ice. There was no way she could fight them. There was nothing to do but to comply. She prostrated herself and the security detail confiscated their weapons and packs. They then handcuffed them while they were still on the ground. They took them out of the park and into the center of town where the town hall was located. They marched them up the steps to a room where they helped them into hard metal chairs to wait.

"We'll be alright," she said looking at the kids. Both were pale and frightened. They nodded their heads at her. A knot of worry was crawling its way around her gut as her mind replayed the incident again. The sounds had come from the direction of the medical tents, she could swear. She found herself straining against the handcuffs, then realized that they were beginning to bruise her wrists and stopped. It was all she could do just to sit still. "Do you think Dad's okay?" Robert asked in a low voice.

"Let's hope so."

They watched as security brought in two men. They were wearing jeans, military style boots, and tan bush-style shirts with rolled up sleeves. One of the men had a large bruise on the left side of his face, and the other man looked like he had been roughed up. His lips were swollen. There was blood on his face and collar. Then there was a sight that made her relax. She felt like crying as Alfred walked in. There were two security men with him. They carried his pack and rifle. He was moving his left hand gingerly, and the side of his face looked like someone had punched him, but he was okay. He saw her and veered away from the men who were escorting him, got on his knees and threw his arms around her. Samantha started to cry. All of a sudden the need to be away from this place and back at the *Rabbit Hole* was overpowering.

She watched as he pulled up a chair beside her. He looked at the kids and smiled. There was a crooked grin on Robert's face and Candice just looked angry. "Why did they put us in handcuffs, Dad?" she asked.

"The way I figured it, they must have immediately gotten a fix on anyone who had arrived over the last forty-eight hours or so and rounded them up. The reasoning behind it would be whomever had set the bombs must have arrived recently, purchased or smuggled in the items, planted and detonated them. It would have been smart for them to have set the explosives and then left, but maybe they didn't have the time to leave, or maybe they stayed to watch the effect their handiwork would have on the encampment." Alfred looked sideways at the men the police had taken in. Samantha followed his gaze and suddenly she had a gut feeling her husband was right.

"Can I just sit down next to my family here, fellas?" He wasn't cuffed and he spun around in his chair and crossed his legs in front of him.

"No problem, Mr. Aimes," the big security guard said, stowing his gear away with the rest of the confiscated equipment. They then unlocked Samantha's and the children's handcuffs. The guard and his partner had helped Alfred to his feet after the explosion had blown most of the medical tent away, killing a doctor and a nurse. The two dentists had escaped. The older man had been hit by some shrapnel and had to be taken to another medical facility in the center of town. They had spoken with the dentist who had treated Alfred, and realized that if he was still in the chair at the time of the explosion, both could have been seriously hurt.

Samantha looked at their surroundings. They were in a waiting room outside a door that led into the interior of the building. Light came through a rather large window to the left. There was a desk in the far right corner and behind it a man sat with a walkie. It squawked and cackled. They all heard when the voice said, "Send in Alfred Aimes." Samantha's breath caught in her chest. Alfred got up and walked to the door. He turned and smiled. "It will be alright, you'll see." Then he stepped through, and she saw that an older graying woman, wearing the camo of the security force, greeted him and closed the door. Once again Samantha began to wish they had never left the *Rabbit Hole*.

The woman escorted Alfred down a long corridor. There were rooms with heavy steel doors on either side. At the end of the corridor she opened another door and he stepped inside. What greeted him was a nice wide office with a single large desk in the center of the room. Behind it sat someone Alfred had known very well in a past life. Despite his reassurances to his family, he wasn't quite sure how this was going to go. The woman closed the door leaving them alone, and the man behind it rose and smiled at Alfred.

He was wearing a camo shirt and pants. He had red short hair, was rotund in stature, and his grin was infectious. Alfred couldn't help smiling, a little in disbelief.

"Goddam, Jasper!"

"Alfie, damn, damn, I can't believe it."

Jasper had run a small gun shop in Binghamton before the Collapse. He had sold Alfred the two Mini 14's that he had used to protect his family. In their past lives they had become friends and had even gone on a few hunting trips together. Jasper had guessed that Alfred was a prepper and was always generous with advice and encouragement. The two had lost contact when things had gone south and the grid came crashing down. They shook hands and Jasper indicated for Alfred to have a seat.

"I can't believe that you and your family survived. How did you do it?"

"We got out of town at the right time and bugged out, to a real secluded spot. This is the first time we have been around so many people in months."

"Well, I am sorry that on your first time here, you almost got blown up." Jasper's face became somber in the glow of the soft office lights. "I already know Alfie that you had nothing to do with what happened. I know from the dentist that if he hadn't let you out of that chair for a few more minutes, I would probably be telling your wife that we were sorry for her loss. I know that the two men we have in custody sitting out front are the ones responsible for the bombing. The third man was shot trying to escape through the woods north of town. These two will be tried and most likely executed for terroristic acts upon US citizens."

Alfred listened to all of this quietly, relieved that he and his family were not considered suspects in the attack. But the more he looked at Jasper's body language the—more unsettled he became. "Okay, Jasper, you got something to tell me. Go ahead."

The small redheaded man shifted in his chair and looked squarely at Alfred. "You were always pretty perceptive. Alfred, your father came through here about four months ago. He and four others from Utica decided to join us rather than try and go it alone."

"My dad!" Alfred couldn't believe what he was hearing. "My dad survived? How did he manage it? Is he still here?"

"His group was part of a small prepper crowd that had banded together and watched out for each other. They had heard our broadcasts over the ham and decided to come and check us out. When they arrived, they decided to stay. Tobias and I became good friends, and there is no doubt that if he had stayed he would have become one of the real leaders of the settlement."

"So, he's not here then?" Alfred felt a pang of disappointment.

"Oh no. Alfred, your dad went to join the New York City Militia."

"You mean the one being led by the man they call the Dove?"

"That's the one."

"No, I know Dad, he wouldn't join that band of thugs."

Jasper looked hard at him again. "Why don't you think your father would join the Dove?"

"My dad fought in Iraq in Operation Iraqi Freedom and he served in Afghanistan as a colonel in the Army. He was a career soldier; he believed in the Constitution. He wouldn't join a bunch of thugs."

"Yes, I remember you speaking about him when we went hunting and at the shop. That's why we sent him east. We needed a man on the ground who could take care of a very delicate mission for us."

Alfred sat up, his hands went to the edges of Jasper's desk and a sharp hiss of breath escaped him. The skin on his hands broke out in goose bumps. "Okay, Jasper. What's my dad into?"

"You got to really understand the world as it is now, Alfred." He reached down and opened the bottom drawer of the desk and fished out a bottle of whisky and two glasses. He filled one and held the bottle over the second. Alfred nodded his head and Jasper poured a shot into the glass. He then corked the bottle and replaced it in the drawer.

"When everything went to hell, our government collapsed, society imploded. Our politicians realized early on that the situation was ungovernable. You can't govern those you can't feed. We suffered a lack of leadership from the bottom up. The local community leaders recognized that they could not help their people so they had to look out for themselves and their families. Most have been killed. This went on all the way up to the higher echelons of our government. There is even a rumor, a pretty good one making the rounds, that most of congress including the President himself was taken out by some rogue group." He sighed and took another sip; Alfred took a sip as well. The hot liquid felt good; it made the side of his face ache less.

Jasper continued, "Well, we have been monitoring events all over the world. We have a pretty extensive ham radio network, dedicated people who are committed to passing on the truth. These reporters have told us basically the same story. Their country has descended into anarchy. There is this organization called the Bilderberg Group at the center of all the chaos. It's even been suggested that they have had some shady ties with the Illuminati and some of the larger more powerful neo-fascist groups in Europe. Their militias and armies have now gained control of a lot of territory on every continent. It's pretty clear that this group is behind the militias trying to take over parts of the United States. There are two groups, the New York City Militia and the Albany Militia that have gained substantial territory, not only here in New York, but all along the eastern seaboard. We are supposed to be in the Green Zone."

"You seem to know a lot about the people who now want to run things."

"We know a lot about them because, just like them, we have a substantial spy network in place. It's all like a game of chess now, they move and we counter. The Albany Militia sent a few messengers here a few weeks ago asking us to send a delegation to some meeting in Albany. We did. My people had a few questions like what they stood for, what were their group's goals, etc. When my people got back we were told that the goal was to consolidate and pacify the eastern part of America and to bring law and order as well as a New World Order. That's the part that really got our attention *New World Order*. They are not even trying to hide it anymore. They are very confident that they'll just roll over any one who is not on board with their new outlook on governance."

"Well, have they rolled over anyone?"

"We got reports all up and down the eastern coast that they have done just that. It's not only in the east, either, Alfie. I want you to understand that this is all over the continental US. Well, what used to be the USA, anyway. These bastards are carving up the country, the whole damn world. It's unbelievable, but they are doing it. They used the Collapse and all the chaos that was triggered to put their own agenda into play."

Alfred took a last gulp. He realized that although he had been listening to Donald Rovey's twenty minute bulletins every night, he had not grasped the whole scope of the dilemma that the vacuum in power had created. He was still waiting for the other shoe to drop; he was waiting to hear what his father's role was in all of this, and it gave him a queasy feeling in the pit of his stomach, one that all the scotch in the world couldn't cure.

"I've been listening to Rovey every chance I get. Why has he not just come out and broadcasted all of this?"

"Well, Rovey's one hell of a newsman, but he's also a patriot. He's working with us. No sense in letting on just how much we know about them. This group, we have been told, manufactured enough biological weapons to kill half the people in the world. They have used different types of virus strains to further decimate the world's population. They have used very virulent strains of H1N1, the Nipah virus, and the most deadly and frightening, Ebola. Every country, every major city has been infected. It has been a diabolically clever thing to do because they can wage warfare against a much more powerful enemy and win, without risking assets. In the chaos that followed the Collapse, all they had to do and did was to release one or a combination of these bio agents and watch the already weakened populace die off. The viruses get results pretty quickly too. All across America, Alfie, they have been releasing these terrible weapons. The best estimations are that before the Collapse there were approximately five hundred fifty million people living in the USA. We now think that there are only about one hundred million left. And they would like to half that total at best."

"What you are talking about is completely insane. Why would anyone want to kill so many people? What could be the purpose?" Alfred felt a coldness spread through him. If what Jasper was telling him was true, this was a whole lot bigger problem than the Collapse had been.

"You are right. It is insane. Alfred, these people believe that their vision for all of humanity is the correct one. They believe that they are on a mission to save us from ourselves. They would like to bring the population down to what they believe the planet can sustain indefinitely. They are trying to establish a one world government. I've seen some of the documents that contain their philosophy. They intend to divide the survivors into different castes. Workers, mechanical, instructors, farmers, scientists, military, logistics, builders, clerical and kings. The surviving populace will be sorted, and everyone else and everything else that does not fit into their categories will be either severely restricted and controlled or forbidden. All of humanity will be working toward a common goal, and in their twisted little philosophy, a common good."

"That is one heck of a social engineering project. There is no way this group could really succeed is there?" Alfred asked the question but already his mind began to tick over. Jasper gave him time to think about it for a few minutes, and he could see that Alfred was now really beginning to understand that their world, their freedom, was in mortal peril. Alfred was also beginning to get angry. It wasn't fair, he thought. The survivors had suffered a terrible blow when the Collapse occurred. He and his family had taken precautions, fought off marauders, done their best to ride the disaster out. He was figuring that one day, someday soon, there would be a restoration of some sort of order and things would begin to get better. Now listening to Jasper, he realized that the Collapse was just the beginning of the nightmare. Monsters had seized their chance for power. Men who had made plans and waited for almost a century had taken their opportunity to subjugate humanity. It chilled Alfred to the bone when he thought of just how ruthless and merciless one had to be to initiate mass killing on a global scale. He saw in his mind's eye millions of people dying from the diseases inflicted upon them, bodies piling up and rotting in the streets and homes where they had died in agony.

"When I first started getting these reports of what these people were doing, I couldn't believe it. They have been successful in the killing of billions and they are not in the mood to stop anytime soon. Not until they have achieved their objectives. I have been getting reports from all over the continental US; they have already pacified the west coast. The central territories are still in play. Texas is fighting off a takeover of its territory from the Mexican drug cartels that were never stopped when we were powerful enough to do it. These cartels have thrown in their lot with the Bilderberg Group. Most of the northeastern seaboard has been pacified, but there are still some major holdouts in New Jersey, Pennsylvania, New York, and Maine. They have us in the crosshairs now." He smiled wryly.

"These are the people who gave our delegation an ultimatum. These are the people who placed three explosive devices in our community and took the lives of three people. These are the people who are now massing troops inside Binghamton and are getting ready to push into and pacify Cortland, Chenango, and Broome counties. We will be fighting them any day now, Alfred. We had gotten word that they were going to receive two of these biological weapons. Your dad decided to go and try to destroy them before they could be used. He left here months ago and has been working undercover since. We got a coded message from him three days ago that the canisters had arrived. I believe the particular concoction they have decided to send our way is a virulent strain of Ebola. If they succeed, Alfred, they wouldn't even have to fight us. They would just lob those babies in or find a way to release it on the community and watch us die. It would spread like a plague all the way to the Great Lakes. They would probably just wait another three months and then it would just be a matter of setting up shop."

Alfred felt a chill despite the whiskey in his gut. He realized that he and his family were caught in an inescapable web. A lot had been made about bug out locations. He had even read that some people had plans to bug out to very remote camps miles away from people. He understood that the situation was such that nowhere was safe anymore. He guessed that a small group of people could go undetected in a major wood or swampy area, but if these imperialist armies got control of the world then it would all just be a matter of time. For Alfred living at the *Rabbit Hole* was as much as he was able to stand. They had a cabin, a garden, and although small, it was a home. Living in a tent, constantly on the move, forever trying to avoid detection by an enemy that would kill him and his family was almost too much to bear. He knew that with these hostile militias seizing and consolidating territory it would only be a matter of time before they were discovered at their hideout. He could intuit what Jasper was going to say next, and when it came he was not surprised in the least.

"Listen, Alfie, the fact that you survived, that your entire family survived means that you understand how to take care of yourself. Your dad is pretty much running the show himself. He's going to need some help to destroy those weapons. Would you be willing to help your father?"

"You mean go in incognito and help him to destroy those canisters?" He looked at Jasper for a long time, then said, "I don't think I have much of a choice now, do I? He is my father, and even if I didn't give a damn about him, the fact that this army could control this area and possibly release deadly pathogens that could kill everyone would move this problem to the top of the list." Alfred thought once more about his family. He did not want to see them dying, choking out their last breath, bleeding from every orifice. He did not want to have to pledge his life and service to a bunch of murderers. He looked at Jasper and nodded. "I'll go, but I will have to let my family know what's going on. If they decided to stay here will they be taken care of?"

"Yes. I know that Samantha's a nurse. We could put your family in a small house on the outskirts of town until you got back."

"Well, I am going to have to run this by them. Samantha is not going to like me going, especially after what happened to us a few months ago. She is just getting back to normal."

Jasper didn't ask what happened to them. He didn't need to. "Okay, chat with your family tonight, and let me know for sure in the morning. If not, then I will have to send someone else, but I would prefer if it was you."

Alfred nodded. "How have you been Jasper? How did it happen that you became the leader here?"

"Can't say things have been good, Alfie. When this all started I was in charge of a small group of preppers in Broome County. People from all the surrounding towns heard about us on Facebook, and they would contact me. Originally there were about sixty of us, but when things began to go south, more people found their way to the group. When the breakdown happened we had it planned that we would all bug out to Marathon. We would meet up with the local law enforcement who we knew, and we would help to defend the town and maintain law and order. That's what we did. Then we realized that with everything falling apart we had to make this community a beacon of hope and stability. Every person who could make it here and wanted to stay had to understand that they would have to contribute. Duties rotated every three weeks. People had to understand that the old laws, the

US Constitution was in effect. This was not a fiefdom. Everything is decided by committees. Everything is debated and voted on. A pain in the ass, for sure, but it helps to bind the community together because everyone feels they have a stake, everyone now feels like they have a good cause. There was an election for who should be in charge. I was elected Community Leader for the next six years. Then there will be another election when my term runs out.

"I lost one of my two sons, and my wife is here in the town with me. But we have had a whole community that has helped to protect us, and it has been hard. It must have been a nightmare to have done it the way you did. I know what you are thinking, Alfie. You are thinking 'My God, I came so far.' Your family unit is still intact, a major miracle, and you thought you had outlasted the worst of it and now this. I know how you feel. We are all now being called upon to decide the fate of humanity for many years to come. We have to stop these folks or at least cause them so many problems they will be set back.

"When I decided to become a prepper, I had made that choice because I thought that we were due for some kind of black swan moment. I had the gut feeling that the way we treated the environment, the economy, our enemies, that something was going to reset our clocks. I did not want my family to be caught out, so I did what I could. You did too, as well as many others. I had no desire to play survivalist for real, still don't, I just want it all to end, but it happened. These Bilderbergs, they waited and when they saw their chance to grab power, to remake the world according to their design they took it. They all want to be kings, Alfred.

"On the outskirts of Whitney Point there's an old graphite mine. There's about six hundred feet of pretty large tunnels. They went pretty deep into the side of the mountain. The main shaft is large and runs about two hundred feet. That's where your dad is going to drive that truck with these biological weapons, and not only destroy them but seal the whole thing up by collapsing the shaft. That was the plan. We have enough intelligence to know that their biological stash is now stretched very thin. There is just so much they can make and so fast. This will buy us some time."

"As I said I will talk it over with them, but I don't think they will say no. I can give you a very strong yes right now. I'll do it. I don't have a choice, and I think they will see it that way as well. I will leave in the morning. I will have to explain everything to Samantha."

"Thanks, Alfred. I hope you and your father are successful. There will be a small team that will accompany you. You will meet at a set of prearranged coordinates."

Alfred looked at him. "Team? Who else is going?"

"We knew that we had to act on this so we had a team on standby. The fact that you showed up is a miracle that I intend to act on. They are a group of very determined people. Not crack, obvious commandos. People who can blend right in. Walk about Binghamton and in town without attracting too much attention to themselves and help get the mission done. The toughest thing will be to get the truck out of the city."

Alfred had heard enough. "Have everything ready for me when I come back in the morning. I want to get back to my family."

"Sure thing. Here is the address and location of the small house that Samantha can have while you are out." He handed Alfred a small note with the address, and a set of keys. Alfred then found his way out. When he got there, Samantha and the children had all their gear back. Everyone wanted out of the town hall. When they left the men were still sitting handcuffed to the chairs, and were about to be taken in to see Jasper. Alfred took one good look at the manacled men, and there was something about the look on their faces that unsettled him. They looked defiant and completely unafraid.

Samantha was relieved when they walked out of the town hall. They moved away down the street and Alfred directed them to a secluded spot. There were a few benches near the school's field. He had them sit down. Checking to see that they were completely alone, he related what Jasper had told him. Samantha felt a stone drop in her stomach. At first she wanted to just scream at Alfred. She wanted to shout in his face. She could tell that she hadn't done a good job masking the fact that she was mad, because Alfred looked positively alarmed, and the children began shuffling their feet nervously as they watched them.

She had just wanted him to say to her "Let's pack it in and go back to the hideout," but she knew that wasn't going to happen. She knew that it couldn't happen, and she lashed out in the only way she could. "I hate that scheming Jasper. I hate him, hate him." She began to cry softly and the kids really began to get nervous. Alfred, who had been sitting beside her, reached across and drew her to his shoulder. She felt her anger melt away, into him. "It's so hard, Alfred, it's so hard. How can we keep doing this?"

"The days of stability and peace are gone, Samantha. We are now in a time of uncertainty and darkness. I think if the right people come out of this on top, this time will be known as a dark age in humanity's history that we managed to overcome. If the imperialists win, then they will call this the age of opportunity that ushered in their golden age for mankind. I think I was still holding onto the hope that all we had to do was wait it out. Just survive and wait it out and somehow everything would work itself out and some semblance of the world we knew, the way we were living would find its way back. But now I have to look it in the face. I have to look the ugly truth in the face and accept that it really is all gone.

"America is gone, at least the one we knew. We can try to create something good and great; we have the blueprint. A place where people are safe to pursue happiness on their own terms. What these people have in mind for the world, for us, is misery and slavery. I don't know about you, but we did not fight off all those threats and go through all that hardship just to become slaves."

She looked at the children and saw that Robert was nodding his head in agreement. Candice looked pensive and angry, but it was she who spoke up.

"You have to go help Grandpa, Dad. You have no choice. Shouldn't we come with you?"

"No, I think you guys should stay here. I think you really do not have a choice but to stay here awhile and see how all this goes. I think that in the next few days something big is going to go down. The problem is we can't wait this one out at the *Rabbit Hole*. We are isolated, but not isolated enough." He looked at Samantha and squeezed her hand. She squeezed back and nodded.

"Listen," she said. "Don't be a hero. These canisters, destroy them if you can but if it means you need to get yourself killed, walk away, Alfie, we need you."

He nodded, and smiled. He knew that Samantha loved him. But he also knew that they would be trying to release one of those canisters here and his family would be in danger. His mind was already made up that if he could, he would not allow that to happen.

"Listen, we have been invited to dinner."

They looked at him completely shocked. "Dinner, are you kidding, Dad?" Candice hunched forward and looked at him. For just one fleeting moment Samantha saw the teenage daughter she knew inside that solemn, serious demeanor.

"Yeah, remember the family Robert and I met, the Meehans? Well just before all this went down I ran into to Jim and he's expecting us. We should get going. After we leave we can check out where you guys will be staying until I get back."

Samantha shook her head. It would be nice to sit with some people and have a meal. A real meal, like in the old days. Then after the children were bedded down, she would take care of Alfred. There was intensity in her feelings for him, and she wanted him in her bed. She wanted to make love to him because it could well be the last time they would be together.

Chapter Nine

Your face, my thane, is as a book where men
May read strange matters. To beguile the time,
Look like the time; bear welcome in your eye,
Your hand, your tongue: look like the innocent flower,
But be the serpent under't.
William Shakespeare

The Aimeses found the Meehan's tent. Jim invited them in and the two families found each other very congenial and well matched. There was an immediate warmness toward the other family. Samantha found Ellie kind and down to earth. With the Meehans, there was the general feeling of what you saw is what you got and they made the Aimeses feel immediately at home. Phillip was the same age as Robert. He was a slim, intense young man with sandy hair, and he had the deep green eyes of his mother.

He shook hands with all the Aimeses, and he and Robert struck up a conversation on the future of America. Candice found herself suddenly a bit shy around him, and she felt her cheeks heat up when he smiled at her. The Meehans had two folding tables which Ellie started to set up, and Candice went over and began helping.

"I hope you like my cooking," Jim remarked.

"I am looking forward to it. I am going to have to be very careful. I just had a tooth removed." Alfred smiled and patted his stomach.

Soon both families were sitting at the table and before they began eating, Jim said grace. They sat at the small makeshift table, on folding chairs, and understood that for just this short time they were lucky to be alive and with their loved ones. Jim's cooking was pretty good. Grilled spicy venison with baked potatoes and vegetables. Alfred chopped up the venison fine and ate a tasty liquid mess. There was a jug of Kool-Aid on the table and when they were done, Jim fished four Genny Lights out of a cooler and handed them to all the adults. They talked about this and that, then Jim looked at Alfred and said, "Let's go take a turn around the camp. We need to talk."

He looked at Samantha who nodded, and the two men left the tent and walked out into the pleasantly warm twilight. The camp was abuzz with activity. All around were the sounds of people coming home from their various duties and jobs. Alfred was amazed at just how orderly and clean everything was. Jim took a sip of his Genny Light and said quietly to Alfred, "We have some important work to do, you and I."

"What do you mean?"

"As soon as your family walked into the camp, we knew who you were. You had given your information to the guards at the gate. I am part of security, and I immediately figured out who you were. I remembered that we had a Colonel Aimes here a couple of months ago and I also remembered that you said your name was Aimes when we met at the farm. I began to think it was not a coincidence, and I called it in to Jasper who immediately asked for a description of the family. He then asked for you to be followed discretely, which I did. It was not by accident we bumped into each other near the med tents." Jim smiled at him. Alfred nodded and took a drag of his beer. The Genny was cool and smooth.

"When those bombs went off we knew that you had nothing to do with it, but we took you and your family in anyway. I knew that Jasper had been looking for a team to go out there and help the old Colonel and who better than the son? I know that he spoke to you and it's a go."

Alfred looked at Jim and smiled. "So it was very fortuitous for me to turn up."

"Ah, very fortuitous indeed. I will be going with you."

They walked along the perimeter of the camp counterclockwise. Alfred noticed that Jim would check around him to make sure they were not overheard. "The plan is that you will spend the night at the small house they gave you, and then you will leave the camp alone. When you do you will head into the woods off Interstate 81, a mile down, and turn off the road toward these coordinates and wait for the rest of the team." He took out a pen and said, "Hold out your right palm." When Alfred did he wrote the coordinates into his hand. "You will wait in the small copse until the rest of the team catches up to you. There will be, me, you, another fellow who's a medic, the colonel's old lady, and a crazy priest who Jasper got to volunteer. Now before we get back to our families, especially our wives, I want to ask if you are really on board with this. This is one very dangerous jaunt we will be going on. You have a family to think about. We might not come back."

Alfred sighed in resignation. Once again he found himself doing something, risking his life willingly, because of the circumstances. Fate was always forcing his hand. He felt that knot of worry in the pit of his stomach. He nodded. "What choice do I really have? My dad needs my help, and the thing he has to destroy can kill millions if it is used."

Jim nodded in agreement and they found themselves back at his tent. They went in and rejoined their families and chatted away into the night. Then they walked with the Aimeses to the house that had been assigned to them for the time Alfred was gone. It was a small one-bedroom cape with a tiny living room and a small kitchen. They did set up a small chemical toilet in the bathroom. The plumbing didn't work, and there was no electricity. The family dropped their gear onto the floor of the musty living room, and then they bid the Meehans goodnight and settled in. They unrolled their bedrolls. The adults took the single room while the children stayed in the living room.

Alfred lay on his back staring up at the circle of light the flashlight made on the ceiling. Samantha pulled her roll over and joined him. She rolled onto her side and propped herself up on her elbow to look at him in the dim light. She reached out and ran her fingers gently over his face. "Alfred, I am scared. I don't want you to go. I can't imagine, I can't image, oh God." She said softly and began to cry. He reached up and wiped the tears from her eyes.

"I don't want to go either. But I don't really have a choice. I will try to come back, Samantha. I will try my damnedest to come back. I love you. You are my heart, my special one, my wife. I have been a lucky man knowing you, Samantha." He began to cry as well, and his wife slipped on top of him, wiping the tears from his eyes. Then the man and his wife made love. It was strong, it was passionate, they became one, a single comingling of flesh and consciousness, and when they had exhausted each other they laid in an embrace until they both fell asleep.

The Bunker-England

Journal Entry 144,

I feel even worse today than I felt yesterday. It has been eight days since I buried Trisha and had that horrible confrontation with those two people. I have been having nightmares about what I did. After I killed those two people and buried the bodies, I went back down into the bunker. That night I got a serious case of the shakes, just couldn't help it. I think it scared the kids. I had never killed anyone before, and it has weighed on me, it's eating at my mind. I see that man and that woman and their smashed faces in my dreams. I see that man looking at me with his dead eyes. I wonder if I had just stopped and talked to them, would things have gone differently. Maybe not. They had discovered the bunker and they would have wanted to know all about it. If they had left, they would have known its location, and what would have happened if they brought back more people and tried to get in? No, killing them was the right thing to do. Am I a murderer? Will I go to hell for what I have done?

People used to write about killing all the time. They made a lot of movies about it, but nothing can come close to how I feel now since I've done it. It's horrible. I will always see their faces. I will see them in my dreams, their blood will always be on my hands. I try to think about how everything has gone and keep asking myself if things would have worked out better if I had made other plans. I keep going around and around on this one issue. I have gone back through my entries and I write about it constantly. I sound like a broken record but I can't help it. There were prepper groups around the UK before it had all hit the fan. If I had joined one, or started my own, would that have been better? Would Trisha be still alive? Would I have other people's blood on my hands? I keep going around and around in my head. Killing is personal. Well to me it is.

The kids were terrified when I came back down. It was bad enough to lose their mother, but I think they heard everything I was doing to those people. Bea kept asking about the woman who was screaming. Hell, I don't even remember her screaming, really, and my memory of the incident keeps getting murkier and murkier. I only see it clearly in my dreams. In my saner moments I console myself with the fact that from what I have heard on the ham, about all the fighting and all the death and killing, I would have been forced to kill long before I did, if I had stayed topside. The kids are still alive and although their mother couldn't take it anymore and killed herself, most of the family is still here.

From what I have heard on the ham, it's hell out there. It seems like people have been dying off in droves. Don't really know what that is about. There has been even worse news; the Prince has surrendered. It's bad news because at least with the royal family we knew what we were getting. They had been around for centuries. These new people in charge have been broadcasting day and night over the ham and regular radio stations. They are saying that the UK is now part of some European Precinct. That's the word I don't like, precinct. The broadcasts keep saying the same thing. The one that is really creepy is on the upper channels. It is the same woman with a high nasally voice. She has an accent I cannot place, maybe French, maybe German. She keeps saying that they will be bringing back order and the new world will rise from the ashes stronger and purer. Her voice makes me want to crawl into bed and cover my head.

I miss Trisha, I miss my wife. I miss her talking to me and discussing things. The girls have been very quiet. I could hear them crying in their bunks at night. They are trying to do the best they can. Cathy has really stepped up. She has been cleaning and trying to take care of the bunker. She has been asking me all sorts of questions about things she was never interested in before. It is nice to be able to teach her about how things work.

I haven't been feeling well for the past day or so now. Don't know why. I figure that maybe because of all the stress I am coming down with the flu. If I get sick I will have to try and isolate myself in the food section of the bunker, and when I get well I will have to disinfect everything. There were no books about bunker sickness protocol. I had a lot of those people's blood on me when I came back in. I tried to clean myself the best I could, and I dumped the clothes I had worn when I went outside. Still it really might be nothing, it could just be a twenty-four hour bug. I'll probably be as right as rain in a day or two. I just don't want the kids to get sick. Hmm, I don't know maybe thinking about it is just making me feel worse, but I am feeling a bit nauseated. I am going to go to bed now. I'll write more tomorrow.

Alfred hugged and kissed his family and checked in with Jasper according to plan. Jasper also gave him extra rounds for the Colt .45.

"The rest of the team has been briefed on this. Make sure your weapons are not visible. One plan is that you will walk in and say that you want to join up. I am sure that they will keep you isolated in a barracks until you go for your interview, then you will be assigned a Company Commander. You will go about your duties, and you will be keeping your eyes open for your dad. You will have to find a way to make contact and figure out how to get the weapons out of Binghamton to the disposal site and destroy them. A lot will be riding on this. The other plan, if everything works out and you guys get there without having to split up, is that you meet your dad at your old house, Alfred. That's where he is staying." He looked at Alfred, his eyes sad. "This is crazy, isn't it? You just take care, Alfred, and God speed."

Alfred shook his hand and left. It was 6:30 a.m. The sun was out. It was a beautiful late spring day. As Alfred walked out of the Marathon Settlement he noticed just how quiet everything was. Here he was on the outskirts of a small town in upstate New York, on a major Interstate, and there was no sound of traffic, or machinery, or people, just the sound of the wind and birds. He began to wonder if it would ever get back to what it was. He then thought about the mission he was on, to destroy cylinders of a mutated virus that was made with just one intention, to kill people, and a certain darkness wrapped itself around his heart. Humanity would be very lucky to survive itself. He passed through the last checkpoint on his way out and walked about a mile down the Interstate before crossing over to the woods that ran along the road. He got his compass and walked along the bearings given, to the small grove of trees where he was to wait for the other team members to show up. He picked a spot where he was concealed and settled in, and his mind wandered to his family. He wondered what they were doing and how Samantha was coping.

About an hour later Jim came into the copse, then another hour later a middle age woman. She was familiar and Alfred realized that it was the woman that had led him in to see Jasper yesterday. His jaw throbbed and he popped an Extra Strength Tylenol. He looked at the woman; she was of average height, and a little soft around the middle. She wore jeans and a tan long-sleeved shirt. She had a small blue knapsack and he could see the bulge of a pistol in her waist. Her hair was tied in a long gray braid and her face one whose beauty was fading into a plain lined mature attractiveness, was flushed and determined. She smiled and hugged Jim.

She introduced herself to Alfred. "I am Anne. Your father and I became very good friends in Utica. When things went south we were part of a group that looked out for each other. We became a little more than just friends, Alfred, and when he decided to come join the outfit here at Marathon I came along. I am very happy to meet you." She smiled, and he could see why his father would have liked her. That smile made her mouth crinkle at the corners like his mother's did. Feeling a little awkward he shook the hand she offered, and they sat back down to wait.

The next member of the team was a young man who looked like the slightest wind could knock him over. He was rail thin, very handsome, and there was a scholarly air to him. He shook hands with Jim and with the others before introducing himself. "My name is Timothy. I was a high school science teacher before it all went to hell. When Jasper heard of my qualifications in science, especially in biology, he briefed me on the threat and I have been studying as much information as

I could get my hands on about these biologically enhanced diseases. He figured having me along wouldn't be a bad idea. Let me just say that the stuff we are going to destroy is seriously lethal. If the containers were to be punctured in any way and this stuff was allowed to escape with us in the vicinity, I can assure you that we would all be dead in a few days. And most likely with time, the majority of New York would be under a serious threat of infection.

"I am going to volunteer as a medic because they are going to vaccinate their army against infection. I will try to get my hands on some of that vaccine and see if I can get it back to our people to replicate. I know you all understand what these people are trying to do. A year ago, if anyone would have said that I would be standing in the woods with a group of people on some sort of suicide mission to protect innocent people from madmen who want to kill ninety percent of the world's population, I would have thought they were absolutely crazy. But here I am, here we are. It's official. It's not us who are mad, it's the rest of the world." He adjusted his backpack and sat down near a pine tree. He then shook his head and added, "No, no, maybe we are all a bit mad now. Maybe at this point we are all a bit crazy." The others followed his lead and sat back down, and the wait resumed.

Almost exactly an hour later the final member of the party came into the copse. It was a well-built older red-haired man wearing a priest's clothing. He was dressed in a black long-sleeved shirt, black slacks and a light black windbreaker. He had the white collar around his neck. He carried a backpack and a bed roll was slung under his right arm. He shook hands with everyone, and when he got to Alfie his face lit up in a huge grin. "So we met again, huh? Hello, Alfred."

"Well, hello, Archbishop O'Riley. Good to know you are still alive. How did you survive? We heard a lot of shooting."

"Oh, you know God takes care of those who take care of themselves." The priest smiled an enigmatic grin. "How is the family?"

"They are well. Why would you come on such a dangerous operation?"

"Your man, Jasper, is a shrewd one. When he contacted me and asked if I would consider going along I realized that I couldn't refuse. The words of Edmund Burke came to mind, *the only thing needed for the triumph of evil is for good men to do nothing.* I can't sit around and do nothing. I can't sit around and watch the four horsemen of the apocalypse walk through the land and do nothing. I figure we have to fight until we draw our last breath. We cannot allow this evil to have a foothold in the world, unopposed. So here I am." He shook hands with Alfred and then turned to Jim. "Binghamton is a good day's walk from here. Are we all clear on what the plan is?"

Jim said, "I think we all have an idea of what we are supposed to do. We follow plan A. There is a safe house on the outskirts of the city. I think it was your old home, Alfred. Your dad picked it. We will meet there and your dad will take you, me, and Timothy in as prospective recruits. We will be processed and given our assignments, which we will do while keeping tabs on where those bio cylinders are stored. Anne will get a job housecleaning. From what we heard they can't seem to get enough people to do the grunt work, so she will slot right in. Timothy you will be taken to the doctors' barracks where I am sure you will be put through your paces and given a spot as a medic. The plan is we all keep a low profile and when your father gives us the go ahead, we swing by the safe house, pick up our guns and meet him with the truck. We'll drive it to the mine where we wire it and the tunnel, and blow them both up. If all goes as planned and there are any of us left, we will light out for Marathon, mission complete.

"To avoid suspicion after meeting at the safe house, we are supposed to enter the city at three different entry points. Your dad will tell us how to go about all of this. You all know the plan so that if something happens to any of us along the way there, the rest of you can continue with the mission." He looked at them and smiled grimly. The members of the group, being introduced, set off for Binghamton—five people on whose shoulders rested the fate of millions.

When Alfred left, Samantha felt like burying her head in her bedroll and sinking into the depression that was waiting like a long lost friend. That's how she felt, but she forced herself to do the opposite because the one thing her stint at the *Rabbit Hole* had taught her was that having a project, something important to do was integral to survival. She decided to volunteer her services at the medical tent after paying off the debt of maple syrup that Alfred had promised to the dentist. She took Candice along; her daughter had all the makings of a really good field doctor, and she was anxious to keep her medical education progressing. Robert said that he was going to volunteer for the security detail while they were staying here, until Dad returned. He had heard that there was going to be a trial for the men who allegedly carried out the attack the day before, and he wanted to watch it.

It was with some sense of purpose that the family left the home that was given to them as compensation for Alfred risking his life. They got unto the main street and then they split up. Samantha headed toward the medical tents, and Robert went to a newly built enclosure that was set up near the river on the south side of the town. The silty land close to the river was cleared out, and light aluminum tiered stadium benches were put in for people to sit and watch the proceedings in the small square enclosure below. People started to call this meeting place the Forum. Samantha knew that her son was very interested in how the compound was being run and governed, and he wanted to watch the trial of the two men who were charged with the bombing. She watched her son walk away; he was actually excited. She turned and went up two more streets before turning into the tented mall. They had left their gear at the house, and she carried only a small canvas bag with the maple syrup and a couple of sandwiches for lunch. Both women were armed and carried openly at the waist. Samantha had her .38, and Candice carried the 9mm Beretta they had taken off the dead Dove soldiers on the road.

She went into the first new medical tent, found the dentist that had worked on Alfred, and gave him the jar of maple syrup. She had to leave because the man started blubbering and crying. He said something about pancakes and maple syrup with his grandmother. The sight of a grown man crying and blubbering like that was just too much to take for Samantha, and she actually fled the tent with a laughing Candice in tow.

They went out the back and into the other medical tent, which was installed where the last one had been. The smell of the blast was still present and they could see the filled-in outline of the hole it had created when it went off.

The sight in the tent was orderly and a bit somber. They could see the main triage center at the other end, and there was a man and a woman seeing patients. There were two other women wearing a white armband with the universal red cross on their upper left arm. One of the women seemed awfully familiar as Samantha got closer. The woman looked up and at first her mouth dropped open like she had seen a ghost, then she ran forward with a grin that lit up her small pretty face.

"Samantha, it is you, right? Samantha!"

It was Candice who placed the woman first. "Geez, Mom, it's the lady we saved on the road next to our place. Julie!" Candice, who rarely smiled, was grinning again from ear to ear. So many bad things had happened recently. Seeing that the woman had made it safely here made her heart leap with hope. Maybe Dad will make it back, she dared to hope.

The woman hugged Samantha, and there were tears in her eyes. "Good to see you, Samantha," Julie said.

Samantha hugged her back and began to cry too. "Good to see you, too." She never thought she would ever see the woman again. It was good that she had made it safely after all.

"How is your niece? Is she well?"

"Nancy is fine. We managed to lay low during the day, moving only at night and get here safely." She looked at Samantha with a frown of concern. Is there something wrong? Do you need medical help of some kind?"

"No, we are fine. I was just coming to volunteer my services for a few days while we are in town. I used to be a nurse in my former life. My daughter has had extensive training as well. She is a good medic."

167

"Jesus, miracles do happen. We lost two people yesterday when those Royalist assholes blew up the tent. Any help we can get here would be welcomed." She turned and beckoned the women forward. The man who was in charge saw them coming and his round red face screwed into a look of complete annoyance. "Bert, you can relax. These two are volunteering to help. Samantha here used to be a nurse and her daughter is a medic."

Bert's face relaxed and he actually smiled. He extended his hand and shook Samantha's. "My name is Bertrand Wood. I am an emergency physician. I practiced for fifteen years at Cortland Hospital before it all went to hell. Where did you used to work?"

"Binghamton General. I also did some time in the ER at Wilson."

The man smiled and scratched the sparse gray hair on his head. "Well I can sure use the help now. We lost two people yesterday. That doesn't stop the people who need medical help." He motioned with his head to the entrance of the tent, and Samantha could see the long line of people already waiting. "Are you comfortable diagnosing and taking a quick history?"

"I am. My daughter can take care of most types of triage."

"Good, good, just run everything by me before we decide what to do. You will need to scrub up. A hand washing station is over there. Gloves and masks are over there, and we have a good supply of medicine in those two large trunks." He pointed out where all the things were located. The hand washing station was one that used to be found at large fairs, the foot-operated kind. Samantha and Candice washed and gloved up. At Julie's direction they also put masks on. Then they went to work.

Robert was excited. He took his seat in the stands at the Forum. He was lucky to have gotten there early enough so he was able to get a spot three rows up and center. He was able to see and hear all. When society breaks down, this is one way people still try to find justice, he thought. Philip Meehan came in later and Robert saw him take a seat way up in the top tier closest to the entrance. Robert wondered if his friend had spotted him, but his attention was grabbed by the arrival of the twelve-person jury. There were five women and seven men. They took their seats in a row of chairs that were set out in the enclosure. Then came the Judge. He took his seat behind a large table. He had a briefcase, and when he sat down he opened it and took out two folders and a sheaf of official looking paperwork. There was a hum in the crowd up to this point, but there was a hush as soon as the two suspects were brought in. Finally the lawyers came in. The defendants were represented by two lawyers, and the town of Marathon had its two prosecutors.

The tall man wearing a suit who had come in with the Judge was the court clerk, and he called the trial to order.

"Order, this trial of James Lloyd and Patrick Mckenner is now called to order, Judge Thomas Kendrick presiding."

"Thank you, ladies and gentlemen, you may sit. Let's hear the charge against these men," the Judge said.

"James Lloyd and Patrick Mckenner are charged with the crime of planting explosive devices in the town of Marathon, New York. Those devices killed three people: Dr. Martin Pike, Tamera Williams who was a medic, and Mary Felinni, a sanitation worker. The devices also injured twelve others who are now being treated at the Medic Trauma Center in town. These two men are charged with terroristic acts against the people of Marathon," the clerk read from the charge sheet.

"The prosecution can now make their statements," the judge said.

The lead prosecutor stood up. He was a thin, tall black man, going gray at the temples. His glasses winked in the sun as he looked at his notes and began. His serious gravelly voice rang around the Forum.

"Ladies and gentlemen of the jury, I would like to say I am glad and honored that you could take the time out of your busy schedule to help us out today. The case before us is very grave. If these men are found guilty they face death by firing squad. The town of Marathon will show that these two are the perpetrators of a brutal and vicious crime. We will show using a timeline and eyewitnesses, as well as physical evidence that James Lloyd and Patrick Mckenner came into this town under false pretenses. That they placed the devices and detonated them then attempted to flee before they were discovered.

"When we established this settlement as an American Free Zone where people could come, live and work, as long as they protected each other and abided by the American Constitution, we thought we understood what a challenge we had undertaken. But that challenge has proven a gargantuan task. We have had to integrate everyone into a town that was already populated and governed. We had to protect it from marauders and cannibal gangs, and individuals who took it upon themselves to take advantage of the chaos and commit horrible crimes, thinking there would be no consequences.

"Ladies and gentlemen of the jury, when you registered to become free citizens of this community you voluntarily took it upon yourself to become protectors of the ideal that was born when the Founding Fathers won us independence so many years ago. We will show in open court before everyone why these men are guilty, and you will get the chance to carry out justice. Justice that is not ordered by one man or carried out by secret edict but according to the Constitution and the Code of Laws of the United States of America. We made the choice when we came here to follow the ideals of the Constitution. We knew that the world had changed. We know that reestablishing the USA may not be in the cards but we as free citizens refuse to be intimidated, to be shackled, or to give up our Constitutional rights.

"These men that you see before you have decided to give up their rights under the Constitution. They decided to become agents of terror, yes, that's what these men are, make no mistake. In the old days the USA had to deal with enemies who hated what our country stood for and who wanted to destroy it. They used the very same methods carried out by these men. Remember 9/11, remember the Boston Attack, the beheadings and women, children and service members killed in random terrorists attacks on US soil. Remember Syracuse. I can see as I look around this audience that we have a few survivors of that attack present here. These men, these villains, they came into our town, saying they wanted to trade, and instead they planted explosives and murdered three people of this town. These people whom some of you knew were not bad people. They did not deserve to have their lives ripped away from them."

KARL A.D. BROWN

Robert listened to the oratory of the prosecutor and found himself completely absorbed in the proceedings. He looked around the crowd and could see a few people; some were disfigured and there were others who wore the yellow ribbon that signified that either they were survivors of the Syracuse nuclear attack or had family or friends who had died or survived it. He remembered the day of the attack and the shock and horror he had felt as he had watched it all unfold on the various news channels. His parents were not aware how deeply that incident had affected him. Up to that point he was just a regular fourteen-year-old boy, not really paying too much attention to the world or its problems. His biggest issue at the time was whether Brittany Quinn, a bubbly fourteen-year-old redhead, liked him or not. For weeks he had been working up his courage to ask her out on a date. The day he decided to pop the question was the day his parents decided to pull him and his sister out of school for safety concerns. His parents were proved right because they never went back. He wondered if Brittany was still alive, or had she perished with the millions that had died on the North American continent.

He had heard his father say many times that the old USA was probably lost for good. That maybe the best they could now hope for was a new America, forged on the precepts of the Founding Fathers. He was beginning to see that maybe his father was right. As he sat in the stands watching the trial of the men accused of terroristic acts, he realized that in a post-apocalyptic world, this trial, this way of meting out justice was perhaps the best that free people could do. He understood even though he was young that in most encampments or small communities the decisions of guilt or innocence, life or death was determined by one man or woman. That made him uncomfortable. It bred despotism.

Robert also realized that he would fight for this way of things if he had to. He realized that these people had a vision of the type of community he would like to live in. He wanted to be a free citizen, not a pawn of the state. His attention was now being drawn back to the proceedings as the defense took to the floor. The man who was the lead defense attorney was a white-haired man of about sixty. There was a serious scholarly air about him. His skin was tanned and leathery, and his eyes were bright and piercing blue.

"Ladies and gentlemen, most of you know me, I have taken my turn at guard duty and trash collection, as most who are citizens of this community. You know I believe in the law. You know I believe in the truth and the Constitution. The Sixth Amendment to the United States Constitution guarantees the right of the accused to a speedy trial by an impartial jury, to have witnesses obtained in their favor. I will show that these accused men are not only having their rights violated, but also that there is a conspiracy at work. A political conspiracy cooked up by the Council to maintain their power and to lay the foundation for hostilities with the New York City Militia, whom they see as the enemy."

Robert sat up on his bench, and there was a buzz of voices in the crowd and the judge tapped his gavel for order. What the hell, was this lawyer serious? In his bones he knew the men must be guilty. They had to be. He and many others had thought that they were there to just see the case laid out and proven against the men. This was completely unexpected to say the least. The defense was actually going to present a case. The lawyer went on with his address.

"We will show that the state cannot prove its case beyond a reasonable doubt. All it has are conjectures about who these men are. You will see in the end that these two men are innocent."

He sat down and at once began speaking to the men in hushed tones. The judge called for order and instructed the prosecution to begin its case. The prosecutor produced a large chart that showed the men's whereabouts over the last forty-eight hours, and he showed that they had come into the town as prospective settlers and that they were only lightly armed. They were searched but no explosives were found. They were allowed to keep their firearms and were given a seventy-two hour pass, which could be extended indefinitely if they decided to stay. The chart showed that they were given a small campsite in Camper's Lot on the north side of town. This was the very place where his family was assigned to camp before his father became entangled in what really was tantamount to a suicide mission.

The men had gone there and set up camp. They then went to several venders in the Tent Mall in the park. It was shown that they were spotted at different points around the camp's limits. The presentation gave the overall impression that the men were spying out the town. They were even shown crossing the river at one of the shallow points and crossing over to the other side, which was less populated and, as the prosecutor postulated, it was probably there they dug up the supplies needed to carry out the plot. The most damaging evidence came last when the men were seen at the location of the attacks and were then subsequently arrested. One of the men tried to fight and was shot dead by the town's security force. The others were captured using non-lethal means; one was maced and the other was tasered. The order had come down from the town's council to capture them alive for interrogation at all costs.

The men's backpacks were searched, and although nothing incriminating was found, when they were subsequently strip searched, one of them was found to have a New York City Militia military tattoo of the Dove on his back.

The prosecutor laid out the bomb fragments and explained the type of device that was used to the jury. Robert realized that they were really lucky that no more people had been killed or hurt, because the power of the devices was devastating. The whole presentation took two hours.

There was a break for the people and the court staff. Robert used one of the porta-potties set up outside the Forum, then went back to his bench and quickly ate a day old cheese and jam sandwich he had in his small canvas messenger bag. He was washing it down with water when Philip came and sat down on the bench beside him. He, too, had taken the break to grab a meal, his a bit more substantial than what Robert had. There was a lot of meat and cheese wrapped up in thick bread. Philip caught the look and asked, "Do you want a bite? I can cut this in half."

Robert ground his teeth and said, "No, I am fine. Heck of a thing going on, isn't it?" He forced a smile and nodded toward the jury that had begun to come back in and reclaim their seats.

"Yeah, I am pretty skeptical about the prosecution's case. I mean they have nothing conclusive."

"I think that it's going to be hard not to convict them, though. They are known to be the Dove's men. They were in the vicinity of the attacks when they went down." He was about to say more when the judge tapped his gavel and the trial resumed with the defense making its case. The attorney for the accused made a pretty convincing case why the jury shouldn't convict his clients. He argued that his clients were part of the New York City Militia but had left, they had decided to make a home here for themselves. He said that his charges had no idea how to make explosives and that the explosives were planted there by someone else. He said that there was no forensic proof linking his clients to the bombing and that the men were being railroaded. He then went on to say that the whole thing was a false flag concocted by the Town's Council to make a case for engaging the New York City Militia in hostilities. When the defendants' lawyer was done, Robert found himself questioning his original conclusions.

He sat with his friend beside him and marveled at the defense council's argument. It was convincing, and the men stood a real good chance of getting off. He looked at his watch and realized that it was almost 3 p.m. almost a whole day had gone by. The trial had proved to be a welcome distraction from the fact that his father was gone. Both sides wrapped up their case and the jury went into the town hall to deliberate. The judge told the audience that the horn which was used to warn the camp of danger would sound the minute the verdict was reached. The people were invited to come and hear the verdict and see justice done.

There was a buzz about the place. Robert understood that he was seeing the execution of law in its purest state. Here in Marathon, after the calamity that had plunged the entire world into an age of darkness, men were given the right to a fair trial and judged by a jury of their peers. There were other settlements around, and most of them would have chosen to go about the process in a much different way. He and

Philip had been walking in the direction of the Tent Mall in the park. He intended to drop in on his mother and sister, and Philip had volunteered to tag along. About halfway there Robert sensed that something was wrong, but he couldn't put his finger on it. It wasn't until they came up to the dirt track that led into the mall that he realized what had been bothering him.

"Hey, Philip, where's your bag? Did you forget it?" Philip's green messenger bag was missing.

"Damn. I must have left it under the bench. I was so excited I completely spaced. Damn, it should still be there. I'll go back and get it."

"Listen, why don't you run on back and I'll go find my folks. Meet me at the Security Center."

"Sounds like a good idea."

"Sorry, I'll just wait outside for you. See you soon."

With that the young men separated and Robert made a beeline for the medical tents. He walked up the dirt pathway toward a small line of people. When he got close enough he could make out his mother examining a man seated on a stool. Samantha looked up. She smiled and waved when she saw him. Robert was struck by how professionally capable she seemed. She had gloves on and had a stethoscope around her neck. He was just a few feet away and was about to ask about her day, and if she would be ready to go soon, when there was a distant and loud bang. Seconds later the alarm went off and he could see people moving toward what he figured was an explosion.

"Mom, I think I better go see what that is all about."

"Be careful, Robert." His mother had stopped examining a patient, who had now also gotten to his feet and was looking in the direction of what most likely had been an explosive blast. From within the tent more people came out, among them, his sister. He handed her his messenger bag and trudged off to find out what exactly had occurred. He followed a small group of people who were also making their way to the scene. The crowd grew and he found himself retracing his steps. The closer he got to the Forum the tighter the sheet of anxiety drew itself around him. He found himself at the back of the crowd, but he was tall and could see into the Forum over most of the heads. The security people were checking out a huge mangled hole in the aluminum benches where he and Philip had been sitting. He felt his skin prickle as ice crept up his spine. After standing there for a few minutes he could hear the security officers talking to each other, and when he realized that no one was hurt he breathed out a sigh of relief. He worked himself toward the back of the crowd and finally found himself free of most of the onlookers. He felt the blood hammering away at his temples as his feet began making a beeline for Camper's Lot at the edge of town. In his mind a cold thought was beginning to form. He felt his chest tighten and as the ugly thought blossomed, he broke into a slow trot. He got to the outskirts of the settler's tent city, ran down four rows, and made for the tent at the end of the end column on the other side of the settlement. The tent flap was closed and when he was just a few feet away from the entrance Philip stepped out. His jaw dropped when he saw Robert, and then he smiled.

"Oh, what a relief. I heard the explosion. I had come back home to grab some more sandwiches and something to drink when I heard the bang."

"Philip, did you go to the Forum after you left me?"

"Yeah, I went to get my bag and then I came here. What exactly happened in the Forum?"

"There's a big hole in the bench we were sitting on."

"Jesus, was anyone hurt?"

Robert sighed and pointed at the bag on Philip's shoulder. "You were the one who did it."

Philip's face darkened in a look of what seemed to be honest bewilderment. "I don't follow. What are you saying, Robert?"

"I am saying that you were the one who left the bomb in the stands."

"I don't like being accused of things I had nothing to do with."

"Your bag. Is that the one you had in the Forum?"

"No, the one I had at the Forum was filthy after I had left it under the seat. I'll go get it, and you will owe me an apology."

He turned and went back into the tent. Robert could hear him talking to someone inside. It sounded like Philip's mother. A hand fell on his shoulder and he almost jumped out of his skin. He turned around and realized that two men were behind him. One he recognized. His mind searched for the name for a second, before he remembered who the short, squat red-haired man was. He had his fingers to his lips indicating that Robert should remain quiet.

"Stay here, we don't want them to know we are here yet."

The other man quickly and silently slipped around the back of the tent. Jasper ran to the side of the tent close to the opening. He drew his pistol and remained out of sight. Robert's head swam, what in God's name was going on here? What had he gotten himself into?

Jasper then mouthed silently, "Call him."

"Philip, you need to come on out and explain to me what's going on."

The boy who had been his friend came out of the tent. In his hand he held a Taurus .45. Robert felt a well of sadness creeping over him and growing alarm. The horrible implications of this discovery chilled him to the bone. The sadness quickly fled and was replaced by rage. "So what does this mean?" He nodded toward the gun.

"We can stop playing dumb, Robert. How did you know for sure it was me?"

"The bag. The one you had at the Forum was green. The one you have now is gray. You planted the explosive, didn't you?"

"Yeah."

"But what I don't understand is why you would do such a thing. You believe in forming a free society just like I do."

"Oh, don't be daft, Robert. Months ago when the grid came down and it all went to hell I was in New York City. My family was killed by a bunch of hungry marauders. I saw my sister chopped to pieces. I managed to escape. I was lucky. I found the Dove and he took me in. He is a strong leader, a good man, hard but good. These people, these preppers and old Constitutionalists are just in the way of a new world, a better world."

"I think you are wrong. These people you have given yourself to are killers and despots. You are fifteen, Philip. We are young men. When he told you to come here to do this, did he give you a choice, or was it a command?"

"It doesn't matter, strong men have to command, strong men have to…" Jasper didn't wait for him to finish his sentence. He didn't ask him to drop his weapon or to surrender. He shot the boy in the shoulder of the arm that held the gun. Philip squeezed the

Taurus' trigger by reflex before the pistol fell out of his hand. He went down clutching his shoulder, screaming from shock and fright. Robert staggered back. His hand went to the side of his face, and his fingers came away slick with blood. Philip had come within a whisker of ending his life.

Screaming erupted from inside the tent. There were sounds of a bad scuffle. Two quick pops of a pistol ended the screaming and scuffling. The altercation had now begun to draw a crowd of onlookers. Two more security officers materialized out of the crowd.

"Take both boys to the medic tents. That one should be in cuffs." Jasper pointed to Philip, who despite his shattered arm was rolled on his back and cuffed. The boy screamed as the broken bones in his shoulder grounded together. They were then escorted by the two guards to the medic tents. Robert felt his heart tripping in his chest. His first thought was that his mother was going to be seriously pissed off. He just seemed to have a penchant for getting shot. He walked holding a towel someone had given him to his face to stop the bleeding. Philip got about half way there and then collapsed in a heap. The officers grabbed him by the shoulders and carried him the rest of the way.

When he got to the medic tents, he saw his sister attending to a woman with a small child who seemed to be coughing and wheezing pretty badly. When Candice looked up and spied him he saw the look of concern. She uttered a small shriek and ran toward him, the small coughing patient she had been tending momentarily forgotten.

"It's okay, it's okay, Dice. Just a scratch, that's all."

His sister removed the towel and after dabbing at the wound she sighed, relieved. "It's not so bad, but it will need a few stiches. It might leave a scar. How did this happen?"

He nodded toward the officers carrying Philip. "That idiot almost killed me. He is not who he appeared to be. None of them are." He saw the look of alarm return to her face. His little sister was no fool.

"Dad, Dad's in trouble, isn't he?"

"Yeah, and we have to tell Mom."

They had followed the officers into the tent and watched as they took the moaning boy to a cot. They had him sit upright. The doctor and Samantha had just finished wrapping a woman's broken tibia and had not been paying attention, but all that changed when she realized who the two young men were. She looked at her son's face then glanced at the boy sitting and bleeding on the cot, and an icy murderous rage coursed through her. The doctor told the officers to remove the handcuffs and when they did, Philip cried out. His eyes rolled up and he collapsed. Robert noticed that his mother had also quickly summed up the situation and she asked one of the officers where she could find Jasper.

"He's going to be back at the town hall. This little discovery has got him all worked up," the man said.

Robert saw his mother look at both of them, and he knew she was going out of her skin with worry, but when she spoke her voice was calm. "Listen, Candice, get that wound flushed, treated, and sewn up. Then meet me over at the town hall. I want to hear what Jasper is going to do about all of this." She turned and walked out of the tent. Robert wanted to go with his mother. Dad was in trouble, big trouble, but he knew he had to let his sister treat the wound because in this new world of nineteenth century medicine, a flesh wound could kill if infected. He would not be able to help his family if he was running a fever. So he sat and let Candice work.

Samantha's heart rammed up and down in her chest as she walked quickly toward the town hall. As she got to the steps that led into the building, she saw Jasper coming from the opposite direction. He saw her and nodded, a look of hard resignation on his face. "Let's talk in my office," he said. She followed him into the building and he took her straight to his workroom in the back. He showed her a seat and as she took it, she began to feel a little lightheaded.

He saw her distress and poured her a glass of water, which she sipped. He then sat himself and said, "This little spy problem is worse than we had thought. I guess you saw your son." She nodded and drank a little more. "Well, the man who is leading the infiltration team is the chief spy among them. That doesn't bode well for the mission and the people who undertook it. I looked into who was the chief guard the day the men showed up and found Meehan's name on the roster as duty supervisor. It didn't ring any bells at first. There are only five men qualified for the job and he was on duty that day. I happened to hear the explosion and when I went out to see what was up, I saw your son at the scene. There was just something in his disposition and the way he made a beeline for Camper's Lot that made me curious.

"I had a report that your boy had been sitting with Philip in the very same spot that was now a mass of mangled metal and I began to wonder, so me and a couple of officers followed him. Then it all kind of clicked. I was the one who shot Philip; he shot your son. One of the officers went inside the tent and we

183

found the Meehan woman trying to send a message to the New York City Militia. She had a small powerful radio and was using Morse code, no doubt filling in her superiors about the trial and the success of their attacks. Before she died she said something about doing it for the cause and for Meehan's daughter. The story they told us when they arrived was that their daughter was dead—that she had drowned while they were hiding out... It appears that daughter is still alive and is being used as leverage for them to carry out the Dove's dirty work."

Samantha began to get her composure back. Her anger returned and it made her feel strong, rather than worried, as she listened to Jasper's story. She saw that he had stopped and was looking at her expectantly, so she obliged him with the only question that mattered.

"So what are we going to do about it? Those people who are following Jim to Binghamton have no idea who he is and what he is capable of. My husband, your friend, is with them. His father has infiltrated the Dove's army. These are all good brave souls. Are they now going to be sacrificed?"

"No, they can't be left to fail. Their mission, their purpose, is too important. Those biological weapons must be destroyed at all costs. We and our only ally to the north are the only thing standing between them and complete control of the Northeast. We are an important enough problem for them to use those weapons against us. As a matter of fact, I think they will do it sooner rather than later, so that's why I am going to roll the dice here. I am going to attack the Dove. We leave in twelve hours. He's got a small army in Binghamton. At last count he has about forty thousand troops in and around the city. I am going to take in thirty thousand of my best people and see if we can take them down."

Samantha looked at the pudgy redheaded man and realized that he was a person who was now in his element. He was clever, and he relished these little problems. "I'll be tagging along," she said as she got to her feet.

"Well, I kind of figured that you would. What about your children?"

Samantha thought about it and realized that she could insist that the kids stay behind, but she doubted that they would. There was no way for her to go and for them not to know. For a fleeting second she considered staying behind and keeping them safe. That would be the thing to do. Alfred would be the only one in any danger. Then as quickly as the idea came, she dismissed it. Jasper saw her hesitation and said softly, "You're thinking about their safety, aren't you? You don't think they would stay behind while Mom goes after Dad. Well there is an auxiliary unit that will stay out of harm's way until they are needed. A group of two hundred reserves that we can call in if we need additional help. How about we assign the kids to that unit?"

Samantha felt like she could scream. A year ago if anyone had told her that she would be chatting about putting her children in a company of auxiliary soldiers who potentially could be in harm's way, she would have said that they were crazy. She swallowed hard and nodded to Jasper. "Good enough. I guess I have things to discuss with my children. Where do we meet, and at what time?"

"We meet here at the town hall at 4 a.m. We will take care of a bit of business, then we will be on a fast hike to say hello to the Dove."

She spent the next couple of minutes talking to Jasper and then she left to find the kids. She found herself twisting her wedding band, and as soon as she was away from the town hall the tears began to come freely. Then she realized that there was one other option she didn't think about to keep the children safe. She could have asked Jasper to throw them in a cell in the small town jail until it was all over. But as soon as the thought came she rejected it. She knew that some of the volunteers who were going into the thick of the fight would be as young as her own children, and they would be expected to perform their duties. The world was now a hard place. We are now in a time that will be remembered by parents as the 'End of Childhood.' She understood that Americans hadn't had a period like this in a very long time. Probably not since the Civil War when boys as young as twelve volunteered to serve in the army. Her feet took her to the front of their temporary residence where the children were waiting. Robert's wound was sewn up neatly.

He was sitting on the front step and Candice was sitting beside him. They both stood up and looked at her expectantly. "What did Jasper say?" Robert asked.

"He basically confirmed what I am sure you all had figured out. Jim's a traitor. He must have helped those men plant the bombs. He will turn on your dad as soon as he gets the chance. Jasper's decided to take the fight to them. I guess he is figuring that he might be able to get lucky if he can catch them unawares and unprepared."

Robert thought about the new information for a while before asking, "When do we leave?"

"Four in the morning."

"That would mean that we could be there at sundown tomorrow evening, figuring we would march through the woods rather than using the main roads where we would be spotted. It will be brutal, but if we could get there without alerting the Dove we might just be able to pull it off. We would need a lot of luck though, and no one gets that lucky. Best case scenario is that we get most of the way there and he meets us in the woods and we fight it out." He frowned. "Wouldn't it be best if we leave now, Mom? We could make better time."

"No, I don't think they would allow that for obvious security reasons. Plus I think the best way to actually get to your dad is to go in with them. If we went alone we would have to get in without them knowing we were there and try to locate your dad. No, the best plan is to go in with them."

"I agree," Candice said. "We have to get in and find him and get him out." Her small face hardened and then she said, "We will have to deal with Jim, won't we, Mom? We might have to kill him."

Candice's words opened more unseen wounds in Samantha's soul. The world is truly insane when children have to kill, she reflected. She looked her daughter steadily in the eye and said, "Yes, if we find him and your father we may have to kill him because he may want or have to kill us." She sighed and said, "Let's get inside and have something to eat and get some rest. We have to pack light and be ready for a fight. When we get to Binghamton, Jasper said that you two are to stay behind with the auxiliary squad. They will only be called if they are needed."

"Sorry, Mom. There is no way we'll let you go in there by yourself after Dad while we stay behind," Robert said.

"You will stay with the reserves until they call you."

"Mom, I'm with Robert on this. We fight well as a team. We should be together."

Samantha sighed, fully understanding just how cruel life and fate was; it seemed crazy that her kids were basically defying her. But she understood on some level that because the world had changed, people had to as well. Her children were fighters now; it was a relationship shift she had not really seen coming and would struggle to understand. They ate a hearty meal of meat, cheese, and bread. They emptied their beat up Maxpedition backpacks and refilled the built in water bladders from the Berkey water filter in the kitchen. Each person had about two hundred rounds of ammunition for every gun they carried, and they would hump that on the trip along with enough food for about four days. They also had the slingshots that Alfred had made. Samantha figured they would come in handy if they needed to be quiet; a shot to the head could drop anyone fast. She and Robert had survival knives in a sheath that they wore around their waists. Candice still had the small machete in its canvas sheath that they had carried, really for practical camping issues, but now it, too, became a weapon of war.

When they were done they went outside to the small deck. The settlement was a beehive of activity with vehicles going to and fro, and groups of people scurrying here and there. Samantha understood Robert's urgency; every fiber in her body wanted to just put on her backpack and walk out of the camp. But she resisted the urge. Her best bet to finding Alfred alive was to stick with the Marathon Militia. It was difficult passing the time; it seemed to slow down to a crawl as evening eventually passed into night. They went to bed and slept uneasily until Samantha's watch went off at 3 a.m. They got up and stretched and shook the cobwebs from their heads. After a quick light meal and a drink of water, they piled the gear they would be leaving behind into a corner of the living room, took one last look around, and placed the key under the mat and left. As they walked away from the little house, Samantha wondered if they would all make it back. She wondered if Alfred was still alive.

Chapter Ten

"Loyalty means nothing unless it has at its heart the absolute principle of self-sacrifice." Woodrow T. Wilson

The Bunker-England

Journal Entry 145

It's been awhile since I have been able to write. I have been as sick as a dog. I even thought of going above and hiding in the woods behind the house until I got better, but whatever I have is already here in the bunker, so what's the use. The kids have been exposed and we have all been breathing the same air, using the same bathroom. There is no escaping germs in a bunker, damn. Bea also has a fever, so I figure she's got whatever I have. Only Cathy seems to be fine. The fever and the headaches are crippling. I think I passed out while in the bathroom last night. I woke up in bed. Cathy must have dragged and lifted me up into the bunk. It must have been horrible for her to see me like that; I can't imagine her dragging and lifting me either. I must weigh about one hundred fifty pounds now. I've lost a lot of weight in the past couple of months.

This is one of the better spells. I hope that whatever this is passes. I need to be here and healthy to take care of my daughters. If something happened to me it would be horrible. Who would take care of them? I keep thinking about my bunker idea. I wonder if other people who went with bunkers had a better or similar experience. I come again to the question that still plagues me to this day. Would it have been better to have joined a community rather than opting to outlast the chaos in a bunker? Would Trisha be alive if we were part of a group?

Christ, my hands are shaking. This fever makes me want to curl up into a ball and scream and scream. I think if I was alone I would probably do that, but I can't. It would terrify the children. I guess those people I killed up top must have been carrying some kind of disease. I got a lot of their blood on me when I took care of them. I have been sick for two days now. Yesterday was bad, but I think I am now in some kind of lull before it gets bad again. I told Cathy to make sure that she keeps me and Bea hydrated if it gets bad enough where I can't help. Then she is supposed to use the bleach cut with water to wipe everything down and to keep the bunker as clean as possible.

How did it all come to this? How could we have screwed up the world so much that we are now fighting for our very survival? My children, God, what kind of world will they now have to live in if they survive? I can't see any light at the end of the tunnel for us, for humanity. Christ, I think just writing this has tired me out. I have to stop now, my stomach feels like crap. Will have to use the toilet. Til next time.

The infiltration team was making good time toward its destination. They decided that they would not stop to camp for the night. It was just safer to keep moving. They kept off the roads and avoided going into any towns along the way. The great thing about I-81 was that there was plenty of cover along most of the road. Alfred was sure that if they had gone into any of the towns they would have made contact with people. The world was not quite as empty and desolate as it seemed, at least not yet. People had just become more adept at keeping out of sight.

He still could not get his head around the amount of people who had died off in the last eight months. The fact that they had seen absolutely no one since they began their walk along what used to be one of the busiest highways in New York chilled him. They passed overturned and burnt vehicles from time to time; the bodies that they passed along the highway told their own personal stories of tragedy. They told of running battles, robberies, executions, and cannibalism. Some-one should be documenting all of this, Alfred thought. Maybe if they did it would prevent us doing it to ourselves again. Every single building along the highway was smashed in and burnt out. They trekked by what used to be a rest station. On the road near the shoulder they passed the desiccated body of a woman, she was wearing a yellow sweater and white jeans. Below her was a small child. Alfred felt something wring inside him. The story here he could see, she was attacked over by the rest station, grabbed the child, and made it all the way over here before she was cut down by bullets. She had tried to protect the child with her own body, but whatever they had used had shredded her back, killing the child as well. He could tell that the bodies had been there for a long time, and they were partially eaten by animals.

The priest saw him looking and said softly, "I saw a lot of death in New York City and it made me half mad for a while. So many people died in their apart-ments, the streets, subway tunnels. I remember the screams and the smell. For four months New York City stank. It became a bloated corpse and the survivors were the maggots. This man they call the Dove, I saw a lot of his handiwork in New York and in the towns that he "conquered." He is an evil man, Alfred. He will not stop all this, and that's why I picked a side. These men, these Bilderbergs, Royalists, whatever they are calling themselves now, are not about life. They are all about death and fear and darkness. What kind of men makes plans to kill off two thirds of the world's population?" The priest shook his head. He would say no more for a while.

Alfred looked around at his little group and felt a prickling of pride. These were all good people and he knew that they all had a story to tell.

Jim was listening to the conversation and added with a sad crooked smile, "Parents, good parents will do anything for their children. That woman was a good parent. She tried to protect her child. She was a hero and no one will know about her sacrifice."

"We know," Anne said softly. "We make sacrifices for family and people we love. We will kill for the ones we love. I've always wondered, though, what the hardest choice is. Is it sacrificing oneself, like that heroic mother did, or is it having to kill the people we love? When does love cross the line from being a beautiful thing to an abomination?"

"It becomes an abomination when it becomes self-ish and kills instead of nurtures," Timothy added.

"I guess her sacrifice wasn't in vain after all. Are we not doing the very same thing? Every person here is willing to give their life to right a wrong that involves the people or an idea they care about," Alfred said. He was thinking of his own family and in his heart he was grateful that they were safe and out of harm's way. He hoped that he would one day be able to see them again.

Jim kept them going at a pretty quick pace. Alfred understood the man's reasons well. The faster they all got to the rendezvous point the quicker they would be able to get on with the mission. They were all lightly armed. If they were apprehended before they got to the safe house it would be easier to make the case that they were a group of volunteers, rather than enemy combatants, since they were not carrying rifles. They took a brief rest after about four hours of walking. At one point they figured that they were being followed. Somebody was tracking them for about a mile before they left. It made the hairs on Alfred's back stand up knowing that back in the woods there were people checking them out. They were on guard knowing that they could be attacked at any minute; thankfully that was not the case. Whoever they were, they decided to leave them alone.

A mile before they could see them they smelled the crucified victims of the Dove. Fifteen minutes later they came upon them. They lined both sides of the road. Cross after cross, the ones at the ends of the row were still alive, and their groaning and screams made Alfred feel like running and screaming himself.

"Oh my God, oh my God!" Anne said, her voiced strangled. She was breathing hard and kept her eyes on the blacktop. She could not look at the ruined men and women who were nailed and left to die. There was the sound of feeding birds and rats that had made their way up the poles to the victims and the buzzing of flies, swarms of them that would attack the living as well as the dead.

"There's the exit," Jim said. Alfred could hear the relief in his voice, seeing that the crosses ended at the exit. "We cross here and we then go from yard to yard, street to street, quietly until we get to your house, Alfred. That's the rendezvous."

Alfred felt his breath catch in his throat. He followed the group across the road, up the ramp and down into a small stand of trees that fronted a few burnt out houses. In the heat of mid-summer he felt his skin get cold. Binghamton was his neck of the woods, his town before it had all gone south. He had run from this place with his family because they had understood that to stay would have been suicide. Looking around he recognized his surroundings. How many times had he driven down this very street? He remembered how busy it was, how the McDonalds at the intersection always had a line at its takeout window. Not anymore. Everything was smashed in and it looked as if a running battle had been fought in the small parking lot.

He was also surprised that they had been able to get into the city that easily. Jim quickly filled them in. He told them that according to intelligence, the Dove was not really concerned about this area. They had their camp set up downtown and that was where they had their checkpoints covering all the roads into and out of the downtown area. They ran only occasional patrols in the outer town's limits. Jim also told them to be careful because the people who lived in the town's outer limits were really part of a large gang that was known to practice cannibalism. That was enough to get everyone on high alert. They moved quietly from house to house, street to street, until they worked their way up into the hills surrounding the town. Those hills were once farm country, and where locals who valued their privacy lived. It was where Alfred and his family had lived. Finally after a few hours they made it to Pine Road.

Alfred felt like a man in a dream. He walked down his old road, his stomach a jumble of knots. He went by the Janus' house that was now just a yawning burnt out husk. He came to the Parsons' house and stopped. He could feel the impatience from the other group members but he couldn't help it. He had to stop as the memories flooded back in.

"These were good people who lived here. Their names were Martha and Dean Parsons. They were an old couple, retired, looking to live out the rest of their days in peace. Marauders ran a truck into the house and shot them to death." Alfred remembered that day and a shiver passed through him. Apart from the destroyed homes his street looked pretty much the way he remembered it. They walked down the street past sections of road edged with pine trees, turned a corner and then he saw it. His house. The front was boarded up the way they had left it, but then as he got closer he could see that the door was patched together with two-by-fours. Someone had broken in and someone had repaired it. The group didn't linger but went around the back where they were out of sight of the road.

"Must be something, Alfred, to be back here?" Jim said and put a comforting hand on his shoulder. "We should just sit and wait. Your father should be along soon."

"No need to. I know where a spare key is for the door." He went quickly to a small flower pot that was overgrown with weeds, lifted it, and there was the small aluminum tin can where they had left the spare set. He then looked at the shed where he had originally stashed supplies and saw the door had been smashed. He didn't look in. He figured everything left that had value was gone.

He saw the tree where the marauders' truck had crashed into and burnt. It still looked pretty bad; a good portion of it was gouged out where the truck's battering ram had slammed into it. This had been the same gang that had attacked and killed the Parsons. They had waited four days after attacking the old couple then they came back and attacked the Aimes's house. Alfred and Samantha had fought them off, killing them all. Nature and time had done a good job of making the tree and the grass where the truck had exploded and burnt appear almost natural, like the tree had suffered some kind of lightning strike. The area around the trunk that had burnt when the truck caught fire was now overgrown, and Alfred figured that in another year it would be very difficult to tell what had happened here.

He walked back to the house, keys in his hand, and a feeling of heaviness came over him. He and Samantha had lived in this place for twenty years. This house had been the center of their universe, their anchor. That anchor had been taken away from them, he thought, then realized that thought wasn't quite true. The *Rabbit Hole* was now their anchor. He got to the door and his hand trembled as he slid the key home and opened it.

He took them up through the basement. To his astonishment he realized that the Sunrnr inverter and the extra power module were still there. It was just one of those fantastically strange things that emphasized the inexplicable randomness of the universe. Here was probably one of the most valuable assets in the house and no one had taken it, incredible. Then he realized that most people probably would not know what they were looking at. He looked in one corner and saw that it was cleared out and was being used by someone as a place to sleep. There was a bedroll and a few personal items. He figured that his dad must stay here from time to time. But why not use one of the rooms upstairs? He kept his mouth shut as he went through the basement and up the stairs to the first floor. The sight that greeted him was truly a shock. He understood why the person had chosen to sleep in the basement. The carpeting was ripped up in places and there was a layer of soot over the walls. He figured that whoever had broken in must have used the fireplace in the living room to keep warm and to cook. The place also had a rank smell of old urine, and there was the smell of something else he could not quite recognize.

The group let him go, they understood what he was going through. He went into the living room and swept the place with his flashlight. The area around the fireplace was burned and spotted. He also noticed that there were large spots that looked a lot like blood splatter. He shuddered as he wondered what must have taken place here in the months his family was gone. The couch was missing its cushions, the television was smashed and shoved into a corner, and pictures of a happier time were smashed on the ground. Some of the walls were smashed in, and in the kitchen someone had gone through the cupboards. Alfred found himself standing on a lot of broken glass and plates. It all had the distinct feeling like someone had gotten angry and went on a rampage.

He then went into the master bedroom where he and Samantha had lain together and discussed the future. The mattress was off the box spring, and all the clothes that had been in the closets were on the floor. Someone had gone through and took what they needed. The place smelled rank as though a wild animal had been living in it. His temples felt like they were going to burst. He sat down on the mattress. Switching off the flashlight he could feel tears welling up in his eyes. The darkness covered him like a blanket. All the horror that they had been through, the marauders, the cannibals, the men who almost killed him and his family at the *Rabbit Hole*. The weight of the new world just seemed a bit much. He knew in the dark then, sitting on the ruins of what used to be his bed, that the world he grew up in, married, and had children in, was well and truly gone. There was no going back now, only forward, to what he had no idea.

He closed his eyes and wondered if he pinched himself and opened them, would he discover that it was all a dream. He found himself thinking about his wife. In his imagination he saw her smiling, younger, face full of excitement and hope when they moved in and were in this room in a much smaller bed for their first night. They had made love and he had made promises. He had made grand statements, the grandest that everyone makes, but know deep down is utter baloney. He had said that they were going to be alright. He had told her that this was the place they would spend the rest of their lives.

He sighed and was about to get up when a loud, commanding and amplified voice cut through the darkness, finding him and making him quake inside with fear.

"You people in the house. You are under arrest for trespassing and suspicion of terrorist activity. Come out with your hands up."

Alfred pushed himself up off the mattress and simultaneously pushed the fear away. His body felt cold and his senses came on with the clarity of the hunted animal. He heard footsteps running toward his room. It was Anne. "Alfred, you back here?"

"Yeah, what's going on?"

"There's a small squad of the Dove's men outside."

"Jesus, how did they find us?"

"Don't know. Maybe someone saw us coming down the street and called it in."

"Well let's go downstairs and see what they want."

Alfred followed Anne back downstairs into the living room. The front door was in a small vestibule and Jim was standing behind it looking out. The others were on either side of him. "How many are out there?" Alfred asked.

"Probably about ten. Yeah, I count ten."

"I think we will have to fight."

"I think you are right," said Jim.

"Here's what I think we should do," Alfred said, automatically taking charge of the tactics. "Me and the priest here will go out back and come around at them from opposite sides of the house. Jim, you and Timothy go out front and face them. Be ready to go for your weapons and get in among them. One disadvantage of their rifles is that it won't be as easy for them to pick their targets at close range. Anne should stay undercover on the porch and do as much damage as she can. Hopefully we can get them all before they get us." Alfred could see the huddled figures in the house nodding at him in the semi-gloom. He and Archbishop O'Riley went downstairs and carefully went out the back. He breathed a sigh of relief the group had not had the foresight to send people to cover the rear. He went left and the archbishop went right. This was good because they could use the side of the house as cover. The two people in the hot zone would be Jim and Timothy, and he hoped that they would just come out with their hands up and walk right out to them before the shooting started. He saw Jim come out with his hands up, and he saw Timothy do the same. He saw as Jim walked across the porch to the steps, then he did something so horrible at first Alfred could not believe he had seen it.

Jim pulled his weapon and shot Anne in the side. He was behind Timothy so the medic did not know what was happening. He had heard the shot however and ducked instinctively reaching for his pistol at the same time. One of the soldiers shot him in the chest. The man was dead before he hit the overgrown lawn.

Then Alfred heard the rapid fire of two pistols from the opposite side of the house and saw a couple of soldiers cry out and fall. The soldiers then began to scatter, firing at the archbishop. Jim had dropped to the ground, trying to make himself a small target. Alfred decided to concentrate on the soldiers and he took careful aim and dropped two more. The training at the *Rabbit Hole* paid off as his aim was just as good and deadly as the priest on the other side. He slammed himself against the wall of the house as the soldiers opened up with their M16's. He got down and hugged the dirt on the side of the house. He got his breathing under control and his .45 banged twice. One man went down gasping horribly, holding his throat, and the other one crumpled over his weapon, his dying finger clamped down on the gun's trigger as the weapon sent a stream of lead in a downward arc that caught one of his comrades in the leg. The wounded man dropped his weapon and began screaming, a high pitched shriek that made the hairs on Alfred's arms stand up. He was silenced by a bullet to the side of his head, one that knocked him over onto his stomach. The other two soldiers had managed to get behind their lorry and used it as cover.

Alfred then heard the sound of vehicles coming up Pine Road. This was bad; they had reinforcements coming. They had to go. He motioned to the archbishop and they both sprinted for the back of the house and into the thick woods on the other side. Alfred ran into what he knew was the thickest part of the woods. If they could get to the other side before the Dove's militia could cut them off they might be able to find a place to hold up and hide. He ran, and the archbishop followed him. *Jim, that sonofabitch, Jim,* Alfred's head pounded. They humped it up a small hill and were almost to the top when he saw something that made him pull up suddenly, breathing hard. In their haste they had ran into some kind of camp. There were a lot of makeshift tents and lean-tos. Three men wearing black clothing came toward them, rifles raised.

The big man in front spoke, his voice had a high, mechanical, and unnatural sound like someone who had his larynx removed, "Hold it right there, padres."

For one insane moment Alfred was going to try and shoot his way out, but he saw about twenty more people melt into the encampment from the trees.

"Alfred, listen, we can't escape. We have to do what they say," Archbishop O'Riley said. The man's face was beet red and he was breathing hard. He placed his .45s on the ground and stood with his hands up.

"Look at them. They are cannibals. We do that and we are dead."

"You don't have that quite right, padre. You see, if you don't drop that pistol you are definitely dead."

Every fiber in Alfred's body rebelled against what he was going to do. He reached down and placed his weapon in the dirt. When he did, he heard the clicking of multiple safeties being reset. He stood up. He wanted to cry out and stomp in rage. The man who had been talking to him smiled a grotesque grin. Alfred could see that the left side of his face had been badly burned and his ears were missing.

"Now, I am glad you decided to do that, padre, because I wouldn't want to have to kill you. Well, not before we have a chat first about some very interesting things."

A man and a large woman quickly secured Alfred's and O'Riley's pistols. Then they were taken to a large teepee like structure. The man opened the entrance and motioned for them to go inside. "Go on in, padres, there are many things we have to parlay."

When Splinter heard the news from his people in Marathon, he went down and laid on the bed in the large room adjoining his office that he had converted into a bedroom. He gave orders that he was not to be disturbed for any reason. He needed to think. The message was short because it had been interrupted. He didn't know if his spy had been discovered and that bothered him. And what bothered him more was the knowledge that a man he had trusted more than anyone had played him for a fool. Tobias Aimes was a spy.

He ground his teeth and looked up into the ornately paneled roof. His hands twisted the sheets and a growl escaped him. A murderous rage made him tremble. A spy, a spy. He had put that man in charge of the 'Hammer Project', the most important project in his administration. He was so close to having his own kingdom; he was going to be a very important man, venerated by history and loved by all. He would be known as one of the new Founding Fathers of the New World Order.

He had worked it out and realized from the message that was relayed that they should put a watch on the house that the elder Aimes had been using as his domicile. That watch had yielded results. He had been contacted when his men saw the group near the home, and he had dispatched a small tactical unit to grab them. Then that went into the toilet when somehow his soldiers had failed to capture all of the saboteurs. They had shot and killed one man, and another a woman who was injured he had them bring here. She was in a room just down the hall, and he would see to her later. The other two men, Aimes' son and some stupid priest, had escaped. They had killed eight of his men. The thought rankled him and he groaned again. That had all went down a few hours ago. He had been busy then going through the paperwork his captains from the city had messengered to him. He took pride in reading each request or report carefully before replying. When he was done he was exhausted, and he decided to take a few hours rest. Now that he was awake, the Aimes business began to really bother him. He looked at the clock. It was 5 a.m.

He got off his bed and he decided to pay the elder Aimes a visit. He had chatted with the man earlier when they had first taken him, but the old soldier had nothing to say. He was planning on being a whole lot more persuasive now. He changed his clothes, putting on green fatigues; he didn't want to get blood all over his regal whites. He walked down the hall and went down the stairs in the back of the building to the large sub-basement area where the man was kept in a small cell. The guards saw him and jumped to attention.

"Open up."

They opened the cell door and came into the room with him. One backed away and stayed by the closed door. The other gave the guard his rifle and was prepared to help Splinter with the interrogation. The old colonel was sitting on the floor. His hands were handcuffed in front of him and his face was badly bruised.

"You ready to talk, colonel?"

"Why am I being held here? I have done nothing. I am loyal to the militia cause."

"We know you are lying, colonel. A group of my men ambushed the Marathon squad and now we have a few of them in custody. The ones that got away will be caught sooner rather than later. We know that your son was involved in this act of terror against the state."

"What state? We are a paramilitary group bringing back law and order to the country. We do this so that the people can reelect their leaders and we slowly work our way back to a unified and strong country. Isn't that supposed to be the plan? Or have you completely ditched the pretense and now are finally admitting the truth, that you and the Bilderbergs are destroying the world and remaking it in your twisted image?"

"I don't really know what you are talking about. I have a powerful ally. They have their plans and I have mine. The area that I have taken with sacrifice and blood are mine and mine alone. I do not intend to take orders from anyone. I intend to rule the conquered areas as well as I can. Wherever the militia go we bring order, justice and peace." Splinter looked at the man, a growing disdain filling him. It was idiots like this who always stood in the way of progress. The old society was flawed with its corruption, aimless multiple distractions, and moral decay. The country he was trying to create from the ashes of the old would be a shining light of order, dynamism, and justice. He had had enough of the old man.

"You will tell me everything now or you will lose everything. Do you understand? I want to know everything about your operation and about the people in Marathon. I want you to tell me where your son is hiding, and we will deal with him and these preppers and constitutionalists."

"I have nothing to say to you."

"You will. You will." Splinter said, his breath coming in excited gasps.

They stripped the old colonel naked and hoisted him up to a hook in the ceiling so that his feet dangled just off the floor. Splinter then used a whip to beat him until most of his skin was shredded, and blood ran freely dripping onto the floor beneath him. Still the old man refused to say anything. There was nothing to say. He knew nothing of his son's whereabouts. But he also knew that if they thought he knew, that would give his son time. The longer Splinter was here working on getting the information out of him, the less attention he was spending actively trying to capture the infiltrators. When his tormentor broke his left arm with an iron rod, he screamed and cried and wished for death. He fought them when they used a welding torch to burn his ears off.

A couple hours later, Splinter looked at the ruined man he had created and sighed. Pushing his glasses up his sweaty nose, he felt strangely relaxed and loose. It was obvious that Tobias had nothing to tell, as far as the skinny pale man with the short, brown receding hair was concerned. The old man knew that some people were coming to help him destroy the canisters. The colonel had made arrangements for them to rendezvous with him at that house on Pine Road, but he was lucky. They were contacted by the woman who had been posing as Jim Meehan's wife, and she relayed most of the plan before they lost communication. He would run patrols outside of the city, and most likely they would get the rest of them soon. It was almost a guarantee that someone would know where they were and they would pass on the information for food or a favor.

"Crucify him today at twilight. I want this traitor to suffer. I want him nailed through the heels. Make sure it happens. This will be the punishment for anyone who betrays us." He then left the guards to their duties. When he got back to his room, he went into the bathroom and stripped off the bloody fatigues. This residence was the only one in the city that had running water and electricity. He ran the water in the shower until it was steaming hot and then he stepped in. He let the soothing hot water wash the blood from his body.

He felt oddly at peace with himself. Family is hell, he thought. The colonel was protecting his son. Despite his anger he felt a certain envious admiration for the man. He had taken his ears and burnt half his face off, and he still didn't tell about his son. He dried himself and looked into the mirror. Could he have done the same for a family member if he had to? He looked into his pale blue eyes and shook his head. His father had been a bastard and his mother, she was a sniveling coward who never protected him when he was a child. He shook his head again at the thought. Can't say that I would have. His mind then turned to Jim Meehan who had betrayed a lot of people because he wanted his daughter back. Meehan was locked in a room in the building which stood beside this one. His daughter was with him. Splinter wasn't sure what to do with him yet. He could offer him a position in his organization, let him go on his way, or just kill him and the little girl. He would sleep on it. He was about to turn in when he remembered that there was one other prisoner he hadn't seen to. He shook his head. It was turning into a busy morning.

The woman Meehan had shot was just a couple of rooms down the hall. They had brought her here because they had all thought that she was going to die, and maybe he would have wanted to do a quick interrogation. He grunted, wrapped his robe tightly around himself, and padded down the hall in his slippers. The guards saw him and immediately straightened to attention. The soldiers on the first two floors of this building were all his personal bodyguards. They were used to seeing their boss in various stages of undress. He had selected these men because they had proved to him that they were loyal. They would carry out any order without question. He nodded to the men at the door and they opened it.

He could see that the woman was lying not on the bed, but on a small cot they had assembled for her. There was a lot of blood on her shirt and the yellow sheet she was on. She moaned and he saw her hands tighten on the sides of the cot. Her face was away from him, and by the looks of the wound and what he was told he knew that if she got treatment in the next few hours she would most likely survive. Maybe he could use that as the incentive when he interrogated her. He could offer her treatment for information. If he left her untreated, then in the next few hours the wound would become infected and he could then see her dying slowly and painfully from the infection.

He was about to tell the guards to wake her when she turned and he saw her face. For a second the world fell away from him, and he felt short winded and faint. He took a deep breath and walked over and looked hard at the woman. Suddenly he felt cold and he drew his robe closer around him. Then the woman opened her eyes, and he knew his first assumption was right. He watched as her eyes swam around in her head and then her fever delirium passed and there was a sudden lucidity. Her eyes scanned around the gloomy room, then they came to rest on his. For a moment there was some confusion, the woman's brow wrinkled. She took a deep raspy breath, one that Splinter knew must have hurt, then she said the word that made him bolt from the room. He ran-walked past the startled guards, who looked in and quickly closed the prisoner's door. He went back to his room and laid on his bed looking up at the ceiling. The word that the woman had said was swirling around in his head. No, it could not be possible, she had called him "Son."

The Bunker-England

Entry 146

I'm really sick, and I think I'm losing the fight. I'm writing this in bed. I'm lying on my side and using my right hand to make what might be my last entry. I will not write anymore, not while I'm sick. If there is another entry from me then it means that I am well, and if not then I guess I will be with Trisha and Bea. Yes, Bea died last night. I can still see her body at the far end of the bunker. My daughter, my little girl, died from whatever sickness I brought into the bunker when I went topside. I think I know what this might be, and I have no way of treating it. There was talk on the ham of some kind of Ebola-like virus that was being used to kill people. I think that maybe I caught it from those people I killed. I got sick and Bea got sick almost immediately.

I think that it had manifested so quickly because we're not really healthy and our immune systems have been compromised. Living on all this packaged and tin food has not been the healthiest thing to do. What I would do for fresh meat, vegetables, and sunlight. We also neglected to store multi vitamins—a big mistake. All I am doing now is thinking about how everything went wrong.

My hand is shaking from the fever that has been wracking my body. It took my precious Bea very quickly, two days and she was dead. She had the fevers, then she was bleeding from the eyes, mouth, and nose. Half the time I could do nothing for her because I was also sick. It has all fell on the shoulders of Cathy who has been trying to nurse us. I was in a fever delirium last night and when I woke up Bea was gone. I kissed her one last time and Cathy carried her over to the ladder that leads outside. I told Cathy to wait another day to see if I get better. If I do then I will take Bea out and bury her. If I die then she should wait for night, then go topside and bury our bodies as best as she can. I hope it doesn't come to that. I just can't write anymore, my head aches and my eyes hurt.

Alfred and the archbishop sat in the tepee across from the large man with the destroyed face. He offered them a bottle of gin, which both men refused. He held the hole in his throat closed and took a careful swallow. His eyes widened and his jaw clenched as the liquid took its effect on him. After about a minute his ruined melted lips arched up in a smile which revealed that he was missing a number of teeth. His one good eye looked at Alfred with an intensity that made him uncomfortable.

"Before those bastards nuked Syracuse I was an engineer with Lockheed Martin. I am a very educated guy." He chuckled grotesquely at that like it was an inside joke, then he continued. "Can you believe that? I had a nice home, a family, and a life. Those fanatics blew up the city and took all that away from me. I was in the blast zone, you know. I lived in an apartment complex near the university. The blast destroyed the apartment and killed my family. At first I was sorry that they were gone, but when I realized what had happened to me and what would have happened to them if they had lived, I was glad that they were gone. I did what I had to do to survive. My brother, the only family I had left, was killed here in Binghamton when he went out on a food raid." He looked at the two men seated in front of him and shook his head.

"We all did what we had to do to survive," Alfred said. He knew full well that people who were cannibals carried a particular scent and this man reeked. He probably became a cannibal out of necessity, but he must have continued his abhorrent practice. Alfred looked at the man and realized that he was most likely crazy. He had probably lost his mind when the bomb killed his family and melted away his skin. What Alfred could not understand was why he was chatting with them now.

"My name is Alfred Aimes. This gentleman is Archbishop O'Riley," Alfred said.

"I had a name once. Now everyone just calls me Mushroom."

"Well, Mushroom, what do you want from us?"

"A little birdie told me that those fine, nice folks from up there in Marathon are coming to put the hurt on the Dove. I agreed to help them. Those padres killed and crucified a lot of my people. I owe this Dove a lot of pain." He chuckled dangerously. "You probably saw a lot of my people on your way in. On a good day we can smell the crucified here in our camp when the wind blows this way."

"You said you heard that people from Marathon were coming to put the hurt on the Dove. What do you mean?"

"Well, I have ears in the woods and villages around the county. An invitation was sent out to either help or stay out of the way. A large force of people are on their way here, and I don't think it's to ask the Dove to a tea party. I intend to help those people get rid of the Dove's militia."

Alfred caught O'Riley straightening up at the news in his periphery vision. Then he decided to take a gamble. "The Dove has a weapon, and if he is able to use this weapon he could kill millions of people. We came here to get that weapon and destroy it."

"Yes, I know where it is. There is a large warehouse on Marsh Road. Before the Collapse they used it to store salt for the roads during the winter. That's where they got it locked up. They have thirty soldiers guarding it. We have about a hundred people living here in camp. About eighty can fight. I propose we help you get that thing away from those tree-nailers and destroy it."

"I say that sounds like a plan. Thirty guards, that's a small army and I am sure they are well armed. If you get us in we can destroy it," Alfred said.

"We have a plan up our sleeves. We knew that it must be something really important out there by the salt warehouse and now we know. We will leave early tomorrow evening. Please, do not leave the tepee." With that he got up and left.

"What do you make of all of that?" O'Riley whispered.

"Well, I think our man Mushroom is crazy," Alfred whispered back. He laid on his back and crossed his arms, looking up into the dark center of the conical ceiling. He kept his voice low, knowing that they were probably being spied on. The priest shuffled over and sat next to him.

"This is really all bad," O'Riley whispered. "Our mission was doomed from the start. Did you see what happened with Jim?"

"Yeah, I saw him shoot Anne. He was a spy, and if I see him again I will kill him. They knew where we were so he must have tipped them off. I can also assume that my dad is either in custody, dead, or on the run."

O'Riley nodded, then said, "I agree. I think that the Mushroom man here is crazy. I also think that maybe he has an alternate agenda."

Alfred looked hard at the priest and nodded slowly. "I agree, I think he sees these weapons as an opportunity."

"Well, we need his help to get to them. Then we will have to get them into that mine, destroy and seal them away. This is going to be a very delicate operation," said O'Riley.

"The question is why doesn't he just kill us and take the weapons himself."

"The Mushroom Man may be crazy but he's not stupid. He wants us around just in case something goes wrong, or if there is something special that needs to be done to the weapons. Plus I think he needs the extra guns. He probably figures that we are Special Forces or something," O'Riley whispered with a smile.

"I think you may be right. I think the way to play this is to act like we are a crack team. We get the specifics of his plan and we discuss it with him if we believe it will work. We will tell him that we will need some serious explosives to destroy the tanks and that we know how to do it safely. Let's see if he plays along." Alfred sighed, images of his family tried to force their way into his mind, but he pushed them away, and instead he saw Anne, Timothy, his father, and Jim. That was the way to keep his focus, getting the mission done and being ruthless was his way to survive and see his family again. "We will try to coordinate our mission with whatever is really going on with this so called attack against the New York City Militia. Oh, to hell with that let's call them what they are, *the Royalists*. Maybe that can buy us an edge."

"Sounds like a plan, all we have to do is to sit and wait for Mushroom." The priest then stretched out on his back and clasped his hands across his chest. They didn't have to wait too long and when Mushroom came back into the tepee, they talked and made plans.

Jim sat on a wooden chair in a small room with his back to the wall. He couldn't help looking at his watch. It had been about twelve hours since the encounter at Alfred's house. This is where they had put him after he had returned with them. They had Diane, his daughter, and he had done what he did to get her back. That little girl was his only connection to a life that was once filled with happiness, laughter and hope. She was all he had. The story he had told Alfred that day at the farm wasn't all lies. He and his family had hidden out at the camp, but after the people who had been hunting them had gone, the Dove's men had come and shot his son and wife before taking him and his daughter alive. They gave him a choice to join or die, so he joined. He had been one of the very few soldiers who had a family of any sort. He was assigned the most menial duties, but that all changed one day when the supreme leader himself paid him a visit.

He had dropped off his daughter at the home of a woman who watched the kids of workers and soldiers during the day. He had known that his day's duties were going to be horrible. The army had just moved into the small city and they began *sanitizing* it. Meaning that they had searched all the homes and businesses to locate any bodies that were not buried. It was the *sanitizer unit's* job to remove those bodies and take them either to a mass grave or to a burn site for disposal. That was his job. He went straight to that morning's location, a huge two-story supermarket. There were thirty-two bodies on the first floor alone, and they had found eighteen more upstairs. He had gone to the small van where they stored their gear and began to put on his white protective suit. He put his mask on and then his goggles. Some of the workers would leave their hoods down because it would get so hot in the suit some people would pass out. Jim always zipped his suit up to his neck and pulled the hood over his head. The way he figured it was, there were a lot of diseases that were killing people and he didn't want to go that way if he could help it. He still had a little girl that needed him and he didn't want to get her ill as well, so he was careful.

He pulled his gloves on and walked into the building. He found the supervisor, a man named Cliff Maxwell, standing in the inner vestibule where all the grocery carts had been stocked. The soldiers had rigged up a generator and the store was brilliantly lit. For a second before he saw the carnage in the empty aisles, things were almost normal. Cliff was dressed just like

215

him; he was a man who wasn't taking any chances either.

"You will take the upstairs. Jose, Mirrela, Victor, and Tibs are already working. We will remove the bodies, bleach spray only. No deep cleaning. We will leave a warning on this building that if they want to use this place, someday they will have to scrape and disinfect it themselves. We are just snatching, spraying, and burning today."

Jim nodded. He was thankful that they wouldn't have to stay and deep clean the place. That meant scraping the human blood and body fragments off of the walls, furniture, and floor. Sometimes they would have to rip up the floors, carpet and get rid of some of the furniture. Then it all had to be sprayed again with bleach. It was hard, horrible work. He left Cliff and walked through the store carefully, trying not to step on anything that could possibly penetrate his boots or suit. His eyes summed up what must have gone on in the supermarket. He looked at the stripped shelves, broken bottles, and corpses and came to the conclusion that the dead people must have taken over the supermarket. They probably had taken it by force, or maybe they just took over the building and were using it as some sort of base. It was obvious by the amount of bullet holes in the shelves, walls, and counters that there had been a fight and the dead people were the losers.

The old corpses still gave off a sharp, cheesy-like rotting smell that got into the sanitizers' pores and clothes. The victims in the store seemed to be mostly young. He counted thirteen women and the rest appeared to be men. All were in varying stages of decomposition, all had been partially eaten by animals and insects. Jim was aware that this was what had happened all over America. People had died off in droves and now the survivors had to find a way to dispose of all the bodies. He heard from the other soldiers that even after eight months of cleanup by the militia, they had not gotten to a quarter of the dead in New York City. He was told that they had huge furnaces going day and night to incinerate the bodies. He imagined that it was the same all over the world. When a city lost three quarters or more of its population, the survivors were tasked with the disposal of the bodies or else they themselves would eventually perish from any of the many diseases caused by the rotting corpses.

He was told that for almost two months, New York City stank so much that it drove a lot of the survivors crazy, and he believed it. Every time the Dove's army took over a town or city they had to sanitize it. It was a job that would take months, but Jim and the other sanitizers understood its necessity. This was something that he certainly never thought about when he was prepping with his Christian group. As preppers the members of his group had thought about various end of the world scenarios but looking back he couldn't remember if they ever discussed cleaning up after a major catastrophic event.

All the lower rank, which was everyone below a lieutenant, took their turn on sanitizer duty. It always struck him as somewhat ironic that here they were busting their butts cleaning up the dead when they were actively creating more with their *patrolling sorties* and the daily executions.

He climbed the stairs and saw that Victor and Mirrela were getting ready to take the first body out to the dump truck. There were no body bags. The sanitizers used solid aluminum stretchers that had high side and end railings to prevent the bodies from falling out. "Check off this mold cake will you, Jose," Mirrela said before reaching down and lifting her end. Jose nodded and crossed the body off the list as proof that it had been removed from the building. Jim was used to the crassness of the people who worked sanitizer duty. It always bothered him that the dead were not respected. People had become so inured to death that the dead were just seen as an inconvenience. Everyone called the dead *mold cakes* now, and it troubled him that no one had a problem with that.

He got to work helping Tibs drag a body out from behind a desk. Parts of the woman had gotten fused to the floor and it was hard lifting the body into the stretcher. Tibs took a look at where the body was stuck on the right side, the flesh under the shoulder where the woman who had been wearing a spaghetti-strapped blouse had rotted and attached itself to the floor. The man shoved the desk out of the way and then gave the corpse a savage kick. He then kicked the right shoulder of the dead woman again. This time her shoulder cracked but the body was still attached. His movement of the corpse made the rotting, cheese-like smell waft up, and both men moved away a few feet instinctively before going back. Tibbs aimed another well placed kick and the desiccated body made a dry tearing sound as it came loose from the floor.

Jim helped the man lift the body into the stretcher, and they crossed it off the list and carried it gingerly down the stairs, passing their colleagues who had deposited their earlier load. Outside there was a ramp that was attached to the back of a large dump truck. The men carried the stretcher almost all the way up, and then Jim, who was in front, placed his end down. Tibbs pushed it the rest of the way to the edge then tipped it up. The body fell into the truck, joining the others that had been removed.

They worked like this for a few hours, stopping only once to eat. They had only one more body to remove before moving on to the next listed location. Everyone was happy that they were about to leave the enclosed claustrophobic room. Then he heard it. A child shrieking somewhere downstairs. It was hard to hear distant sounds clearly through the hazmat suit, but he noticed that they were all looking at the door which lead downstairs.

"Now what do you think that's all about?" Victor asked as the shrieking grew closer. They could now hear the crying child and the boots of men coming up the stairs. Jim suddenly felt a chill hand brush his spine. Three men came into the room; two were guards and one was the Dove himself. He was wearing rubber gloves and a mask. He told the other sanitizers to get lost, that he had some business to discuss with Jim.

He felt his world wobble and for a minute he found it hard to breathe. The two guards had his daughter between them. Jim went forward toward his child, but one of the guards pointed his pistol at him and smiled. His daughter was crying, and Jim knew why. She had seen some of the bodies in the building and was freaking out. He felt a sudden violent murderous anger toward the men in the room.

"Why have you brought my daughter here?"

"I am here to offer you a job, Mr. Meehan."

"What, has that got to do with my daughter?"

"Well let's put it this way. Before I make the offer I wanted it to be very clear what you had to lose if you fail me. My offer is simple. I need spies who can infiltrate the Marathon Settlement and send me reports on what they are up to. I think you would make a very good spy. I also need people who I know will not turn.

I will keep your daughter safe and sound until you return. Say hello to your daddy, Diane."

The Dove nodded at the men and they let the little girl go. She ran over to her dad and was about to hug him when he said, "No!" She stopped and looked at him. "Wait honey, I don't want you to touch me and get sick," he said in a gentler tone. He took off his gloves, unzipped the suit and pulled the hood off. He ran his hands through her hair. She was pale and frightened, that was clear, but what enraged Jim the most was that they had brought her here. They had brought her to this place of horror and death. He really tried to shield her as much as he could from the dreadfulness of the world they were now living in; she had seen her brother and mother die. The sights she must have seen as they brought her here must have really scared her. He held her close and felt her shaking, and again that murderous rage flooded through him. He knew that if he got the chance he would kill these men, no questions or doubts about it.

"Say goodbye to the little one. For now she will stay with me at HQ. Don't worry we will take good care of her. After all we want your complete cooperation," Splinter gently took the girl's arm.

"You, you can't, you can't..."

"Yes, I can, Mr. Meehan. You will finish up your day here, then you will come and see me at HQ this evening. I have a lot to tell you about your new assignment."

Jim made a motion to get to his daughter and one of Splinter's guards swung the butt of his rifle. It connected solidly in Jim's midsection and a sharp bolt of pain shot through him, making him drop to his knees. He remained that way, his head spinning, gasping for air as the man who had the power of life and death over him said softly, "Come immediately after work, Mr. Meehan. You have a more important task to do now." With that the men holding his daughter hostage left the room.

As he lay upon the hard cot he remembered how he had finished his shift like a man in a dream, and when he reported to HQ he was shown in, and standing by Splinter's desk was Colonel Tobias Aimes. Aimes was the one who briefed him on his mission. He was given a new family, a woman who worshiped Splinter. There were a lot of people who actually believed that the maniac was some sort of Savior, and they latched on to him and the militia with a sort of religious fervor. If the Dove had told the woman to jump off a building, Jim had no doubts that she would. The young man who was to play his son was also of the same cadre of unshakable believers. Apart from adults who had joined the militia, there was also a large contingent of young teenagers among the ranks. These were kids who had seen unspeakable things, and the militia had taken them in. It had given them food, a purpose, and power, and they imbibed the propaganda the militia's Department of Truth spun. The boy and the woman were selected because of their loyalty to the militia, and he was chosen because of his attachment to his daughter. Hence, he found himself part of a new family. For a week they rehearsed the story that Jim told them about his own family, until they all knew it well enough for them to recount it in a believable way. They used it to get into the Marathon settlement, and for six months he lived among the people he would betray.

He shook his head and rubbed his burning eyes. There was a sound on the other side of his door. He swung his feet off the bed and waited for them to open it. When they did, there was a squeal of joy, and a child with light coffee skin, wavy black hair, and hazel eyes ran in and launched herself into his arms. He slid off the cot onto his knees and hugged his daughter. For two minutes nothing else existed for him. They held each other and cried. He then got a hold of himself and took a good look at Diane.

She was a little taller than he had remembered. It's amazing how they just get taller, especially when you are away, he mused.

"They won't take me away again, will they, Dad?"

"No, I think we are good now." He looked past her to the two smirking guards. "When are you going to let us go?"

"That's up to the boss man. If he thinks you have done a good job then you might well walk out of here. By the way, that old colonel, he's going to be nailed tonight. Just for that I would make you a captain. I hated that old fart." The guards then locked the door and he could hear them laughing on the other side. What they were going to do to the old soldier sickened him, but he also realized that he could rationalize his actions. He had done what he had to do to protect his child.

Jim realized sitting on the cot, holding his crying daughter that it hadn't taken much to shake his moral compass. With society in shambles, ordinary people found that they had to throw their values out with the old world. When the country could not provide protection and order, when people preyed on each other, Jim understood that what he believed was his unshakable ethical and moral compass was not entirely practical.

Many people had to face that reality in the post-collapse world. Most lost the battle, and many killed themselves or went insane. Jim reckoned that a lot of people actually killed themselves or were killed because they just could not cross the threshold into damnation. He figured that if he lived long enough in this new world, he would one day meet the ultimate test, and he shivered. Up to this point everything he had done he had done for his child; he could rationalize all his decisions and justify his actions. That was something that never really came up when he met or chatted with other preppers in the *Old World*.

He leaned back on the cot as his daughter actually began to fall asleep. He gently placed her head on the cot's pillow and sat down on the floor. His mind went back to those pre-Collapse days when he decided that he had to start preparing. Just like Alfred and many people living in the crazy days before the Collapse, he became alarmed when he realized that there was no institution he could trust. He remembered the thing that finally pushed him over to the prepping side. It was when it was revealed that there were actual black sites in the USA. He read all the alternate news sources, especially *Wide Awake News*, *The Daily Sheeple*, *Natural News* and *Blacklisted News*. He would supplement this by reading the *American Prepper's Network* website, as well as *The Organic Prepper* and *The Prepper Journal*. He shook his head; all those websites were gone now. The internet was dead, the world with its cell phones and twenty-four hour news channels, family summer vacations, ball drops in Times Square, his wife and son all gone, all dead. His daughter began to snore, and feeling the weight of what he had done and a burning heavy sorrow, he closed his eyes. With his back to the wall he slowly fell asleep.

Chapter Eleven

"If there must be trouble let it be in my day, that my child may have peace." Thomas Paine

The Marathon army that gathered on Main Street spilled over into Brink Street. The sky was just beginning to lighten, and the morning was cool and clear. There were close to thirty thousand men and women. When Samantha showed up, people were already forming into squads. It seemed that Jasper, the Sheriff, and the local community leaders had been drilling the free citizens for this for a long time. Samantha and her children noticed how everyone just knew where to go and where they belonged.

She and her children stood on the sidewalk watching everything, then a familiar face came into view and the woman's eyes lit up when she recognized her rescuer.

"Samantha, oh my God. So good to see you." It was Julie Matson. Samantha smiled and embraced Julie carefully. They were both packing a lot of gear. "Imagine coming into town to trade and getting yourself caught up in all this. You are coming with us?"

"Yes, I am but we have no idea where to go."

"Well, why don't you come with me to my squad, we can always use another nurse."

They followed Julie through a very congested area of milling people and came finally to her group. The people in the squad smiled and nodded when they joined them, and a tall man wearing a red beret reached into a bag and gave Samantha and her children green arm bands with American flag badges sewn on. "My name is Lieutenant Gordon Kniffen. Every squad has a different color arm band and a different military objective. Once we are there we will go and secure our objective and hold it until we are relieved. Most people here know each other. We have gone out and drilled a few times. I expect everyone to follow my orders. If you have a problem with that you can leave right now. This is a volunteer army, not a dictatorship like the army we are going to engage."

Samantha nodded and slipped the arm band on, as did Robert and Candice. The squad leader acknowledged that as acceptance of his rules and left. They all took off their packs to give their backs a rest before the march.

Julie then asked, "Why join if you are just here for a few days?"

Samantha had never explained to Julie why she had volunteered her services at the medical tent the previous day. They never had much time to catch up. It had just gotten too busy.

"We got here and trouble just seemed to find us. Alfred, my husband, is in Binghamton, and he is in trouble. That's why we are going. We are hoping to find him and get back to our place. We should never have come here." Samantha shook her head in genuine regret. She saw Robert shift uneasily and realized that her son thought that coming here and being part of this was important. The trial of the men and that boy, Philip, was postponed until the army returned. She knew that her son was drawn to what was happening in the settlement. Candice, she knew, was more or less on her side. She just wanted to find her dad and get as far away from all these people as possible.

She wondered if her husband was safe or if he was already dead. She wondered about his extracted tooth and whether he was in pain. She wondered what was going on back at the *Rabbit Hole*, if her garden was sprouting. As she stood in the crowd of nervous, excited people all she wanted to do was to go home. They were all going to fight in some noble cause; all she wanted to do was to find her husband and disappear with the children back into woods. She looked at Robert and realized that he might be a problem. He might not want to stay at the homestead anymore.

They waited like that for another hour as people buzzed up and down and the squad leaders got their people and themselves sorted out. Then the leader of the Green Squad finally came back and slipped on his pack. He was grinning and his face was flush with excitement.

"All right, listen up. We are going to quick march for the next twenty-nine miles. We estimate that it will take us about fourteen hours to reach the objective. All you should have on you is food, your two primary weapons and ammo. Anything that will slow you down should be chucked at the ditching station at the gate. We will hold it until you or a family member claim it. Our squad's objective is to get into Binghamton's City Hall and secure it. We move quiet and we will keep our voices down. We don't want them to know we are coming until we are already there." Samantha heard other squad leaders relaying orders, and then there was a torrent of movement as people swung backpacks on and they began to move out.

It was amazing how quickly it all went, soon they were a mile beyond the settlement and moving at a very quick pace. They hugged the cover of the woods next to I-81 North. Samantha noted the strategy employed to keep them moving. The squad leaders and their lieutenants marched outside their respective groups and the squads would try to keep up. She wondered about the older people in the group and how they would fare. It was one thing to get to the objective quickly, but they also had to have the physical reserves to fight.

Samantha knew from experience that fighting for her life tended to burn up her reserves of energy quickly. She hoped that the people she was traveling with would not be so exhausted that they would not be able to perform their jobs under fire. She wondered how many had actually been in a combat situation. She looked around her at the people in her squad. There were people of all races. Most looked to be in their thirties, but there were a few who seemed to be well into their sixties. The ones that broke her heart were the young fighters, the teenagers. Her own children were in that group. Once again it struck her just how insane it all was. Here she was marching off with her own children to engage in deadly combat. There were a few like her, with a son or a daughter. There were also a few teenagers who were by themselves, and she guessed that they must have lost their parents and were now on their own.

She felt a stab of guilt. Her generation would always be known as the ones who brought this destruction upon the world. They would bear this mark always. The brisk trek did a lot to help her clarify one thing that her own personal tribulations had clouded out. As she looked at the young people, she understood that all the adults had a huge responsibility. They had to try to set things right. They had to try and leave a much better world behind for the next generation. What these

Royalists were doing was wrong. They had used a worldwide economic catastrophe to further their own New World Order agenda, had murdered billions, and would murder billions more. She was going to Bing-hamton to try and find Alfred, but she reluctantly realized that she had to take this small step for freedom. This was going to be very difficult. Clarity came with her thoughts and she understood that there was no way to avoid the terrible trials that were surely to come. It was one hell of a thing being a survivor, she thought. Surviving just means that the trials are not over. Life after the black swan event was relentless. Surviving was one part preparation, one part luck, and the other part was hard work.

They marched through tall grass and brush that caught at their clothing. Mosquitos took a liking to them and swarmed with a vengeance. Horse flies attacked and drew blood. They trekked through tall, thick bush and woods that were nearly impassible in some places. Small streams were forded and Samantha wondered how the enemy could not know they were coming. They seemed so loud to her ears. Candice kept to herself, but Robert was soon chatting quietly with everyone around him.

Candice took her slingshot and killed a couple of squirrels. Robert also pegged a few. Food on the way to war. The army stopped for a scheduled hour break and the Aimes clan quickly skinned, gutted, and roasted the squirrels. It felt good to have warm meat. They shared what they could with the rest of the squad. Julie ate her small morsel hesitantly with bread; she had never had squirrel meat before and she began looking at the Aimeses with a bit of awe. After about a forty minute rest they got back on the march.

Three hours later Samantha realized that they were crisscrossing the Castle Creek stream. Alfred had each of them memorize maps of the area. She had always thought that he was a bit OCD on the issue, but now she was grateful. She realized that if she was ever on her own without a guide or even a compass, she could find her way home. The thought of Alfred made her eyes get teary. She had been completely blindsided by the Meehans, if that was even their real name. She wondered how she could not have known or intuited that they were lying. If she came across Jim-the-liar-Meehan she would not hesitate to kill him. Then her nose caught something. It made her crinkle her face with disgust.

"I think we are here," Julie said, also crinkling her face. "When I came through here on my way to Marathon you could smell them."

"Smell what?" Candice asked.

"The crucified," Julie said. "That crazy Dove, or whatever his name is, nails people to trees for sport. It is said that starting a mile outside of town on some of the major roads he uses trees or has had special trees cut down to nail his victims. It's his version of justice."

"It's his version of terror," Robert said with disgust. "We can't let the bad men win," he added. It would be a statement that Samantha would remember at crucial times in the future. One that would shape her young son's life forever.

Suddenly the entire group came to a halt and the squad leader called them together in a huddle. Samantha could see the other groups doing the same.

"This is where things are going to get mighty interesting, folks. We will either be able to drive these clowns out of the city or we will get ourselves shot or nailed along with all the other sorry crucified bastards."

He held up a crude and large but accurately drawn map. "Our objective is five miles from here. We are going to take the direct route straight into town and hit them hard. The word is no prisoners, except high ranking officers or the Dove himself. The squads that are supposed to take key bridges into the city are already gone. I would think that in another half hour or so Binghamton is going to sound like Iraq during the Gulf War. Halfway up the road here near the firehouse is where we will meet another squad. People who were part of the Dove's army but defected. They will help us fight our way into town and into the main offices. Three other squads are going to swing around and come at the city here and here."

As he pointed, Samantha could see that the plan was to encircle the city and fight their way in from all sides. Jasper had been busy; she shook her head at the audacity of it.

"What we are about to do will require you to leave all fear, all mercy behind. The people shooting will kill you if given the chance. My advice is to kill them first, no mercy." We'll take a thirty-minute break. I want you to have a light meal, rehydrate, pee, do whatever you have to do. Then we will move out."

Samantha nodded at her kids and they all sat together with Julie. They checked their weapons, had a light meal, and then they actually went into the woods and peed. Samantha then sat back down, gathering her strength and nerve. She looked at her children and felt a sense of dread. They should be in school, she thought. Candice was actually lying on her back looking up at the darkening sky. She looked absolutely relaxed using her pack as a pillow, and her rifle was across her waist. Robert reminded Samantha of Alfred; before a fight, his jaw had that same clenched look of absolute determination, and his normally kind eyes were hard and glittery. She looked at Julie who seemed nervous.

"How do you guys stay so calm?"

"Just think about the mission and nothing else. Think about all the things you may have to do to kill and stay alive," Samantha said.

In the distance there was the sound of automatic gunfire and a couple of explosions, then more distant gunfire. So, it's really begun, Samantha thought.

"All right, Green squad, on your feet. We are moving out," the leader said crisply. Soon the men and women of Green squad were on their feet, moving toward the sound of gunfire and death.

The Bunker-England

Entry Number 147

Dad died two days ago. Everyone is now gone. Mum, Dad, and Bea are all dead. Everything is so hard and horrible. End of the world, end of everything, end of my family, end of my life. I cannot believe that some people actually thought that the end of the world would have been cool. Some of my friends use to play those zombie video games where the zombies took over everything and the humans were on the run. They would shoot the zombies and kill the people who attacked them. They actually thought that the end would be like that. Them surviving, always surviving. Mum said something telling before she died. She had asked Dad what was the point of surviving if the world was shit? Dad had said that surviving meant hope. I don't know who was right. All I know is that surviving is hard and scary and because things are not the way it used to be, I don't know where to go from here. I guess I'll just stay here until I can't anymore.

I couldn't believe some of the stuff Dad wrote about us in this diary. He wrote in it whenever he could, so I guess I will keep it going. The last two days have been hell. When Bea died, Dad was too weak to bury her outside. She had lain in her bed for the first two days and then she began to get a bit stinky, so he asked me to move her to the foot of the stairs. It was one of the hardest things I have ever done. The hardest thing I ever did was to move Dad outside.

I had tied a long piece of rope around Bea. Then I went up the ladder and opened the hatch. It was so nice and scary being outside. The air smelled so good, and the sky and the clouds made me cry. I wanted to run through the woods and down to our old house, until I remembered Dad saying that it had burnt down. I wanted so badly to be normal again. I think I sat and cried for a while, then I wrapped the rope around a tree and began to pull Bea up. Dad had told me how to get them out of the bunker if this happened. He had told me to wrap the rope around the tree and use it as a fulcrum. Still with Bea it was hard work. It took me almost half an hour to haul her up to the opening. I had to tie the rope off and reach in and pull her out onto the ground. Poor Bea. She had died with her eyes open. I had tried to close them but they wouldn't stay shut. She was very pretty when she was alive, but death had taken that beauty away. Her face had begun to get blotchy and her stomach had swollen. She would fart from time to time and it stank something awful.

It was really hard grabbing and hauling her out of the bunker. I actually had to reach in and grab her under the arms and pull her out. I thought I would throw up. I got her up and out. Realizing she must have weighed only around sixty pounds I began to cry because I didn't know how I would get Dad out. He was so big and heavy.

I laid Bea out, and then I decided to rest a little and get Dad. I needed some time before I went back into the hole. My arms and legs felt weak, I guess because I haven't been walking around like I used to. I had become frail. I was really out of shape and maybe all that canned food we have been eating wasn't the best thing either. I gathered myself and went back down. I tried lifting Dad from his bunk and all I could manage was to roll him off. It was so horrible when he hit the ground. He was beginning to smell too.

I realized then that I could not lift him and carry him to the ladder. There was no way I could ever lift his body out of the bunker. I started to cry again, and I think maybe I went a bit crazy then. I must have blacked out because when I came to, an hour had passed and I was still leaned up against the bunker's bulkhead with Dad still lying face down at my feet. I realized then what I had to do. It was either I would wrap Dad up in garbage bags and shove him into a corner of the bunker and hope that when he rots it doesn't stink too bad, or I could cut his body up and haul the pieces out.

I grabbed him by a foot and dragged him into the bathroom. I placed him over the small tiled area where we would sometimes take a barrel shower. I figured I could cut the body up there and wash the blood down the drain, then disinfect the whole place when it was all done.

I went to Dad's tool box and I got a handsaw. I also got the sharpest knife I could find in the kitchen. When I went back over to Dad, I realized that I suddenly had to go. I ran to the toilet and crapped; it was hot and mostly liquid. I felt like I needed to vomit too. I got up and leaned over the toilet but I only dry heaved; nothing came up. My chest felt like it was on fire and I think I must have passed out again, because I remember hitting my head against the toilet, and then I just remember looking up at the bowl from the floor. I got myself up and leaned against the toilet bowl. My head felt like it was going to explode. I must have sat that way for a long time until the pain in my head began to go away. Then I got to my feet. My stomach still felt queasy, but I could not put it off any longer. I had to do it.

I walked over to Dad. Then I took off all his clothes. I turned him over so he was face down. I couldn't stand to look at him. I started to cry again and I kept saying 'sorry Dad. I'm sorry.' I took the saw, placed it against the back of his neck. I lost my nerve and got up and walked all the way to the other end of the bunker, beside the ladder that led up and out. I looked up and saw that the sun was beginning to go down. I couldn't believe how much time had passed since I took Bea out, and that's when I really made up my mind to do it. I walked back over and I put the saw to his neck again and this time I began to cut. I sawed through his neck. I hit bone, pressed the saw down, and kept going until his head rolled away into the middle of the shower floor. I thought that there would be a lot of blood, but not much of anything came out. Then I started to work on his legs, sawing through one then the other, then I removed the arms. Finally I realized that I had to cut him in half, so I picked a spot in the middle of his back, and starting at the sides, I cut through his ribs. This was really hard. At one point I thought the saw was going to break. It got stuck in the bones and I had to remove it slowly. Then I started to cut again. This was the worst, as a lot of what was in him came running out. That really sticky thick liquid. Then when I was almost done, there was a loud wet popping sound and the stink was almost more that I could ever imagine, as a thick brown and red liquid came out and spilled all over the floor and across my shoes. His intestines slithered out. I think I began to scream because I tried to shove it all into the shower along with the head and arms. It kept slithering all over the place and it stank something horrible. I got myself back under control until finally I got him cut in half. Then I got some thick black trash bags and I put the body parts in them and tied them off. They were still pretty heavy but at least I could get them out of the shelter.

I don't know but it must have been another half hour for me to take everything up and out of the bunker. I piled the body parts next to my sister. It was getting dark and I was feeling sick and tired. I just couldn't dig their graves. I just didn't have it in me. I felt like I was about to collapse. So I shut the hatch of the bunker and I cleaned up the mess inside the bathroom area. I got a couple gallons of water from the hand pump and washed off as best as I could. My plan was to bury Dad and Bea in the morning. Just couldn't do it then. I crawled into bed and I must have fallen asleep. I don't really remember anything, just that I came awake with a feeling of real panic. I think I must have been having a nightmare, then I must have fell back asleep and slept all the way through to the next day.

When I got up, I realized that the place still stank really badly. I went into the bathroom to pee in the toilet, I saw that I hadn't really done a good job of cleaning up. There was still a lot of blood and rotting pieces of flesh on the shower floor. I got on a pair of rubber gloves and cleaned these up, then got a shovel and went up the ladder to the outside.

The animals had been at the bodies. I could see that the garbage bags had been eaten through. There was a big hole in the plastic I had wrapped Bea in. Something had eaten away some of her belly and a lot of the flesh on the side of her face and one eye was gone.

I started to dig a hole close to where Dad had dug the hole for Mom and the people he had killed. It was hard work. It took me about four hours to dig a hole that I could stand in up to my knees. I decided to go a little deeper and dump everything in. There were just so many rocks. I couldn't believe it. At one time I thought that I would have to stop and maybe continue digging the next day because my arms and back were hurting so much. I started to feel nauseous again, and I decided I had to stop and eat something, so I did. I went back down into the bunker and opened a packet of Wise Emergency Foods. It was pasta and vegetable rotini. It tasted really good and it helped me to get my strength back. Then I went back up and dug for a few more hours until the hole was about as wide as the shovel and as deep as my shoulders.

I dragged Bea and the bags with Dad over and dumped them in. I then filled the hole and realized that the burial had taken me almost an entire day, nine hours. I still can't understand how I just seemed to lose track of the time like that. It was a bit creepy, as if I was alive and breathing but I was just inside a fog, a dream. I could see and feel everything happening but it was like I was outside my body watching myself working and crying. So I buried my dad and my sister. I figured when I felt a bit better I would make a cross and put it by their grave.

I came back down and used bleach to clean the floors and everything I could think of. I had to go topside a few times because the bleach was strong, but I wiped everything down. I think the place now still smells like bleach, but I can still smell the rotting scent of the bodies somehow. It must all be in my head. I took the sheets off Mum's, Dad's, and Bea's beds, bagged them up and took them topside, then I wiped everything down, even the exit ladder. I also made the cross for the grave.

So here I am. I am fifteen and now an orphan. I am a survivor, I am afraid and alone, hiding in a hole in the ground. I miss my family, I miss my life before the end of the world. I may be wrong but that's the way I feel about all of this now. There won't be anything left to come back to, as Dad was hoping. I think that we started something we might not be able to stop. I hope that I am wrong but I can't help but despair like Jonah in the belly of the whale. Will write more next time.

Harry Lambert watched as his men mounted the M270 MLRS rocket launcher in place. It was midafternoon and he and his army had finally cornered the Massena Militia. They had them nicely surrounded in the town of Potsdam. Lambert's face was one of grim determination; he meant to finish the job on these troublemakers. He hated these survivalist, preppers, whatever they called themselves, with a vengeance. They lived in a world of self-delusion, refusing to acknowledge that the world as they knew it was over. They refused to accept the rule of the Royalists. They actually believed that they were fighting for a country that still existed. They refused to lay down their guns and surrender. They actually believed that they were making history by defying the authority he represented.

After the meeting in Albany, it was very clear which one of the groups would be a problem and which ones wouldn't. The larger groups such as the Marathon, Genesee, Buffalo, and Massena groups all felt that they had the manpower to defy the Bilderberg mandate of surrender. The smaller, less organized groups had more or less complied. He was about to destroy the Massena group now. He would show them no mercy. They had their chance. Unlike Splinter he had no intention of using the biological canisters, at least not yet. Having those canisters meant having an enormous power chip that he had no intention of cashing in. He fell back on his military training, and for him it was a cerebral experience trying to outthink and kill the enemy.

Lambert had been very successful in bringing some of the holdout groups into his fold, but others such as this one had refused to swear allegiance to the Bilderbergs. They had openly defied him. He had chased them through three villages until he finally managed to cut off their escape by outflanking them. His army would now shell the village day and night until every house was flattened. Then they would move in from all sides, mopping up. This little operation had cost him one hundred and twelve people. He had killed around four hundred of theirs. Each town the Massena's had fallen back to, they had hoisted the American Flag from some roof top with a stupid sign that read, "Come and Take It." This time he would break them, he had to. Despite all the military aid he got from the Bilderberg Group, he knew that it was not limitless. This campaign had stretched his supplies almost to the breaking point.

That's why he would throw the kitchen sink at this little operation now, in the hopes of crushing it. With this problem out of the way he could lick his wounds and resupply his army, then move on to the next objective.

So it was with a special intensity that he was focused on the map of the town and the surrounding roads. He had every one blocked and those stupid rebels cornered like the cockroaches they were. The launch team was adjusting their weapon's trajectory when the field radio operator held the phone up to him. He took it.

"Yes."

"We are ready on this side, sir." His other captains were all ready with their launchers. This was good news.

"Okay, go ahead and cook the bacon."

"Yes, sir."

With that he gave the phone back to the operator and went into the small tent. He needed a drink of water, and the thought of supplies made him want to examine the contents of the next scheduled delivery. He pulled a small aluminum folding chair next to a large heavy footlocker. He opened it and began to root around when his phone man came to the tents' flap and said without looking in, "Decoded message just came in, sir. This is high priority."

Lambert got up, opened the flap, and took the message from the phone man's hand. He sat back down by the footlocker to read it. *Large force seen moving towards Binghamton. Attack imminent.* He dug into the footlocker again, reaching for his satphone he needed to contact Splinter to warn him. He more or less figured that his military counterpart to the south would know that there was a hostile army incoming, but he would make sure he got the information. Lambert had a very elaborate spy network in place. His agents infiltrated every group of interest, and one of them had just sent him this little bit of intelligence. The way he figured it, Splinter had his spies as well. There were even a few double agents he knew of personally that were in his own camp. That skinny little bespectacled psycho had been trying to keep tabs on him. Lambert also knew that he had spies in the Marathon settlement so he figured that he must already know about this troubling development. Everyone had spies. He dialed in Splinter's number and waited for him to pick up.

On the second ring there was an ear splitting series of explosions. The rear artillery had opened up on the village. He couldn't hear the phone ringing anymore. He put a finger in his ear, trying to focus in on the ring. Pick up, damn it. He was about to put the phone away and try again when it went to message retrieval. He shouted into the phone, "Diefenbacher, this is Lambert, there are people on their way to attack your position in Binghamton. They are from the Marathon group. I will call back as soon as I can." A movement caught his attention. He turned just in time to see an unknown man in his tent. There was also another one outside and about to enter. The man had his rifle trained on him and it was just because his foot got entangled in the tent's canvas that Lambert was able to react in time. The man's gun began its deadly chatter as the Albany Militia leader dropped the receiver and threw himself to the gunman's right. He felt a sharp, hard, jabbing sensation in his left side that knocked the wind out of him as he managed to wedge himself between the two metal supply lockers near the tent's entrance. The men wasted no time. They intended to kill him, and he heard the one who had shot him run forward. Sucking in air and grunting in pain, he pulled the Luger from his waist holster, and aiming upward anticipating where his attacker would appear, he managed to get four rounds away. The man had to expose himself to get a clear shot over the storage lockers, and the first bullet went through his mouth and exited the back of his head. The second bullet grazed his ear but he was already dead. The other attacker lobed a grenade up and over the lockers. Lambert desperately threw himself over the trunks. He caught the man completely by surprise, knocking him over. He then grabbed him by the shirt and spinning him over, used him as a human shield. The grenade went off and he felt as the shrapnel from the lockers tore into the man's body and half the tent disintegrated in flames.

Lambert's world began slipping away as he lost consciousness. Everything seesawed for a second and the world began to go gray. Those cockroaches had tried to kill him. Somehow they had infiltrated the camp and had gotten close enough to actually put a bullet in him. He shoved the man's corpse off and the world went black.

The archbishop was quiet for so long that Alfred believed he was asleep. He was almost drifting off again himself when there was a commotion outside. Killing all those hours in the tent was about to drive him out of his mind. But in a strange way he sensed that he needed the down time to recharge. There was a loud flurry of shouts and screams.

"What the hell is that all about?" the archbishop said as he sat up and got to his feet. They both looked at each other and decided to step outside the tent. When they did they realized that it was late evening.

The camp was a flurry of activity. They saw really for the first time that the campsite was divided into two circular camping areas, with a kind of open lot in the center linking the two parts. Everyone lived in tents and lean-tos. Some of the lean-tos were made with tree branches and leaves, while others were cobbled together with anything that could keep out the wind and rain. He shook his head wondering how they had made it through the winter. There was a gathering and a movement of people, and Alfred just followed the crowd into the open area, which obviously served as a meeting place. Pushing his way through the black-clad stinky individuals, he did notice that a lot were hobbling around on makeshift crutches, and some of them could hardly walk. The archbishop noticed as well and asked a woman close to him, "Why are so many of your group on crutches?"

"They got scurvy. I think we all got a touch of it really," she said as she drew her hand over her nose to wipe away some snot. "We had a nurse, or doctor, whatever you want to call him. He said a lot of the people in the camp had it. Says it's caused by a lack of vitamin C. She turned her dirty, greasy face to them and they could see she was also missing a few teeth and her gums were bleeding. She turned her attention back to the main action now in the square. "They got some of the tree-nailers, I see. Good, I hope they gut them good and proper for what they do to those poor souls."

Alfred felt queasy. He had a bad feeling in his stomach about what was going to happen. It was not his first time in a cannibal camp, and that initial experience had been more than enough for a lifetime. It was one thing to shoot a man, it was another thing to kill him with a knife. He felt the missing tooth throb in his jaw as he became tense. The archbishop was looking on impassively. Suddenly Alfred felt trapped. There was no way he could walk away now; it would be noticed and he could not jeopardize his leadership of the team to destroy the weapons. If he walked away it might be perceived as weakness, so he had to stay and watch the horror show that was about to enfold. Both men were crying and begging for their lives. There but for the grace of God, thought Alfred.

Mushroom walked into the square. He barely seemed to need the crude thick crutch under his right arm. He drew a mask over his head, covering his face. Only the eyes and mouth were cut out so he could see and talk. This had a feel of a well-worn ritual to Alfred, and he was soon proved right in his assumptions. Two big heavily armed men with rifles slung, and large sharp knives in their hands, guarded the two men who were on their knees. The captives' brown uniforms were bloody and dirty. Mushroom then held his hands up and appealed for calm. His black-clad brethren hushed at once.

"This here trial is hereby called to order." His in-human mechanical voice rattled. "These padres were seen guarding and nailing the prisoners to trees on Front Street. They were taken by Bernard and Paxton here when they slipped into the woods for a comfort break. Take a good look everyone. We have all been in town. We have all been out to the human tree garden, and we know all the tenders of that garden. Are these men planters of human trees?"

"Yes," came the damning cry from most of the people standing in the camp.

"Then these men are guilty as charged. We have meat tonight." A loud and horrible cheer went up from the crowd. Mushroom motioned to one of the black-clad men. He reached down and grabbed one of the men by the hair, forcing his head back and exposing his throat. The executioner then expertly drew his knife through the man's neck, cutting off the screams. The victim's hands came up, trying to stop the red jet that issued from his throat, but he was losing a lot of blood fast and his choking struggles soon faded as life left his body. The executioner then used the knife to saw through the neck and the head popped off. The body fell and the huge man held the head up so everyone could see. There was a huge roar of approval from the crowd again.

The other man tried running. Mushroom, moving with a quickness and dexterity belying his size and limp, struck out with his crutch and knocked the fellow in the back of the head. The man fell in a heap. The other black-clad executioner caught him up by the hair and slashed his throat. The man's eyes flew open like window shades and his eyes bulged as his life's blood streamed down his brown shirt. His arms flailed around like a blind man. Alfred felt his whole body go cold. He knew that the man was in immense pain; the executioner did not stop to let him bleed out but held him fast and kept on cutting, the large serrated knife sawed through the neck's tendons and bone. Finally the head came lose and the body fell in a useless heap. He held up the head and showed it around the camp. There was a loud chilling cheer around the encampment.

"Justice is a beautiful thing," Mushroom said. He took off the mask. "These nailers killed some of our people. They have paid the price. Eye for an eye." He smiled and walked over to Alfred and the archbishop. "We leave in another hour. It will be about an hour's walk from here. We will take our best people, about fifteen. There will be two women with us. Their job will be to distract the guards. They are known by the soldiers and they will get them away from the camp to a place where we can kill them. Then we will be able to get into the warehouse and you can take the canisters and destroy them." He looked at Alfred with his one good eye, while the other dead milky one moved about disquietingly in its socket.

"Sounds good," Alfred said.

"Hanson. Give these padres back their gear. They are going to need them. We will have to kill a lot of brownshirts to get those canisters out of there." Alfred and the archbishop followed Mushroom's gaze, and a tall thin man nodded and ran to carry out his chief's orders. "You can wait by the tent while we get ready to go. I'll come to get you when it's time." Alfred nodded, and he and Archbishop O'Riley walked back to the tent.

When they were inside, the archbishop whispered. "Jesus help us, these people are all insane."

Alfred nodded. "Yeah, but we need them to get the canisters."

"I say once we have loaded the canisters on the truck, we should just drive and get the hell away from these psychos. Do you also think that Mushroom may become a problem?"

"Yeah, he is a problem. I don't trust him. Most of the time I think he is just measuring me up when he looks at me. I just can't put a finger on what I see in his eye. I think if we keep our own focus on the objective, which is to get the canisters to the mine and destroy them, then it is still all pretty clear."

Hanson came to their tent and he returned their weapons, ammunition, and backpacks. "A show of good faith from Mushroom," he said before he left. Alfred checked his .45 and the extra clips of ammunition on his belt. They inspected their backpacks and found that they were untouched. Then they sat down to wait for the cannibal chief to send word that they were ready to go.

"Alfred, are you a man of faith?" the archbishop asked quietly.

"I really can't say that I am a Bible thumper. But I do believe in God, if that's what you are asking."

"That's precisely what I am asking. I think that all this, this tribulation, these horrors are all a test of faith."

"That might be, but I think that every man and woman are free to make their choices."

"Look at what those crazy devils did to those men. Did they deserve to be murdered?"

"I don't see how any of that is a test of faith. All I saw was a group of insane people killing two men. My motives for coming on this mission and taking these risks are for my family, and the fact that we cannot allow evil men to run the world. That, I think, was my choice, and not a part of some holy mission," said Alfred.

"That's where you and I differ. I think that everything is part of God's plan. I believe our destinies are fixed. I think that every action, life, birth, and death serves the will of God."

Alfred looked at the priest and asked, "So you are saying that the deaths of those two men were all for a reason? That it was all part of some grand master plan?"

"That's what I think. I think that fighting these evil men is my destiny. I think establishing a New America is also destiny."

"All I want to do is to get rid of these canisters that can kill millions, which includes you, me, and my family. Then I intend to tell those people at Marathon to pack sand and just disappear with my family, away from all this madness."

"Somehow I don't think that's what is in the cards for us." The priest smiled sadly. "I think we all have a part to play in this drama, we all have a destiny we cannot escape."

"I think people make their own destiny and that nothing is predetermined. We both want to have a better world, so we will work in our own ways to achieve that. This destiny talk is a little crazy, priest."

O'Riley smiled, "I guess my line of work makes me believe that there is a bigger force at work here. I lost and found my faith again. I think you will one day realize your destiny, your part to play in this drama."

Alfred grinned. He liked the priest. He liked the fact that even in these grim times there were people around like O'Riley, men of faith but also of intellect, who were curious about the truth and trying to peer and make sense of all the dark metaphysical and existential mysteries.

The rank, cheesy smell told them that Mushroom was here before they saw him. He poked his thick crutch in through the tent's flap, moving it out of the way, and his good blue eye locked on them. He gave Alfred that singular penetrating gaze, then nodded. "We are ready to go. Let's get those canisters." The two men slung their backpacks and holstered their weapons. They had a bit of a hike to the suspected warehouse. Alfred's mind was now completely focused on the objective.

As they trudged out of the camp he noticed that all traces of the bodies were gone, and the great big fire pit at the second smaller camp was being set up. He ground his teeth, bringing a sharp stabbing pain from his extracted tooth. What a world we live in when I must accept help from people who kill and eat other people. He was at the front of the group along with

O'Riley and Mushroom. The man moved quickly despite having to use the crutch. A few others were also using crutches but it did not slow them down. The people in black seemed excited and eager at the prospect of killing more brownshirts. Alfred looked at Mushroom and once again that feeling that he had been missing something came back to him. One thing he did understand, and because his life would probably depend on it, was that he would have to determine the man's real motives if they managed to capture the weapons. As they left the camp and walked off into the twilight, thoughts of his family wormed their way into his mind and his gut clenched in a spasm of apprehension. He just wanted to get the job done and get back to his wife as quickly as possible.

The stench from the crucified men and women got worse as they trudged up Front Street, which ran parallel to the Chenango River.

"Do you hear that?" Julie asked.

Samantha actually held her breath as she walked and listened. At first she had thought it was just the gurgling of the river but as they approached the crucified victims she could hear it, a great buzzing sound. Then she saw what was causing it. A great wave of flies rippled off the crosses in a black swarm, then returned to their pinned meals. She reached into her backpack and pulled out a large bandana, folded it into a triangle and tied it over her face. It made the sweet, nauseating smell of the rotting corpses a bit more bearable. Robert and Candice followed suit, and Julie also tied a piece of cloth over her nose.

As they walked between the crosses, Samantha could not keep herself from occasionally looking up.

The sight of all those rotting, nailed bodies sent a chill along her spine. She had actually thought that nothing could surprise her at this point, but she was wrong. The people who did this must be cruel beyond bounds, and she found herself getting angry. If the Dove had thought that all these victims would demoralize people, he was wrong. It definitely was a weapon of terror, but instead of frightening the people it only served to make them angry.

She noticed that Robert and Candice were looking up, too. Her daughter was coolly taking it all in, but Robert was mad. "Mom, how could they do this? These people are American citizens. These people had rights. This, this was just wrong."

"That's true, Robert, when it all collapsed it affected people in many different ways. I'm afraid in some people it brought out the worst. I hope we can take back Broome County and stamp out this madness." She turned away from the sight of a crow ripping into the body of one of the victims. The flies did not seem contented in eating the crucified; they also began tormenting the living as they trudged up the nightmare road of suffering. As they rounded a slight bend, the squad leader put his hand up and backed them up a few steps. About three hundred yards ahead two men had just finished putting up a new cross between two older ones. They could hear the screams of the victim from where they were.

The men were so engaged in their work and tormenting the crucified victim they did not see the squad that had just rounded the corner and ducked back out of sight. Samantha peeked and saw the men take a piece of wood and hit the victim on the side of the right foot. The man screamed hoarsely in response.

"I guess we could get two really fast runners to run them down and shoot them so they can't give away our position," the lieutenant said.

"Or we could try to pick them off from here," Samantha said.

"Think you can make the shots?"

"Yeah, I think we can get them from here," Samantha said. She looked at her children and nodded to them. "This will have to be quick and accurate."

They got down on their bellies and crawled forward until they could see the men. Still at work, they were beating the poor nailed bastard with two-by-fours. She, Robert, and Candice took aim with the M16s. "Aim for the body, not the head. We want to make sure we drop them." She breathed out. They were all in the prone shooting position. She fired, a single, hollow, deadly pop. Her target went over like someone had pushed him from behind. The other man didn't have time to react. The two siblings rifles also popped, and he went down like a sack of apples.

The lieutenant waited a few seconds which seemed like forever, then he gave them the signal and they approached the two men carefully. There was a moan, and the man Samantha had shot turned over to face them. There was a pooling red spot on the left side of his shirt. He tried raising his arm in supplication, but the lieutenant's pistol banged twice, and he stopped moving forever. "Okay, let's pick up the pace," he said gruffly as the squad went by the bodies. The two-by-fours that they had been using to torture their victim lay in the dirt. Samantha heard Candice gasp and followed her daughter's gaze upward to the nailed victim. At first the face didn't register; the man was so badly beaten, he was almost unrecognizable.

"Grandpa," Robert said through clenched teeth.

Oh, damn it, Samantha thought. This is not what she wanted at all. This was a bad sign, a really bad sign of what may have happened to the team. Jim must have succeeded in warning the Dove's militia and they had been caught. A savage sinking feeling thrummed through her body. A horrible thought came unbidden into her mind. What if Alfred was also nailed on one of these crosses? She looked up at the destroyed man, a man who was once a proud member of the US armed forces, a real patriot. She looked at his smashed body. They had stripped him naked and nailed him to a roughly made wooden cross. They had driven ten inch spikes through his palms, and what really horrified Samantha, because she understood the physiology of the human body, was the sight of the nails through his heels. The nails cracked the heel bones and so every movement must be excruciating. The Romans had sometimes used the same technique of torture on especially horrible criminals. They had tied him to the pole under the arms and across the chest with pieces of foul looking rope.

Samantha understood that his suffering must be terrible. With every breath his body shivered and when it did a low moan would escape him. Blood ran down his body from the many cuts he had received from the beatings. Horrible burn marks covered almost every inch of his skin. The squad had stopped at Candice's cry, and the squad leader looked at them with shock and sorrow. Julie began to sob.

"Tobias," Samantha said softly. "Tobias, can you hear me?"

The man shifted his head and groaned. His eyes were swollen shut so he couldn't see, but he could hear and he shook his head.

"Tobias, did they catch Alfred?" Samantha asked.

"I don't know," he said.

"I'm so sorry, Tobias. The two bastards that did this to you are dead."

The man smiled, which turned into a grimace of pain as he coughed, and a bubble of blood came up from his destroyed lips and teeth.

"We are here, Candice, Robert. We came to find you and Alfred." A tear ran down the left side of Samantha's face.

Candice began to sob. She heard the subtle change in her mom's voice and knew that something bad was on the way. The sun was almost gone from the sky and twilight was coming on. The smell and the flies, which were beginning to swarm again, made her feel like screaming. Robert was looking on, his face a mask of suppressed rage.

"There is nothing I can do, Tobias. Your injuries are just too extreme. Even if we took you down, you would just die painfully. I can hear your breathing; I know they punctured a lung. Almost all your ribs look broken, and I can see that they broke both your feet," Samantha said.

"Sam, Sam, don't worry about it. You know what you have to do. I've lived a long and good life. You and the children were a blessing. I love you and Alfred and the kids. Do what you have to do, Sam."

Samantha unholstered her .38 revolver. "Goodbye, Tobias." She took a deep breath and fired two bullets into his chest. She heard the man breathe out like a collapsed balloon, then he was still. She would come back one day and take him down if she got the chance. Now she had to move on. The two children and everyone in the squad were looking at her. Candice's face was white and there were fresh tears on her cheeks.

Robert took a shaky breath and turned on his heels. Samantha took the lead and nodded at the lieutenant.

"Okay, let's get moving, we have some Doves to kill," he said.

As they walked away from Tobias, Samantha hoped that she wouldn't find Alfred nailed up because she knew she would not have it in her to ease his suffering that way. She would come apart and that would be very bad. She found herself looking at every cross they passed with dread. They successfully made it to their rendezvous with the other team, and when they moved out toward their objective under the cover of darkness, the air was filled with explosions and the sounds of gunfire. Samantha actually found herself looking forward to dealing out some justice on the people who had killed her father-in-law and possibly her husband.

Chapter Twelve

"The whole life of an American is passed like a game of chance, a revolutionary crises or a battle." Alexis de Tocqueville

Alfred followed Mushroom and his band down Morgan Road, and past the Ross Park Zoo. They were making a beeline for the warehouse on Rush Avenue, where Mushroom figured they had stashed the canisters. The men in black blended into the twilight, and they moved cautiously now past rows and rows of militia vehicles, until they could see the top of the long one story building.

The two women who were supposed to provide distraction were sent ahead, and Mushroom smiled and waited. A couple minutes later one of the women came running back, barefooted. She had left her stilettos behind. The right side of her face was bruised and she was bleeding from the mouth. She ran to Mushroom, caught her breath, and said, her voice remarkably steady, "They've got Angie. We went in as planned. The guards were willing, but some captain drove in. He was shouting that they were being attacked and that they were now in code red. He said if anyone came near the facility they were to shoot to kill. That's when he realized that the men were about to have themselves a little fun. He hit Angie in the face with his pistol, and he hit me a few times, then someone called him on the radio, said attackers were overrunning the city and that they were to pack up The Hammer and move it. That's when I ran. Didn't think I would make it. I just jumped the fence and ran like hell. I expected to be shot, but I guess they were just thinking I'm just that hooker Donna, and I ain't even worth a bullet."

"You did good, D," Mushroom smiled. "We'll get your sister back."

Mushroom led them to a couple of huge trucks that were parked right beside the fence. Alfred could see why the man had picked this spot. They were close to the large door that led into the warehouse. All they had to do was to cut the fence open and they could get close to the loading dock relatively quickly. It was obvious that he had done some surveillance of the facility before. He leaned on his crude crutch and motioned to the people around him.

"All right, you all know what to do. We were planning this even before these hotshots showed up." He grinned that strange grin again at Alfred and O'Riley. "Let's see if they have your death juice."

The slightly insane glint in the man's eye made Alfred's stomach clench and once again he reminded himself to never drop his guard around him.

"The only bad thing is now they will be on their guard since there are attacks going on all over the city," Mushroom said shrugging his shoulders in resignation. "Here's what we'll do. We managed to put together about four pipe bombs. Pretty powerful if they go off. Let's cut this fence open first. Then we light the fuses and toss them toward the guard station, one and two, there and there." He pointed at the two sandbag bunkers that had been built in front of the dock.

Alfred also noticed that another four guards walked the perimeter in teams of two inside the fence, going in opposite directions. There were also another four guards in a guard house at the front of the building. They sat inside the shack watching the heavy front gate. He wondered how many men were inside and how well armed they were.

This was going to be a major firefight at really close quarters. He also understood that the only reason they had not been spotted yet was that these eaters of men were dressed all in black and were really, almost uncannily quiet. He figured that this was what it was like for them when they were hunting people. He looked around quickly and realized he was right; they were predatory and dangerous, and it radiated off them in waves. Once again he intuited that the only person he could trust on this little jaunt was O'Riley. He looked at the priest. The man seemed relaxed. He had the look of a person who believed completely that he was doing the right thing. He figured that O'Riley had already said a quick prayer and had put himself in God's hands. He looked completely focused on the task.

Alfred wished it was the same for him, that singularity of purpose, because something was gnawing at his consciousness. He kept coming back to the way these people smelled. He had smelled it somewhere before and it worried him like his throbbing missing tooth that he could not put it all together in his mind. Something about Mushroom really bothered him. He remembered when the man first saw him when they had rushed into camp. There was something in his face that was mostly masked by the man's horrible disfigurement. It was surprise and recognition. Was it recognition that they were from the Marathon Militia, which he was expecting, or was it another kind of recognition. Could the man had known him from somewhere else? He had never seen Mushroom before, he was sure of that, and he figured that there was no way the man could have known him. He pulled his .45 from his holster. He felt hot, pumped, and ready to go. Despite his misgivings he still had a job to do. Before this was done there was going to be a lot of killing.

The men silently took two of the explosives out of their canvas bags and lit them. They watched the fuses burn down to the right length, then they tossed them at the sandbag bunkers. Their aims were true and the bombs fell on the other side of the sandbags, which had not been really built up. The guards saw and reacted, but it was too late for them. The pipe bombs blew apart, sending deadly shrapnel flying that impaled the screaming, running men. They went down howling in pain. One stopped moving, but the other kept screaming. A piece of metal had taken his hand off below the elbow and his life blood ran out of him as he thrashed around, sending dark scarlet squirts unto the graveled surface.

Mushroom's people did not scream and rush forward. They went through the fence, silently, their feet hardly rustling the stones on the graveled surface. The many hard months of living in the woods, hunting men and game, had made them well suited for an operation such as this. One woman lashed out with a machete and the dying man's head rolled away from his body. Someone else quickly stabbed the other guard a few more times to make sure he was dead.

They heard the alarm go off inside the building and they heard the running footsteps of the other guards who were patrolling the perimeter. About five of Mushroom's soldiers were inside the fence. The rest were concealed in the shadows of the parked trucks outside. Mushroom didn't hesitate. He nodded toward the bunkers and the men reached them just as the guards came into view. Alfred, who was in a prone position peeking out from behind a sandbag, immediately realized that the guards were well trained. They too flung themselves down on their bellies and opened up with their Kalashnikovs. Their rifles were full auto and a hail of bullets hit the sandbags, a few finding their targets. One man began unhooking a grenade from his utility belt and was about to pull the pin while the others covered him.

Alfred took a deep breath, exhaled slowly and pulled the trigger on his .45. He saw the stones next to the man's right shoulder shatter. One soldier noticed that his partner was being shot at and swung his rifle toward Alfred. There were now a couple of bolt action rifle pops coming from Alfred's position as well from behind the men through the fence. The man who had been aiming at Alfred uttered a small cry and slumped forward. Alfred squeezed off two more rounds. He saw the man hold his arm and drop the grenade. He then shot him through the neck.

The other two guards, realizing that they had lost their advantage with their two comrades dead, did what appeared to Alfred a remarkable thing. They grabbed the bodies, and using them as shields stood up and tried running for the right side of the building, away from the gunfire. They didn't make it because there was no way they could shield themselves from two sides at once, and some of the bullets also went through the bodies and hit them. They fell dead in a bloody mess on top of their human shields.

They were quite close to the loading docks, and Alfred could hear the pounding of boots on the other side of the metal door. He then realized to his dismay that there was a face peering down at them from the single solid fiberglass window in the center of the door. He visualized what the man had seen and realized that for them it wasn't good. The door thrummed and began to move upward. Damn it, they were coming out. They figured they could take care of the threat themselves. This was a real dilemma. Alfred's mind ticked over. They did not know where the canisters were located. They had to be really careful about firing blindly into the building. But what to do? This fight would have to be up close and very personal, hand to hand, until they figured out where the biological weapons were located.

"We can't fire in without knowing where the canisters are," he said to Mushroom. O'Riley also nodded his assent. "Well, we've got to think of something fast because they are opening the door."

Alfred looked up. The face was gone from the window. He ran for the bodies, O'Riley following him. "Okay, everyone grab a body or a sand bag. As soon as they open those doors, we go in fast, try and get in among them, then use our pistols or machetes." He grabbed one of the bloody corpses from the yard and dragged it over to the door. As soon as it was open high enough, he grabbed the cement dock and hoisted himself and the corpse up. O'Riley was on his left.

Alfred ran for the kneeling cluster of men who were just assembling themselves. His quick crazy charge caught them by surprise. A couple men still managed to open fire, but he had the body by the back of the shirt and barreled into them. He knocked one man over and fell on the floor among them. He hooked his knees into the corpse and spun over unto his back. He brought his .45 up and fired two bullets into a man who was scrambling to get out of the way. The man collapsed. Alfred felt the body jerk a few times and felt a burning just below his knee. He fired at one of the men who had been firing at him. The bullet hit the man in the face, smashing his skull. Alfred heard screaming, shouting and the deafening roar of gunfire at close range.

The priest had done the same, charging into the men, but O'Riley threw the body at two men who were scrambling backward. It threw off their aims, and it was all O'Riley needed. The two Glock .45s popped twice a piece. One man threw himself down. He fell on top of his weapon which discharged, then his body twitched and was still. O'Riley coolly aimed at the other man and fired twice, hitting him in the chest.

Alfred's heart hammered as he scanned the room. More brownshirts, now running toward them. Some actually took cover behind a couple of forklifts. There was a metal table pushed up against one of the walls. He ran, slid under it, and used his legs to lift and flip the huge table over, flying cans of soda and papers flew into the gunfire and carnage. So much for not firing in the warehouse, he thought grimly. Combat sometimes didn't go the way it was planned. Things just had a way of taking on a life of their own. He shoved the table forward so he could have a better vantage point to return fire. O'Riley ran and jumped over the table, joining him.

There was a major fight going on near the door of the warehouse. The rest of the canni gang had finally come into the storeroom, and after shooting their way in, they drove the guards back into the kill zone. The black garbed men were quiet and fearless. The difference in the fight, Alfred noticed, was that Mushroom and his men were not afraid to die and they attacked with a scary silence that unnerved the guards. They hacked at the brownshirts with their machetes, furiously but methodically lopping arms and heads off, one by one. The sporadic gunfire was punctuated by the meaty kill sounds of metal cutting through flesh and bone.

Alfred and O'Riley made sure that the other guards were kept busy by sniping at them. This prevented them from getting a free shot at the black-clad dervishes in the middle of the warehouse. Alfred switched his clip for a new one and quickly checked his leg. A bullet had passed through his pants and grazed his shin. He was just wondering how they were going to get at the men behind the forklifts when O'Riley nudged him.

"See that forklift over there? It has that huge metal tank loaded on it. I say we rush it. Bring the tank up to give us cover, drive it around one of the sides and kill the workers of iniquity."

Alfred checked it out and smiled. It was a good plan. In all the mayhem, he realized that he had developed a sort of tunnel vision. He had stopped seeing the entire staging floor and had been focusing just on his targets.

O'Riley bolted for the forklift with Alfred on his heels. They got on, and O'Riley slid into the driver's seat, with Alfred standing on the step and holding on to the roof of the cab. The priest used the key and starter button and the forklift came to life. The man did not waste any time. He raised the fork with the steel tank, hit the gas, and the rear wheels spun, almost throwing Alfred off. He quickly raced around the other parked forklifts that the guards were using as cover.

Bullets pinged into the steel tank. The men were firing at them desperately and they were soon exposed and outflanked. O'Riley brought the machine to a stop and jumped off, using the steel tank as cover with Alfred on the other side. The two men made no mistake. The three guards fired their automatic weapons recklessly at their targets. Alfred shot one man in the face, and the priest killed the other two. Alfred held on to the steel tank to get his breath back. He felt drained and cold.

"I think you have been blessed," O'Riley said, smiling as he pointed to the two bullet holes that had passed through the left side of Alfred's shirt.

Alfred checked his side. He was unscathed. Their attention was now turned to the scuffle still going on in the middle of the warehouse. The cannis killed two more men who were fighting desperately for their lives; they had been trying to use their guns as clubs and were hacked to death by the black-clad men. There was only one man left. The six remaining cannis backed him into a wall and Mushroom was about to chop his head off. Alfred realized that he had to stop him. "Mushroom, no, you can't kill him. We need him to show us where they got the canisters stashed."

Mushroom looked at Alfred. The black and white face paint used by the man made his already disfigured face look like a very bad nightmare. The man's eye glittered with an emotion that Alfred knew and understood clearly; it was raw hate. Alfred's weapon was in his right hand at his side and it was all he could do to keep it down and not point it at the man.

"You don't tell me what to do, Pine Street man. You don't give me orders."

"He's right," O'Riley said. "He can show us where they are. It saves us the problem of having to waste precious time looking for it." He looked at Mushroom and for the first time the priest caught a whiff of a seething animosity toward Alfred in the man's glare and body language.

"Okay, priest. This one will live." Mushroom lowered his weapon and two of his men grabbed the guard and shoved him toward Alfred.

"Okay, tell us what we want to know and you will live," Alfred said.

The man looked at Alfred, and collecting all his nerve, he said, "Do I have your word on that?"

"You have my word. Tell us what we want to know and when we are done here you will be left alive."

"In the second part of the warehouse there is a metal screen partition that runs on a rail. The partition can only be opened by entering the security code in the panel. The code word is LOVETHEDOVE, all caps. They are packed on pallets, ready to move."

"Okay, let's check this padre's story out," Mushroom said, his mechanical voice sounded extra harsh and edgy. It brought chills to Alfred's arms.

There was a low cough behind them. Two of Mushroom's men were there, and one was bleeding from a wound to his upper arm. "The guards at the front gate have been taken care of," one of the men reported.

"Good, I guess the others didn't make it."

"Yeah, all dead."

"Okay, go back out front and keep an eye out. If there seems like there might be a problem come back here and let us know." The men shook their heads in the affirmative and left as silently as they came.

They turned and continued toward the metal partition. As they walked by two stacks of empty palates they came up short. On the ground was a beaten and bloody woman who Alfred guessed was Angie. She was on her back, and one black stiletto was lying beside one of the stacks. Alfred could make out the blood spatter all over the ground. He figured they had beaten her with their rifles. Mushroom kneeled down beside the woman, leaning on his crutch. He felt for her pulse. Alfred figured it was a futile gesture, since her eyes had been open but unblinking the entire time. A groan escaped the cannibal, a deep angry growl that rippled through his mechanical voice box. Alfred just registered his arm moving then the captured guard uttered a cry of alarm, which immediately became a death rattle as he fell on his knees before collapsing on his side. There was an ivory handled knife stuck in his chest. It was interesting to Alfred that they could still be shocked by the sudden act of violence they had just witnessed, when they had just finished killing almost a dozen men themselves. But all the men present were shocked just the same.

Mushroom closed Angie's eyes and retrieved his knife from the guard's body. Then they walked to the metal partition, and O'Riley tried the code. The keypad beeped three times and a red light flashed, but the door did not budge.

"Oh, damn, he lied. Now he's dead," Alfred muttered under his breath.

"Let's hope that alarm didn't alert someone somewhere that they need to come and check out their warehouse," O'Riley said, his face grim.

"Stop living in the twenty-first century. All the power in here is run by a generator and a couple of solar cells they installed on top of the building. The odds that they have the capability to warn someone miles away is next to none. No working phone lines, no working cell towers," Mushroom said. "Besides we can always use these." He pulled the other two pipe bombs from his pack. He placed them where they figured the locks were located and lit the fuses. The men had enough time to duck behind a couple of pallets that were packed with more of the steel tanks they had seen earlier on the forklift. They covered their ears and made themselves small as two powerful and almost simultaneous bangs ripped through the metal locks and blew away pieces of the partition.

Alfred watched as Mushroom's men pushed the metal screen open. Mushroom went to the wall and switched on the flood lights. The two huge metal containers with death inside gleamed malevolently on their pallets. One of the cannis whistled. Alfred felt a chill. Nothing but death here, every nerve ending screamed at him. The silver containers were about fifteen feet each. Alfred's mind gave up trying to figure how much cubic feet of gas or vapor both cylinders could hold. Enough to kill every non-inoculated person on the east coast, he thought grimly. Just release in a highly populated area, and the virus would do the rest. The infection would spread exponentially and there would be no cure. Hundred millions more dead. Then the appalling thought occurred to him that this very scenario had already occurred at specific vantage points all over the globe. The monsters, the architects of Armageddon had killed billions in their quest for power. They had used the financial folly of the world and the insanity of racial and religious hate as cover to drive the world into a new Dark Age where they could rule as kings.

Alfred was so wrapped up in his own thoughts, as he stared almost mesmerized by the gleaming weapons, that he forgot his misgivings about Mushroom. He was pulled back from his reverie by the man's shrill mechanical voice. "Okay, Pine Street Man. It's time for us to talk."

Alfred saw that the cannibal chief had the drop on him. His jaw throbbed in time with his heartbeat as he realized that O'Riley had both his pistols aimed at the three cannis and Mushroom, while the cannibal had his rifle unslung and aimed at him, his rotting decaying teeth flashed yellow behind the loose pink ribbons of skin.

Jim had fallen asleep on the floor. His daughter was sleeping on the bunk. When he sat up his head ached and his throat felt very dry. He tried to remember the last time he had eaten something, and he realized that it was close to fourteen hours. Something had jarred him awake. He couldn't quite put a finger on what it was, when suddenly there was the sound of what surely must have been an explosion so close it made him jump to his feet. His daughter sat up slowly, and she began to sob. He sat on the edge of the bunk and put his arm around her. For the millionth time he wished his wife were there. It was hard being alone with a child. How many people had just up and abandoned their families, he wondered.

Tears stung his eyes and he felt the headache growing worse. He wondered about his own ethics, his own soul. He was and still considered himself a Christian. He had sat in church, and with discussion groups talked about right and wrong and what it meant to be a moral person. The deacon at his church would always say that the measure of a person was who they were when no one was watching. Jim had taken this even further and thought it was more about how a person behaved during trying times. It wasn't so much about who was watching but how one acted when the chips were down. He couldn't understand any of it anymore. Wasn't the first priority protecting one's family and loved ones? He had tried to protect his family and that hadn't worked out. He had tried to protect his daughter and they had used that to make him do things that went against his conscience. It was easy to talk about morality and ethics when one was comfortable. That goes out the window when one's family was starving or in danger.

It was also horrifying to live in a world where human life was so cheap, where you were only as valuable as your ability to provide some sort of service. He looked at the state of the world before the Collapse and realized that in countries where people agonized over the loss of one life, there was more personal freedom and happiness, versus the places where life was cheap, and some lives were considered more important than others. Those societies seemed to produce citizens who only valued others exactly like themselves and allowed for no diversity, no freedom of thought. He couldn't imagine the horrors that must have been perpetrated in some parts of the Middle East after the Collapse. He and many others had actually expected one of the super powers to take advantage of the chaos and launch an invasion into their enemy's territories. He remembered how the US military had sent men and planes up to Alaska and the North Pole to counter any Russian insurgency. The American people found out that the Russians weren't the only ones with large secret bases in the Arctic Circle. But the threat never materialized, and the countries had all imploded when their governments could not meet the needs of their citizens. People did not turn their anger outward; they turned it inward upon themselves.

Jim held his daughter as sounds of automatic gunfire came closer to his building. There were no windows for him to see what was happening in the streets below. It sounded like a war zone and he wondered who was attacking the Dove's army. He remembered his wife, the real Ellie, not the Dove's acolyte who had been his accomplice and who he had eventually taken into his bed. He closed his eyes and his wife's face came into his mind. They had met at a church fundraiser. She was beautiful, tall, well-spoken and African American. They became friends and worked on a lot of the church's activities together. He remembered when he first realized that he was in love with her. He was getting out of his car in the parking lot of Algonquin Park, and she was there already, setting up tables with the other volunteers. She had wavy thick hair that came to her shoulders, beautiful dark brown skin, thin graceful features, and she looked and moved like a ballerina. She turned that cheeky mischievous smile on him and he was hopelessly lost. Two weeks later he got up the nerve to ask her out. He was apprehensive because he was white and she was African American. He almost passed out when she accepted.

Jim clung to his daughter, and he clung to the memory of his wife as the sounds of gunfire and explosions rattled and boomed up close and in the distance. There was the sound of running in the hallway outside his cell. A pair of feet stopped at his door. He stood up as the door popped open and a hand tossed in a smoking canister, then the door slammed shut and he could hear the deadbolts being thrown in place. He saw the name on the rolling cylinder and his mind was filled with a maniacal rage. It was Zyklon B. They were gassing him and his daughter like they were rats.

Jim ran and hit the door full tilt with his shoulder. The frame shuddered but held. He held his breath and ran to the end of the room and ran at the door again. He knew he had very little time left. He hit the door with every ounce of strength and force he could muster. He felt his shoulder dislocate and screamed in pain. The top of the door sagged off its hinges. He reared back and kicked out, his boot hitting the door right below the lock and splintering it outward. He limped back into the room, grabbed his daughter by the back of her shirt and dragged her into the hallway. His eyes and ears burned, and he gasped the cleaner air in the hallway, prodding his daughter along because he knew that they had to get out of the building—the gas was still dangerous. As they ran by the other cells on his floor, he unbolted the deadbolts because he could hear the screams and pleading in the other rooms.

His shoulder felt like it had shards of glass inside, and his knees felt wobbly. He also realized that he couldn't put his full weight on his right foot. He most likely had sprained his ankle when he kicked the door down. As he hobbled down the stairs leading to the outside, he heard voices in the enclosure below. He placed a hand over his daughter's mouth and put a finger on his lips. Then he rounded the flight of stairs and flung himself at the men beneath them. His body hit both men in the back, driving them forward into the steel door. Jim's bloodcurdling scream of pain as his dislocated shoulder ground on itself further helped to unhinge the men in the dark. His hand found a holster, and he pulled the weapon and fired point blank into the man's body. The other man fired at him. He felt a burning in his stomach, and he suddenly found it hard to breathe. He pulled the trigger on his own weapon and the man cried out, falling lifeless to the ground.

Jim groaned and pulled the bodies away from the door. "Come on, Diane, we have to get out of here." His daughter came down the stairs and they both stepped out into the sweet-smelling night. He was about to run across the street to a building that looked like a garage, when a large group of people, some of whom he recognized, stepped out of the shadows on the other side of the street. He thought quickly. He couldn't step back into the building because he could already hear boots coming down the stairs, so he headed for the driveway that was between the two buildings. They took cover behind an armored SUV, parked close to some bushes.

He leaned his back against the vehicle and sat down. He had a feeling that he might not get back up. His shoulder was out and throbbing horribly. The bullet in his stomach, which at first had been numb, was now becoming unbearable. He couldn't see the wound in the dark, but he knew that he was most likely mortally shot, and that he may have a few minutes or a few hours at most. His daughter was sobbing and crying as she sat down beside him. He could feel her shaking and his anguish crushed him. He had failed. He had failed his wife, his daughter, and himself. Diane jumped when heavy gunfire and explosions erupted from the front of the building, as people tried earnestly to kill each other.

The people he recognized a few minutes ago were from the Marathon Settlement. He smiled grimly at that, because Jasper was a real wily bastard. He must have been planning this little operation for months and he kept it all to himself. His mind went back to all the squad drills Jasper had insisted the volunteer defenders run, all the memorization of the area north and south of the settlement. His doggedness that each member of the defender militia run two miles three times a week, and complete the once-a-week weapons training. He understood it all now as he lay dying beside some car. He agreed with it as well. It was wise for them to attack the Dove's militia here and now. They could chase them out of the county. For the umpteenth time he wished that it had been the Marathon group he had hooked up with, instead of the Dove's, but it was all in the past. He heard the patter of feet coming toward them and he held his daughter's hand, lifted the pistol to his chest, and waited.

Samantha's group was a lot bigger now. They had nine people in the squad originally, but now their number was about three times that many. The people they had hooked up with were out of Middletown, New York. They had traveled all the way here to fight with the Marathon Militia. The man leading them was a brute wearing an eyepatch. He and his group didn't seem so well off but they were eager to fight. They all wore dirty civilian clothes and jeans, and they carried mostly bolt rifles, but they were all of one accord, and that was to drive the Dove out of Broome County.

In the ten minutes that they stopped to link up and properly brief the Middletown group, Samantha had learned a little about the man leading them. His name was Gregory, and apparently the Dove had rolled into Middletown and killed a lot of his people and some of his family. He and these men had sneaked away from the city, which was still under the control of the New York City Militia, to fight here and link up with the Marathon group. Their goal was to prove their loyalty to Jasper so they could join the Marathon Settlement. Samantha had her misgivings about that. These people were a bit different. They were wilder, rougher, and she got the sense that they may have done really horrible things to stay alive during the last eight months. She shoved that all to the back of her mind, thinking they had all done really bad things to stay alive.

Samantha's squad leader didn't waste any time, either. They took cover going from building to building, closing in on their objective, which was City Hall. They were in the heart of the city, and there were gun battles going on all around them as other squads tried to meet their own goals. Up ahead, she saw that a squad was pinned down by people firing at them from the four levels of a garage. Since there wasn't any real way around the garage, their group then came under fire as well. The gunners in the garage controlled the entry into the heart of the city, pinning down squads on four sides.

She saw the two squad leaders chat, shaking their heads furiously. Samantha knew what they were chatting about. The garage would have to be cleared and manned by their own people before any progress could be made to get control of the heart of the city. Somewhere up there were a couple of .50 caliber guns and troops with heavy weapons.

"Okay, let's pool our resources. We are going to have to go up there and clear this building out. Everyone with a semi-automatic rifle or fully automatic rifle will go in." When they did a count of the two squads they had about thirty-eight people. The squad leader then looked at Candice and Robert and asked, "Do you think you can keep that .50 caliber gun really busy? That building over there is clear; a couple of sharp shooters could do a lot of damage."

"I don't want to leave, Mom." Candice shook her head. Robert agreed. He did not want them separated.

Samantha seized upon the opportunity. "I think it would be a good idea. You can give us some serious cover while we go in and engage."

"Mom, it's dark and we can't see anything in there. How are we going to shoot what we can't see?" Robert asked.

"You can see their muzzle flashes."

"It makes sense," the squad leader added. "We will send three teams to engage the other .50 calibers on the other four sides. He went through his squad and picked two more sharp shooters while the other squad leader did the same. "Figure out where the .50 cals are located, get into a sniping position and keep them busy while we go in and clear the building. And we got a surprise for you." The lopsided grin on his face was visible in the waxing moonlight. He handed two small bazookas to the first two teams. "They are already loaded, so keep your fingers away from the triggers. Point it this way, aim through here, and press the trigger here. You got that? Now, here's what we'll do. We will wait ten minutes to give you time to get set up, then we will lay down some fire from here to keep them busy. It's dark so they really can't see much. Good thing they didn't figure a way to light up the street. Fire the bazookas first. Aim so that the shell drops inside among 'em. Then we will go in."

"Yeah, minus the sniper teams there are about thirty-two of us left. I say that we break into four teams of eight. The first team engages the group there on the first floor, and then we split off eight on each floor. We'll check the roof and leave our own people up there to keep control," the other team leader added. "Okay, sniper teams, move out. When you hear us shooting, fire your shells and target those .50 calibers if they are still operational. When we secure the building we will fire a few shots off the roof and you can meet us back here."

The teams split off, each moving toward its objective. Robert and Candice hugged Samantha. "Be safe, Mom," Candice said.

"Yeah, Mom, don't think we don't know what this was, too," Robert said. "See you soon."

"Get the job done," Samantha said. "Love you."

They turned and melted away into the night. Robert had the bazooka slung over his shoulder. They went into the building across the street and up the stairs. They were responsible for the machine gun nest on the third floor. The siblings were not careless. They swept each floor carefully, making sure it was clear. They checked the windows of the last floor and realized that they were still a bit low. They needed to get higher up. They found the door that led to the roof. It was locked. Robert found a trash can and used it to smash the lock. They then went out on to the roof and saw they were about on level with the enemy position, about two hundred feet away.

Candice and Robert carefully ran to the roof's edge. It was surrounded on all four sides by a five foot brick wall. Robert sighted in the bazooka. It was hard to do at night. The scope was pretty much useless, so very carefully he aimed it as he would a rifle and waited. There was the sound of automatic gunfire on the other side of the building. He hoped that the other sniper teams made it to their positions safely. Then all hell seemed to break loose. The main force below opened up at the gun placement on the first floor. That was the signal.

Robert breathed in then out slowly, but before he depressed the trigger, two explosions rocked the garage. The night exploded in light. The .50 caliber gun opposite opened up, and he had to duck as the bullets churned up the cement blocks of the safety wall. He heard his sister cry out in pain. He dropped the bazooka and, reaching down, he grabbed her and dragged her away from the gunfire.

"I'm hit," Candice said. "Oh, hell, Robert."

He threw himself on top of her as the .50 caliber machine gun raked the side of the building, blowing out chunks of concrete. The whole world below erupted in another round of gunfire. Robert reached into his pocket and pulled out the tiny flashlight he always carried. Cupping it in his palm so the gunner across in the garage couldn't see him, he scanned his sister and realized that she was hit through the thigh. She was bleeding out fast. He shrugged out of his backpack and got a piece of cloth he had been using as a sweat rag. He tied it around her thigh.

"Take that sonofabitch out," she said between gasps.

He crawled over and got the bazooka, and aiming quickly, he targeted the gun that was now firing at the street below. There was a whoosh as the shell left the canister, and a loud bang as it exploded amongst the men and supplies. There was also a powerful secondary explosion that shook the foundations of the building. Part of the structure actually sagged and collapsed onto the level underneath. Robert dropped the weapon and scrambled back over to his sibling. She had braced herself up so she was sitting with her back to the wall. There was a lot of fighting going on in the garage now, and he realized that there was nothing he could really do up there on the roof, in the dark. So, he said, "Let's get you inside and really check you out."

They crawled across the roof. Robert grabbed the bazooka on the way. They got to the door, and he helped his sister down the stairs to the third floor. They went through the hall and into a large room that had been an office. He used his flashlight to examine his sister. Her face was pale, and he saw her trembling and realized that she might be in shock. He had her lie down, resting her head against her pack. Then he examined the wound. It was bad, the .50 caliber bullet had torn away a great deal of the flesh and muscle on her left thigh. They were lucky he had tied the tourniquet as tightly and as quickly as he did, or else she would have bled out for sure. He needed to get her to a medic so she could be treated as quickly as possible.

He got her to her feet, and holding her under the shoulder, he began moving her slowly from floor to floor. When she got to the second floor she cried out. She couldn't take the pain anymore. She slumped and passed out. Robert found himself holding one hundred fifteen pounds of dead weight. He placed her down carefully and decided that he would get help. His mother was fighting to secure the garage, but he needed her to come and take a look at Candice. He pulled her into one of the offices and hid her behind a photocopying machine. He elevated her legs and ran downstairs and up the street to the garage's entrance. Two men, wearing the brown of the Dove's militia, came running out of the garage. Robert didn't hesitate. He hit both with a short controlled burst from his M16. There was a lot of shooting going on up ahead of him, and occasionally he heard as bullets chipped and pinged into the walls of the surrounding buildings. His mother was in that hell somewhere, and he needed to find her.

"All right, Pine Street Man, let's talk." Mushroom looked at Alfred, shuffled his feet and made himself more comfortable. His rifle never wavered though it was still pointed at Alfred's chest. Alfred's pistol was in his fist, pointing at the floor. All Mushroom had to do was press the trigger. Alfred felt a chill. He couldn't believe that he had allowed this to happen. The other three cannis had their rifles pointed at either him or the priest. "The first thing I want you to do is to put your pistol there in your waist. Nice and easy now. That's it." The man smiled his grim smile. "Let me tell you a little story. You might be wondering why I didn't kill you straight off or maybe why it seems like I know you."

"Yes, it has crossed my mind."

"Well, about seven months ago, my brother and four others went out on a run to get some food. Those were better times, before the winter and the Dove showed up. There was still enough stuff to scavenge. We would hit all those abandoned homes in town. My brother was a sort of mechanical genius. He had pimped out this truck, placed a huge pointed steel grill on the front of it. Ah, I see that you know this truck. Yes, yes."

Alfred sucked in a breath as his mind went back to a night seven months ago when a group of marauders attacked his house on Pine Street. This was the group that had been responsible for killing and looting his neighbor's, the Parsons', home, a couple of days before they attacked his. Alfred had figured that they would not have been satisfied with what they had gotten from the older couple's house, which wasn't much. He had figured that they would attack his own home soon, and he was right. They had come back in the early morning a few days later. The marauders had tried ramming their truck into his home. It was a simple and effective plan, really. Crash into the house, shoot and kill the stunned and confused inhabitants, and steal their stuff. He and Samantha had dealt out a little hurt that morning. They had thrown Molotov cocktails at the truck, burning it, and they had shot and killed the six marauders in a deadly gun battle in which Samantha herself had gotten shot. This was what had left the burn scars on the tree and lawn of his house. These were the men who were responsible.

That last bit rankled Alfred, and the anger flooded his veins, thinking that these idiots were responsible for him almost losing his wife. His hands slipped into his pockets, making him seem relaxed. His mind churned through all the little things that had been rustling their dark claws over his consciousness for the past couple of hours. The fact that when he had gotten into his old home, the place had been badly ransacked, all the furniture and appliances smashed. Alfred now understood what had driven the destruction; it wasn't people looking for hidden food or supplies, it was rage. It also explained the destruction of the master bedroom and the smashed wedding picture of him and Samantha. That's how Mushroom had recognized him.

Mushroom saw the look of understanding on Alfred's face, and his gruesome smile took on a hawkish and dangerous aspect. "They were supposed to hit the red, brick-faced house. They hadn't gotten shit from the old geezers. We knew that a family was living in that red house, so it was a good target. The morning of the raid they left and never came back. A few days later, when we went down to investigate we found their truck burnt out and their bodies in the old folk's yard, covered by crows. When we went to the red house, your house padre, we found it all boarded up, and there was a great big burn track in the yard. One of the trees was smashed and all burnt to hell. So we figured out what had happened. We also realized that it seemed we had just missed dealing out a little justice of our own. My people all wanted to burn it to the ground, but I said no, let's just get in and see if we can find anything out. We actually spent a few days in your house, and we also saw that picture of you and your old lady in your room. I made sure I took a really good look at that picture, padre. We found out that your name was Alfred and your wife was Samantha. I decided to stick around to see if you would come back. If someone came to live in the house then we would check them out. Imagine my shit-kicking surprise when you came stumbling into camp. Now call that what you will, fate, karma, justice, but now I have to set things right. My brother was my only kin and you killed him. Now I have to kill you. You see the great circular path that we are all on. The great karmic wheel."

"Why didn't you just kill him, I mean us, right then and there?" O'Riley asked. He had both Glocks still trained on the cannibal chief's men.

"I needed you alive, to make sure that this was what we really believed it to be. We have plans of our own, padre. With this in our camp, and with the Marathon Militia chasing those tree-nailers out of town, my people can begin building something here. Hell, if we can get us a pilot and a plane, we can use this ourselves. We can stop living in the woods and become real players."

Alfred smiled sadly, "So with all that you have been through, the personal terror of living through a nuclear attack, having to resort to cannibalism and losing people you cared about, none of that has made you more compassionate, more willing to work for peace. To build something that you can pass down, an inheritance of hope for future generations?"

Mushroom looked at Alfred, his expression one of pity. He shook his head and laughed. "Man's inheritance has always been one of pain and sorrow. I think we have the great ability to fool ourselves. We fool ourselves into believing we can be better than we really are. We fool ourselves into believing that we can have happiness, love, and respect for free, when all those things are taken by force and are all illusory too. So, no, that bomb opened my eyes." He shook his head. "When I found out that my brother was dead, I made a promise that if I ever caught the man who did it, I would take his life and my brother would finally have justice."

Alfred took his hands out of his pockets. In one hand, he had the grenade he had taken from the guard out back during the loading dock fight. It was such a natural movement that he actually managed to pull the pin out before Mushroom could react. He held it in his hand and smiled. Mushroom backed off, his good eye twitching, Alfred stepped to the side and quickly grabbed the barrel of the rifle. It went off as Mushroom pressed the trigger in a panic. He shoved the man into a wall and popped the grenade into the man's backpack. Mushroom cracked him on the head with the butt of his rifle, Alfie's world began to go grey as he scrambled away from the huge cannibal who was trying to get out of his backpack. Mushroom didn't make it. The grenade went off, ripping him to pieces.

O'Riley used the distraction to drop two of the cannis with bullets to the chest and head, respectively. The other one was hit by shrapnel from the grenade. He had been on the wrong side of Mushroom and wasn't shielded by the man's body. The canni collapsed on the floor, writhing in pain, until the priest's pistol coughed. A well-placed shot to the side of his head ended his suffering.

O'Riley saw Alfred trying to get up, but the man stumbled to his knees and vomited up a white liquidly mess. He ran over and grabbed him by the arm to steady him. Alfred took a few deep breaths, and after a few seconds the nausea passed.

"He hit you pretty hard, Alfred. You may be concussed. You are going to have to be very careful."

"Do you think the others, the ones he sent to keep an eye out front, heard the explosion?"

"Yeah, I think they would have heard it, and I think they will get curious and come to investigate."

"Okay, then let's get ready and take care of them as quickly as we can, load these canisters from hell onto a truck, and get out of here."

"I think we should just bushwhack them at the dock entrance," O'Riley said.

Alfred nodded, and the two of them quickly retraced their steps to the dock's door. They were not a minute too soon; they could hear the two men running on the gravelly path that lead up to the entrance. They waited on either side of the door, and as soon as the men popped their heads under the industrial electric roller door, Alfie and O'Riley shot them. The bodies fell back onto the gravel outside. Alfred caught his breath and looked at his watch. He couldn't believe how much time had passed since they first attacked the warehouse.

"It's been almost an hour, and we need even more time to get the bodies and sandbags away from the door, so we can get one of those trucks and load the canisters onto it. Damn, we are going to be here maybe another hour at least." His face knotted with worry. He knew they had to be in a very tight window, because he was sure that as soon as the Dove and his captains realized that they were under attack, they would send reinforcements to protect and maybe move their most precious asset. Both men got to work. It was really a four or five man job, but the two of them would have to do.

Chapter Thirteen

"Sooner or later everyone sits down to a banquet of consequences."
Robert Louis Stevenson

Before the Marathon attack on his city materialized, Splinter had been in bed again. After he had seen his mother, he had actually tried doing some work, but it was fruitless. He tried eating something at his desk but his appetite was gone. All the myriad responsibilities and decisions he made effortlessly now seemed like a huge burden. He looked at all the paperwork and eventually went to his bedroom, which was located in a suite behind his office. As far as he was concerned everything was under control. He could take a few hours to work out why he was suddenly in this malaise. It was late afternoon anyway, and he could do with a rest. He suddenly felt the need to lie down. He wasn't stupid, and he realized that his sudden depression was most likely caused from the shock of his mother returning from the dead.

He went into his bedroom, leaving his work and half eaten dinner on his desk. The room was dark and cool. As he undressed and got into bed the satphone's yellow light had been blinking, indicating that there was a message. It went unseen on the floor, next to his desk. A few hours later, he would check that message and scream in rage. It was Lambert, warning him of the attack.

He looked up into the darkness of the ceiling. Yesterday had been a good day. He had caught the would-be saboteurs and had the last two on the run. He should have been celebrating that. His mind went to his worthless mother in the room down the hall. He got up and paced around his room. Then he got back into bed again. How could she be here? How could she have survived the last eight months? His mother! His mousy, afraid of her own shadow, mother! She had been part of some infiltration team. He felt the laughter bubble up in his throat, and before he knew it, he was laughing hysterically. He laughed until tears rolled down his cheeks. He rolled over in his bed and buried his face in his pillow, and let the laughter rip. When he got himself under control, his mind began to tick over. Things must be pretty screwed up if the best they could send to sabotage his bio-weapons supply was his mother, a priest, and a bunch of people with no recognized military training. They really were a deluded bunch, those preppers and survivalists up there in Marathon. Still, they had killed eight of his men. His soldiers would be getting that traitor's cross ready about now. He was going to be nailed, and the crows and flies would eat his eyes.

"Yes, eat his eyes."

He sat up on the side of the bed. The laughter had left him drained. Damn, I guess if she could survive twenty years of cowering servitude to Richard Diefenbacher, she can survive anything. She was probably dead by now. That bullet in her side would have ripped her insides to shreds. He had not given her any medical help. She would bleed out internally and eventually die. It was an extremely painful way to go.

Should he go and help ease her suffering, maybe? No, there was no going back to that room to help. He knew that although his mother was scared of his father, she had despised her son. He could see it in her eyes every time she looked at him. He was a disappointment. He might not have been as physically strong as his father, but he made sure that he had become mentally tougher. He had from time to time captured little animals around their home and taken them to an abandoned building at the end of their street, where he tortured them. He would listen to their cries of pain, and he would make them scream more. He learned to turn off all the compassionate switches in his head until they no longer got in the way. With that came clarity. He learned to see the world without all the hindering emotional mumbo jumbo that others brought to it. He figured that his mother saw him as cold and detached.

As he ruminated over his past, he became more relaxed. He began to plan. His mother would be dead in the morning. He would get rid of the body, and his life would move on. He would then turn all his attention to Marathon. He would fast track his plans; it was time to get rid of that little problem up north. I'll get up in a few hours and work until morning, he thought, as he slowly slipped into sleep.

While he dozed, Samantha Aimes eased her stepfather's suffering on his cross, Alfred Aimes was about to attack a warehouse with two extremely dangerous canisters of weaponized Ebola virus. Harry Lambert was being worked on by his camp's surgeon, who was absolutely terrified of his patient dying on the table. The man was under no illusions that if he lost this particular patient, he would be dead as well. A young girl in England, alone in a bunker, was killing the rats that had gotten in while the hatch had been open. A man sat in a cell, dozing, holding the daughter that he had compromised all his principles to keep alive.

Splinter began to dream. He began to dream that his father was still alive. He was in a courtroom, but it looked remarkably like his parents' old house. His father sat at the head of the table, his mother beside him. Splinter's old man was blue in the face, and he had a huge distended bulge on one side of his throat. The old man was sitting at the end of the table, looking at them. He tried turning around but he couldn't move. He could sense that there were people watching the whole proceedings, but he couldn't turn to look at them.

"We are here to judge my worthless boy, William," his father said in a voice that came out as a harsh gagging croak. Bits of white and yellow swallowed food came up with the saliva that was ejected from his mouth. His mother sat there looking at him with her sad, deer-like eyes.

"You are just like your father," she said, pointing an accusing finger at him. All the things that made me hate him are in you, and worse. You believe you are someone special, and all you are is a monster."

There was noise like gunfire and thunder, and the house shook. "Are you afraid? I think you are afraid," his father croaked as more thunder shook the house. He tried to speak but he couldn't get his voice to work. His father always had that effect on him.

His mother pointed at him again and said, "You are not special, and I am horrified that I gave birth to you. I brought you into this world, you monster, tree-nailer." There was a knife in her hand and she was waving it around.

Then there was another loud boom, and more noise that sounded like gunfire, and he decided to escape the dream. When his room swam back into view, he rolled over on his left side. That roll saved his life.

A knife went into the pillow and mattress, where his head had been. A choked scream came up and died in his throat, as he scrambled over to the other side of the bed. His pistol was on the night table on the other side. His bare feet hit the cold wooden floor, and he spun around in the almost total darkness of his room to see who had attacked him.

There was the sound of more automatic gunfire somewhere outside, and more explosions. What the hell was going on! The would-be assassin moved slowly around the bed toward him. A thousand questions scrambled through his mind, but first he had to deal with the threat. He was about to call out for his guards when he saw his attacker for the first time.

"You are a monster, monster!" his mother hissed through clenched teeth. Her shirt and jeans were dark-colored in the gloom. Splinter knew that it was blood. She put her free hand on the bed as she moved slowly toward him.

"Put the knife down, Mother."

"When your father died, I hoped and prayed that you would blossom into the person I always thought you could be. Instead, you became this twisted thing."

"You and Father were responsible for the man I became. Don't try to put all the blame on me, Mother. You and Father made me the person I am."

"No, we all have free will, Monster! We can all choose the paths we walk upon, and you chose this."

"What exactly did I choose, Mother? I chose to leave my pointless life behind. I decided to be one of the few people who will leave a mark on history. You're right, I made a choice not to be weak, not to be like you, but to be strong and feared."

The woman stumbled toward him. She held the large heavy bladed knife in front of her, like a vampire hunter holding a cross. She was breathing in painful gasps, and she groaned and almost collapsed on the bed. It was all the chance he needed. He ran forward. She swung the knife upward and the blade cut deeply into his left arm. He rammed his body into her. She was knocked to the floor, the knife clattering across the floorboards, sounding to Splinter like shattered teeth. He landed on top of his mother, and he heard the woman gasp in pain. A rage came upon him as he sat on the woman's chest and punched her in the face. Her head knocked against the floor with a loud sick crack, and her hands fell harmlessly to her sides.

"You made me, Mother, you and Father made me in every way." His fists went flying. He punched her in the face, his fury growing with each swing. He felt a sharp pain in two of his right knuckles and cried out. Splinter backed off his mother and staggered around the room. It felt to him like his brain was in overload, and the room see-sawed as he fell to his knees, holding his hands and crying. When he got his breath back, he stumbled over to his mother and saw that her eyes were open, never to blink again. She was gone.

He got up as rapid gunfire erupted in the distance. He went into the bathroom and quickly washed the blood from his hands. He wrapped a towel around his still-bleeding arm. The Dove chose his white fatigues. He pulled on his pants and a white beret, which he thought gave him a martial air. He buckled his sword gingerly around his waist and shoved his glasses up his nose, looking himself over once more in the mirror. He slung his shirt over his shoulder. He would put it on after a medic took care of his arm. He figured he had dislocated the index and middle finger on his left hand as well. He looked at the body of his mother and shook his head. Thanks a lot, Mother, he thought bitterly. It was time to find out what the hell was happening in his city.

Clearing the first floor of the garage had gone easier than Samantha would have thought, but their luck ran out when they got to the second level. The bazooka squad that had been sent to shell the group controlling that level seemed to have never made it, because the enemy were hunkered down and ready for them. It was terrifying, hearing that .50 caliber machine gun up close, knowing that they were aiming it at her. She hit the deck and hid behind a concrete support. Julie was right next to her. Her head was down and her eyes were shiny. It was dark in the garage; the enemy wanted it that way, so the attackers tossed fuses, which lit up the scene in a bright red glow. She stuck her rifle out and sent a short bust the enemy's way. They were a bit lucky in the way the garage was built. It had these raised concrete walls that they could hide behind and return fire. There was also a part of the level above that had collapsed, leaving large chunks of concrete and metal on the garage's floor.

"Grenades on three. Toss 'em at the gun, and for God's sake keep your heads down."

Julie had a grenade. She pulled the pin and waited for the count. Samantha watched her friend as she did her job. On the count of three, Julie scrambled up, tossed her explosive, and ducked, as the roar of the .50 caliber made the garage sound like a dragon from hell was on the loose. Three of the tossers didn't make it as they were virtually cut in half. One of the brownshirts managed to grab a bomb and toss it back. It fell behind the assault group and exploded, killing two people.

The other grenades went off and prevented what would have been a lengthy and even more deadly gun battle. One of the explosives had actually detonated right in front of the .50 caliber's bunker. It didn't destroy the gun, but it caused enough havoc so that as Samantha rushed forward with a small group of attackers, it made the wounded gunner fumble as he tried to aim the weapon. Samantha wasn't having any of it, and her rifle cracked twice. The man fell over, dead. The close-quarter fighting was fierce as they closed on the enemy. They had to be careful not to shoot their own people. The Marathon soldiers had to be merciless because it was clear that these soldiers were not going to give up their position easily. Eventually the brownshirts were overrun. The soldiers swept the third floor and found there weren't many of the enemy alive there. Her kids had done a fine job. When they got to the roof, the defenders there were ready to surrender. They waved their arms. One of them had a white flag.

"Well, just look at that," the squad leader said. Samantha could see that he was grinning from ear to ear. They quickly zip-tied the seven men and two women. Samantha was about to ask the squad leader if they would now move on to the primary target across the street, when she suddenly felt a sharp ache in her stomach. It was so unexpected and painful, she let out a gasp, and then the throbbing went away. She wondered if it was just because she hadn't eaten in a while. She decided to have something the first chance she got. Her thoughts were just now turning to her children, still in the other building across the street, and she wondered if they were okay.

In the dying light of the fuses, she saw Julie turn sharply and walk over to one of the prisoners. He was sitting with his hands tied behind his back. She didn't like the tense look of her friend, and she followed along to see what the problem was. Julie walked slowly up to the man. There was a fuse glowing nearby, and she picked it up by the safe end and shone it in his face. The man backed away from the bright light. Samantha heard Julie gasp.

"Oh damn, oh damn!"

"Julie, is that you? Is that you?"

"Adam, Adam, how, what are you doing here? How are you alive?"

"Oh Jules, you know how it was. I, I just couldn't handle it anymore."

Adam, oh Adam, you are alive. My God, I thought you were dead. I thought someone, somewhere had killed you. I thought you were dead!"

"I'm sorry, Jules. Look, I just couldn't handle it anymore. I just couldn't look out for you and the kid anymore. It was just too much, too damn much."

"But you stockpiled all that stuff, you taught yourself the ham radio, you said you were ready, that we would get through it."

"It's one thing playing those games in your head, Jules. It's another thing living it. I guess when it came to the test, I just didn't have it. I didn't have it, Jules. I couldn't handle the responsibility of taking care of you and the kid like that. It was too much. Too much! It was one thing when we both had regular lives, and you pretty much did what you did and got through the day, and I would, too. There were hospitals, the internet, television, and the police, but when those things went away, when it all became real, and it wasn't just a hypothetical anymore, I couldn't handle it."

"You sonofabitch, you goddamn sonofabitch! So it got hard and you ran out on us. You left us alone in that house, and you went off by yourself, you sonofabitch! You left me and Nancy to fend for ourselves. I am your wife, you sonofabitch! I am your wife! I thought you had been killed! I cried over you. I thought you were a hero, that you went scavenging and you died trying to take care of us. I mourned and asked God to take your soul, and I hoped every day that you did not suffer."

"Mom." Samantha turned away from the drama. It was Robert, and she could see the concern in his face, even in the dim red light. She felt her chest tighten. Candice should have been with him. Her heart sped up in anticipation of the next words out of her son's mouth.

"Candice has been shot."

"Oh my God, oh my God. Is she, is she…"

"No, she's alive, but she's been shot pretty bad in the leg. I need you…" He didn't finish because the sound of automatic gunfire ripped through the night.

Julie emptied half a clip into the body of the man who had promised to love, honor, and protect her. She let out a primal yell of rage as the gun chattered, sending its load into the body of her husband. Two soldiers from the squad rushed forward, shocked by the sudden act of violence against a prisoner. She aimed her weapon at them and yelled, "Stay the hell away from me! Stay the hell away from me! That sonofabitch had it coming! He had it coming. God forgive me! God forgive me!" Then she sat on the ground and began to cry, long deep sobs raking her body.

"Oh shit, what the hell!" Robert was stunned.

"Don't swear, Robert. Let's go see to your sister."

She turned and walked away from her friend. The squad leader looked as she turned to walk away. "My daughter's shot. I'm going to help. Any problems with that?"

The man shook his head. He was looking on in bewilderment, trying to make some sense of the scene he had just witnessed. "If you can, just meet us by the building."

Samantha nodded, and she followed Robert out of the smoking, red-tinged garage. As she walked across the street, she heard gunfire inside the building Candice was in. Robert broke into a run, and she gasped again as the pain in her lower abdomen flared up. She clenched her jaw against the ache, and followed her son into the building where people were trying to kill her daughter.

It took the largest forklift, but Alfred and O'Riley finally got the two canisters loaded on to a flatbed truck. They had located four really large transport chains which they used to secure the canisters to the bed of the truck. The priest threw his backpack with the C-4 onto the seat and climbed in. Alfred backed out and drove carefully through the gate. O'Riley watched their cargo carefully, and saw the chains were holding.

"Okay, the mine is about half an hour's drive from here. Let's take our time and get there," O'Riley said.

"Let's hope we don't run into... Oh, damn." Alfred uttered a sigh as he looked in the side mirror. The headlights of a military-style lorry pulled in behind them. Just before they pulled onto the ramp to I81 North, a Jeep pulled in behind the lorry.

"Any suggestions?" Alfred asked.

"Not really. I say we just keep on driving ahead to the mine; when we pull in we can fight it out. You realize why they haven't attacked us?"

"Yeah, they don't want to damage the merchandise."

"Agreed, those two canisters are probably worth millions of dollars. Christ, I'm still thinking in the old way. Our money isn't worth anything anymore. Their value is in what they can do, the millions of people they can kill. Whoever gets hold of them has a lot of power. So it's really precious cargo. They won't risk anything damaging the canisters. I figure they'll just follow us until we stop."

"Yeah," Alfred said, his stomach in knots as he drove. He forced himself to think. "Yeah, we drive this sucker right into the mine and force them to come in after us, fight them in total darkness. It's our best shot. Then we wire the C-4 and blow the mine entrance first, then the truck, once we are outside."

"Sounds like a plan to me. Let's make sure we are ready." O'Riley took both his .45s out of their holsters and reloaded the magazines. He checked and reloaded his extra clips. When he was done, he still had twenty rounds left in a pouch in his backpack. The truck suddenly swerved, and Alfred looked like he was about to faint. The priest grabbed the wheel as Alfred regained control of himself. He began to dry retch and O'Riley was happy that the man didn't vomit in the cab.

"What the hell!" Alfred gasped.

"I think you are suffering a concussion from the blow you took to the head from Mushroom's rifle," O'Riley said, eyeing his friend with growing concern. Alfred got himself together, and the priest let go of the wheel. He realized that he had to keep an eye on him just in case.

"I think you might be right." The pain of his missing tooth went up a notch, and he popped another pill. He handed the priest his weapon, and O'Riley repeated his earlier task, checking and refilling Alfred's clip, as well as making sure that his friend had extra clips ready to go.

"I think if you are going to carry extra ammo, the best way to do it is in pouches," said O'Riley.

"I usually just carry preloaded clips. But I guess you might be right. I've seen some people carry the extra ammo in the boxes it was bought in. But in an emergency, I can see just opening a pouch and shaking out a few rounds better than fiddling with a box. Something to think about."

They drove the rest of the way in silence. Getting off I81 North, they drove into Whitney Point and made for the abandoned mine. The gate was open and Alfred rolled right on through. They went by a couple of buildings and some large abandoned pieces of machinery. It was almost total darkness, the moon hidden behind a thick cloud. Alfred slowed down. He was searching for the large entrance that went down into the mine. O'Riley happened to look through the glass window in the back of the cab and realized that two men were in the truck's bed. He could just make out their silhouettes in the dim moon light.

"Roll down your window, Alfred, and when I say 'firing now,' take your hands off the wheel and foot off the gas and cover your ears. Alfred understood what the priest was about to do. He slowed the truck down to a crawl.

"Firing now." Through the fiberglass, O'Riley aimed one of his pistols at one of the men and fired. The man crumpled forward. The other man lifted his rifle and managed to get off a couple of rounds. The bullets punched through the steel shell of the cab and left holes in the windshield. O'Riley took aim and fired carefully, two bullets taking the man in the chest as he fell off the side of the flatbed. The back wheels of the truck rolled over him. The vehicle jumped as it crushed the man's body to a bloody pulp.

Alfred gave the truck a little more gas, his ears ringing from the shots that were fired in the cab. Up ahead, he spotted the opening to the mine and drove the truck straight for it. "Look, I'll go all the way down to the end of the tunnel, then I'll kill the lights and we go out and deal with the assholes."

The priest nodded, his own ears ringing from the two shots he had fired in the cab. Alfred drove the truck straight into the man-made cave. A din of gunfire erupted from behind the vehicle. O'Riley couldn't see anything through the shot-out window in the back of the cab. He was very uncomfortable with the cargo they were hauling, and now that there were bullets flying, it made him catch his breath and involuntarily duck. They drove the truck all the way into the tunnel, until they got to a fork that led to two smaller passages. It was the end of the line.

Alfred killed the lights, got out of the cab, and felt his way to the truck's right rear wheel. He heard the priest somewhere up ahead. He was sure that the man must have taken cover behind a large piece of old machinery they had gone by, then total silence. The tunnel was cold as a chill wind blew in through the main entrance. He began to wonder what had happened outside the mine, why were they shooting at each other. Then he heard it, the stealthy sound of people who did not want to reveal their location, coming into the tunnel. Suddenly there were two flashes and a couple of loud deafening bangs. The men had lobbed a couple of flash bang grenades. His eyes became even more useless as the white flash imprinted itself on his retina. He knew that it would be a few seconds before it would go away. He couldn't help thinking that maybe the thing about fighting in the dark, or near total darkness, was just to close his eyes so that if they did this to him, his eyes weren't rendered totally useless.

There was a pop and an exchange of heavy gunfire. Alfred crawled back into the truck. He switched on the engine and killed the lights, then he put it in reverse and gunned it. The vehicle careened backwards, smashing through the squad of attackers. He felt several bumps as the truck went over bodies, smashing and breaking bones. When he judged he was far enough, he switched on the lights and ducked. There was the now-familiar dull, popping sound of O'Riley's Glocks, as well as a short burst of automatic gunfire. He could hear O'Riley's Glocks answer, one short gasping scream, then another pop, and silence. The only sound was the truck idling. He carefully raised his head and heard O'Riley calling his name. Alfred sat upright and saw the priest waving him forward. He put the truck in drive and eased back to the flat spot before the forks. Killing the engine, he left the lights on. He noticed O'Riley going through two large canvas sacks that were stashed just inside one of the smaller tunnels. He reached inside one and held up a small electronic device.

"Detonators." I will have to wire the canisters and the tunnel entrance. Good old Jasper, I swear the man always has a rabbit up his sleeve. He gave us C-4 and detonators, but he made sure that he stashed some away here, just in case." The priest shook his head, and Alfred had to admit that the leader of the Marathon Militia was always thinking two steps ahead.

"What do you think that was all about? Who were those men, and why did they kill the Dove's men?" Alfred mused. He shone his flashlight at the bodies, and noticed that the men they had just killed were wearing all black camo. "What does it all mean? Look, O'Riley, those weren't brownshirts. Who did they represent?"

"I don't know Alfred, but we got a job to do."

"You're right. Let's get on it."

They worked for an hour, carefully wiring the canisters, then the tunnel entrance. They ran the wires to a mound about two hundred feet outside the entrance. They took cover, and Alfred flicked the first switch. The explosion took down the tunnel entrance. It was an impressively powerful blast that collapsed the tunnel walls. There were a couple of dull yellow flashes and then a low rumble that shook the earth, as tons of rock and dirt fell in on itself. He then flicked the other switch, and he was sure he heard a secondary rumble deep inside the tunnel. The plan had been to blow up the tunnel entrance first to seal in the deadly biological agents, then destroy the canisters themselves.

Alfred sat down and leaned against the large gravel mound. He dropped the detonator triggers and looked up into the cloudy night sky. There was that bout of nausea again, and he realized that he must indeed be concussed. He felt like he could lie on his back and look up into that dark sky forever. He was so tired. He heard the priest talking to him, but he tuned him out. He wondered what was going on with his wife, how they were doing back in Marathon. Rest, yes, just rest awhile, and in a little bit we will take one of the vehicles and drive back to Marathon. Oh, Samantha, I need to see you. I love you. The world swam away from Alfred Aimes as he passed out.

Candice wanted to scream. She couldn't believe that anything could hurt so much. She groaned and turned on her side. She reached into her backpack and took out her flashlight to shine on her leg. She shook her head and lay back with a despairing grunt. It looked really bad. Robert had done a good job of tying the leg off, but the cloth he had wrapped around it was soaked through with blood. She leaned back and looked up at the dark ceiling. For the first time, the fact that she could actually die crystalized itself in her mind, and she felt her insides turn to water. She was afraid. She felt tears stinging her eyes. It just didn't seem fair. She was going to be fourteen this year. Last year this time, the big thing was playing soccer for her middle school and going to the mall with her friends. She had been into her music, and her cell phone had been the center of her life. Now here she was a year later, having to shoot people who were trying to kill her and her family. It all seemed too crazy. How could things change so fast? She wondered if any of her friends were still alive. There was the sound of automatic gunfire and explosions coming from the garage next door. It sounded like a serious fire fight, and she hoped her mom and Robert were okay.

Her leg really began to hurt. It was a weird pain, deep and throbbing. She hoped that Robert would be back with her mom soon. She hoped that her mother could so something, and that she wouldn't die or worse, lose her leg. That thought made her want to cry. It would be awful to have to lose her leg. A loud bang downstairs interrupted her thoughts. There were people moving about down there. It wasn't Robert, she was sure of it, because he wouldn't make so much noise.

She wondered if it was a Marathon squad checking out the building, but she doubted that, too, so she took her little flashlight and quickly did a scan of the room.

It had been a very small office. Robert had moved the photocopier from the wall so he could hide her behind it. In the far corner was a steel computer desk with a chair, there was an Apple desktop computer still on it. Well, there was only one thing to do. She placed the flashlight in her mouth and stood up on her good leg. She shoved all her weight against the photocopier and shoved it up against the door. She then took the computer off the table as quietly as she could she could. But as she bent awkwardly to put it on the floor, her leg banged into the small steel chair and she cried out. She hit the chair exactly where she had been shot. It was so sudden and jarringly painful that she could not stop her cry. For a second the world turned red, and the pain, jagged and merciless, made her curl into a fetal position and bite down hard on the flashlight. She wouldn't scream again.

Candice felt hot, and she took deep breaths, trying to ride out the pain. She heard them coming up the stairs to her floor and figured they must have heard her. She quickly hopped up on one leg and turning the desk over on its side, shoved it against the backside of the photocopying machine. She then got down on her belly, pulled the 9mm, and waited. They were moving around outside, checking the floor out. The footsteps stopped in front of the door. She heard them try the lock and push against the door. The photocopier was heavy, and so the door didn't move much.

"I heard someone."

"Yeah, me too."

"I bet you they are in there."

"Listen, whoever you are, you need to give yourself up. We know you are in there and there is no escape. You need to move the junk away from the door. We promise we won't hurt you."

Candice didn't answer. She scrunched down as much as possible behind the desk. She tried to see if she could tell how many were actually out there. There were two distinct voices, but she also sensed that there was a third. She was not going to give them any information, so she remained quiet. Her silence seemed to enrage the people outside the door. There was more chattering of automatic gunfire across the street.

"We got to get this done, man. We have to clear this building, then meet the rest of the company and counter-attack the garage."

"Look, we're giving you to the count of three to come out, or else we are going to start shooting our way in. We order you, in the name of the Dove, to come out with your hands above your head."

They started to count, and she made herself as small as possible. Then they opened up with their M16 rifles. The roar of the bullets was deafening. They came through the door and smashed into the photocopier. The shooting stopped, and the voice on the other side of the door called out. "Are you still there?" he chuckled. She lifted her head but couldn't see much in the dark. The photocopier looked beat to hell; that much she could make out. She figured that the door and part of the wall was probably shredded. She holstered the 9mm and brought up her own rifle. Aiming for the voice, she sent a short burst at the door and to the side where she thought they might be. She figured that they might not have taken cover. Her short burst was answered by return fire, but it seemed she had done some damage, given the scrambling and sounds of distress on the other side of the wall. This was confirmed when someone shouted, "They shot Croust. Damn, he's dead, man." She didn't wait for them to start firing at her again. She opened fire, another short, controlled burst. She heard swearing and more scrambling on the other side of the wall.

"You in there, you're dead, you hear... dead."

In the dark she scrambled and found her backpack. She wanted it close. She had an extra clip in one of the external pockets and would need it soon. She kept her head down and suppressed a gasp. Her leg felt like someone had jabbed needles into her raw flesh. She beat her hand on the floor, grabbing at the filthy carpet. Just then the Dove's soldiers opened up on her again. She could hear the bullets rip into the photocopier, and she heard them slam against the steel table. It seemed like it went on forever. The soldiers emptied their clips into the door and wall. It all seemed a horrible, surreal nightmare to Candice, as she laid flat in the dark. She began to cry as the pain, hot and deep, made her want to scream. She tried to get up but she found that she could hardly move. She reached down to feel for the cloth on her leg and realized that it wasn't there. A feeling of horror overcame her as she understood that Robert's tourniquet must have fallen off. She didn't dare use her flashlight, but she understood she must be bleeding out. She knew about blood loss and realized that the weakness she was feeling was probably a sign that she was dying. Her heart must have been pumping her life's blood out onto the floor while she had been returning fire. She tried lifting her arms but they were as heavy as lead. She heard the soldiers in the passageway reloading. It suddenly didn't matter to her; she would be dead soon anyway. Living in this messed up world was so hard, it was good to just let go. Then suddenly there was a volley of gunfire outside the door. There was return fire and a lot of screaming, all the intense sounds of a life and death struggle unfolded beyond the door.

There was a familiar voice and she heard the photocopier being pushed out of the way. She tried lifting her hand again but it was just too heavy. The voice was her brother. She couldn't see him, although he had a flashlight in his teeth as he moved her away from the overturned table. She felt another pair of hands on her thigh. She knew those hands; they were her mother's. She heard a curse and knew her mom didn't like what she had found. It was weird the way her consciousness worked. She just couldn't hold on to anything. She heard another loud curse, and then she felt a pain that made her scream. It felt like someone had reached into the wound and was poking around. The pain was just too much and before passing out Candice felt regret. She would have liked telling her mom and brother how much she loved them. She didn't think she was going to make it.

Splinter's left arm ached. His medic had just managed to staunch the bleeding. His mother had really done a number on it. She had cut through his forearm all the way to the ulna. He was lucky that the blade had missed his arteries. He was still bleeding like a stuck pig, and it hurt.

He forced himself to sit still on his desk and watched in irritation as the medic worked on him. He had his shirt off but his undershirt was on. His round glasses slipped down his nose, and he subconsciously pushed them back up. The medic had cleaned the injury and was now closing it with some sort of glue. He wrapped the wound in a bandage.

"That's the best I can do, my Lord."

"It's fine, fine," he said as his mind ticked over. He had taken over twenty emergency radio calls from captains all over the city. They were under attack, and they were losing. He never anticipated that the Marathon Militia would do anything so daring. He had the city, and now he was on the verge of losing it. Had lost it! It seemed impossible. All the key areas had been overrun, and they were making a beeline for his headquarters, fast. His jaw flexed as he ground his teeth. They must have had excellent intel.

After his mother attacked him, he had walked back into his office. He had his white shirt in his hand, and he hung it up on a hook on a hat rack that was by the door. He had immediately sent for the medic, and while he was waiting for the man to show up, he cleared his desk and saw the satphone's light blinking. Groaning internally, Splinter opened the case and dialed his message box. There was only one. It was Lambert, warning him that an attack was imminent. He heard the message time and groaned again. If he had been working, instead of resting, he could have probably gotten the situation under control, but it was too late for that now. He did, however, radio in to all his captains, and after getting a clear idea of what was occurring, he decided to evacuate. He would fall back to Orange County. He could take stock in Middletown and figure out where to go from there. He told his captains to burn any documents of value, and he had ordered the evacuation of his headquarters. They had two modified school buses out back where they were packing all the important documents and supplies required for him to transfer his base of operations. He could hear the bustle of activity in the building. He was also tying up loose ends. The man, Jim Meehan, that he had detained in a cell, he gave the order to gas him and the child, as well as all the other detainees in the building. He did a quick mental calculation. There were ten people he had locked up for differing reasons.

He made the decision to kill Meehan because the man was not loyal to him. He was loyal to his child. That's why he had been able to use him to spy, root out, and betray the infiltration group. But now the man had outlived his usefulness. It was a mercy having him get a few hours with his daughter and them dying together. It was the best possible outcome for the both of them.

He had ordered his captains to fight a strategic withdrawal. That was, to hold certain strong holds as long as possible, then withdraw. The goal was to have most of his Binghamton battalion intact so they could regroup at Middletown. He had over sixty thousand personnel in the besieged city, and he intended to save most of that force so he could one day come and take back his territory. His personal armored SUV was downstairs. He would be escorted by a small force along the way back to Middletown.

He had sent a squad of some of his best people to go out to the warehouse and get the Bilderberg's canisters, with the plan to rejoin the retreating force on the road. Those canisters were supremely important. He had every intention of retrofitting a small plane and flying at night, spraying and infecting the Marathon Settlement. All the scientists and mathematician eggheads working for him had assured him that in doing so, he would surely kill at least ninety-nine percent of the group. Infecting that settlement was the best shot at making sure that they got the best bang for their buck. And for the people who would flee the dying town, they would carry the disease into every single group or settlement that killed or took them in. Their bodies would infect all the larger animals, and those animals would also carry the disease into other areas. In less than forty days, the pathogens released from the canisters would have killed over one hundred thousand people, and it would keep killing for a very long time. Eventually the entire north and central area of New York would be empty of everyone except his and Lambert's vaccinated personnel, and those naturally immune. He would have contaminated his sector, which would complete the *seeding* of the entire north eastern seaboard of the North American continent.

He put his shirt on and straightened his beret. His soldiers came in and under his direction, he told them what to take and what to leave behind. They packed away the array of long-range walkies and the satphone. He also told them to booby trap the rooms. He smiled at that, knowing that he could take some of those interlopers out in the process. Always hurt your enemy when you can, he thought grimly. There was even gunfire in the other building across the street now, and his mind raced because he never figured they could have fought their way into the heart of the city that quickly. Then he realized by the shouting going back and forth that the building wasn't under attack. His soldiers here had gotten word that a prisoner had escaped. He shook his head at that, because it reminded him of something he had to do himself, a little loose end before going.

Sitting on the edge of the desk, he grabbed the only radio left and called his personal body guards into the room. The two men came in. They were expecting the call because it was time for them to evacuate the building. Splinter settled back. This had to be done, this cleaning house. He drew his sword.

"Four months ago in Middletown, you allowed those child-eating, smelly dogs to almost kill me. They had somehow managed to sneak a weapon into my office. You allowed that to happen. There have been other lapses, but today was the last straw. You allowed an old lady to sneak out of her room, grab a kitchen knife from my desk, and attack me in my own room. I could have been killed."

The two men looked at each other, then back at their boss, a look of nervous consternation on their faces. Then one of the men slouched and looked hard at his chief. They had spent a lot of time around the man; they knew that he was dangerous, and they knew not to underestimate him. But he was small; he had the look of a nerdy professor rather than the brawn of a hard man. He always commanded from a position of strength. Now here he was alone with two men packing rifles, men who were ex-army in another lifetime. He sat there holding his sword while his world, as far as they saw it, was crumbling.

"Are you saying you have a problem with us?"

"I am saying that as of today I am terminating your services."

"You are just one man. There is no one here to help you if we decide to take you out right here, right now…" The man stopped in mid-sentence, a look of surprise on his face; somehow Splinter had shoved his sword into his chest. As he crumpled toward his killer, the other guard lifted his rifle and fired a racking burst. The little man in the glasses used the body as cover, pulled his own Luger, and shot him twice in the side as he tried to run through the door. The man fell to the floor, grunting in pain. As he turned around to bring his rifle up, Splinter kicked it out of his hand. Then he took the sword and drove it into the man's neck, almost severing the head from the body. The man choked, convulsed, then died.

Splinter wiped his sword clean on the corpse, and looking around the room one last time, he decided that those rebels would not have this place. He ran down the hall to a storage closet. There was a small can of gasoline. Grabbing it, he went back to his office and poured it over his desk, then made a trail that went back into the room he had been using as a bedroom. He poured the last of the liquid over his mother, took a match and lit it. This was good, he thought. It was cleansing. This was a clean break, one from which he would retrench and build on. He dropped the match. The flame bloomed as he walked out of the room.

As he went down the corridor he saw three other men who were part of the headquarters guard detail. They immediately took up an escorting detail around him, and without question or hesitation they guided him out of the building toward the car at the side of the building. An enormous racket was going on in front of the building. There was heavy gunfire and a few explosions that sounded like grenades going off. His mind ticked over. He was about to get into the vehicle when someone stumbled out of the darkness behind the car. The man held a gun, and Splinter could see by the moonlight that he had been shot in the stomach. His guards trained their weapons on the man and were about to kill him when he stopped them.

"No!" he had recognized the man. It was Jim Meehan. There was a small sound of terror behind Jim; it was his daughter. "You kill me, and my guards will kill you and your daughter. What is it going to be?"

The man's hand trembled. Splinter smiled and got into the vehicle. The guards followed suit and they drove away around the other side of the building, away from the fire fight on the other side of the street. As the car sped away through the night, he decided that he would make these men his personal body guards from now on. He also realized that he had lost a major objective tonight, and it may cause the king makers in Europe to doubt his abilities. If he had someone in his organization that had lost a major piece of territory and an invaluable weapon, he would have had the bastard crucified. So he knew he had to watch his back. His SUV caught up with the rest of the retreating army making their way out of the city, a long motorcade of heavily armored vehicles. Yes, they would probably want to kill him and replace him. He would have to show them that he was the only qualified candidate for the job.

Chapter Fourteen

"In all things it is better to hope than to despair." Johann Wolfgang Goethe

The Bunker-England

Journal Entry 148

Something interesting has happened. Where to begin. Well, there are rats in the bunker. I remember Dad had killed a lot of them months ago. These must have gotten in when I had the hatch open, or maybe Dad hadn't gotten all of them. I don't understand how they can hide in here. It's a sealed metal structure. I woke up two nights ago hearing squeaking noises. I almost freaked out. I hate little hairy animals. I hate rats, period. I got up and switched on the main bunker lights. The three overhead LEDs light up the place really well, and I walked through the entire bunker, thinking that maybe I was just hearing things. It's tough being down here all by myself, with just the ham radio for company. I talk to myself all the time now. Maybe I am losing my mind.

I didn't see or hear anything, so I went back to bed, but this time I took a torch with me. I laid down for a few minutes and what do you know, the squeaking started up again. So I shone the torch in the direction of the pantry and on the fourth shelf there they were about four of them, with their shiny eyes and twitching noses. I had made some bread and they were into it. I couldn't believe that I had missed them the first time. I just laid there. I didn't really know what to do. Then I figured if I got up and got Dad's hammer from the tool box, I would be able to track the little shits down and bash their brains in.

The thing about it too, was that after I got up and went to the tool box, they must have been watching me all the time, and they didn't move. They just sat there on the shelf looking at me, brave little tossers. So I shone the torch in their eyes and when I got close enough, I swung the hammer and clipped one on the side of the head. The others ran. The little tosser didn't die immediately; he just twitched around on the shelf. I used the hammer's claw to drag him then I aimed and bashed his head in.

I had seen where the others had ran behind the big bags of rice. Dad had packed maybe twelve huge bags of rice up against the corner of the pantry section of the bunker. I began to move the bags, and by the time I had got to the last four, I saw them. They were living in a small nest in one of the bags, and as I looked at it I realized that they had used hair they had picked up from around the bunker.

I acted quickly and got two more. The last one ran by me. The little creep actually ran over my leg and went into the bathroom. I pulled the curtain that was supposed to give us privacy, and there it was hiding behind the toilet. It had wedged itself in the farthest corner and was looking at me in a real sad way. It didn't matter to me, I just gritted my teeth and smashed his body in with the hammer. I sat on the floor and caught my breath for a second. Then out of the blue, I got the fright of my life. A loud knock went through the bunker.

It sounded like someone was at the front door of our old house, and using the knocker, but instead of rap, rap, rap, it was boong, boong, boong. It was deep, it was loud, and it scared me shitless. I went to the periscope and carefully took a look around. Didn't see anything at first, but then I saw two women, hitting the handle of the hatch with a large rock. I think I almost passed out, I got so frightened. How the hell did they find the bunker? Dad had hidden it away so well in the woods. Then the answer came to me. It was so clear. When I had buried Dad and Bea, I had made crosses and placed them on the graves. I think these people probably saw the crosses and then saw the hatch.

I had a problem then. What should I do? Should I just stay quiet and hope they go away? Or go up and ask who they are? Should I go up and kill them? I looked at all the options. If I let them go on banging, they could attract other attention to my bunker, and they could damage the lock with the rock. I could invite them in and have some company, but I could see that going badly because they were older than me, and would want to take charge of everything. They could also just kill me and take over the bunker. They could go and tell a larger group about the bunker and they would probably try to get in. I paced up and down the floor as they banged that rock against the latch. I was horrified when Dad killed those two people, but now I could understand why he did it. You just could not trust anyone. This is a horrible way to live. After a while I calmed down. I sat down and thought it through. It didn't matter to me that they were two women instead of two men, they were still dangerous.

I imagined that living in the dangerous world above, the people would lose most, if not all, of their morals. It was all about survival. This was now about my survival. There was no Dad and Mummy around to protect me anymore. I had to take care of myself. I guess it was just that simple. The people above were a threat, so I had to neutralize the threat. I shook my head at the fact that they must have found the graves almost at the same time I found the rats. They must have been close and heard me banging below. I imagined just how curious they must have been, and hopeful. It all didn't matter to me anymore. I pulled on my jeans, tied my hair in a bun, got Dad's shovel, shoved a long-bladed knife into my belt, and climbed up the ladder. They were banging on the hatch door relentlessly. I knew how I would play it. I would be the frightened young girl who had just lost her family then I would just go at them. My heart was beating really hard in my chest.

I unlatched the door and swung it open. I went up the ladder and stepped out into a clear twilight sky. They backed off and looked at me. Two women, one was older, maybe in her fifties. The other woman was maybe in her late thirties. Her hair had a lot of gray in it, but not as much as the other woman. That's the thing with the end of the world, no one has any time to dye their hair anymore, I guess. They both had aluminum baseball bats and knives.

"Oh, thank goodness. I am so happy that it is two women and not men."

"How many are there below?" the younger woman asked.

I decided to ditch my first idea on the spot, I didn't want them to believe that I was alone. "There are three of us below," I lied. "Two other women and myself. We have been helping each other. Listen we can help you as well. They relaxed, and the older one actually sat down in the dirt beside the hatch door and began to cry.

She wiped her eyes and said, "It's so nice to find someone who is actually decent. We've been on the road alone for four days now, since our husbands died. I can't believe how bad it all went, and how quickly it all just dissolved. How could England fall apart so easily? I mean we have all this history, for god sakes. We survived the Saxons, the War of the Roses, the Black Death. We fought the Nazis and won. So how could it fall apart so quickly? We had a strong government and military. But none of that mattered when they couldn't feed the people fast enough. Weeks without food, and no government can stand. Oh, yes, I remember being hungry. I remember how terrifying that was, starving is worse than just dying. You'll do anything for food, anything. Everything just broke apart. We fought for everything. We either had to fight people or join them to fight others. Meanwhile, you hope that everything will get better but it just got worse and worse. And then the sickness, God I never saw so much flu and pestilence. It seemed like the Four Horsemen of the Apocalypse were set loose. I don't know how we never fell ill, but everyone in our first and second group eventually got sick from something and died.

"We listened to all the bulletins on the radio, until they stopped. My husband always said that when the Western and Asian powers collapsed, the religious fanatics in the Middle East thought that they were being rewarded, for the forty year jihad they had fought against the west. They thought it was all God's plan, and for a couple of months, they went around killing all the people whose faith were different from theirs. They even killed those of their own, who they thought were heretics. Then like everyone else they all just began to die. Sick men cannot fight, and soon there were not enough left to wage war. The world is now empty. So much death. Everywhere we go, we cannot escape the smell. The smell of human putrefaction and decay. In America and Russia I heard they are just as bad off. Everyone thought that they would try to annihilate each other, but it never happened. What would be the point? Mutually assured destruction. So the missiles never flew, and we all just died slowly and painfully." She looked at me, then the other woman. "I am so tired of all the killing. We can help each other. I can tell by your body language that you are thinking of trying to kill us."

I think I must have gasped because I had been gearing myself up to swing at the younger woman with the shovel. I guess to people who had been out there in the world, surviving and fighting every day, I must have seemed pretty transparent. Was I about to make a colossal mistake? I could just change my mind and tell them to go, but I understood that wouldn't work. They would either try to kill me themselves to get at the safety and stores below, or they would find others and eventually they would bring them back to the bunker. The bunker was pretty secure, but I wasn't stupid enough to think that it was impregnable.

I could go through with my original plan and try to kill them, but I was sensing that I had lost my moment. It's easier to kill people when you don't really have to think about it too much. It's harder to do when you have some kind of human contact with them. I guess a real survivor would have buried her feelings deep, pitied them, but swung the shovel anyway, caving in the younger woman's skull, but I found that I couldn't do it. I don't understand why I couldn't do it.

"What're your names?" I asked.

"My name is Louise and this is Joyce," the younger woman said.

"My name is Catherine," I said. "Are you alone? Does anyone know you are here?"

"No one knows we are here. The world is a very dangerous place for men, but it is a very hell for women. We've heard now since the Prince was defeated that people are being rounded up and used as slaves or soldiers. We were looking for a place to kill ourselves." She looked at Joyce and smiled wearily. "That's why we were in this part of the woods. We just happened to stumble on the graves, and then Joyce saw the door to your hatch. I wouldn't have known what it was, but she did. There are not a lot of bunkers around England. As far as I was concerned, that kind of crazy survivalist bollocks only goes on in the United States. Then we heard the banging, and we really began to wonder what was going on. We decided to take a chance. We got that rock and began to bang on the lock. We are actually at the point where we believe that our lives aren't that important anymore."

"What happened to your husbands?" I asked.

"Lloyd, Joyce's husband, was killed fighting for the Prince. The Prince won the battle at Falkirk but he was defeated by this Count Archibald at Bosham. The rest of the Royal family is in hiding, God help them. A lot of people died at Bosham, but it wasn't all from the fighting. As a matter of fact, people began to get sick and die before any of the real fighting began. I think some of the medics were saying that it resembled Ebola, but they couldn't be sure. It went through the army like a wildfire. When Archibald finally showed up to fight, the Princes' army was in no shape to contest the battle. We had just beaten them a few weeks before at Falkirk, and it seemed an unbelievable turn in fortune. They came through and took the town. They captured the Prince and dragged him out in front of the Holy Trinity Church and cut his head off."

I shook my head. I had heard a lot of this on the ham. That horrible woman with the nasally voice kept repeating that the English were beaten and were now subjects. "I heard all about it," I said.

"Well, Lloyd was killed trying to protect the Prince. Shot through the chest. We snuck in and found him in a pile of bodies near the Manor. We couldn't even give him a proper burial. We had to leave him there," Louise said.

"They didn't bury the bodies of the dead; they just left them there. I think it was done intentionally, to spread even more disease. But to think of my Lloyd being eaten by dogs and crows, it made me want to throw myself into the sea. I can't remember the next few days clearly, but Louise and her husband, Hugh, cared for me, keeping us hidden and scavenging for food, until he got sick. A few days later he was dead. Bleeding from the eyes and skin. We buried him and we thought that we would have gotten sick, but so far we have been spared," Joyce said, wiping her eyes with the back of her hand.

"We kept moving, trying to stay ahead of Archibald's troops, then we decided to end it here. We can't run anymore. There is nothing left but a lot of suffering and pain," Louise said.

"What's the worst thing you have had to do?" I asked.

"We have had to kill people to get food. In the old days, right after everything went to shit. I am not proud of it, but I killed a man who had a couple pillow cases of food. I figure that's why God punished us by killing our husbands, especially making sure that mine couldn't be buried. That his body would be eaten by animals," Joyce said.

"How do you feel about the killing you have done?" I asked.

"I, and I know that Joyce will back me up on this, I have carried those killings around with me. I think about them all the time, I know I will pay for them, if not here, then in the afterlife," said Louise.

I looked at the two tired dirty women in the dying light of the evening, and I realized that I didn't really want to kill anyone as well. I made a decision that I know my father would not have approved of. My dad would have killed these women already. I am not my dad. I chose life. So I said, "Okay, you can stay with me, but understand that this is my bunker, my rules."

"Now that you are here, I don't know if I want to go below with you," Joyce said. "I came here to put an end to my life. To end this nightmare. I don't even understand why I would want to prolong this anymore."

"Listen, why don't you come below and if you feel like you still have nothing to live for in a couple days, you can go above, make your peace and end it," I said.

Louise went over and placed a hand around her shoulders. "She's right."

"I also want to say that there is no one below, only me."

They nodded. I went down first, hauling all my weapons back down, then they followed. I locked us back in and showed them around my small home, which would now become theirs as well. Joyce sat down on the floor and she began to cry. She looked at the pile of rats and said, "There was a time I would have done almost anything for a couple of rats." Louise held her and nodded her head in acknowledgement. I told them that we were not that bad off yet.

The rats I would get rid of later, and I would also get rid of the crosses on the graves. They had attracted the attention of these women and they might attract others. It's late now, a lot has happened today. I think it has been a good day, in a bizarre way. It's a good day because I didn't have to kill anyone, and no one was trying to kill me. I will keep writing in this journal. I understand why my dad spent so much time recording our ordeal. I hope that everything works out here. Til next time.

Candice had stopped bleeding again, but Samantha knew that her daughter needed a transfusion. That wasn't a problem really, as she was also B positive. The problem was that she needed to find the right medical supplies, and she had to do so quickly. Robert was carrying her, and although Candice was upright and hopping weakly on one leg, she was practically semi-conscious. They got to the side walk outside the building just in time to see the lights of a small convoy of armored SUV's roll away on the other side. More ominously, the headlights of two trucks turned onto their side of the street. The Dove's men piled out, and while the first group ran for the garage, the second group took up positions behind three large cement pots that in the past were used to grow a variety of beautiful flowers.

Samantha grounded her teeth. This was the last thing she needed now. She and Robert ducked back into the building just as the shooting started again in the garage. The full moon was now high in the sky, and it was easier to see what was going on than earlier, when it was practically dark. "Robert, you think you could go up on the roof again and see if you can pick off a few? Make sure they can't see your muzzle flashes."

Robert nodded and left. Samantha waited with Candice, who was resting against a wall just inside a closet. She made sure her daughter was okay and went to crouch down at the window, to see what was going on across the street. She could clearly see two of the men from her vantage point, but she didn't want to tip her hand or let this become some kind of protracted gunfight. There was a single pop from above, and she saw one of the men keel over. She hoped that Robert had figured out how to make himself invisible. There was another pop, and another man went down, then in quick succession another and another. She saw the men lay flat on the ground, trying to make themselves as small a target as possible. She could hear them shouting at each other and gesticulating wildly. It was obvious that they were trying to figure out who was shooting at them, but they couldn't figure out exactly where the sniper was. Samantha smiled grimly. She knew that Robert was a very good shot, and she found herself urging her son on to kill as many of the men who stood between her and getting Candice some help. Her attention was caught by the blossoming fire that began to light up the interior of the third floor of the City Hall. The flames illuminated the entire square. Then an explosion went off in the building. It was hard to determine where.

Samantha saw something that made her heart skip a beat. There was a tremendous thunder clap of .50 caliber machine gunfire coming from the second floor of the garage. It raked the men's position, smashing the cement pots and kicking up a lot of dust. She figured that this little development meant that the squad that had gone inside had been neutralized. Incredibly, there were still a few men left alive, and they made what could only be described as a suicidal break for cover to the other side of the building. Two of them had the lower half of their bodies shredded by the .50 caliber bullets. The survivor lunged for the side of the building and made it, just as another short burst kicked up the dust and ripped out a part of the building's wall. There was a small interval of silence and then there were three quick shots. From around the corner, a man stumbled out into the fiery hellish light of the raging inferno of the building.

His face made Samantha's throat go dry, and a rage which made it hard to breathe rammed through her veins. Jim Meehan emerged from the side of the building, and he was waving his hands over his head. He was shouting something that Samantha couldn't hear. Then he fell down and rolled unto his back. He got up and made it to his knees, and looking at the garage, he waved his arms like he was beckoning for help. The man fell on his side. Samantha could see his face clearly in the flickering light. He was screaming, and his eyes seemed insane.

There was another explosion, and glass and debris from the building rained down around the prostrate screaming man. Two men from the garage very warily made their way over to him. That's when Samantha left the window. A part of her wanted to question Meehan about her husband, but she went back to check on Candice. Her daughter was breathing unevenly, and in the light of the flashlight she looked really pale. Robert rejoined her, and once again he lifted his sister to her feet. She moaned and cried out in pain. Samantha felt like screaming herself. They went outside the building again and crossed the street. There was now a group of people around Meehan. He was waving his arms and gesticulating wildly.

Samantha walked over and immediately took the opportunity to speak to her squad leader. "I'm a nurse. I think I should set up a med station."

"Well, we can't set it up here. We need to get out of here. This building's gonna burn and there is nothing we can do to stop it. It might even take a few of the other buildings along with it." There was another bang, which made them all jump.

"I think someone either left some explosives behind, or someone booby trapped the place and now the fire is causing the explosives to go off." The squad leader looked at Samantha, then he shrugged in the direction of Meehan. "Is there anything we can do about him? He's been trying to say something, but we can't understand a word."

Samantha felt really annoyed. She didn't care about the man who had betrayed her husband. But she needed to know what happened to Alfred and the team. Her daughter needed medical attention, and they were just standing around twiddling their thumbs. Despite the anger and the fact that she should really take her revolver and finish Meehan off, she knelt down and quickly examined him in the heat and light of the burning building. She saw right away that he had a very serious stomach wound, and she also understood that he was not coming back from it. She saw that he had also been shot through the chest. He was pretty much done. She began to lean in to talk to him when he reached out with his left arm and gripped her wrist tightly. Her first reaction was to pull away, then she looked at his face and realized that he was trying to say something. She leaned down and said, "Jim, do you know who I am?"

"Yes, Samantha, I know who you are." Her ear was right by his lips, but his voice was barely audible.

"What happened to the team, Jim? What happened to Alfred?"

"I had to do it. They had my daughter. They had my Diane." He coughed, and Samantha could see specks of blood on his chin. The smell of copper and stress wafted from his body.

"What happened to them, Jim?"

"Timothy and Anne didn't make it. Alfred and the priest got away. I don't know if they were caught. That's all I know. I am sorry, Samantha. But I had to do it, that maniac had my daughter."

Samantha felt her world wobble a bit. *Alfred and the priest got away.* Her temples pounded. For the first time in hours she felt real hope. The man grabbed her wrist tighter and with a great effort, he said, "My Diane, she got hurt when that soldier came around the corner. Please go and check. Please go!"

"His daughter is around there." Samantha pointed. One of the Marathon soldiers went to check, and he came back with a child in his arms. He placed her on the ground beside Jim. Samantha checked her over quickly. There was a deep gash on the left side of the child's head. The bullet had gouged out a two-inch track and had left a deep cut, but the skull was not pierced. The impact had knocked her out cold.

"She's alive," she said.

"Please, take care of her. Please! I am sorry for what I did." His breath caught, then he exhaled one last time and died. Samantha felt like screaming. The sight of the dead man and his unconscious daughter, and the people who were at the scene seemed ghastly and surreal, like spirits in hell. The smoke from the burning building was now really beginning to make its presence felt, and soon they were all coughing, their eyes tearing up. The heat, and the sound of the raging fire, drove them away from the building into the side street. One of the men carried the unconscious child. Samantha looked and saw that Jim was enveloped in thick, black smoke. He was dead, and there was nothing else they could do for him.

"They have set up a medic station about two clicks from here, at the intersection of Fayette and Court Streets. I don't have any transportation, at least not yet, but why don't you go there and get yourself set up and tend to your daughter? I think we got it here. Our objective was to take that building, but the assholes set it on fire, so I guess our part in this little caper is over. We will be sending our wounded there as well. They will need your help," he said. "I would send Julie along, too, but I don't think she's in any shape mentally to deal with anything else right now."

Samantha nodded, and slipping an arm around her daughter's other shoulder, she said to Robert, "Come, we have to get there as quickly as we can. Candice, darling, hang on, we will get you there and you will be alright. You will be alright."

"Mom! Mom!" Robert cried out in fright. Candice jerked; her body began to shiver violently.

"Oh God, she is having a seizure. Set her down. Set her down! We have to get her mouth open and put something between her teeth so that she doesn't bite her tongue."

Robert quickly reached for his flashlight and placed it in her mouth. His sister bucked, and her body went rigid as she shook and her eyes rolled upward. Then she stopped and went as limp as a noodle. Samantha cried out and placed her ear on her daughter's chest. She couldn't hear a heartbeat. She tried finding a pulse. There was none.

"No, no, no!" She began CPR, alternately pumping Candice's chest and blowing into her mouth. While his mother worked, Robert watched in horror. This was insane. He felt himself go cold. He was about to lose his sister. The building burned, and in the distance there were other sounds of battle going on. He watched his mother working frantically to save his sibling, and he prayed.

Samantha could feel her arms going numb as she worked desperately to get Candice back. Finally, she gave up, and a low raspy moan escaped her. She pulled her hat off and grabbed her hair. She began to cry in earnest. A hole opened up inside her, and she felt that she was going to go crazy. She screamed. It was high-pitched and conveyed the primal sense of a grievous loss.

She got up and circled Candice's body, shaking her head and moaning. No, this couldn't be the end, it couldn't; she just hadn't tried hard enough. No, she had to try again. She got down, and placing the heel of her hand against her daughter's chest, she began to give CPR again, thirty compressions and two rescue breaths, another thirty compressions and two rescue breaths, on and on it went. She was crying and screaming. The people around her backed away and watched the mother's struggle in awe, in remembrance, of all the people and everything they had lost. A mother, father, sister, brother, spouse, hope. Then suddenly Candice's eyes flew open, and she drew a breath and coughed. It was a moment Robert would remember all his life. He felt a chill like a higher power had granted them a boon, and when the universe gave you something there was always a reckoning. He watched as Samantha hugged

Candice to her chest. Tears stung his eyes. He walked over, kneeled, and put a hand on his mother's shoulder. "Let's get her to that medic station, Mom, there's no time to lose."

When Alfred finally came around, he found that the priest had placed his backpack under his head. The man had also built a small fire, which kept the chill from seeping into their bones. The flickering light cast an eerie glow around the mining site. "How long was I out?"

"Around two hours."

"That cannibal really gave me a bash on the head, Christ." He reached up and rubbed his temples. Another familiar pain in his jaw throbbed in counterpoint to his temples. He did a quick mental calculation and realized that the time for another pill had long past. He sat up and retrieved the bottle from his backpack, then dry-swallowed a capsule. He got to his feet; it was time to get going. He longed to see his family again. The priest kicked dirt over the fire, and he led Alfred to one of vehicles their pursuers had driven. The Jeep had almost a full tank of gas.

"It was the only one that didn't have any bullet holes in it," O'Riley said.

"Good choice. Let's get on the road." Alfred was in no mood to do the ultra-safe thing and walk back to Marathon. He was ready to reunite with his family as quickly as possible. He didn't trust himself and left the driving to the priest. In the blossoming day, they were able to get a good look at the condition of the interstate. They weaved around abandoned or burnt cars, saw the long dark traces of human misery in every looted derelict or decaying body lying in the road.

Alfred marveled at the amount of opened and ran-sacked suitcases and bags. It also struck him just how quickly the roads had broken down. The interstate had huge potholes as a result of the long, cold winter they had experienced. With no one to fix them, he figured they would only get worse. Even the roads in Bing-hamton were pretty bad.

Whoever took control of the surrounding counties had a big job of marshaling resources to supply the basic needs of the surviving communities, including providing adequate security. He didn't envy Jasper one bit. He listened to the hum of the vehicle and lost himself in his thoughts. He wondered if the garden he had started with his family four days ago was doing okay. When he got to Marathon he would tell Jasper what happened, and they would leave immediately. He didn't want to have anything else to do with the settle-ment. They got to the checkpoint without any incident. The guards, after a cursory search and radio confirma-tion from Jasper, let them through. They also got wind that some big operation was in play. They pulled in next to the town hall. Alfred got out.

"I'm in Row E, tent five, in Camper's Lot. Come see me before you and your family go," O'Riley said. He then waved and drove off.

Alfred went up the steps. He was met just outside by four armed guards. They asked him to leave his weapon with them. The request made him uncomforta-ble, but he could understand. Jasper had to be even more careful now, he mused. He went down the hall and was made to wait a few minutes in the small waiting area before Jasper stepped out of a large, well-lit meeting room. The room was buzzing with noise and the sound of a lot of people on radios. The militia leader waved him into his private office, which was semi-dark and quiet by comparison.

"Is it done?" Jasper asked.

"Yes, but we had a lot of serious problems."

"Such as our man Meehan, I suppose."

"You know about that?" Alfred somehow got a tingle. He didn't like where this conversation was heading. He didn't like the way Jasper was looking at him.

"Yeah, there was another act of terror here. When you were gone, another bomb went off. We found out that the boy pretending to be Meehan's son was the one who had detonated it. We got to the scene and followed your boy, following Philip. When we got to the tent, we actually intercepted the woman operative sending a coded message to the Dove's headquarters in Bing-hamton. She panicked, exchanged gunfire with my man, and died. I would have liked to have kept her alive, but that wasn't to be. Your boy did really well, but he did get injured when I apprehended Phillip. Nothing serious!" He held his hands up when he saw the dark look of concern on Alfred's face.

"That's when I decided to go after them in Bing-hamton. I figured that they were so used to being the aggressor that they wouldn't be expecting us to come at them, and my hunch proved to be right, thank God. We got lucky and chased them out of the city and the county. When your wife heard that Meehan was a traitor, she went with the militia to Binghamton to find out if you were okay. I don't know any more yet. I've been kind of busy."

Alfred sat down heavily in the visitor's chair, on the other side of Jasper's desk. He felt like his world just fell out from under him. "Listen, put the word out for Samantha. She is a nurse, so she would gravitate toward first aide and helping people. If and when you contact her, find out if she and the kids are okay, and let her know I am fine, that she should get here as soon as she possibly can. Sorry Jasper, but it's time for us to go home," Alfred said.

"You got my word, Alfred. You did us a huge service. You got rid of their ability to deploy those bio weapons against us. I heard that it will take them some time to be able to manufacture more, and we are not the only group fighting back. All across America they are finding it very difficult to subjugate the survivors. Seems we got some fight left in us after all. I can tell you that since we have chased them out of Binghamton, the counties of Cortland, Broome and Tioga are now under our control. At least for the moment," Jasper smiled, and in that smile Alfred could see how terribly tired his friend really was. He got to his feet.

"I'll be at the house. If you hear anything, send someone to get me." The two men shook hands and Alfred saw himself out. He collected his weapon from the guards outside. His stomach rumbled, and he realized that he was ravenously hungry. He walked down to the tent market. Compared to the hundreds of vendors present the first day when he and his family came in, today there was only a handful. There was only one food vendor open, an old man who moved around on one leg and a pair of crutches. The man must have been eighty, but he moved with a quickness and purpose that made Alfred smile despite himself. He wore a chef's apron and hat. When he turned around, Alfred could see that he had a pistol tucked into his waist.

"What'll you have?" The man smiled at Alfred.

"It all smells good. What do you recommend?"

"The best thing I've got is a venison barbeque burger." The man chuckled when he saw Alfred's jaw drop. Have a seat and I'll cook you one."

"That does sound good, but I'll take some soup." Alfred sat at one of the small tables in the tent and watched as the man went to work. He rummaged around in his backpack and found a small bit of gold. The man brought his soup over, a really hearty broth made with venison burger, and Alfred realized that this was a version of hamburger soup, which he loved.

He tucked in with gusto. His jaw throbbed, so he ate as carefully as he could, and when he was done realized that he was sweating. The man noticed and smiled "I've got a few Cokes left—"

"I'll take one." He threw the gold bit to the old timer. The man got a small chisel and a hammer, and knocked off a piece of the gold expertly for himself, and then handed Alfred back his piece. He then went about cleaning dishes and left Alfred to his thoughts. Sitting in the tent, he relived memories of outdoor barbeques with friends, and all the New York State fairs he had taken his family to in Syracuse. Samantha had loved going to the farmer's market every summer in Otsiningo Park in Binghamton. Alfred shook his head at the memories. He popped the Coke and took a swig. It was a taste he had relished since boyhood, making him groan with pleasure. He also realized that it tasted a whole lot sweeter than he had remembered. He put that down to the fact that almost everything he had eaten and drank over the last seven months was made from natural ingredients. He enjoyed his Coke, maybe the last one he would ever drink, he mused, and when he was done, he thanked the man and walked slowly to the house Jasper had loaned the family.

In a corner of the room he had shared with Samantha, he found his rifle. He set to emptying the backpack and repacking the stuff he had left behind. He then unrolled his bedroll and stretched out on his back. He had only meant to lie down for a little while, but he fell asleep. He was awakened by a loud banging on the front door. He got groggily to his feet, but his head cleared quickly as his heart rate ramped up. News, Jasper must have news, he thought, as he opened the door. A young man wearing green fatigues smiled and said, "The Commander said to tell you that he spoke with your wife. She is fine and the kids are okay. She said that Candice got hurt but is all right. They will have to stay in Binghamton a few days until Candice is okay to travel. She also said that they will hitch a ride back on one of the transport trucks. She said to tell you that she has a couple of surprises for you." Alfred smiled and shook the messenger's hand. For a moment he felt at peace, and he decided to savor it, because he knew it wouldn't last.

Harry Lambert laid prostrate on a bed in a large house that his men had selected as his headquarters. It was a place for him to recuperate. The bullet had passed through his left side and had smashed a rib. He was lucky that he had an excellent surgeon on staff. The man went in and managed to repair the damage, but it had been a very close thing. Lambert knew that he had almost died. The thing that really grated on him was the fact that although his army had managed to take the town, eventually most of the rebels had escaped. His intelligence network had sent him a lot of coded messages confirming that they had joined up with another group based in Vermont. So both he and his prey had lived to fight another day. It would be awhile before he was fully mobile again. The doctor had said six weeks. It was mid-May. That would have him fully ready to go late July. He found himself grinding his teeth; it was a huge set back. He had wanted to get most of the fighting done by September, before autumn set in. Then he could use the remainder of the year to consolidate his territory and make plans for early spring. This had thrown a wrench in all those plans.

His satphone beeped. He reached gingerly across and pulled to him the chair with the silver humming case. He quickly spun the combination, and the top popped open. He grabbed the receiver and lifted it to his ear. A very familiar, gravely Austrian voice spoke in his ear.

"So you have survived, Herr Lambert?"

"Yes, your Excellency. They tried to kill me but they did not succeed." Lambert waited for the man to speak. He knew that he had to tread very carefully here.

"We have consolidated the UK Precinct. Russia is close to falling; the Chinese are decimated. That Precinct will be under our control very soon. The religious fanatics in the East wanted Armageddon, and when we gave it to them, they decided they didn't want any part of it, but we gave it to them anyway." There was a long bemused chuckle on the end of the line. "What I found out was that they were fine with Armageddon, as long as they thought they were in control and winning. As soon as they realized that they were being wiped out and that we didn't care about them or their beliefs, that we had a plan, a goal that didn't include them, they suddenly began to care about life and getting along." Another cold chuckle sent icy chills up Lambert's spine.

"Most of the world is now ours, only America is giving us problems. We killed their entire government; we triggered long-dormant vaccine viruses that we had seeded into the population. We used biological weapons, eighty-five percent of the population is now deceased, but still they are a thorn. Still they rebel, and cling to their extinct Constitution, and they kill our soldiers with their guns." There was a sigh as the man caught his breath before he began to speak again. "We had made certain plans, just in case you and Deifenbacher failed." The man cleared his throat, and there was a long intentional pause that made Lambert's heart lurch, and he looked around wildly for his weapon. To his horror, he realized that he was unarmed in the room. He was about to sit up, which would have been extremely unwise in his condition, when the voice purred, "The Board still believes that you are the right man for the job of controlling the Green sector. We have put in play events that should eliminate certain nuisances. You will be getting confirmation messages soon. I want you to rest up, Herr Lambert, you are going to be a very busy man." The line clicked off, and Lambert relaxed back into his bed. His head felt like it was going to explode, and his bladder felt heavy. He suddenly had the urge to pee very badly. He took a couple of deep breaths to calm himself. He had known just how powerful and ruthless his employers were, but the fact that they were out conquering the world and still had the time and the ability to take care of a few nuisances in Lambert's neck of the woods made him realize that not only was he being monitored very closely, but they had agents among his personnel and every other vassal's as well. He had always intuited it, but knowing it for certain now filled him with serious unease.

He composed himself and reached for the bell on the desk by his bed. Two nurses came in; one male and the other female. They wore green fatigues and the white armband with a red cross on their left arm. They slipped his bedpan under the sheets, and after he relieved himself, he had them bring his personal firearm to him. Lying on his back, he slipped the Luger out of the leather shoulder holster and checked the clip. Then he placed the pistol on the bed next to him. He began to calm down. If they wanted him dead, he would already be. They had killed the world's most powerful men, some of whom had hid in bunkers miles below ground. Killing Harry Lambert would be an easy proposition, he concluded. He settled in to wait. He figured that he would be getting some pretty interesting news soon.

It was with a heavy heart that Splinter walked back into his old headquarters in Middletown. Those rebels had chased his army out of Binghamton and out of Broome County. He sat in his old office and contemplated his predicament. He knew his Bilderberg overlords would try to come after him. He wondered how they would do it. He didn't think that they would just shoot him in the back. They were too aristocratic for that, people who didn't matter maybe, but with him he was sure they would want to make an example. He knew less than Lambert about the internal machinations of the organization, but he knew how he would have dealt with a failure the magnitude of his. He would have personally chopped the offender's head off. So he figured they would come looking for him soon. He was under no illusions that they had agents watching him, keeping tabs. He didn't panic, but rather he felt something in his head switch off, and calmness descended on him.

He called and had a couple pounds of C-4 delivered to his office. He also had a Kevlar vest and a police riot helmet sent to him. He decided that since he couldn't pick the time, he would pick the place. He closed his door and wired his office. There was a large pen in a penholder on his desk. He decided he would use this as the trigger. He ran the wires through the bottom of the pen. It took a bit of ingenuity, but he managed to set it up so he could use the action of the pen's push button to complete the electronic circuit. He placed the pen on the edge of the desk. He then positioned an envelope over the tip of the pen to hide the wires that ran under the desk, to the explosives he had planted and hidden around the office. The riot helmet he hid on the floor under his desk. The Kevlar vest he now wore under his shirt at all times.

For the next twenty-four hours, he had all his meals brought in to him. He actually got to work, reorganizing his army and consolidating his losses. He checked in with his captains in New York City and other strong holds, and he also put the word out to his people that the loss of Binghamton would be avenged soon. He kept his bodyguards outside the door of his office, and the only time he interacted with them was when he needed food or messages run.

Two days later it happened. There were two quick pops outside his door, then a knock. He got up. There was that feeling that he was outside his own body again, as he walked over to the door and opened it. There were four men standing there. Two he hadn't seen before. They were dressed in all-black fatigues and carried HK33 rifles. As they barged their way in, bringing up the rear were two men that surprised

Splinter. One was the captain he had left in control of New York City, Borso, and the other was his chief intelligence officer, Cole. They were dressed in brown fatigues like the rest of his men. Splinter went to his desk and sat down. The two men who worked for him, and who were now betraying him, sat in the two available chairs. The Bilderberg soldiers stood grim-faced with their rifles trained on him.

Borso placed a computer on his desk. "Open it. Someone wants to have a chat."

Splinter flipped the lid open, and as the screen came on, he again had to wonder how they had contrived to have this kind of satellite access. The same man who had spoken to him when Lambert visited came into focus. The man's face was of bemused venomous arrogance.

"Sorry to have to meet again under such trying conditions, Herr Diefenbacher, but I think this is very important. There is a certain formality that has to be established when we relieve a high ranking member of our organization of his or her post."

"Are you sure we can't work this out? What happened was just a temporary setback."

"Herr Deifenbacher, we know that not only did you lose six thousand men, but also two canisters of a most precious weapon. You had an occupying force of sixty thousand, and you were defeated by a rabble of no more than thirty thousand. This smacks of gross incompetence. You are a lord in our organization, so we cannot just shoot or poison you. The Board demands that strict protocols be followed."

Splinter sat back in his seat, took the pen, and held it in his lap. He kept his eyes on the screen. The men were busy listening to their Supreme Commander and were not fully engaged in watching their intended victim.

"These protocols include making sure that the disqualified Lord is present, and his demotion or elimination is witnessed by his successor and a member of the Board," the Count continued. "These conditions are now met. Your successor will be Lord Borso. He understands your organization, and he seems to have the necessary qualities—what, Herr Diefenbacher!"

Splinter ducked beneath the heavy table and managed to slip the helmet on before one of the soldiers began reaching for him. He pressed the button on the pen and nothing happened. He almost screamed in terror and fury. The man had grabbed him by the shoulders and was about to yank him out, when he pressed the button again, and this time there was a couple of thunderous explosions. The world under the table went silent for Splinter, as a sharp pain flared in his head. The explosions had blown his eardrums. The desk and floor moved and shook, shards of wood ripping into his skin in a million places, as the desk shattered into two pieces, falling apart. He was in agony as he crawled out into the smoke and swirling dust. He vomited and it splashed in the helmet, running down his face and neck. He reached and pulled the helmet off.

Two walls were blown out, and a part of the roof sagged then fell in, letting in a ray of light. He crawled around in the rubble and saw that one of the soldiers was still moving. He tried to stand but his knees felt like jelly. He gave up and crawled over to the bleeding, twitching man. He found the soldier's HK33 and shot him once in the chest. He shot the other men for good measure, he saw Borso crawling away.

Then he heard it, the warbling sound of the computer. It was under a large chunk of sheet rock. The case was badly damaged and the screen was cracked, but it was still on. The Supreme Commander was still there, but the image of his face was cracked in two, the distorted image looked like the misshapen reflection of a fun house mirror. He could see the man's lips move, but he could not understand what he was saying and didn't care. He had a message of his own to send now, and he hoped the Austrian shit understood it loud and clear. He dragged the computer over to the crawling Borso. He grabbed the man by the shirt and turned him over onto his back. Somewhere in the deep recesses of his brain, he understood that the man was really already dead; half of his face was missing, and moist pieces of his brain could be seen in the dust beneath his head. The one remaining eye that looked at Splinter registered only terror.

Splinter placed the computer by Borso's head, grabbed the man by the throat and squeezed. The man's hands came up feebly as his life ebbed out of him. He bucked as he tried to breathe, but soon the movement stopped as the surviving eye went glassy and fishlike. Splinter turned to the man on the screen, who had been watching in keen interest. He caught his breath and said very slowly, enunciating every word because he knew that the microphone must have been damaged.

"Our deal is off. I'll do things my way." He then crawled, picked up the rifle, and shot the computer to pieces. Yes, he would do things his way from this point on. He was so exhausted, he fell on his back, and although he tried to stay conscious, the world wobbled then went gray. Blackness swallowed him. He lay in the wreckage of his office until his men found him.

Alfred woke from a dream. He could not remember what had awakened him in the quiet of the night. He got his answer when there was a knock on the door. He got up, shrugged into his shirt, and slid the .45 into his shoulder holster. When he opened the door, O'Riley was standing on the steps in the dark. Alfred could tell that the priest was agitated.

"Something's happened. Come with me."

"What's going on?" Alfred asked as he followed O'Riley, who had begun jogging.

"They've killed the Command Team. Jasper's dead."

"Wait, wait, how did it happen?"

"It seems that they used some kind of nerve agent. Somebody seems to have released it in the command center. Everyone was there except for the Sheriff and Jasper's son, Marcus. It appears pretty much all the people who had founded and kept this place going were in the room when it was released."

Alfred found himself grinding his teeth. It just never ended, all the bad stuff just kept on coming, it seemed, with no end to it. They got to the building and found that there was a small group of armed men outside. There was a genny growling nearby, powering the lights that lit up the surreal scene. A man wearing a star held his hand up for them to stop.

"Thanks for coming, O'Riley. Are you Alfred?"

"Yes."

"Jasper had filled me in on what the two of you had done. How you saved the settlement. This is very bad. It couldn't have happened at a worse time. I know that he was about to consolidate our victory in Binghamton and get the ball rolling on reaching out to the various surviving groups in the counties. That's all up in the air now. Marcus has been coordinating things in Binghamton. I have taken on the investigative duties here. It's a real blow."

Both men shook their heads. "Listen," said Alfred, "I'll help out until my family gets here, then I am heading back to the homestead."

"Good enough. Most of the people who were in that room were on the town council. They supervised things from garbage collection to security. They sure picked the right moment to attack; it seemed from what the investigators have told me that they used some sort of fast-acting neurotoxic gas. They found two canisters. Both were released at different points of the room. It is assumed that this was a suicide mission. One of those dead people in the room did this."

They backed away from the steps to allow a group of men and women dressed in yellow decon suits to go by. "Who have we told so far?" O'Riley asked.

"Well, all the captains in the field know. We plan to leave a small force in Binghamton, and when everyone else is back, we will make the announcement in the Forum. We should have a strong provisional council in place by then and be able to carry on."

"Well, I'll help anyway I can," O'Riley said. "I was about to move on myself, to see what that other survival group up there in Rochester is like, but I'll stay now."

"Thank you. We need all the experienced leaders we have. We need a new Head of Security. Do you think you can handle it?" O'Riley nodded and scratched his head.

"Marcus needs someone to help him coordinate the army in the field." He looked at Alfred, who also nodded. "You two should go see Marcus right away.

He's set up an emergency central command station in my office."

They had to move out of the way again as two teams of stretcher bearers came down the steps. They had two bodies wrapped in dark plastic. They placed the bodies gently at the bottom of the stairs, then went back in. Alfred and O'Riley took their leave and went down two streets to the Sheriff's Office.

There they found Marcus and a group of people amid a slew of cackling long distance radios and paperwork. He looked up at them, his face despondent and strained. Alfred he knew from the days he used to hunt with his father, and O'Riley from the time the priest had spent at the settlement. Both men asked what they could do to help, and over the next few days they went about their duties diligently. O'Riley immediately tightened security protocols, and Alfred went about making sure that the day to day military objectives were carried out. Alfred found Marcus a less assured version of his father, but he was competent, and not prone to taking chances, something Alfred thought was a disadvantage in these dangerous times. Jasper had understood that *fortune favored the brave*. Alfred carried out his duties and kept his own council. Finally, he got the word that his family was leaving Binghamton on one of the troop trucks that had begun to ferry personnel from the city.

He was standing in the Marathon cemetery. The council members who were killed were now being laid to rest. O'Riley was performing the funeral ceremony. Alfred knew that he was reading from Ecclesiastes.

"There is a time for everything, and a season for every activity under heaven: a time to be born and a time to die, a time to plant and a time to uproot." Then he closed the Bible and switched to the famous 23rd

Psalm. Everyone joined in, including Alfred. *"The Lord is my shepherd; I shall not want. He makes me lie down in green pastures. He leads me beside the still waters. He restores my soul. He leads me in the paths of righteousness for his namesake. Even though I walk through the valley of the shadow of death, I will fear no evil, for you are with me; your rod and your staff, they comfort me."* O'Riley paused to clear his throat, then he said, "Let the Lord take these brave souls, let them have their rewards in Heaven. We will miss them. They were our comrades in arms, they were our friends, and they were family."

Alfred watched the rest of the ceremony with a feeling of loss. There was just so much death these days. He thought that he would have been inured to it, but it still affected him. Most of the people who were killed in that control room had at least one loved one who would now mourn their passing. Everyone standing in the cemetery, and that was nearly the entire town, understood what a huge loss the town's council was to them and the cause. They were shocked by the thoroughness of the assassination; in one fell swoop, their enemies had taken out most of their leadership. The thing that bothered Alfred was that he did not know who the responsible party was. Was it the Dove, was it the Royalists, or was it an unknown enemy, yet to rear its head? Alfred himself still was not convinced that the assassin had been one of the dead. Being on the Provisional council, he was in the second row behind immediate family and loved ones. He watched as Marcus threw dirt on his father's coffin. Then he got up and began to make his way through the crowd. He wanted to be back at the house. His family might be there, and he needed to see them now, to hold them close. He knew that everything was fragile, and that time and luck was short and fickle.

Alfred walked up the street to the house. As he approached it, he saw that there was a dim light on in the living room. He stopped and composed himself. The door opened, and Samantha rushed out and ran down the walkway, into the street, and into his arms. They held each other and cried.

After they got themselves under control, they walked up the short sidewalk together. Alfred realized that he held on to his wife like a man holding on to a life vest in heavy seas. When he got inside, Robert was standing just inside the entrance. He hugged his boy, and his son hugged him back. He couldn't stop himself from crying. Then he saw Candice sitting up, with her injured leg on a small cushion. She was pale and small, but she was smiling. She was holding the hand of a girl of around eight.

"Who is this?" he asked.

"Her name is Diane. She's Jim's daughter. I think she will be a part of our family now. She will be my sister," Candice said as she held out her arms and embraced her father. She found that she could not stop herself from crying as well. When Alfred finally broke the embrace, he hugged the girl who had lost her entire family, and welcomed her into his own. He knew he would get the story from Samantha later on.

"Alfie, your dad's dead. The Dove crucified him. I had to ease his passing," Samantha said quietly. Alfred had been sitting on the floor with his back to the wall, looking at the people who were the center of his world.

"Dad, Mom has something important to tell you," Candice said.

Robert was nodding and smiling. "Yes, it's big," he said.

Samantha got on her knees at her husband's side. She ran her fingers through his hair. She touched his cheek and wiped a tear from his eye. "Alfie. Alfie, I'm pregnant."

Harry Lambert laid in his convalescent bed. It had been a stressful couple of days since he had last spoken with Count Gustave. There was a knock; he had his hand under the sheet; the Luger was pointed at the door. Despite what the man had said, Lambert did not trust him.

"Come in."

"These messages came in high priority, sir." The radioman gave him the three slips of paper and returned to his post.

He unfolded the strips and read them. Message one read, *Town Council of Marathon Settlement liquidated. Jasper Filitree among the casualties.* Message two read, *Leadership council of Genesee Survival Township liquidated. Bonnie Connolly and Jesse Cook among the casualties.* Message 3 read, *Attempt on New York City Militia failed, Diefenbacher known as the Dove survived. No further attempts will be made at this time.*

Lambert began to relax for the first time since he regained consciousness. He was still in the loop. If they wanted him gone, he would be dead already. He had to get his strength back as quickly as possible. He always knew that he had made a deal with the Devil, but he never knew the extent of that deal until now. He understood that to the people he worked for, he was just a tool to get a certain job done. He knew that they had a plan, a plan to conquer the world. He had always thought that they had shared the plan with their high level associates, but now a shred of doubt was beginning to creep in. There was something about being a king who ruled by the proxy of a stronger power. There was something that chaffed at him, and he realized that he was tired of being an employee; he wanted to be the boss. The undisputed boss. For the first time in his life, he began to get a glimmer, a clearer sense, of what his destiny might be. Along with the desire also came the sense of foreboding. Remember your Shakespeare he mused. Macbeth wanted it all as well. Just be careful you do not end up like the Thane of Cawdor. He shifted in his bed, and suddenly he felt ravenously hungry. He began grinning despite himself; he realized that the game for the world had really just begun.

Alfred and Samantha couldn't help holding each other as they saw the homestead through the trees. It had been three weeks since they had left their home to check out Marathon. Old habits came back, and they stood quietly in the tree line, observing the house until they were satisfied that it was safe. They walked with their children into the clearing, and when they opened the front door, Samantha spun around and threw herself into Alfred's arms. They kissed, and she could see that there were tears in Alfred's eyes as well. Candice limped by, using a stout piece of wood as a cane. Robert helped her into a chair by the stove, and their new sister came in timidly. She had not spoken since she woke up in the medic station in Binghamton. She ran to Candice and hugged her. That was another peculiar thing. She had attached herself to the Aimes girl, and when she cried at night only Candice could get her to go back to sleep.

Samantha and her husband deposited their backpacks in their room, then went outside to have look around the place. They inspected the root cellar and checked the four storage containers. Everything seemed okay except for a few food items they had to discard because of spoilage. Slowly they began to shift mentally from a large community to homestead life. Alfred began sizing up all the chores he would have to do, and Samantha also realized that she and Alfred would have to have the chat they had both been avoiding since she told him that she was pregnant. They would have to decide very soon how they were going to prepare for the baby. For now though, for the first time since the Collapse, they actually had a sense of optimism.

"Do you think the verdict for those men was fair?"

"Sure, all things considered they got a fair trial. They were found guilty by a jury of their peers. That was a far better chance than trial by the Dove. They were then taken out six hours later and shot."

"Do you think that the verdict was influenced by Jasper's death?"

"No, it seems like the evidence was pretty overwhelming."

"What about the boy, though. Do you think his verdict was fair?"

"Yes, all things considered, his jury came back with a fair verdict. They found him guilty, but they considered his age and that he was manipulated by the adults around him. Ten lashes and sending him on his way was fair."

"Robert liked him. The way he cut him down after the whipping, and saw to his wounds, that was compassionate." Samantha reflected on this a second. The fact that her son was still able to forgive Philip, after all he had done, gave her hope. She understood that the world really belonged to Robert's generation, and if her son could still find it in his heart to be kind, even after all they had been through, then there was reason to believe that, given the chance at a fair and open society, people would be able to build something great from the ashes of the past.

They stood and looked at the garden they had planted. It had been untended, but most of the seeds they had sown were now small plants. Some had gotten eaten by insects, and there were rabbit tracks around, but most had made it. It would now be tended and protected, and Alfred knew that with a little bit of luck, they would be able to get a good harvest. They looked around at the homestead. There was full acceptance of the world as it was now. It had been the toughest thing for them to come to terms with, this new world, but now they understood completely that the life they had known was gone. Something new was being born. The new world was not going to allow too many passengers. It was going to take commitment, faith, hope, and blood, to survive and thrive.

The Collapse survivors were now already writing a new page in the history of mankind. The Aimes family had no interest in power, but they did have an interest in justice and making the world a place where people of courage could aspire to be happy. Samantha held Alfred's hand. The sun was beginning to set, and the homestead and the people on it knew peace, at least for a while.

"I love you, Samantha."

"I love you, Alfred."

In the quiet New York woods, a man embraced his wife, and when they kissed, for a while, they were happy.

The End

Afterword

If you enjoyed this book, please feel free to leave an unbiased review on Amazon.com. See how *The Prepper* series got started by reading *The Prepper Part One: The Collapse*, also available on Amazon.com in print and e-book format. If you would like to switch genres, but still want the adrenaline rush of a fast-paced adventure story, check out *The Shaker of Worlds* by Karl A.D. Brown.

As I was writing *The Prepper Part Two*, I had done a lot of research and came across many of the products and websites mentioned in the story. After some thought, I decided to leave the names of the products and websites in the text. A number of these products and websites are well known to the prepper and survivalist community anyway, and some readers, I thought, would probably have some fun checking into these products and websites for themselves. I am in no way associated with any of these products or websites.

I would like to acknowledge D.C. Snyder for being my reader and editor. I would like to say thanks to Carol Thompson for her editing services. I would also like to thank www.ebooklaunch.com for their cover art and formatting services.

Made in the USA
San Bernardino, CA
24 February 2016